Legend of the
Book Keeper

Legend of the
Book Keeper

By Daniel Blacaby

Published in Boise, Idaho by Russell Media
Web: http://www.russell-media.com

This book may be purchased in bulk for educational, business, ministry, or promotional use.

For information please email info@russell-media.com.

ISBN (print):   978-1-937498-04-7
ISBN (e-book): 978-1-937498-05-4

Library of Congress Control Number: 2012935683

Printed in the United States of America

Dedication

To my beautiful wife, Sarah—
You are my unwavering constant.
The greatest depths of my creative imagination
and fantasy pale in comparison to the
joy of spending my reality with you.

Acknowledgments

This book is the direct result of the investment of countless amazing people. If I were to record thanks to every person whom I owe my gratitude, I suspect this list would quickly exceed the length of the novel itself. So to list only a few:

First and foremost—a sincere thanks to my family. I consider myself incomparably blessed to have been born into such a loving, fun, and supportive family. Thank you for always encouraging me to pursue my dreams.

Also, a special thank you to my "second family," Rachel and Ryan. It is a great privilege to be welcomed into your family. Thank you for trusting your only daughter/sister to this shaggy-haired nerd.

To my patient editor, Anna "Passive-Voice-Slayer" McHargue. If not for you this book would have many errors and MANY more severed heads.

To my publisher, Mark Russell. Your enthusiasm and belief in this story have been contagious. Thank you for your putting faith in a geeky writer with a wild imagination.

To Olivia Tether, Anita Broussard, Brad and Mary Keel, and Elena McHargue for being my guinea pigs and providing great feedback and suggestions.

To Dr. Collier, Dr. Sepko, Dr. Thompson, Dr. Shin and the rest of the NGU English department for being able to look past the "less-than-attentive" C+ student, investing in me as a person, and bringing out my best (with the obvious exception of *Advanced Grammar* exams . . . *shudder*).

To G. R. S. Blackaby, whom I never had the privilege of meeting in this life, but whom I have gotten to know through your books. Your passion for classic literature has remained vibrant and inspiring even four generations later.

Lastly, to Chevy, the best one-eyed, poorly disciplined, socially awkward, shaggy dog a guy could ever be stuck with.

Chapter Titles

Prologue

He was dead.

The precise moment of the soul's mystical voyage from this world? Unknown; forever a secret for the damp stone walls to hoard and cherish. However, that which *was* irrefutable was the absolute certainty that he was dead—completely dead.

Crackling flames, liberated from the solitary confinement of their lamps, danced a wild, savage dance, reflecting off the harsh surface of the walls; rouges in a room infiltrated with midnight blackness. The steady hum of nighttime's wonders seeped through the open window, providing the crazed inferno their tribal rhythm. Slyly escorting the midnight drone was a scent—a most peculiar scent. A prodigal aroma having returned from an exceedingly lengthy absence only to find itself a complete stranger in its own home; it was the distinctive scent of *change*.

In the center of the room, blind to nature's passionate carnival all around him, lay the corpse. Two lifeless eyes fixated heavenward, thin windows into an empty dwelling. The thick skin of the man's face was coarsely pale, as though warmth, finally accepting the inevitable, had swiftly fled its longtime dwelling place. The most telling feature of the empty corpse, however, was the mouth; gaping wide open. Not open as it had been on so many occasions to release waves of laughter, nor as it had been to engage in three million delightful conversations: open as though agonizingly torn beyond capacity by a soul departing its earthly vase. In all, he had the look of a man who had carelessly left Death off the invite list to his banquet, only to, with great surprise, discover that it would be the celebrated guest of honor.

Hushed whispers cut sharply through the thick tranquility, a regiment of life in the lifeless room. Two hooded figures, both of short stature, huddled in the adjacent corner, bystanders to the serene scene. Their whispers were exchanged with frantic urgency.

"You are absolutely positive he's dead? No trickery?" The voice of a woman shot out to the figure on her right. She leaned forward for another glance, but kept her distance; fearful that what she witnessed might actually be reality. Her voice was husky, crafted by the erosion of sorrow. The return whisper came volleying back in the form of a male's voice, calm but with the subtle hint of shakiness that exposed its true composure,

"As sure as this night is dark as sin. I've checked every vital sign. Nothing points to foul play. I can't explain it. He's simply . . . gone." The last word was uttered with the conviction of a man unable to accept an obvious truth.

"What does this mean? How could this happen? How are we going to explain this? Everything is going to change. Everything is going to crumble."

"No, we keep it secret. No one can discover what happened tonight. Nobody. We trust in only ourselves. Its revelation would be utterly disastrous. Do I have your word?"

Silence.

The women's heavy eyes peered urgently toward the deceased body; she was praying for a final miracle to pinch her and awaken her from her nightmare. At last, her shoulders sank as she released the last traces of denial, "Yes, brother, you have my word. But this won't stay hidden forever . . ." Her voice trailed off. For a moment their minds were unified in a singular train of thought—a train quickly running rampant off the tracks. They knew her final statement held prophetic truth. They both understood the repercussions of the dark, veiled funeral service: A power long maintained—now faded. A secret long kept—soon unveiled. A city long lost—ready to be found.

PART ONE
THE BOOK

1
An Odd Discovery

There was absolutely *nothing* ordinary about Cody Clemenson. He was in no shape or form bound by the mundane, restrictive chains of normality imposed upon his peers. Granted, at 5' 4" in height, he was bashfully flirting with the average stature for fifteen-year-olds. And it probably shouldn't be overlooked that his report card had the steady tendency to follow suit with his alliterated name. Actually, he had never really excelled in *any* particular area or at *any* particular thing. In fact, when all the variables were considered, it seems as though Cody Clemenson was exceedingly ordinary after all.

Cody pondered this utterly dismal realization as he sat restlessly in his 9th grade science classroom. Lounging in his back-row desk in Slacker Row, he twirled his pencil clumsily between his index finger and thumb. His shaggy brown hair hung in front of his sky-blue eyes like wrinkled curtains as he stared mindlessly toward the amateur doodles scratched into his desk. The doodles were all akin: Cody's shirt bursting open as muscles rippled underneath.

In several, the addition of a cape and swooning girls had been added.

The irritating hum of Ms. Starky's, (or Ms. *Shark*-y as she was spitefully referred to by her class), scratchy voice droned on and on as she shared a less-than-tantalizing lecture on the Scientific Method. It wasn't that Cody lacked interest in the lesson; it was simply that he could think, off hand, of approximately 56,433 and a half other places he would rather be at that precise moment. And, one place in particular.

"*Pssst!*" The whisper exploded like dynamite in the comatose room, the shrapnel tearing Cody from his dream world and back into reality. Finding his bearings he pivoted to see who had so rudely intruded upon his daydream. It was Sean Schneil. Cody groaned.

Sean was the embodiment of a try-hard, striving with painstaking effort to fit in everywhere, effectively fitting nowhere. Greasy, fire-red hair and a freckle-infested face, Sean cherished nothing more than to be involved in the action. From under his desk his gangly, splotchy arm produced a folded note, "It's from *you-know-who . . . ,*" he whispered loudly, oblivious to his volume. The unnaturally, and slightly freakish, large smile on his face hinted that he was clearly pleased to be included in the moment of mischief. Cody quickly unfolded his letter:

CODY

Still up for Wesley's after class?

JADE

Cody grinned. Glancing up from his desk, he gazed at a head of long, charcoal-black hair in the front row. Jade—his best friend. In truth, her birth name was Mari Shimmers. That name, however, had been relegated by her school-mates to little more than obscure trivia as her prominent fiery green eyes had quickly earned her the nickname, Jade.

Cody recalled the moment he met Jade at the beginning of fourth grade. Her divorced parents had decided it was in her best interest to stay with her mom in America rather than her military father in Europe and transferred her into Cody's class mid-year. Although Jade's dress was extremely plain when compared to her image-conscious peers, and she rarely made use of makeup, her face radiated a compelling attractiveness with two large dimples, light freckles, and, of course, her trademark green eyes, which captured the look of the rising sun reflecting off the damp forest leaves the morning after a violent rainstorm.

Despite joining Cody's grade, Jade was a full year older than her classmates, having been put back a year due to her military father and her constant need to transfer. This did not prove to be a hindrance, however, as she excelled academically and was quick to make friends. In many ways, she was everything Cody was not. Her bold outgoing nature stood out next to his stark, introverted demeanor. No doubt, the influence of military life shined through as well as she had developed a precise, analytical mind. Cody, on the other hand, seemed to always be lost in his private thoughts as he explored fantastic worlds and journeyed to magical realms. However, the two had struck up an immediate and surprising friendship. Some suggested it was because Cody had also dealt with the painful experience of his father walking out on his mother, and indeed that had undoubtedly played a supporting role. More probable, as Jade would quickly testify, was that she wrote all of Cody's essays.

As if sensing Cody's stare, Jade swung her head around and smiled, her piercing eyes peering at Cody. Cody smiled back, confirmation that the afternoon's excursion to Wesley's was a go. Wesley's, or rather *Wesley's Amazing Used and Rare Antique Book Store*, was the duo's favorite after-school hangout. Apart from broken families, the pair was also bound together by another chain: a mutual obsession of classic books.

From some vague distance, Cody heard the words, "Excuse me, Mr. Clemenson." He flushed. Glancing up, he flipped his hair from in front of his eyes. The moment he did so he immediately wished he could undo the deed. Standing directly in front of him was Ms. Starky, who peered at him disdainfully. Cody gulped.

"Mr. Clemenson, would the student's foot size in this experiment represent the controlled, or independent variable?" Cody didn't even begin to have a clue as to what the answer was . . . or what in the world a variable was. He cast a desperate look toward Jade, but knew she couldn't save his bacon this time. There would be no fooling Starky this time.

"Um," he began slowly, searching for rescue, "Well, Ms. Sharky . . . I mean . . . Starky. . . . argh . . ." Sean let out an uncontrolled hiccupy laugh that sounded like a seagull choking on *Cheetos*. Unfortunately, Starky did not find humor in the situation. Squinting together her eyebrow-less eyes, she muttered, "Well, Mr. Clemenson, it looks like you will have the privilege of staying after class with me today . . . again." Cody winced, and cast a sheepish look over to Jade. The Wesley's excursion was indefinitely postponed.

"It's about time!" Jade cried as Cody came straggling out of the school thirty minutes later. Cody tossed up his arms. "You think *you* had it bad? At least you got to wait outside, not with JAWS!" Jade let out a gentle smirk and continued in a motherly tone, "Well, for one, her name is Ms. Starky, not Jaws. No need to be rude. Secondly, the foot size in her question was the independent variable. And thirdly, you might be happy to know that I graciously spent my time waiting for you by finishing your algebra homework. Congratulations, you should have an A." Cody flashed a smile of gratitude, reminding himself again why their friendship worked with such perfect harmony. With this, the two began their delayed trek to Wesley's.

Coming to a crosswalk Jade pressed the walk button. "So, aren't you going to tell me what Ms. Starky had you do for all that time in there?" she persisted. "I'm assuming it wasn't tea and a game of checkers?" Cody shrugged, "Oh, you know, just the usual. Had to write a few hundred lines and listen to the *'you're a disappointment to your ancestors'* speech again." These appointments with Starky had become somewhat of a regular occurrence; often scheduled into his agenda a week or two beforehand.

"So, what did you have to write this time? I-will-not-be-an-embarrassment-to-fifteen-year-old-boys again?" Jade prodded with a mocking grin. Crossing the street, Cody thought for a second, "Um . . . I can't remember. Something like that. They all start blurring together, ya know?" Jade hung her head. After years of friendship she was still amazed sometimes by Cody's apparent selective memory. He could instantly rattle off the birthdates and a variety of random facts about authors who had died centuries ago, but could not recall the ten words he had just spent half-an-hour repeating. *Silly boy!*

The friends turned into a long alley between buildings, a shortcut to their destination. Although the town of Havenwood, Utah was small, the two had not yet reached the age where shortcuts and secret passageways had lost their intrigue. The pair had spent hours scurrying through the streets in one adventure or other; over the years they had run from Indians as well as from invading cut-throat pirates looking for plunder. Their passageways now carefully held these memories the way a glass bottle holds a tiny boat. Over time you may forget how the boat got into the bottle, but you never stop appreciating the nostalgia.

On this late afternoon, however, a foreign smell invaded their sanctuary of familiarity. Cody's nose sensed it the minute it arrived, much the same way a dedicated librarian itches when a book is inversely replaced. He instantly knew they were not alone in the alleyway. Turning into view appeared a large man, cloaked in a long, black coat. The tall figure walked with the sway of one well acquainted with authority, and with the haste that seemed to proclaim that his business was his own. Jade forcefully yanked Cody against the wall as the figure briskly passed by, the tail of his coat bushing against Cody's sleeve in the narrow passageway. A sharp chill shot down Cody's spine.

Although the figure's face was downcast, Cody caught a glimpse. It was a face he had never seen before. As the man reached the end of the lane he turned and disappeared as quickly as he had arrived. And, just like that, all returned to normal. The smell of alien cologne had stained the air the way a scar remains long after the cut has healed.

"Who do you think that was?" Cody spouted out the moment the stranger had vanished. "He gave me the creeps!"

"Just an ordinary visitor. It's none of our business; probably a book collector come to visit Wesley's. Speaking of which . . ." Coming to the end of the alley, their destination came into view. *Wesley's Amazing Used and Rare Antique Book Store.*

Honest to its name, the bookstore dazzled the eyes of even those accustomed to its splendor. The building itself was not an average bookshop but a converted mansion. The oldest building in town and the last landmark of the city's past now long forgotten. Around the front of the building was a magnificent porch carved out of gray stone, tightly hugging the house as its staunch confidant. The faded, wind-brushed bricks that fashioned the walls appeared feeble, as though a stiff breeze might tip the scales in favor of Father Gravity; yet faithfully they stood. Covering these walls were leafy vines that had slowly slithered up over generations and now clung to the walls like leeches. In the front, two black, stone lions stood imposingly as guardians on either side of the pathway leading to the house; their marble eyes staring at every visitor as though judging his worth.

Two breathtaking, sizable bay windows, covered by thick, black drapes, shielded the store in a blanket of mystery. The town's children unanimously concluded that the mansion was haunted.

However, for the store's most frequent visitors, these ghost-legends took no hold. Cody pranced up the chipped front steps and—*SMACK!* "Ouch!" cried Cody grabbing his now throbbing forehead. Jade shrugged once again; having witnessed another prime example of Cody's poor memory. What offered the crushing blow was the ever-familiar wooden sign reading: **Wesley's: Your Home for Rare Books Since 1683.** The store had just relocated to their town roughly four years ago when Wesley had arrived and quietly purchased the long-abandoned residence.

The melodic clattering of chimes announced their entrance. Despite their weekly visits, the two friends never ceased to be taken aback by the magnificence of the store. Walking through the front door was like stepping through a time-portal to an ancient era. Full-bodied knight armor stood at attention at the entrance. A royal red carpet lined the wooden floor, and an enormous chandelier hung from the ceiling, all thirty of the candles wielding flame. Having neglected to make acquaintance with electricity, the caretaker hung wall-mounted oil lamps that served as the large building's only lighting. The house was three stories tall, with the top story presumably reserved for Wesley's living quarters. And yet, it was not the scale of the store that continually amazed them, nor was it the ancient decorations—it was the books themselves.

On every wall, floor to ceiling, were rich oak bookshelves brimming over with books of all colors and sizes. The floor itself had become a spellbinding labyrinth, with stacks of books piled one-on-another higher than even the tallest man could reach. A customer could get lost in the expansive maze of books and have his decaying bones found again only years later. The books appeared to be in no apparent order, instead being simply shoved into any niche that would hold them. The air had the overpowering smell of leather and paper. It also had a coarse texture as millions of dust grains floated weightlessly.

Cody glanced up as he heard slow footsteps descending the spiral staircase from the third floor. In polite terms, as Jade preferred to put it, Wesley had pulled his weight in helping the family business sell books since 1683, as their slogan boasted. In other words, Wesley was not a young man. Reaching the bottom of the stairs, the elderly bookkeeper glided toward the customers with agility uncommon for his age. "Ah . . . I should have known it would be you two," he said in a slow, rich voice. "It's been two whole days. I was beginning to get worried." An awkward silence followed. The statement had been uttered in such an emotionlessly neutral way that it left Cody unsure whether it had been intended in joke or earnest. The old man appeared oblivious to the silence and in no particular hurry to fill it with further words. After several uncomfortable moments Cody opened his mouth to speak but the elderly man turned and looked toward the two friends, as if to notice them for the first time. "What will it be this week? More Dostoevsky for you, Master Cody? Perhaps *The Idiot*?" Once again Cody was struck silent, unsure whether the suggestion had been meant in seriousness or in jest.

Before Cody could gather his wits to respond, Wesley smoothly vanished and took his post behind the front desk, commenting, "You don't need any help. . . ." Ready to leave Wesley's awkward presence, Cody was relieved to hear Jade call for him.

Quickly navigating through the stacks of books, he found his friend surrounded by a pile of George Eliot works. "Jade!" He cried, catching his breath, "You're not supposed to leave me alone with that crazy old man, remember!?"

Jade laughed. "Don't be a baby. Didn't your mother ever teach you how to talk to grown-ups?" she chided him. "Now go find some more of your useless fantasy garbage while I pick a book that actually talks about the *real* world." It was a disagreement that went back to the first time they had entered *Wesley's* and had threatened to tear apart their blooming friendship: Jade was a reader of historical fiction; Cody adhered to the school of fantasy and science-fiction authors. In order to save the friendship, they had adopted the necessary plan of splitting up and shopping in private.

Cody, taking leave of his friend, circled around the perimeter of the maze of books in order to avoid coming into contact with the strange store owner. Reaching the staircase, he quickly ascended to the second floor. Although the shop had been organized with no apparent pattern, one could find various stashes of similar books; Chaos masquerading as Order. The particular pile for which Cody was probing was a hoard of greats containing H. G. Wells, Tolkien, Bradbury, C. S. Lewis and more that fate had led him to on his previous visit.

At last he found his treasure trove, hugging the corner of the room firmly, towering ten-feet high against the wall. Cody's mouth began salivating at all the classic goodies before him. Scanning the mountain for new immigrants to the pile, his eyes bulged; a first-edition copy of T. H. White's *The Once and Future King* sat as the steeple of the stack. Cody cherished the classic story of King Arthur and his noble knights.

He scanned the room for a stool to reach his coveted prize but came up blank. He briefly considered asking Wesley for a hand, but quickly dismissed the idea, opting to avoid enduring any more cryptic conversation with the ancient bookkeeper. The solution presented itself in the form of a stubbed toe. "Ouch!" Cody yelped.

Glancing to his throbbing foot he saw a stack of Jane Austen novels littering the floor. *Perfect!* Shuffling them across the floor with his foot, he pushed them up flush against the larger pile. Then, his footstool in place, carefully ascended the Austen books. They wobbled beneath him like a swinging bridge. As with most areas of his life, Cody had not been gifted with exceptional balance, and as he tensely teetered back and forth on the books, he began to rethink his plan. He reached out his hand, his fingers brushing against his desired classic. *Just a bit higher.* Rising onto his tiptoes he grabbed the novel, but the sudden shift in weight caused his homemade stool to implode.

Cody tumbled out-of-control toward the wall and crashed into the mountain of books, which swayed slightly just before crashing down around him. The splattering of books upon the floor echoed like thunder within the antique shop. Fear seized Cody, wrapping its firm hands around his neck and stealing his breath. He paused, breathless for a second, waiting to hear if either Jade or Wesley had heard the commotion. After another moment of silence, he let out his breath. The coast was clear.

He half-heartedly turned around to examine the aftermath of his clumsiness—and released a startled yelp. The top portion of the book pile had come crumbling down, and behind where they had once been was a door. Above the frame of the door was one word: **Restricted**. It was written in blood.

2

A Midnight Visitor

Jade stared unimpressed at her anxious friend. "A door?" she issued in a bored, irritated tone. "You rushed me out of there like a bomb was about to detonate because of . . . a lousy door?" She shook her head disbelievingly, "I really hope you have a better explanation because I had a classic *Middlemarch* in my hand and . . ."

"You're not hearing me, Jade," Cody cut her off. "Okay, okay. So a door isn't anything to sound the alarm about, but what about the word *restricted*? And, in case you had forgotten, it was written in *blood*!" Cody struggled for breath. Following his accidental discovery of the hidden door and without wasting any time to clean up his mess, Cody had dashed wildly down the stairs, grabbed Jade, and dragged her out the door before Wesley was able to question them. Pulling Jade by the arm, the duo had scurried down the alley. Only when they were a good six blocks from the store had Jade finally managed to demand an explanation.

"Or red paint," she insisted in her rational voice. "You do realize that Wesley is going to think we shoplifted the way we dashed out of there," Jade continued, still unable to grasp the significance and reason behind their impromptu mile dash. Cody collapsed onto a sidewalk bench, inhaling rapidly.

"That's the least of our worries. It was blood. I'm positive! What would a man need a hidden door labeled with blood for?" Cody asked, as if there was only one logical conclusion to be deduced. Jade stared blankly. Exasperated, Cody bit his lip, "For storing dead bodies!"

At this Jade couldn't suppress a laugh. "So, you think Wesley is a mass murderer do you? You do realize he's . . ."

". . . like eight hundred years old, I know," finished Cody, "but still, you have to admit it's not normal. He's clearly hiding *something* back there." Jade sighed, placing her arm onto her best friend's shoulder, "Cody, maybe he is. But whatever it is, it's *his* secret. It's of none of our business." A crack of thunder exploded in the dusk sky and the first drop of rain splashed on Cody's shoe. "It's getting dark, and a storm's rolling in. Get some sleep, Cody, and I'll see you at school tomorrow. I'll walk myself home." The two friends diverged toward their homes. After a few feet Jade paused, and turned around, calling, "Cody!"

"Yeah, Jade?" Cody answered while fitting his jacket's hood over his head.

"Sometimes people's secrets are just better off left alone. Forget about the door."

With those final words the sky flashed pure white and the rain began to pour.

Cody rolled over in his bed. Noisy raindrops pelted against his window and the wind howled against the house. His bedroom seemed to sway like a pendulum against the unrelenting onslaught of the storm's breath. He rolled over again, smothering his head underneath his thick pillow. The crackling of thunder erupted overhead. Cody squeezed the pillow tighter around his face. *Blasted rain! Blasted wind!* He was in the middle of turning over once again when something caused him to pause; he could have sworn he heard something. Straining his ears he heard it again. "Cody . . . Cody . . ." It sounded like someone whispering his name.

It's just the wind playing tricks on me. It's been a long day. It wasn't his mother calling. She was away in New York for business, a regular occurrence ever since Cody's father abandoned them. He didn't think Jade would be calling him from outside in the miserable weather. "Cody . . . Cody . . ." He could not deny it this time; someone, somewhere was calling his name. He felt a tingling sensation rush across his skin. *Who? Who? Who?* "Cody . . . Cody . . ." He could hear a slow creaking sound. *Is it coming from my closet?* he thought, petrified. He could hear the faint sound of breath seeping through the door cracks—he was not alone. The creaking noise continued. Cody squinted open an eye; shadows were moving across the ceiling. He took a deep breath and tossed away his pillow. Sitting straight up he screamed at the top of his lungs, "What do you want from me!"

There, standing unmoving before him in the open closet was a figure. Light from the window reflected off a ghostly white face as it stared back savagely: the pale face of Wesley. In his left hand was a serrated knife. Above the closet door, **Restricted** was written in fresh blood. "Cody! Cody!" The wraithlike man shrieked in an inhuman voice, lunging forward . . .

With a jerk, Cody rose up in his bed, drenched in sweat. In front of him was his closet—both doors were fastened closed. The sound of Cody's racing heart was the only noise audible above the fierce offensive of the outside storm. *I've been dreaming.*

Cody glanced over at his clock, debating whether to call Jade and tell her about his nightmare, but he decided against it, knowing what he would get; another motherly lecture on the need to forget all about Wesley and that stupid door. No, it was too late now to simply forget that door. His nightmare had ensured that. For whatever reason, he and this door were now interconnected and there was only one way he was going to get it off his mind—he was going to have to go through that door . . . and he was going to have to do it tonight.

3

Opening the Door

An eerie fog settled in on the town of Havenwood like a hungry vulture following behind the passing rainstorm. Early remnants of frost seemed to proclaim the coming of the night's nipping chill. No lights were shining; all of the town's people lay nestled in their warm beds, shielded from the bitter night. All except for one . . .

Cody pulled his jacket up to guard his face from the wind gusts careening against it. The idea to enter the mysterious doorway seemed a good one while Cody lay in the warmth of his house. Rushing, completely drenched down the alleyway toward Wesley's, he began to realize the rashness of his plan. *I've come too far to turn back now.*

Coming out of the alley, Cody saw the familiar mansion. Only not all was familiar. Standing out like a neon light from the rest of the unchanging scene was a wooden sign in the front yard. The sign read: **FOR SALE.**

Cody panicked. *Does he know?* Surely the new sign could not be a reaction to his discovery. But Cody couldn't dismiss the odd timing. *He knows.*

Cody shuffled under the doorway ledge of an adjacent building. He needed a plan, and he needed it quick; otherwise he would freeze to death in the storm. Wishing Jade was nearby, Cody scanned the house. He was positive the front door would be locked. *Backdoor perhaps?* He tried to recall the backside of the house. Even though he had been in the store countless times, he could not recall the existence of a back door. He bit down hard on his lip, a nervous habit that emerged anytime he was straining his brain, which of course, was not very often.

Finally, it came to him. *The window.* Apart from the large, draped bay windows in the front, the house had a surprising lack of additional windows, especially considering its great size. There was only one rather small, circular window on the top floor, which must have served as Wesley's peephole to the outside world. *Or to scout out his next murder victim.*

Another window was located on the left side of the building on the second floor. Clearly, though, without a legendary growth spurt in the next few moments, Cody knew it was not an option. That left only one hope: the back window. The window was of medium size, but large enough to crawl through, and if Cody's memory served him right, which was rare, it should enter into the room that primarily housed poetry.

Determining that this was his only reasonable plan of action, Cody squatted low and sprinted toward the house, hiding behind parked cars and bushes along the way. *For all I know old Wesley is scouting out that peephole right now.* Reaching the store, Cody silently scaled the walls around the large house until he came to the backyard. What he saw next shocked him. In the middle of the backyard was a large hole dug into the ground with a shovel sticking upright. By the look of it, the dirt was fresh. *He's going to bury the bodies!*

Cody sensed his quest was becoming more direr by the second. He examined the back of the house. Just as he had remembered, there was the window, his one glimmer of hope. Rushing toward it, he was pleased to find it had not been completely closed. A sliver remained separating the glass and the window sill. Sliding his fingernails under the crack he heaved with all his might—it didn't budge. *It's jammed.*

Cody looked around him for something to use as leverage. His eyes fell on the shovel. Dashing back into the rain he quickly retrieved the tool. Returning to the window, he slipped the spade under the crack. Applying all his weight, he pressed forcefully down on the handle. With a thud the rustic window dislodged and opened up. Eager to gain shelter from the storm, Cody crawled through the window and into the house—the house of a murderer.

He collapsed on the floor. The temperature inside was nearly as chilly as the stormy air outside. Gathering himself off the floor, he removed his drenched jacket and shoes, laying them by the window for his departure. He didn't want to risk his soaked sneakers squeaking and revealing his intrusion.

Tip-toeing to the door, he cautiously stuck his head out of the room. As expected, the floor was empty. The house was dark, with the only light coming from the chandelier candles that still faintly flickered. Ducking down to conceal himself behind the piles of books, Cody made his way toward the stairs. Reaching them, he knew he would have to temporarily forgo his cover. Taking a deep breath, he stood and dashed up the spiral stair-case. Without stopping at the top, he turned down the hall, weaving his way around piles of books and corners, until he finally threw himself against the wall and sunk down to the floor. He had reached the spot. Looking at the wall erased any doubt that the 'For Sale' sign corresponded with his discovery. In the place where the revealed door had been, now, once again, was a neat pile of books. *Wesley knows.*

Just then he heard a creaking noise. Cody froze. The sound was coming from above his head. He could make out slight bowing of the ceiling. *Wesley's awake! And he's walking around.* Cody could think of only a few reasons for Wesley to still be awake, and all of them meant that Cody would be dead by the end of the night. He swallowed hard.

Every fiber in his body was screaming at him to return home, but thoughts of the horrifying nightmare were too great to overcome. He had come too far to turn back. His desire to open the door trumped all rational thinking. As quietly as he could, Cody began removing books one by one.

The footsteps overhead continued in frantic bursts of movement. Wesley seemed to be riled up. Removing the top several rows of books, the red letters once again came into view: **Restricted**. Looking closer, Cody confirmed his earlier thoughts. The letters were indeed written in blood.

Exhilaration shot through Cody's body. With increasing pace, no longer worried about noise, he continued to remove book after book. The polished oak door came back into view. Cody felt every hair on his arms stand straight. Having removed most of the books, Cody knelt down and pushed the remaining books aside with reckless abandon, too possessed by a savage yearning to worry about noise. The last book fell limp to the ground.

With the door fully revealed, Cody was surprised to discover that it was not full-sized. In fact, it resembled a child's playhouse door. *Odd* thought Cody, pondering how an elderly man would be able to enter the door. Reaching a shaky arm out, he grasped hold of the handle. Adrenaline pumped uncontrollably through his veins like a drum. He braced himself for what he was about to witness; Cody turned the handle and opened the door. Ducking down, with a final pause, he entered the room . . . and gasped.

The scene before his eyes was shocking.

4

The Man with the Knife

Time was running out. The man glanced around his messy room. *Everything is going to change tonight.* With haste he raced back to his closet and grabbed another bundle of clothes, stuffing them into an overflowing suitcase. The boom of thunder outside startled him. *Yes, time is very short.*

It had happened as he had feared, yet the moment had still found him unprepared the same way one still flinches when anticipating a needle. His secret had been discovered. Shuffling over to his lone window he peered anxiously out onto the street. It was empty. *How much longer do I have? They could be on their way this moment.* This last thought sent a jolt of terror down his spine. *I'm getting too old for this.*

He grabbed his wallet off his desk and flipped through to survey his cash. It was not much, but it would be enough to get to where he needed to go—that being as far away from Havenwood as absolutely possible. The man returned to the window that once again revealed he was still alone on the dreary night. He watched as a hawk flew gracefully into the fog. *Am I too late?*

This was not the first time he had had his secret discovered, but it was the first time the intruder had been allowed to exit his store unquestioned. He glanced at his watch, it was a quarter to two in the morning; time was running out.

How much had the boy seen? Had he been inside? Surely not. If so, he would have known. He would have been dead by now. *But this weather?* Clearly, this was a bad omen. Something sliced through his thoughts, paralyzing him. The man dropped to the floor and pressed his ear against the dusty wood. His worst fears had been realized. *Somebody's entering the hidden room!*

The man jumped up with unnatural agility for a man his age and dashed to his nightstand. Opening the top drawer he began tossing out papers and trinkets until he found what he was looking for—a sharp, serrated knife. He staggered toward the stairs. *This is it*, he grimly determined, *or the world as we know it is doomed.*

5

A Scarlet Letter

Cody rubbed his eyes and stared back into the small room. *How could it be?* He glanced around the room; he had expected a lot of things. He had prepared himself for the most horrific sights. But what he now saw before him was the last thing he had ever expected to see. The room was filled—with books. An initial feeling of disappointment was soon consumed by the uncomfortable feeling of a tightening stomach, the kind you get when you realize you have just made a terrible, terrible mistake. It had never crossed his mind that his theory could be incorrect; it had all seemed so logical: the door, the blood, the sign, and the freshly dug grave. *Jade was right. Jade's always right.* It suddenly dawned on him that with the absence of murdered bodies, he now had no conceivable reason to have broken into an elderly man's house and trespassed onto private property. Cody sickly began to think that Wesley was not the man who was going to end the night behind bars.

The room was not large, about the size of a small bedroom or large bathroom. After entering through the child-sized door, the ceiling once again rose to standard size. The two flanking walls, mirroring the rest of the store, were covered with large bookshelves. Various trinkets and unusual objects decorated the shelves. The center-piece of the room, against the far wall, was an extravagantly carved podium with a single book resting on it.

What is the book? Cody wondered as he walked toward it. His eyes explored the room. The spines of the books were too worn down and tattered to make out the names or authors. But what really captured Cody's attention were the unusual objects on the shelves. Many of them looked like travel devices, perhaps a sexton or a compass, yet like nothing he had ever seen before. As to what purpose they served, Cody could only speculate.

Approaching the book on the podium, a decoration on the final shelf drew his attention away. It was a picture, framed by an elaborate silver frame. There was nothing out of the ordinary about the frame, however, what was *inside* the frame left Cody speechless. The picture was of Wesley, looking many years younger, shaking hands with a familiar man. The man was George Washington.

Cody was no history scholar, but he remembered enough from the history essays Jade had written for him to understand that George Washington lived around the seventeen hundreds. *How old IS Wesley?* Shaking his head, he returned the picture to the shelf. *All this adrenaline is making me crazy.* Gathering his wits, he realized that the man with Washington could easily be one of Wesley's ancestors. Or at worst, it was merely a photography trick. Several of the boys in his school had played a similar prank on him a number of years back by photo editing Jade into a picture with Jules Verne in an attempt to make Cody jealous and profess his love for her. It hadn't worked then, and it wouldn't work now.

Besides, the more pressing concern was the large Book lying, unopened, on the podium before him. Cody's first impression was that it would be a Bible or a Koran, or some other significant religious book. Now that he stood before it, he realized his assumptions had been wrong. *It's not the first time I've been wrong tonight.*

The Book was larger than the average novel, closer to the size of a traditional magazine. It had a dark brown, leather cover, which was tattered and clearly showed the wear-and-tear of its age. Along the edges of the front cover, various cryptic symbols created a border around the perimeter. The only other marking, placed directly in the middle, framed by the symbol border, was a large scarlet 'A.'

You have got to be kidding, thought Cody. *All this trouble for a lousy Hawthorne novel?* Reaching down, Cody picked the Book up with his hands. It was remarkably lighter than he had expected. In fact, it felt almost weightless in his hands. He also noticed that the pages were not regular paper, but rather a tough parchment. *Well, here goes nothing.* Inhaling deeply, he anxiously pulled opened the cover. The first page revealed two very important facts to Cody. The first was that the Book was definitely *not* the famous classic written by Nathaniel Hawthorne. And secondly, the Book was clearly not written in English.

Running his eyes across the page he could not recognize any familiar word. The letters seemed similar to English; in fact several of the letters, such as the vowels, were almost identical to English. However, there were many letter shapes that Cody had never seen before, and unfamiliar accents marked the majority of the letters. *What is this?*

For lack of a better idea, Cody cleared his throat and began sounding out the first line as best he could. The words slipped awkwardly off his tongue. The instant he finished the sentence, a roaring clash of thunder shook the house, knocking Cody back against the bookshelf. Regaining his balance, he opened his mouth to attempt to read the next line, but didn't get far.

"What are you doing!?" Cody's stomach jumped. He turned to the open door way. In the archway stood a frantic-looking Wesley; he was wielding a knife. Cody unconsciously concealed the Book behind his back, "I . . . um . . . I . . . Sir . . . I'm so sorry . . . I just . . ." Cody stuttered.

Wesley wasn't paying any attention to him. The old man's eyes scanned the room until they stopped at the empty podium. "No! Where is the Book?! What have you done with the Book?!" Wesley was in a state of hysterics, and Cody knew that the knife he was holding was not intended to butter a late-night slab of toast. Cody understood his chances of survival were slim and brought the Book out from behind his back.

"I . . . ah . . . just wanted to look inside. I'm very sorry, Sir. I couldn't read it so you don't have to worry. I'll leave you now, I just . . . "

At this comment Wesley's eyes flared up and blazed like a forest fire. "You tried to *read* it! You *fool!* What would possess you to do something so stupid! So, I'm already too late; we're doomed!" Wesley screamed.

A bead of sweat ran down Cody's forehead. Clearly he was missing something. "But, Sir, why are you doomed? I'm afraid I don't understand."

Wesley pierced Cody with a penetrating stare and a crooked smirk formed across his face causing his rough forehead to wrinkle and his face to take on a demented appearance.

"Clearly, Master Clemenson, you misunderstand me. *I* am not doomed. *We* are doomed. This *world* is doomed."

Cody shuddered; his head was burning. *It's just a stupid book!* The conversation was brought to a quick silence. A loud thud was heard from above their heads. Once again the floor began to sag under the pressure of footsteps clicking across the floor like fingers tapping on a table. Cody shot a glance to Wesley for an answer. Wesley's face had gone completely pale. "It's here," he whispered in a terrified voice that seemed distant and not directed at anyone in particular.

"Who's here? What's going on, Wesley?!" But the elderly man had already disappeared out the door. Cody followed him at a sprint. The footsteps overhead were growing louder and were accompanied by a steady banging. *Thud.* Whoever was upstairs was trying to get through Wesley's bedroom door. *Thud.* By the sound of it, they would soon succeed.

Wesley had run to his desk and was hurriedly flipping through his files and tossing papers into the air muttering, "Out of time, out of time." Cody caught up to him and stood petrified watching Wesley scrounge around his desk like a madman. Terrified as he was, Cody knew it was unwise to interrupt the elderly man. *Thud.*

At last, Wesley seemed to have found what he was looking for—he pulled a large sword out from the cabinet beside his desk. The sword looked like something from the medieval days. Next, he pulled out a smaller dagger. Grabbing a piece of paper, he tore it in two and began scribbling madly. Without a word, he took one of the sheets and pinned it onto the wall with the dagger. Cody opened his mouth to question the strange turn of events but Wesley held a finger out, "Don't talk. Listen . . ." *Thud.* "There is no time for me to explain. But there might still be hope. Take this," he said, shoving a crumpled piece of paper into Cody's hand, "And I want you to run. Find somewhere safe. This letter," he said pointing to the paper he had just given Cody, "will guide you from there." *THUD*—The upstairs door had been breached.

Cody glanced with horror to the staircase but Wesley grabbed his shoulder. Wesley's face had changed. His eyes no longer burned with rage, but looked weary, almost sad, "Boy, I'm sorry it had to be you. Destiny is a sly devil, my lad. The code is now in your hands. Now run. And under *no* circumstances let anyone read that Book. Only *your* eyes, do you understand? Otherwise all is lost. I'm so, so sorry." With these final words, Wesley ran toward the stairs, sword in hand.

Cody didn't need to be told twice. Shoving the book underneath his shirt he ran to the front door. He fumbled franticly with the lock. He heard a chilling scream from upstairs, but didn't intend to wait around long enough to find out from whom. With the door finally open, Cody dashed out into the pouring rain and ran as fast as his legs could carry him.

Reaching the alleyway, Cody turned back for one final glance at the mansion. The place looked desolate, all the childhood ghost stories racing back to Cody's mind. *What just happened in there?* Suddenly he saw the drapes in the bay windows shuffle. Pressing himself against the wall, Cody squinted his eyes. Although the fog hindered his vision, he could make out a faint shape standing in the window. Leaning forward for a better look, he saw two softly glowing red slits. *Eyes? What on earth is in there?* The shape moved. The red slits turned, and for a brief moment, locked eyes with Cody.

6

The Unseen

The telephone stared mockingly as the middle-aged man paced back and forth in the miniscule, dimly-lit room. The lone clock ticked forward as though coated in heavy tar. The man curled his plump upper lip into his mouth and rubbed it with his tongue; he was no coward. He had stared down the face of horrors that had turned even the strongest of men into whimpering children—and without so much as a blink. No, he was no coward. Death was as much a mundanely routine part of his life as flossing his crooked teeth. No, he was no coward.

He continued to repeat this thought to himself as a bead of sweat zigzagged down the wrinkles of his forehead, slid over his nose, and tumbled off his sharply-defined chin. He cast another nervous glance at the telephone sitting lonesome on the brittle wooden table. *Why hasn't he called yet?* A startling sound echoed in his ears. His arm lurched out with savage speed and brought the phone to his ear, "My lord, I'm . . ."

A blank dial tone greeted him. *It's just the bloody birds.* He replaced the phone and resumed his pacing. The clock now showed that the anticipated call was two minutes late. *He's putting me in my place.*

At last the phone vibrated on its bearings; its loud ring filling up the room. The sound sent a shiver down his back. The phone rang again. *Blast!* He pulled the phone to his ear, "Forgive me master for being unable to answer on the first ring. I curse myself for keeping you waiting." Silence. The man knew his life was dangling by a thin wire; his master was not one to be kept waiting. At last a voice responded; it was slow and emotionless, "I trust it will not happen again. Report before I regret my unwarranted display of mercy." The man exhaled an audible sigh of relief before he could stop himself, "You are most merciful my lord. Events have been . . . put into motion. The first casualty has been claimed. 'That-which-arrives-in-the-dead-of-night' has awoken. The old man has fallen. The Book has been seized by a young boy. My men have just narrowed down his location. Are we to engage?"

The phone was once again silent. The sound of puffing smoke was faintly audible. *Just answer; is this all a game to you?* The cold voice returned, "Yes, but with caution. The boy will be oblivious to the situation. Do not take unnecessary risk, CROSS must remain invisible. We do not exist. I will not accept otherwise." The man shuttered; he had not the slimmest doubt that the caller was a man of his word.

"I understand, my lord. The target is just a young boy; am I to assume that casualties should be avoided?" The unseen man's chilling voice responded, "A young boy, a pregnant woman, a carefree child, a proud grandfather—a threat to the cause is intolerable regardless of which insufferable form it takes. If the boy will not cooperate—eliminate him without hesitation. I can assure you, if you fail, you will not receive the same hesitation from me." The sound of dial tone once again filled the man's ear.

"Good-bye to you, too," he muttered bitterly into the receiver. The moment he did, he instantly scanned the room. *You fool, he could be watching you! His web is omnipresent.* At last convinced that his imprudent jab had gone unnoticed, he exhaled and collapsed into a wooden chair. Every time he made contact with his master he felt as though he was playing a terrifying game of Russian roulette. He wiped the sweat from his brow—*I've survived another round.* He looked to the corner of the room where a swarm of flies buzzed around an unrecognizable object on the floor. The smell was vile. *Charlie.* His predecessor; at least what was left of him.

Charlie had displeased the master. The consequence had been a well-placed bullet from behind. At the master's request, Charlie had been left to rot. The man looked away; the sight of the decaying body was sickening.

He reached into his coat pocket and pulled out a metallic object; a shiny six-shooter revolver. He cocked it open and smiled. It was fully loaded. With a fluid movement he flicked it closed. *It's time to go to work.*

7

The Intruder

An explosion of thunder ripped apart the night sky; causing the earth to tremble in solemn reverence. Jade yanked up her covers earnestly and watched the heavy rain wash down her bedroom window like a waterfall, blurring her vision to the outside world. She squeezed her eyes shut—it certainly wasn't the first time she looked out into the world only to see haze and disorder.

A loud crash resounded from the living room. Jade kept her eyes closed; the familiar smell of stale liquor informed her that her mother had returned from her nightly excursion to the bar. Slowly, and as delicately as she could manage, she rolled over to glance at her clock—1:15 a.m.

There was another loud crash, followed by the cringing sound of shattering glass. "MARI!" screamed a husky voice, "Mari, you wretched, useless child! Get your ugly, flabby butt out here and help your mother! MARI!" Jade squeezed her eyes tighter. With a resonating thud she knew that her mother had just passed out on the floor, once again leaving Jade alone. The bitter taste of moist salty tears rolled over her tongue. She despised herself for her weakness, but allowed the tears to trickle gently over her small cheeks.

Reaching over to her nightstand she twisted on her dusty radio. Soft, classical piano music began to seep gently through the speakers. She took a deep breath. *I miss you dad* she mouthed silently. It had been eight years since her world had come crashing down. Everything had been so perfect before. Her parents were in love and she had been happy. She clenched her fist. *But that was another lifetime ago. At least I have Cody . . .*

Suddenly, Jade was pulled away from her melancholy thoughts as a familiar voice sounded through the radio. **"We interrupt our scheduled broadcast for an important announcement . . . this is Sheriff Messiner speaking. Havenwood is being put on a code red alert effective immediately. A man has been murdered tonight. This is the first murder in Havenwood in over thirty years. The victim's body has been brutally mangled and disfigured, but we confirmed his identity: The bookstore owner, Wesley Simon."** Jade choked and covered her mouth with her hand. **"We strongly encourage all of you still awake to remain inside, keep your doors locked, and report any unusual activity immediately. We are in pursuit of a suspect. We have reason to believe he is still in Havenwood and is highly dangerous. We thank you for . . . "**

BANG! Jade screamed before she could catch herself. Out of the corner of her eye, she caught the faint silhouette of a figure through the window. The enlarged shadow projected upon her bedroom wall advanced toward the front door. *Thump . . .*

thump . . . thump . . . she watched silently as the shadow ascended the stairs and reached for the door. With a soft creak the doorknob twisted and the figure entered the house.

Stay calm, Jade. There was a soft squeaking as the old wooden floor of the living room bent beneath the weight of the intruder. *Mom!* The sound of the steps confirmed the intruder was heading directly toward her room. Noiselessly rolling out of bed, Jade pulled her bedside lamp from the wall and readied it like a club. The footsteps were getting closer. Her bedroom doorknob began to twist. Jade drew in a deep breath and backed herself into the shadows. Without a sound the door gently swayed open.

With a wild, savage scream Jade lunged forward and raised the lamp. She froze, staggering into an abrupt halt. Standing, framed in the doorway—was Cody. All the color was drained from his terrified face and his eyes bulged as though in a deep trance.

Jade swiftly pulled him into her room. "What are you doing here! You scared me to death! You shouldn't be out tonight; they just reported on the radio that Wesley is dead!"

For the first time Cody raised his eyes to meet hers and what she saw in them was pure fright. He nodded. "I know Jade, and it's my fault he's dead."

Jade felt the color drain from her own face. "Cody, what are you talking about. What have you done?"

Cody shook his head as though fighting to break free from the merciless clasp of a dream. "I don't know. Something giant, something—terrible . . . " his voice trailed off.

"Cody, what is it! What happened tonight?" Jade demanded.

Cody's arms shot out and grabbed Jade by the shoulders, giving her a rough shake. "Aren't you listening?! There's something out there! Something . . . huge. We can't stay here. We're not safe. It's coming!"

8

Wesley's Riddle

Cody flushed as he looked around Jade's room. Their friendship was close, but had mostly taken place in public places such as school and around town. Now, as on the other few occasions he had been into her room, he felt uncomfortable. He felt his cheeks begin to burn so he hastily turned to face the wall. He had quickly filled Jade in on the night's events and now sat shamefully on the floor awaiting her response.

Jade was pacing back and forth. "I told you to forget that stupid door . . . why can't you *ever* listen to reason?" she scolded sharply. "This is no game, a man is dead. Dead! This is clearly larger now than we ever suspected." She flopped down onto her bed. "And you say the murderer saw you? It won't take him long to figure out you're here." Jade sighed, "But we don't have time to dwell on your inexplicably dim-witted stupidity. Come on, let's have a look at this book of yours . . ."

She leaned down in eager anticipation as Cody removed the Book from his backpack. His hand wrapped around the smooth leather cover. "Ah!" he screamed and winced in pain. A sharp wave of pressure, like an electric current, shot up Cody's fingers, ran along his arm, and burrowed into his brain. A deafening, high-pitched ringing sound erupted in his ear-drums. Clamping his eyes shut, he grabbed his ears, squeezing violently, desperate to release the tension. The pressure on his brain clamped its vice-grip tighter and tighter and tighter. Cody yelled in agony. Then, just as soon as it had swept in, the pressure vanished, like a breeze flowing through one window and out the next.

Cody slowly dropped his arms and opened his eyes. *What just happened?* He brought his fingers up to his sweat-drenched forehead, searching for any evidence of the sudden attack on his brain. His investigation was interrupted by the impatient voice of his female companion, "Well, are you just going to sit there or do you want to hand me that book?"

Cody looked at the worn leather Book; he was tightly squeezing it in his right hand. He looked back to Jade, who appeared completely oblivious by his sudden attack. *I need to get some sleep; my brain is going rogue.*

Without a word about his recent episode, he passed the mysterious Book toward Jade's anxious hands. She was taken aback by its simplicity. She had expected something grand, perhaps a cover comprised of sculpted wooden designs or rimmed with flashy gold. But only the scarlet 'A' jumped out in contrast to the worn brown backing. Cody stared up at her intensely, "Whatever you do, don't open it. You won't be able to read it anyways. By Wesley's reaction, I don't think it's safe," he said, massaging his forehead again. Jade had no intention of challenging his theory, and set the Book down gently on her nightstand, quickly withdrawing her hands as though it were poison ivy.

"We need to hand this book over to the police immediately," Jade commanded. Cody jumped up. "NO!" he yelled before he realized what he was doing. His face flushed again and he sat back down. "I mean, uh, no. Wesley's last words were a strict order not to let *anyone* read the Book. Until we figure out what is so special about it, we have to keep it a secret. Promise Jade?"

Jade scrunched her face; she was not eager to break even the smallest of rules if there was any other way. Finally she sighed, "Promise." She linked her small pinky finger with Cody's, "Pinky shake, never break, or all my books are yours to take. . . . But, dude, I hope you know what you're doing." *So do I!* Cody thought gloomily.

He suddenly remembered the crumpled letter in his pocket. He pulled it out and smoothed out the creases. "This is the letter Wesley gave me just before he . . . well, just before I left. I've read it several times but can't make any sense of it."

"Well, maybe I can help figure it out," Jade countered. Cody knew this was simply her polite way of reminding him that she was the brains of the friendship and he was not. Retrieving the note she read it earnestly,

Fifty-three, less four, until the rite does write,
Iron décor, future war, hides passage out of sight,
Deep contrite, prevents invite, now precious yore,
Must leave Tonight.

Cody waited impatiently as Jade reread the note for the third time. He had every confidence that if anyone could make sense of this riddle, it would be Jade. He could see her deep green eyes twitching as they strained toward the paper. Finally, she lifted her head, a defeated look stealing her face, "It's a load of gibberish. I think our dear friend Wesley lost his mind. I'm sorry, Cody, I don't think this is going to be of any help to us." Cody was not ready to admit defeat. He had spent an academic lifetime not understanding. He hauntingly recalled Wesley's saddened eyes moments before his death. *No, Wesley was not a mad man.*

The clues on the note kept turning over and over in Cody's head. No matter how many times he thought about it, each time made less and less sense. It was like staring at the face of a longtime acquaintance and being completely unable to remember his name.

The one word that kept jumping out and frightening him was the last one: *Tonight.* The only thing Cody *had* concluded was that Wesley did not make it the only capitalized word by accident. Wesley clearly wanted them to leave immediately. *Then leave a simpler message next time!* Cody thought angrily. He attempted to break it down into bite-sized chunks. The first part was a pretty simple math equation, even for him, equaling a sum of forty-nine. The second part would be impossible to decipher until they determined what or who "the rite" was referring to, and what it was writing.

The second line, however, was one that troubled Cody the most. He did not like the sound of a "future war." He decided that the end of the sentence most likely referred to a hidden passageway. *Was this where Wesley had wanted them to go? Were they supposed to uncover the path? But where was it? And where did it lead?*

"Cody?" The voice was Jade's. Cody lifted his head and looked into her weary green eyes, "Any ideas?" Cody felt his shoulders sink, "No, and I have the sickening feeling that we are quickly running out of time. . . ." In frustration he released the letter, allowing it to flutter to the floor, "So, what do you think we should do? We obviously can't go anywhere until we know *where* we're going, and Wesley seems absolutely adamant that we don't delay."

Sheriff Messiner's description of Wesley's death added undeniable weight to the urgency, Jade thought as she nodded with grim determination. "I know. That's why we have to go back."

Cody rubbed his eyes, startled, "Go back where?" The look in Jade's eyes made it clear that her decision had been made, there would be no discussion.

"We're going back to Wesley's."

The chilly night breeze had forced people into their homes, leaving the barren streets in desolate stillness. The families had worriedly tucked their children into sleep before fretfully locking all the doors and windows. All of them were oblivious of the two sharp red eyes gazing at them from the shadows, stalking their every movement. The foreboding figure felt the dense fear rising from the homes and settling over the town like an ominous fog. Another draft of night air blew between the houses.

The sound of sniffing fluttered out from the shadows, barely noticeable over the sound of the gusting wind. The red eyes squinted, the scent in the air was familiar. It was the same odor that had conveniently lingered in the doorway of that old fool, Wesley. Unnoticed by anyone, the red eyes noiselessly disappeared into the night.

9

The Ruby Pocket Watch

Peering across the road, a dark figure stood staring at a small, plain house. Gliding over the road with serpentine swiftness, the figure entered the tiny home. A strong, new scent billowed from the nearby couch. Alcohol. Regaining the initial odor, the dark figure was guided to a small bedroom. The door flew off its hinges as the figure burst into the room. Its dense, probing eyes scanned the scene for its prey—but the room was empty. Sniffing the air again, it turned and left the building. The scent was fresh. It was not far behind.

Staring out across the road from the alleyway, Wesley's mansion looked just as it had earlier that night. The only glaring exceptions were the long yellow ribbons blocking the house off from the public, the aftermath of Sheriff Messiner's investigations. The unfamiliar neon streamers looked awkward against the backdrop of the ancient dwelling. Scanning left and right Jade confirmed that the coast was clear. Motioning behind her to where Cody was crunched down low against the wall, she signaled him to follow.

It had taken a lot of guts for Jade to go against her nature and decide to return to the mansion. She gazed back at her friend as they stealthily crept across the road toward the house. His face was pale with fright. *Who can blame him?* thought Jade tenderly. In truth, she felt *inside* just as scared as he looked *outside*. But she also knew that he was counting on her to be courageous, and that to continue on this mission, she would need to suppress her fear. The undecipherable letter had bothered her tremendously, more than Cody would ever know. Up until that point, her practical side had taken control and she was convinced that there was a reasonable explanation behind everything. But now her confidence was rattled. Being unable to solve the riddle had been a harsh blow to her academic pride, and the mention of "new war" had left her nauseated.

"Around back," Cody whispered. The two scurried around the house until they came to the rear. Jade's focus was captured by the piles of dirt in the backyard. "What do you think this is?" she asked. Cody shrugged, "I'm not sure; I had originally thought he had been digging holes for the dead bodies hidden in that room. Whatever it was for, it will now serve as his own grave." Jade shivered at the grim irony of the statement. *Hold it together, girl.*

Removing the yellow tape barricades, she followed after Cody and crawled through the window. With a light thud she fell to the floor on the other side. Had she fallen a few inches farther, her face would have landed on the objects littering the floor: Cody's jacket and shoes, still slightly damp.

"Cody, you left evidence! They are going to be onto you now. I can't believe you were so stupid!"

'I'm sorry, but I was a little bit too preoccupied trying not to get mauled and mangled to worry about covering my tracks. Next time my life is flashing before my eyes I'll try and do better!" For the first time all night Jade let out a slight smile. "*Touché.* . . . Now let's see if Wesley left us any more clues and get out of here before Messiner and the other officers return."

Without another word they ventured forward into the dark house.

Standing in an all-too-familiar alleyway, two red eyes probed the scene of the night's earlier murder. Through the drapes of the front bay window, it could perceive the shape of two children rushing up the stairs. The figure took a slow stride toward the ancient bookstore: the children were impeccably brave—or unforgivably stupid. It licked its lips. They always grew dry right before a feeding.

A pile of books carefully concealed the restricted room. Cody quickly pushed the books to floor, once again reveal-ing the oak door. Jade followed Cody through the small opening. Both were disappointed to find the room completely trashed. "Looks like Wesley's murderer was looking for something," Jade observed. Cody felt the weight of the scarlet-lettered book in his backpack and remembered the unexplainable sensation it had given him in Jade's room. *What are we getting ourselves into?* Jade scanned some torn pages littering the floor. "Well, whoever was here last probably took anything of value. Let's take a look quick and then get out of here."

Cody pushed aside a pile of shredded books. Underneath was a torn picture, the photo he had seen earlier of Wesley and George Washington. Looking over at the shelves he noticed that each of Wesley's unique location devices had been systematically destroyed. *Apparently someone doesn't want us to find this hidden passageway.*

Cody was examining one of the devices when Jade called him, "Cody, come take a look at this." He scurried over to Jade who was kneeling beside the overturned podium. "What do you make of this?" She pointed midway down the neck of the podium. Cody knelt down and examined the wood. There didn't appear to be anything unusual. Squinting his eyes, he noticed a light marking tattooing the wood. A faded capital red 'A', was scarcely visible. The marking matched the symbol on the book's cover.

"Well, this podium was designed to hold the book, so it makes sense right?" Jade didn't look as convinced. Without a word, she raised the podium above her head and chucked it against the wall. *CRASH!*

"Jade! What do you think you're doing? Someone's going to hear! We've got to . . ." He halted midsentence. A faint glimmer caught his eye. Stepping over to the podium rubble, he reached down and retrieved a shiny object that had been concealed within the podium's trunk.

"What is it, Cody?" Jade asked.

The object was circular, the size of Cody's palm. The face was tinted with gold. The back was formed with smooth ruby marble, and intricate symbols were engraved along its side. "Um . . . maybe it's . . . a pocket watch?" He passed the object to Jade. Sure enough, four elegant look-ing clock hands, three long and one short, all moved. The longer hands were colored red, gold and purple, and the short hand was a darker shade of red. Surprisingly, instead of numbers there were pictures. Jade couldn't make out what they depicted. The light in the room flickered. Jade looked out the door.

"We better hurry, the sun is starting to rise. And . . ." She stopped. Cody could see the gears in her head spin-ning, "Quick Cody, walk around me in a circle." Cody opened his mouth to object and remind Jade of their time pinch but she again insisted. Dropping his shoulders, Cody quickly paced around her.

"Happy? Okay now we really need to get out . . ." With lightning swiftness Jade's arm shot out and grasped Cody, pulling him toward her. "What are you . . ."

"Shut up and look!" Jade pointed to the clock hands "They aren't moving, see? But what about when I do this?" She began to slowly circle Cody, holding the device in front of her. The hands began to rotate along with her. "The long red hand points toward you no matter where I move."

Cody clutched his backpack. "Either that or it points to what I'm carrying with me. It's like a navigation device for locating this Book! What about the other hands?" Jade grinned, "I'm not sure, but I have my suspicions that it wouldn't be such a bad idea to follow the *short* red hand if you know what I mean." Cody caught his friend's contagious smile, "I think we just found the direction to the hidden passageway."

BANG! A loud crash shook the house. Dust freefell from the rafters. Cody saw on Jade's face that they shared the same singular thought. *We need to get out of here. Fast!*

Stuffing the device into his pocket, Cody flung his backpack onto his shoulder; Jade was already halfway through the door. "It might be Sheriff Messiner," she whispered earnestly behind her. Cody bit his lip, *or worse.*

They emerged, panting, from the dwarfed hidden door. Standing at the top of the spiral staircase, they gazed down to the front door. It was swinging on its hinges.

We're not alone.

10

The Beast

Cody's heart seemed to burst through his chest. He glanced at Jade, who for the first time that night, appeared frightened. "We've got to keep moving. We need to get out of here. *Fast.*" She didn't answer. All the color in her face had vacated. Her eyes twitched. Cody didn't need to look back at the door to realize their passage down the stairs was no longer an option.

Cody saw it; a figure obscured in the sanctuary of the dancing shadows cast by the swinging front door. A foul stench wafted up to their floor. "Cody, we need to run," Jade whispered, but his muscles had already overthrown the mastership of his brain. He stood petrified as though turned to stone.

Cody could make out two red eyes and heard the faint sound of sniffing. The figure stepped out from its cover. Jade's trembling hand suffocated her own terrified scream. The silhouette illuminated in the frame of the door was not human.

Concealing most of his face, the creature was cloaked in a dark purple robe, which draped over its back and came up in a low hood. From under the cape, the only things visible were two glaring red eyes and a boar-like snout. Beneath the cloak were four scaly feet and giant talons that glimmered from each of the six birdlike fingers.

With deathly silence, the creature rose up vertically revealing its true size. All the moisture in Cody's throat evaporated; the Beast was easily the height of a fully-grown grizzly bear. A bulge pressed against the robe from behind the creature forming the shape of a shell, like an exoskeleton of a beetle. Cody heard Jade's soft cry from across the room; she still hadn't budged from her spot.

Seconds masqueraded as hours as Cody and the creature remained locked in a stare. Cody felt like a helpless prisoner held in place by invisible hooks bursting forth from the creature's eyes. Still void of sound, the hoggish creature lowered back onto all fours—and charged.

The horrifying sight was enough to wrench Jade from her trance.

"Run!" Grabbing Cody's sleeve she yanked him down the hall; the sound of the creature's feet could be heard thrashing rapidly up the staircase. In desperation the two friends reached the second staircase that led up to Wesley's private chambers. "Up! Let's go! Hurry!" The pair dashed up the stairs and slammed the door behind them, quickly fastening the lock.

"Cody, help me move this couch, we've got to brace the door!" Jade screamed over the scraping sound of talons scratching against the wooden floor. They heard a light growl. "Push!" With all their strength they shoved the couch toward the door. The crashing sound of the sofa hitting the door was echoed by a loud thud from the other side. The screws in the hinges loosened. Cody stood staring at the door, "It's not going to hold for long, Jade, we need to get out of here!"

Jade looked around the room. "There has to be a way out of here!" Cody examined the room for the first time. Reflecting the disorderly nature of the store below, the room was a messy collection of scattered objects. Wesley was obviously a world traveler. There appeared to be objects from every part of the world and culture imaginable: An Egyptian vase, an African voodoo mask, a large elephant carved from wood. *It's like he lived a double life,* Cody bit his lip, *or a very long life,* he thought, remembering the framed picture. Looking over to Wesley's bed made it clear to Cody which of these countries was his favorite, a large British flag was pinned over it. Another loud thud on the door brought his sightseeing tour to a halt.

"Jade, we need a plan and quick!"

Jade looked around the room and the realization struck her hard. The only connections to the world outside the house were the small circular window and the door through which she had just dragged Cody. *I've led us into a death trap.*

Frantic, alarmed whispers and the hustling of bodies oozed from under the doors. They were panicking . . . as they should. The creature lowered its head, bracing itself for a final charge against the door. A smile formed on its grotesque mouth, fondly remembering the similar scene only hours earlier. It had waited a long time for that old fool. Its black tongue brushed over its sharp teeth, the excitement of another feeding filled it with a berserk ecstasy. It was hungry again.

With a haunting, shrieking squeal it rammed its powerful body against the door, exploding it off its hinges and rocketing the couch across the room. It looked around; the room appeared to be empty. But that was impossible; they were hiding.

Calmly scanning the room for its prey, it caught sight of a foot, slightly visible from underneath the bed. Letting out another piercing cry, its large body stampeded toward the bed, its razor jaws lashing out at the leg, shredding it into two.

The pant leg was empty. Furiously the creature yanked the pants from under the bed and found itself holding an empty pair of jeans. From behind, it heard the thumping of frantic footsteps descending the stairs.

Jade's plan had worked, *for now,* she thought. But they were far from being out of it yet. A high-pitched shriek, like fingernails on a chalkboard, made her cringe. *The creature took the bait.* Running at full speed they fumbled with the front door. Locked! They heard the large creature galloping down the upper staircase. Cody grabbed Jade and raced toward the back of the mansion. "The door is barricaded from the front, the back window is our only way out!" he shouted

They reached the window. "You first," he commanded. Jade obliged and hurried through. Once outside she looked around; running was pointless. The creature had shown far superior speed—and now it was angry. They needed another plan—and fast.

Furious! Fooled by such a childish decoy. The creature had overestimated the children, but it never made the same error twice. Sprinting at full speed, it reached the back window. Through the glass its red eyes caught sight of the frantic Book Keeper. With a fluid motion the creature lunged toward the window, its weight propelling it through. The wall shattered against its giant mass.

It instantly perceived the girl at the bottom of the Wesley's dug out hole. Dinner in a bowl. The pitiful girl was trying to climb out the other side, but her hands slipped on the fresh dirt, sending her tumbling back down, over and over. Hungrier than ever, the creature propelled itself through the air and landed directly in the center of the dirt hole. Its large, six-inch talons sunk into the dirt and gained traction. Taking a few slow strides toward its victim, it smiled at the pathetic face. Cowardice had a way of staining food with such a delightful flavor not found in bravery. The victim had abandoned her further attempts to climb out and now stared at it helplessly screaming for help.

Opening its mouth, gobs of saliva oozed between its immense teeth. It prepared to lunge, and this time its teeth would devour more than empty pants. It pounced . . .

Something pounded hard against its side, knocking it slightly off balance. Before it could regain its bearings the heavy weight of another collision crashed against it and all went black.

11

On the Run

Cody and Jade took off in a sprint. Their husky breath fought through the deep cramps that assaulted their legs. Neither of them spoke a word. Their escape had been close—too close. The only thought on their collective minds was the need to put distance between themselves and that *thing*. They had been extremely fortunate to have made it out alive, and they were not feeling up to asking Lady Luck for a second dance.

"What happened back there?" demanded Jade, her voice hurried and shaky.

"I . . . I don't know." Cody closed his eyes, "I'm trying to remember . . ."

"Hurry! Hurry!" Cody tumbled out of the window; he could see Jade waving him forward, she was already several feet ahead and running fast. He pushed himself off the ground and sprinted after her, adrenaline gushing through his veins.

CRASH!

The creature had burst through the wall. Cody spun around to see the shadowed demon charging toward them. He felt something catch his foot. "Ah!" His momentum sent him crashing hard to the ground. The Book flew out of his backpack and skid across the dirt ground. "Cody! Help! Help me!"

"Jade!" Pulling himself forward from behind the large dirt pile, he panicked at the scene—Jade had fallen into the large hole. With a soft thud the creature landed ten feet from her. "Please! Cody! Help!" Cody desperately looked around for a solution. "Cody, help!" The creature readied itself to pounce. Without understanding why, Cody reached out and grasped the Book in front of him. He felt a surge of energy race up his arm. Before he could stop himself he felt unfamiliar words work their way up his throat and explode out of his mouth, "Dastanda! Byrae! Gai di gasme!"

Suddenly a giant gust of wind rolled over his back. The dirt pile behind him began to rise, swirling around the hole like a whirlwind. Growing fiercer and fiercer the swirling dirt froze before crashing down like hail and filling the hole, hurling the comatose night back into its silent trance. . . .

Cody slowly opened his eyes again. Jade shook her head disbelievingly. "So, this dirt just flew into the air all by itself . . . like magic? All because you spoke some enchanted words . . . words which, by the way, you've never heard before and can't even remember? Cody, what's going on here?"

"I'm telling you, that's what I saw. I think it's the Book. There's something special about it. It's like the words . . . spoke *through* me somehow . . . like it was just borrowing my mouth . . ." Jade snickered, "Cody, it's a *book*! Books don't *speak*!"

"Don't treat me like a child, I saw what I saw. Besides, either way, that dirt cage won't contain the creature for long. We need to get out of here."

Jade nodded silently—she wholeheartedly agreed.

Running through the streets, they turned the corner and came upon Jade's house. "Cody, grab as much food from the kitchen as you can fit in your backpack. I'll grab whatever else we might need. We've got to be out of here in five minutes." The two divided and set off on their tasks.

Several minutes later the duo reconvened at the front door, both wearing full backpacks. "Ready?" Cody timidly nodded his affirmation. "Then let's get out of here."

"What about your mother?"

Jade looked down at her, still passed out on the sofa. *I'm sorry, Mom.*

Jade shook her head slowly. "We're in too deep now to involve anybody else. The farther away we are, the safer she'll be. We need to leave. There's no time for second thoughts." Jade quickly scribbled a note on a napkin and left it on her mother's chest. Then, without looking back, she turned and left the house. *Is this the last time I will ever see my mother?*

Neither of them spoke as Jade led the way down the street. In the heat of the escape, Cody thought little about the predator. Now, in the silence of the night, he felt terror grip him. *What is that thing?*

When he had first made out the grotesque shape through the window after Wesley's murder, he had refused to accept what he had seen. But now, having stared helplessly as the Beast readied itself to devour his best friend, the reality of the situation hit Cody with full force. He did not know what it was, but he did know what it was *not*—natural. Cody had the sickening feeling that they now were involved in something much larger than either of them could imagine. A rustle in the bushes startled Cody. Jade heard it, too. "We need to keep moving. Let's pick up the pace."

After twenty minutes of tense speed walking, they turned a corner and Cody realized where they were heading. "The train station? Where are we going?" Jade pulled the ruby pocket watch from her coat and motioned to the short hand pointing at nine o'clock.

"West."

They walked up the long set of stairs leading into the station. It was still early, so the large building was sparse with people, only a few officers and travelers scurried about. Jade confidently marched up to the ticket booth. "Two one-way tickets to Los Angeles please, on the next available train." The ticket agent eyed the two travelers uneasily; the full backpacks had not gone unnoticed.

"That's a pretty long trip kids. Whatcha' heading there for at this hour?" Jade's tongue went numb in her throat.

"We . . . um . . . we . . . were . . ." she stumbled. Cody jumped in front of his bumbling friend, "Sir, our mother is visiting our sick grandmother there. She has taken an unexpected turn for the worst, we just hope we manage to reach her before she . . . before she . . ." Cody paused for a moment to gather his emotions. "Before she passes onto the next life. It's just . . . so unexpected. . . ."

The agent placed a hand tenderly on Cody's shoulder. "I'm so sorry to hear that, son. I recently lost my grandfather. Hardest day of my life. Don't cry, it will be all right. Here are four tickets. These two take you to Las Vegas. From there you'll catch a connecting train with these two tickets. I wish you speed." Wiping his watery eyes, Cody took the tickets. He attempted to thank the officer, but emotion seized him so merely nodded his thanks.

Out of earshot from the booth, Jade grabbed Cody's arm. "Sick grandmother, eh? That was quick thinking."

Cody grinned a boyish smile. "What can I say? Lying to get out of trouble is my specialty. I've had plenty of practice with Ms. Starky. Why Los Angeles?"

Jade shrugged. "Because it's far west. I figured we could just mind the pocket watch and wait until it changes, then go from there. It's not much, but it's a start."

They reached docking bay 51A. Luckily, the next train scheduled to Las Vegas was only ten minutes from departure. Punching in their tickets, they stepped aboard. Only a few other passengers were sharing the early morning train with them. Cody stepped into the first empty compartment. "Come on, let's take this one." They moved in, closing the door behind them. Overhead the loud speakers crackled to life: **Ladies and gentlemen please take your seats. We will be departing for Las Vegas momentarily.** Cody leaned his head against the window preparing for departure. He released a deep sigh of relief. They had escaped.

The call of the horn signaled that the train was departing the station. The travelers onboard were busy getting comfortable for the lengthy trip. Had any of them been looking out their window toward the dock, they no doubt would have noticed, jogging alongside the train, a tall man wearing a long black jacket and a matching black fedora pulled over his eyes. With a final call of the horn, the wheels began spinning and the train chugged smoothly out of the station. The boarding dock was empty.

12

A Calm in the Storm

The steady chugging of the train's wheels soothed the two young travelers. With a moment of peace, they began to notice the aches in their legs and the exhaustion that had set in. Just yesterday the biggest crisis in their lives was which book to purchase; now they found themselves trainbound to "The City of Lights," with supernatural forces an unknown distance behind them. *Not your average weekend.* As Cody lifted his stiff legs up onto the seat, a paper in his pocket crunched. Reaching in, he pulled out Wesley's note. Cody knew that the time to figure out the note was quickly evaporating. Sitting up he unfolded the paper:

> Fifty-three, less four, until the rite does write,
> Iron décor, future war, hides passage out of sight,
> Deep contrite, prevents invite, now precious yore,
> Must leave Tonight.

Jade joined Cody on his bench. "I've been thinking about it, too. I keep hoping that as we get closer, something will reveal itself and it will suddenly make sense." She reached into her pocket and pulled out the pocket watch, the small red hand still pointed west. "At least we have this to guide our way. Just give it time, Cody, it will come to us." Her green eyes drooped, struggling to stay open. "It will come to us." Muttering these last words she leaned her head down, nestling it onto Cody's shoulder. He tensed up; his spine stiffening as firm as a plank. Looking down, Cody gazed at the peaceful face of his best friend; her steady rhythmic breathing indicated that she was already possessed by a deep sleep. Cody's muscles loosened.

He had never been very popular at school and third grade had been the worst. He was always slow to learn, and several of the class bullies made sure he was daily re-minded of this flaw. When Jade transferred to his school the next year, she had saved him from a sea of depression and helped him find his place. Looking at the sleeping friend lying on his shoulder, Cody realized that Jade was still saving him. He smiled; it felt nice to let her lean on *him* for a change. Shutting his own eyes, Cody rested his head against the window.

The world blurred into focus. Reaching up, Cody rubbed his eyes. The sound of the train's mundane chug-ging reoriented him to his current situation. He immedi-ately noticed that Jade was gone. Panic stuck. Jumping up, now fully alert, he dashed to open the train's compartment door—and crashed right into Jade.

"Ouch!" she cried, "I'm carrying hot coffee!"

Cody blushed with embarrassment. *What's wrong with me?* He sat down silently, feeling silly for having acted so rashly. Jade handed him his coffee before taking a sip of her own, apparently feeling no awkwardness from the situation. Cody desperately wanted to bring up the sleeping incident from last night, but couldn't think of a casual way to do so. Instead he remained dumbly silent.

Jade set down her coffee. "You were really out of it, bud." The way the sun shone through the window Cody guessed it was mid-afternoon.

"You sleep okay?" he probed.

"Oh, yes, wonderfully. It was much-needed after all this craziness." Cody felt a surge of disappointment in her response; she seemed completely oblivious to the entire head-on-shoulder occurrence. For several minutes neither was anxious to restart the conversation. Both sat quietly sipping their coffee as the sun's beams flashed through the window. It was Jade who eventually broke the vacuum of silence, "Should we have another crack at that letter?" Ready for a change in conversation, Cody pulled out the note. "Read it out loud, maybe that will help change it up— unless, of course, riddles happen to speak to you as easily as books appear to . . ." she added with a playful smile. "I know what I saw," Cody replied stubbornly as he unfolded the note but was in no mood to argue.

Complying with her suggestion, he began to read the words. Halfway through, he was interrupted by the sound of their door jostling open. Raising his eyes from the paper Cody saw a tall man in a long, black jacket standing in the doorway. A fedora rested over his face.

"Pardon me," he uttered with a thick British accent. "Do you two have a moment?" Cody's eyes meet Jade's. The look on her face told him everything. They didn't have a choice.

13

Sir Dunstan

W ithout waiting for Cody's reply, the tall man took a seat on Jade's bench. She quickly got up and took a seat beside Cody, who in turn nervously inched closer to her. The two friends fixated their eyes on their unexpected visitor, who appeared in no rush to introduce himself or explain the situation. The scent of musky cologne vanquished all doubts; this was the very man who had invaded their alley shortcut on the day of Wesley's murder. It was not a coincidence welcomed by the two young fugitives.

Patting down the leather bench cushion, the man made himself comfortable. He removed the fedora that previously hid his face. He was a middle-aged man, although the hard wrinkles sharply carved into his forehead seemed to suggest that he had experienced more life than many men much his elder. His hair was dirty blond with subtle hints of white breaking through, and neatly combed to the side. Beneath his thick eyebrows was a pair of bright blue eyes. He reached to the wall and hung up his hat with a casualness that indicated he found no awkwardness in joining the younger two travelers.

Finally, having made himself completely comfortable, he turned to Cody and Jade, "Allow me to introduce myself," he said with quiet calmness. "My name is Dunstan." He paused, apparently feeling that a first name would suffice, and a purpose for the intrusion was a minuscule and unimportant detail. He turned to the window. "Nice weather we're having, don't you think? Especially for this time of year." He spoke with the tone of boredom awkwardly blanketed with an ill-fitting disguise of pleasantry.

"Um . . . yes . . . Sir. Very nice weather. Can't complain," replied Jade uneasily. The man looked at the piece of paper in Cody's hand. "I couldn't help but overhear you reading as I came in. Sounded like poetry. D. H. Lawrence, perhaps? Good poet, nice and British," he said in the same disinterested tone. Cody shot a side-glance over to Jade. "Um . . . actually no . . . it's a . . . map . . . of sorts," he responded nervously, internally kicking himself for revealing too much information. For the first time something spiked the strange man's interest.

"A map you say? In words . . . like a riddle? Interesting . . . very interesting. So you guys are on a quest? A treasure hunt, perhaps?" The man's tongue came out, resting on his upper lip as he leaned forward. Cody could feel Jade's hand lightly shaking against his leg as she answered. "It's nothing though. Just two kids with wild imaginations. You know how that can be."

At this the man let out a surprisingly jolly laugh. "Oh, don't you kids worry about me. If there's one thing we Brits know a thing or two about, it's treasure hunts! I had in my mind once to head off on a search for the Holy Grail! Can you imagine that! Instead I was forced into a much more meaningful job. But just between you and me, every now and again, I still get that hankering for some Grail hunting. It's in the blood! Your secret is safe with ol' Dunstan. I promise I won't mention it again." With this he heartily slapped his leg and let out another jolly laugh.

"So, what was that meaningful job that put an end to your quest?" asked Cody as he quickly stuffed Wesley's letter back into his pocket. Dunstan smiled, revealing his uneven yellow-stained teeth. "I'd tell you . . . but then I'd have to kill you . . ." He paused, his stern eyes burrowing their way into Cody's soul. Cody realized both he and Jade were holding their breath. Suddenly the man's mouth morphed into a sly grin and he, again, begin to laugh. Cody and Jade joined in half-heartedly.

"So where did you youngins say you were from again?"

"We didn't. But we are from Havenwood, Utah. You ever visit there?"

The man looked to the ceiling thinking for a moment. "Havenwood . . . Havenwood . . . can't say that I have, " he replied at last, the words dripping slowly from his mouth. "But I did know a chap who lived there. What was his name? Wesley, Wesley Simon. Yes, I think that was it. Good man. Nice and British! You ever know the man?" Cody jerked at the mention of the name. *Surely this man can't know. Can he?*

"Um, can't say I know a Wesley Simon. Sorry."

The man didn't seem to be bothered by the reply; he raised his thick blond eyebrow. "Well, when you get home you should look him up. Believe he owns some sort of old bookstore. You two rascals would probably enjoy that, could get some more of that poetry!" With this he gave an exaggerated wink and let out another chuckle. "Elderly man though, should probably visit him soon, never know how long a man like that will live," he added sternly. He gazed stilly at the children.

A voice sounded over the loudspeaker: **Ladies and gentlemen. We have come to the end of our trip. Welcome to Las Vegas. Please return to your seats. We will be arriving at the station shortly.**

Dunstan stood slowly and reached for his hat, having rediscovered his good humor. "Las Vegas! Never been to a city like it. And, I'd bet you thirty pounds that you'll never find a city as wonderful!" Jade smiled, having been put to ease at the man's high spirits. "But don't they call it Sin City? Doesn't sound like such a wonderful place to me."

Dunstan grinned. "True, true. But you see, the key is changing your perspective. Nothing is ever how it first appears. Once you step back and look at what is *not* obvious, then that's the very thing that will become what *is* obvious, and you will never see it the same again!"

Looking at the blank stares, he gave a mysterious grin. "Consider it another riddle for you treasure hunters! Well, I better get to my seat. I hope we meet again, and then you can tell me all about the treasure you discovered! God bless the Queen!" With this odd salutation he opened the door and stepped out; pausing, he turned back one more time. "Oh, and you chaps should probably invest in a new pocket watch if you are going to be doing much treasure hunting. The one you have there seems to be broken," he pointed to the ruby pocket watch that they had left sitting beside Jade on the seat. "At least in England they are supposed to move clockwise! Not counterclockwise. Anyways. Luck be with ya!" He closed the door behind him and disappeared.

The moment he was out of sight the two friends glanced at the pocket watch. The man had spoken the truth. The clock's hands were spinning ploddingly around the perimeter of the device. With a soft clicking noise the clock hands once again returned to a stationary rest. The short hand was now pointing upward at eleven-forty. They had a new direction.

14

Followed

The train station was an anthill of people; Jade grabbed hold of Cody's arm to avoid separation. She had become familiar with the routine of busy transportation having visited her father in England on several occasions. However, for Cody, the venture represented the first time he been farther than fifty miles from Havenwood. As he glanced out over the sea of noisy, rushed people, he secretly hoped it would also be the *last* time he was so far from home.

Pushing their way through the mob of people, they finally found space outside the station. Cody scanned the horizon. The sight was breathtaking. Flashing lights flickered a dazzling tapestry of every possible color as they danced madly to and fro while large fountains spat majestic pillars of water thirty feet high. He heard the faint crackling of fireworks although he could not see from where.

Jade squeezed his arm. "Okay, you and I need to get a room."

Cody choked, gagging over his own gobs of spit. "Excuse me?" he asked blushing bright red.

Jade didn't notice. "A room. You know, four walls and a door? We need to go find a cheap one where we can talk things over and maybe get some more rest. There's no point buying a new ticket north until we have a plan. We need to take another look at that riddle. That creature is fast, but the train should have bought us some time."

"We also need to talk about our good friend, Mr. Dunstan," added Cody. It had just occurred to him that with all Dunstan's cheery disposition and talk of Wesley, he never had given them the reason for his intrusion. The fact that he had lied about having been to Havenwood was unsettling as well.

As they set off toward the hotel strip, Cody was thankful for the rest they had gotten on the train, his legs felt stronger and reenergized. They walked in silence, the reflection of the bright lights flashing against their faces. Internally Cody kicked himself. He wasn't sure what was going on with him. His reaction to Jade's hotel room comment was now the second time that day he had made a fool of himself toward her. *What's wrong with me? It's just Jade; why do I suddenly feel so weird? Pull yourself together!* He opened his mouth but Jade cut him off sharply.

'Don't talk. Just walk," she ordered.

Cody looked at her in surprise.

"Trust me . . . " she whispered, "we're being followed."

Cody suddenly felt an ominous presence behind them. He desperately wanted to look back but didn't dare. *Who could it be?*

The first thought that materialized was the Beast. The image of those piercing red eyes caused his palms to become clammy and tremble. *No.* The idea of the monstrous creature prowling around unnoticed in Las Vegas quickly negated that possibility. *Dunstan, perhaps?* It was the logical guess. "Just keep walking, we'll lose him in the crowd."

Walking as calmly as they could manage, and fighting the overpowering urge to take off running, they briskly headed toward the noise and lights of the main strip. They could hear the soft patter of footsteps behind them. Neither of them dared to look back. *Just keep moving.*

At last their road merged with the central hotel strip of the city. The street was an irritated hornet's nest of people chattering and cars zipping past. As they stopped, the shadowing footsteps behind them froze as well. They could hear heavy breathing. *Whoever's following us is not far behind.* The shadow of a body loomed over them. Its arms slowly extended out toward their shoulders. Jade caught Cody's eye and nodded her head. *Three . . . two . . . one.* On the third nod they took off running, sprinting for their lives. The shadow's footsteps drummed after them, but their unannounced burst had startled the stalker and given them a head start.

They ran directly into the most populated gathering on the street and slipped through the mob by darting left and right. Cody clasped hold of Jade's hand as they pushed their way through the labyrinth. Emerging from the crowd they came to the busy main street where taxis and limos bustled by. Without warning Jade yanked Cody's arm and began to run. The next moment was a blur of lights as the sound of whooshing tires whizzed around him. "What do you think you're doing?! Stay off the road!" screamed a furious cab driver, swerving sharply and narrowly avoiding them.

Reaching the other side of the street, they paused only for a brief moment before Jade grabbed hold of Cody's arm again. They dashed to their right, up a flight of stairs, and through the revolving doors of Caesars Palace hotel. Without looking back to see if they were still being tracked, they sprinted through the lobby. The desk attendant stood up to shout something, but they were already out of earshot.

Sprinting down a long hallway, past several gift shops, they halted; they had come to a dead end. A crowded casino was their only escape; the sound of bells and hollering blasted through the doors from within. Standing directly in front, blocking the entrance was a bulky security guard.

"What do we do now?!" Jade asked exasperated. "We aren't old enough to enter and we surely can't go back. Think! We don't have any time!"

The sound of agitated voices followed by hurried footsteps floated toward them from the lobby. Cody glanced around fervently for a solution, but they had nowhere to go. They were trapped.

He clenched his hands tensely—and paused. The feeling of cold leather pressed against his fingertips. He peered down to his hands in surprise—he was holding the Book. He gazed at it in astonishment; he could not recall removing it from his backpack. Suddenly his fingers began to tingle and he felt his throat clot up, blocking his air path. He dropped to his knees, clutching his neck, as the lump scaled its way up his throat. As the bulge reached the top he wretched his head irrepressibly, *"Bauciva! Gai di gasme!"* He heard himself utter the words as though a distant by-stander to the scene.

Jade cranked her head, "Shhh! We need to . . . oh, my gosh. How in the world?" Cody followed the trail of her wide eyes toward the empty wall—only it was no longer empty; directly across from them, made entirely out of fine polished wood—was a door.

Cody shook his head disbelievingly. He was absolutely positive that there had been no door there a minute ago. He shoved the book back into his bag. *What's happening to me?*

Jade dragged him through the new door and he once again found he was breathing Las Vegas air. "Come on, let's go."

They began to run. "Jade, what happened back there? That door just appeared . . . out of nowhere. How . . . ?" Cody's voice trailed off.

Jade tugged against his arm. "I . . . don't know. Nothing is making sense. But it doesn't matter; I think we've lost him. Let's get inside somewhere before we're seen again."

They turned to enter the hotel directly in front of them. Cody glanced up to see the large flashing sign above the doorway. It read: Treasure Island Hotel. Cody grinned.

Dunstan would be pleased.

15

A Mystery Solved

Unmoving, Jade stared down at the hectic city street; the sea of lights extended far into the distance from her fifteenth floor window. She breathed slowly and intentionally, still trying to calm her racing heart. They had waited for several minutes in the lobby as a precautionary measure, but eventually felt confident they had lost their mystery pursuer.

Cody sprawled out on one of the two single beds and greedily unwrapped a granola bar. "Hey, Jade, heads up." She reached up and snatched the flying granola bar that Cody had propelled her way. "When's the last time we had a bite to eat?" An answer came in the form of her growling stomach. Ripping open the wrapping she stuffed a large bite into her mouth.

Cody ungracefully crammed in his third granola bar, chocolate chips spraying out like debris from a volcanic eruption. "So, what . . . do you . . . figure we . . . should do . . . next?" he mumbled between bites.

Jade pulled out the ruby pocket watch and set it on the desk. As it had before, the short red hand still pointed up at eleven-forty. Snapping the blinds closed to ensure their privacy, she walked over to her own bed and plopped down, sinking into the blankets, "Well, what do we know so far?" She began in a diplomatic tone, "First off, whatever this pocket watch is, it obviously wants us to head north. To where? I'm not sure. Then there's the issue with our British friend, Dunstan. Perhaps he simply was a jolly, lonely old man. But my gut tells me that there was more to his visit than meets the eye. I don't think its coincidence that he shows up in Havenwood on the very day that the city experiences its first murder in decades. Speaking of which, that brings us to Wesley's riddle, which I am sure is the key to of all this."

Cody sat up. "Don't forget the gigantic demon-pig creature that tried to bite your face off." They both involuntarily shuddered. *Where was the creature now? Was it still hunting them? Was it close?* Cody laid Wesley's letter beside the pocket watch. Somehow the two objects were interconnected, but neither knew how.

"Well, now that we are safe from any strange British interruptions, maybe you should try reading the letter out loud again. It can't hurt." Cody was depleted of hope, but couldn't think of a better alternative, so he began reading the riddle slowly:

Fifty-three, less four, until the rite does write,
Iron décor, future war, hides passage out of sight,
Deep contrite, prevents invite, now precious yore,
Must leave Tonight.

As he finished, he looked up to Jade, his face defeated. Her deep green eyes were an inferno. She ran her hand through her thick black hair. "It can't be . . . " her voice trailed off, deep in thought.

"What can't be? What are you talking about Jade?" he questioned. Jade looked up, a wide smile on her face. "It's been in front of us the whole time . . . Dunstan was right . . . "

Cody couldn't contain himself any longer; he grabbed Jade with both his arms and gave her a shake. "Dunstan was right about what? Snap out of it, girl! What are you going on about?"

Jade grabbed Cody's arms on her shoulders and looked up at him. "The riddle, the clues. It all makes perfect sense. Dunstan was right; he said we have to step back and look at what *wasn't* obvious, and by doing so, that's what would *become* obvious. It's worked! It's so obvious now." She was shivering as she did whenever she was consumed with excitement. "I've just figured out the location of the passage way."

The front desk receptionist at the Treasure Island hotel looked strangely at the man before him. Something about the peculiar man gave him chills. *This night just keeps getting weirder and weirder.* Already he had seen two young teenagers dash franticly into his lobby, demanding a room. *Probably runaways* he had thought at the time. Even in Vegas, it was unusual to rent a room out to such young customers.

Now the man standing before him had something unusual in his appearance, but he couldn't quite place what it was. The customer leaned over the desk and whispered, even though they were the only two men in the lobby, "I need a room. Just for tonight. Anything on floor fifteen perhaps?" The attendant looked strangely at the man in front of him, "Um, one second, Sir. Let me check the records." Running his hands expertly across his keyboard he brought up the floor plan for floor fifteen. There was one room available. He opened his mouth to inform the odd customer, but stopped short. That particular floor was the very floor he had just checked the two teenagers in only half an hour earlier. *Something doesn't feel right.*

The man in front of the counter sensed the hesitation. Reaching into his jacket pocket he produced a large wad of bills and dumped it on the counter. The attendant looked from the bills to the computer screen, and then back at the customer, "Yes, Sir, there is one room available. Just give me a moment while I make you a key."

"Are you sure?" Cody could not believe his ears; he had abandoned hope of ever unearthing the mysterious message behind the riddle. Jade nodded adamantly, "Yes, yes. It's actually very straight forward; we just were going about it wrong from the beginning." She paused, being pulled into thought again. Cody clenched his fists. "Well . . . where is it?" he demanded, pulsating with anticipation. Jade grabbed the letter off the desk and pointed to the first line. "You see, we've been doing the math wrong the entire time." Cody felt offended. He recognized his academic prowess wasn't equal to that of his friend, but even *he* was able to handle a simple mathematical equation such as fifty-three minus four. Jade noticed the dejected look on her friend's face and smiled.

"Don't worry, buddy, I missed it, too. You see, we were so caught up on the simplicity of the question that we jumped right over the word *until*. Do you get it now?" Cody nodded his head in affirmation, although in truth he had no idea where she was going.

Jade continued, "The subtraction is only the first half of the problem. It says *until the rite does write*. Forty-nine isn't the *answer*—it's the way to *find* the answer. Like a formula! It tells us that there are forty-nine *more* times, until a particular event takes place. The number we need is how many occurrences have *already taken place*. All we have to do is determine how many *total* occurrences there will be in the end, when that event takes place, and then simply subtract forty-nine from it. *That's* how we get the answer we need."

Cody's head strained to wrap itself around his friend's explanation. Math had never been his strong suit, but he was beginning to understand. "Well, that's great. But we don't know what the numbers are adding up to, so the number is still useless."

Jade pointed back to the riddle. "That's where this next part comes in. *Until the rite does write.* What do we know about Wesley?" Cody was confused by the random question. He knew a few things about Wesley: he had apparently lived a creepily long time, he was completely crazy, he had been brutally murdered, and he had apparently missed the memo that medieval swords were no longer fashionable. But none of these seemed to be of any relevance to the problem.

"Um, I don't know. He was tall?"

Jade grabbed her forehead in frustration. "No, you thickhead, he was *British!*" She let the statement hang in the air a moment, as though it alone solved the mystery. Cody, however, was still lost and, now, incredibly frustrated. "Well, good for him, God bless the queen and all that rubbish . . ."

Jade shook her finger toward him, "Exactly!"

Cody frowned. He had meant the comment sarcastically, "What do you mean?"

"The queen. She's the key," Jade iterated excitedly. "What does every British citizen receive from the queen on a certain day as a ceremonial act, or rite?" Like math, Cody also was weak in social studies. Luckily for him, Jade continued without waiting for an answer, "A birthday card." Cody was fascinated; he had not known that. "So, every birthday you get a card from the queen if you're British? That's a pretty sweet deal."

"No, not *every* birthday, just one special one. They get a signed card from the queen on their one hundredth birthday." Now, it all was making sense to Cody.

"So the numbers in the message refer to years? Forty-nine more years until one hundred makes our number . . ." Cody paused to think, ". . . our number is fifty-one."

Jade stood up and began pacing back and forth. "Our train gate number was fifty-one and there was that British flag over Wesley's bed. You see the answers have been in front of us the whole time." Cody was not ready to celebrate yet. "Well, okay, so the number is fifty-one; what about all this other mumbo-jumbo about wars and iron?"

Jade returned to her bed. "Have you not figured it out yet? *New war*, it does not mean what we thought it did."

For the first time in a while, Cody felt relieved. "Then what *does* it mean?" he asked, his attention now completely glued to his friend.

"It's not talking about a physical war about to happen, at least not in the sense we were thinking it did. *New war*, what else could that mean?" Finally, something Cody could understand, the many hours spent playing video games coming in handy. "Could it mean new warfare *style*? Like weaponry? You know, atomic and chemical warheads and such?"

"Exactly! And where are we right now? Can you not think of anything that comes to mind in Nevada where new war technology is being done in a secretive, iron setting?" Suddenly Cody shoulders sunk, all the pieces finally had reached each other in his mind, "This isn't good. Are you absolutely sure?"

"I'm positive" Jade responded confidently. Cody gulped, "So the hidden passageway . . . is at *Area 51*."

16

The Dwarf

Area 51. Although it lined up perfectly with the clues, Cody struggled to wrap his head around the fact that it was now their destination. Like most boys his age, Cody was wholly familiar with the mysterious U.S. army base and the overabundance of secrets supposedly held there. From the most cutting edge in technological warfare to the Roswell UFO conspiracy, it all existed within the secretive walls of the restricted facility. Whatever momentary relief there was in solving Wesley's riddle was stiffly suffocated by the dense sensation of gloom—they were now going to have to break into the most secure location in the entire United States.

A loud knock interrupted his thoughts. Cody tensed up and dropped to his knees. "Do you think it could be Dunstan?"

Jade crouched down low beside him. "I don't know. It could just be the maid." Another burst of knocking, even louder than before, rattled the door. "Okay, so it's definitely not the maid. What do we do?" They heard the creaking sound of the doorknob twisting back and forth. Cody froze, "Did you hear that?" Jade had just made the same observation, "The doorknob didn't budge. The knocking isn't coming from the front door!" Pivoting around, they stared at the side door connecting their room to the adjoining room. Someone was jerking that doorknob.

"Should we try to escape through the front door?" Jade suggested in a hushed whisper. The moment the words left her mouth she got an answer: a loud banging pounded on the front door. They were surrounded.

They began slowly backing up until they bumped against the pane of the window. Enclosed, and fifteen floors up, they could do nothing but simply wait for the inevitable. Above the banging a muffled voice barked from beyond the side door, "For heaven's sake, Cody, open this blasted door!" At the same time the front door handle began to rattle with increased ferocity. It shook with the impact of a body colliding with it from the hallway.

Jade grabbed his hand. "They know your name?!" Giving her hand a quick squeeze, Cody pushed himself off the wall and grabbed the doorknob to the adjourning room. "Cody, what do you think you're doing! Don't . . ." She was too late; he had already unfastened the lock and opened the door. Framed in the archway stood a stubby man they had never seen before. In a blur of motion, the man's arms shot out and clutched onto Cody's collar. With a violent yank Cody was dragged into the room.

The stench of beef protruded from the assailant's mouth as he slammed Cody onto the floor, his face settling inches away. Hazy eyed, Cody released a grunt as he lost his wind.

Swinging up his fist, he jabbed the man square across the cheek. Dazed, the man loosened his grip. Squirming wildly, Cody struggled free of the man's grasp and bolted back toward the door, but the man's coarse hands latched onto his ankles sending Cody toppling back to the floor.

Jade emerged through the door and dive-tackled the man, his spine crunching under the pressure of her knees. "Let him go!" Jade commanded.

Reaching up to the nightstand, Jade yanked the alarm clock out of the wall and swung it with all her strength. It collided directly into the back of the man's head. He let out a loud *umph* as his body went limp. "Come on, Cody, let's get out of here. Follow me!" They ran to the room's front door, leaving the man wheezing on the floor. Gasping for breath, the man called out, attempting to push himself up with his arms, "Stop, if you leave this room . . . you will . . . die . . . you must . . . trust . . . me. . . . Trying . . . help. . . ." Jade hesitated, her hand already grasping the doorknob.

Heavy pounding was still ringing out from the other room's front door. Whoever was in the hallway was now ramming the door fiercely with their body. Jade knew they would soon break through. Time was no longer a luxury. Whatever she decided, she had to decide quickly. She let go of the door, "Speak quickly, man. What do we do? And don't even think about standing up." The man, still battling for breath, pointed to the door connecting the two rooms.

"Close . . . quickly . . . lock . . . ," he wheezed. His words had been enough. Cody reached the door and slammed it shut, flicking the lock in the same motion. Corresponding with his action was a loud crash. The door in the other room had been breached.

"Shhhh," whispered the man. Jade killed the lights and dropped to the floor. She could feel her pulse pounding against her temple as she locked the breath in her lungs. Voices were muttering to each other in the other room, but it was impossible to make out what they were saying. Cody quietly stepped over and pressed his ear against the wall. The men on the other side did not sound pleased.

"I swear, Sir, I'm telling the truth!" said a rough, husky voice. "I saw them go in, and I never saw them go out," he pleaded apologetically. A loud thump of something banged against the wall close to Cody's position, sending dust soaring around his head. His nose crinkled. Cody bit his upper lip, sweat running down his brow, as he fought the uncontrollable need to sneeze. Jade shot him a death glance, informing him that it was not a battle he could afford to lose.

"It was a simple job," said a second voice that scolded in a cold, authoritative manner. Cody concluded that it commanded its respect out of fear rather than love.

"I apologize, Sir, it won't happen again," the first piped in.

"Oh, shut up you whimpering rat. We hired you for one reason, to handle this matter, and you couldn't do it. Perhaps you'd be better off making biscuits and tea for the rest of the boys when they return from actually doing their jobs. Or maybe . . ." His tone became chillingly serious, "you would like to explain this mishap to the master?"

The first man inhaled, "No, please, Sir. They can't have gone too far. We still have time. I'll find them." The second man remained quiet for a moment, then replied frigidly, "Rendezvous with the others, have them stake out a watch around the hotel. Something tells me they are still here somewhere. They have yet to uncover the meaning behind the Book. They will be vulnerable. If they attempt to escape . . . shoot them."

"Yes, Sir," the first man marched toward the door.

"Don't let me down again."

The three stowaways in the neighboring room kept a panicked silence for several minutes longer, even after the sound of the two men's footsteps had faded away down the hall. Jade was the first to exhale and end the nervous quiet. *AH-CHOO!* Cody's head was cranked back by the force of his sneeze, "I thought I was going to implode!"

Jade was in no mood for joking. She knelt her knee onto the stranger's neck and applied firm pressure. "We don't have much time, man, so you better start explaining yourself and quick."

During the frantic wrestling match neither Cody nor Jade had gotten a good view of the stranger. Now that the dust had settled, their eyes fixed upon him with fascination. He was at least an inch shorter than Cody, although his face revealed him to be at least a middle-aged man. Like a newly constructed bird's nest, his hair was a dark gray, messy tuft on the top of his head. A sparse, unkempt beard formed around his thick chapped lips. Something was unusual about the short man, but they couldn't determine what it was.

The man rubbed his head where Jade had connected with the clock. When he finally spoke, his voice was scratchy and irritated. "Well, I had intended to introduce myself like a civilized man, before the warrior-princess over there thought it would be a great idea to knock my wind out." He brought his hand up to rub the carpet burn on his cheek. "Stupid children."

"I'm sorry, we thought you were . . ." Jade began as she removed her knee, but the man interrupted her. "Well, you thought wrong. If foolish girls like you started attacking people every time they had a rogue thought, we'd have a world of cripples and lames. They'd be giving out wheelchairs with birth certificates."

Jade felt her face flush. "How dare you say . . ." But the man paid no attention to her; instead he turned to face Cody.

"Do you have the Book?" he questioned matter-of-factly. Cody subconsciously reached behind and felt the indentation of the book pressing against the edges of his backpack, grateful that he had not forgotten it in the other room. After all the adventures they had endured over the last two days, he realized that this was the first time anyone had acknowledged the significance of the Book since Wesley. It gave Cody a strange sense of assurance.

"The note!" yelled Jade. It had just dawned on her that they had left Wesley's letter openly exposed on the nightstand. The short man grunted, "Never mind it; it's worthless to you now. You already deciphered the riddle."

"You were eavesdropping on us!" Cody accused furiously.

Again the man let out an irritated grunt. "Well, I wouldn't have been forced to tap into your dull conversations had you not led me on the bloody Boston marathon throughout the streets! So uncivilized, you people . . ."

"So it was *you* who was tracking us from the station! But why?" Jade questioned.

"Ruddy well right it was me tracking you. And to save your toasty American bacon, that's why. Which I just did if you hadn't noticed. Not that my crushed ribcage made me feel unwelcome or anything."

Jade knew it would be pointless to argue with the man. Mustering up all the friendliness she could manage, she offered him a smile. "Well, Sir, what would you have us do next?"

The man tossed his head back in disgust, "What do you think, hunny? I'm gonna bust your hinies outa this fifteen-story prison."

17

Escape

Creaking soft as a cricket, the door inched open. Out of the opened crack stuck a small, roundish head. The bearded face scanned the hallway left and right before easing the door open fully. "Follow me, and don't make a sound or I'll kill ya myself," he commanded to his cohorts as they crept down the hall.

He was sure that both the elevator and stair exits would be under close surveillance in the lobby. He pressed his hunched back against the wall to avoid the moonlight sneaking through the hallway windows; even at fifteen stories up, he was not willing to take chances. These people knew the truth about the Book. That fact alone made them an exceedingly perilous threat. It was going to take a lot of smart planning to get out of this one, *and a whole lot of dumb luck*, he thought grimly.

From behind, Cody and Jade followed him tentatively. Their newly self-appointed leader was a foul little man, but their gut told them that he was trustworthy. Besides, they didn't exactly have an alternative option. The fact that he had remained nameless, though, was more than unsettling.

For the first time, the stranger turned back to examine his followers. "Okay, lads, we're going to have to take the stairs. I have a car parked just outside the lobby in temporary parking. When we get to the lobby, let me handle things. I don't want you brainless oafs ruining our already slim chances. When the coast is clear, get to the car and start the engine. We either leave here tonight in that car or in a body bag." He tossed a set of keys toward Cody who boggled them in his hands.

"How are you going to distract..." Cody began, but the short man had already departed and was scurrying down the stairs. Jade leaned in close to Cody. "What do you make of all this? Is this man one of the good guys or the bad ones?" Cody made no reply; he had no answer. They passed by the tenth floor and kept moving. The man in front continued his constant, distasteful muttering. "You lads and your obsessive desire to build higher and higher ..." The rest of his grumblings were incoherent. At last they reached the ground floor. The dwarf peeked through the window of the door. "Aye, I see three of those mindless goats there now," he whispered. "Wait for my cue; then make a dash for it."

"What about the others? It sounded like there might be more of them. What should we do if run into them?" asked Jade timidly. The man muttered a curse, "Use your own blasted head. You do got a brain swimming around in there, ain't ya?" He grabbed the doorknob. "Oh, and lads," he paused, "try not to get yourselves shot...." Before they could protest the dwarf had pushed the door open and sauntered into the middle of the lobby. Cody and Jade knelt down, leaving the door slightly ajar, waiting anxiously for the man's cue.

In the lobby were three men. A skinny, blond haired man was lounging on a sofa holding a *Women's Home Decor* magazine as his eyes perused the lobby diligently. Another hefty man was propped up against the wall on the opposite side of the room doing the same. A third man, with a prominent scar across his left cheek, was standing casually by the front doors, peering out the glass at the people walking the streets. All three men were wearing long, black leather coats. Cody could just make out tiny wires coming from their ears.

"What a day! Don't yous say gentlemens?" the dwarf called out obstructively loud, plopping himself down on the couch adjacent to the blond man. The coated man looked up, unimpressed by the intruder, before lowering his head back down to his magazine, ignoring the question altogether. The dwarf continued, uttering each word with a drunken lisp, "First I loses the family fortune on a fews games of blackjack, can you believes it?" The watchman again looked up from his magazine disdainfully. "Yes, tragic," he snapped in a bored voice, indicating that the conversation had already reached a point further than he cared to hear. The second watchman continued to scan the lobby. His eyes paused momentarily on the staircase door. Cody winced. After several intense moments, the man looked away again, apparently noticing nothing unusual.

"Just whens I thinks the day can't get any *more* interesting, can you guess whats I saw?" The dwarf continued, swaying back and forth dizzily, "Two teenagers, climbing outs their window!" At the mention of the teenagers, the eyes of the watchmen shot toward the speaker. "Just a walkings and a' climbings down the ledge; don't sees that everyday dos ya lads!" The scar-faced man by the front door quickly disappeared outside. The bulky sentry by the wall inconspicuously set down his brochure and moved swiftly toward the stairs.

"We need to hide!" Jade whispered to Cody, watching as the man came straight in their direction. They scanned their surroundings but there was nowhere to go. The man reached the stairway door. His callused hand wrapped around the handle and began to slowly twist it open. Cody braced himself to pounce.

The sound of a ding sounded from around the corner. An elevator had just opened. The gruff man paused, gave an ugly smile and walked out of sight toward the sound of the bell. Cody let out a sigh of relief. *That was too close.*

Out in the lobby the dwarf continued to blab on to the skinny man with the magazine, whose face had grown increasingly redder with frustration. ". . . I tells ya, she was the purdyest thing I ever laid me's two eyes ons!" He yakked on, "Well, it's beens a whale of a day! I think I should be's off to bed." The man gave a rude grunt, acknowledging that he whole-heartedly agreed with the suggestion. As the dwarf stood up he swaggered back and forth for a minute, before releasing a rattling, wet belch. He took a wobbly step forward and then, with a loud curse, he collapsed right into the lap of the watchman.

This had been the final straw. The vexed man threw up his hands. "Sir, I don't give a hoot about your family fortune or your ugly third wife. I just want to be left a . . . *umph!*" He never had a chance to finish his rant. The dwarf's head came flying up and smashed against the man's lower jaw, jerking his head back. He fell against the back of the sofa, unconscious.

For Cody and Jade, this was the only cue they needed. Jumping out from their hidden refuge, they dashed across the lobby as fast as they could. The dwarf followed close behind. "The car, start the ruddy car!" he bellowed. Cody didn't need to be told twice. Dashing out the revolving door he saw a black BMW parked in the front. Clicking the automatic doors, Cody jumped into the passenger side and thrust the keys into the ignition. The car roared to life. The crackle of a gun-shot rang out. Sparks exploded off the pavement beside the car, spewing chunks of pavement into the air.

As the dwarf reached the door he flung another wad of cash to the shocked desk attendant. "For the damage!" The sound of a second gun blast flew just above the attendant's head. He collapsed to the desk. *I need a raise.*

18

The Hunted and the Hunter

The screeching of tires echoed in the night sky as the BMW peeled out of the parking lot, the smell of smoldering rubber filling the air. Fish-tailing onto the road, its tires gained traction, and it burst off as though launched from a cannon. Moments later, a black van drifted onto the road; with a loud squeal it propelled forward in close pursuit. Despite dusk settling in, the streets were still littered with cars and pedestrians lined the sidewalks. A chorus of horns erupted as the BMW swerved recklessly across two lanes unannounced and veered off sharply to the left. Loud, angry curses flew out the car window in response.

Cody felt his heart race. The hotel lights blurred in his side window as the car gained speed. Glancing to the rearview mirror he saw the black van roughly two blocks behind. Jade squeezed his hand tightly from the backseat.

Lurching across lanes, the car zoomed around a left hand turn and cut down a narrow single-lane ally. An opposing one-way sign flashed across the windshield for an instant as the car exploded past. The dwarf slammed his foot on the gas pedal; the car jerked back as it kicked into a higher gear. The parallel brick walls enclosing the narrow road blurred. Sparks cracked from the side-view window as it nipped against the wall like a match against a match box. The car reached the end of the alley; Cody felt his fingers stiffen around Jade's as the BMW launched out like a bullet. Cranking the wheel, the dwarf sent the car sliding sharply right, squeezing in between two oncoming cars.

The deafening crackle of a gunshot was followed by a loud *TING* sound. The car jerked sending Cody's head whiplashing against the dashboard. Looking back, with a warm dampness of blood accumulating on his forehead, he saw that the pursuers were now close enough to see the whites of their eyes. Holding a gun, a bald, dark-skinned man's arm hung out the passenger side window.

Another shot blasted. The BMW swerved swiftly to the side to avoid it. Up ahead, Cody saw the approaching intersection. The lights turned red. Cody gave a nervous glance to the dwarf; the car continued to accelerate, "The light's red! You're going to . . ."

The driver's arm came flying up and smacked Cody hard across the mouth knocking him back into his seat. "Keep your mouth closed unless you want a bullet sailing through that empty waste of a head!" he growled. Squeezing Jade's hand tight Cody shut his eyes.

The next moments were a blur. He heard the screeching of tires and the blaring of horns. A thunderous smash was accompanied by a dozen yelling voices. The car rattled back and forth violently. From the back seat Jade gave a quick shriek. Then everything was quiet.

Cody peeked open his eyes. In front of him, the open road raced relentlessly toward him. He glanced to his side mirror; a large smoldering pileup of cars now clogged the intersection. They had miraculously made it through with only minor damage. Unfortunately—so had the black van.

A long string of muttered curses flowed from the dwarf's mouth, never finishing one before eagerly pronouncing the next. The road ahead was flat, straight, and deserted. Cody watched as the speedometer climbed to 130 miles/hour. The landscape around them was no longer distinguishable as it whizzed past. Cody grinned; this had obviously been the dwarf's plan all along. On the open road their BMW had far superior speed than the van. They were home free.

"Blast!" the driver yelled.

The car began to gradually lose speed. Cody looked to the dwarf frantically. "Why are we slowing down! We need to keep moving!"

"I'm not trying to . . . we're out of gas!" The dial on the dashboard was completely flush with the E. "You didn't bother to fill it? What were you thinking!" Jade called in horror from the back seat. The car was now rapidly losing speed.

"You think I'm an idiot? It *was* completely full when we left. I don't know what happened . . . I . . ." Glancing out his window, Cody discovered the answer. Gas was sputtering out of the car onto the road. A bullet had punctured the tank. Cody knew they had been fortunate. *Another inch and we would've been blown to kingdom come.*

With a final sputter the car came to a complete stop on the desert road. The trio wasted no time. They grabbed their things and jumped out of the car. Endless desert surrounded them on all sides. The spewing of rocks warned them that the van had caught up.

"Run!" They took off heading in no particular direction. But their escape was short lived. Sand flew into the air by Cody's feet as a gun blast went off. "Stop, or the next one sails through your head." Cody halted and put his hands up. Turning around he saw that the dwarf and Jade were doing likewise. Standing before them stood three men: the dark-skinned man wielding a raised gun as well as the hefty and scar-faced men from the hotel lobby. A chuckle sounded from behind them. The three men took a step aside, allowing a fourth man to step between them. The man—was Dunstan.

"Well, well! So we meet again, young treasure hunters!" He pronounced with a jolly enthusiasm. "I told you we'd meet again, and here we are."

Jade peered at him venomously. "I knew the instant you barged into our compartment on the train that you were evil and crooked!"

To her surprise, Dunstan simply smiled. "Gosh! Awfully harsh words from such a pretty lady."

He chuckled calmly. "You are quick to label us as *the bad guys*. Seems a little unfair considering we hardly know each other! If only we had time to sit and have tea like civilized Brits I'm sure everything would make sense."

The dwarf let out a loud *hmph!* "To the seven circles of Hades with your tea!"

Dunstan smiled at this remark and turned to the speaker, acknowledging him for the first time. "Well, well, well. This is certainly a pleasant surprise! I did not expect to find you here so soon . . . Sir Randilin." The look on the dwarf's face hardened, traces of fear forming on his brow.

A smirk appeared on Dunstan's face. "Oh, yes, my little friend. I know all about you. And your . . . loyalties. Shall I inform the children of what kind of man they are traveling with? Shall I let them know about certain . . . dark deeds? You see children. . . ."

"You keep the blazes out of my life! You hear me! My past is none of your bloody business!" spat the dwarf wildly. "You think you're so clever. You're a lot braver with your goons' guns pointed at our heads."

The sternness of Dunstan's face faded away. "Indeed, having your precious life held in the palm of my hand does give an old man some added confidence." The tanned man cocked the pistol. Dunstan took a step back and motioned him forward.

"Now my good friends. Unfortunately time does not allow for as pleasant an exchange as we would all like, so we must get down to the meat of the matter. If you would be so kind as to hand over the Book to Rodriguez here," he said, motioning to the man holding the gun, "then we can all be on our merry little ways. Agreed?"

Out of the corner of Cody's eye, he saw something move. He was sure he caught a glimpse of a shape before it disappeared into the darkness. Cody glanced to Jade and the dwarf in desperation. "What do you know about the

Book anyway! You don't know what you're doing!" Cody yelled.

Dunstan smiled. "Oh, my naive child. I know a great deal more than you do, I have no doubt. Indeed, I believe it is *you* who is completely ignorant about the power sitting carelessly in your backpack right now. So, come on now, be a good chap and hand it over . . ."

Cody hesitated, scanning the blackened horizon for an escape route. Dunstan's smile disappeared. "Come on Cody, I was really hoping we could be civilized about this. I am much too fond of you to have to order your execution. Hand over the Book. . . ." Cody took a step back; again a shape in his peripheral vision caught his attention. The henchman, Rodriguez, took a step forward. His muscular arms reached out and squeezed Cody by the collar. It was useless to struggle.

The man violently ripped the backpack off Cody and dumped it upside down. Cody and Jade's remaining rations fell out along with the ruby pocket watch. The man reached in and pulled out the worn leather Book; the scarlet 'A' glimmered in the moonlight. At the sight of the Book, Dunstan let out an ebullient yell, "Magnificent!" His eyes shimmered greedily in anticipation of his prize. The subordinate paced back toward his leader, keeping his eyes and gun fixed on the three prisoners.

Dunstan reached out with gluttonous eagerness and snatched the Book from Rodriguez's hand. For a fleeting moment his face morphed into a demented smile and his eyes blazed with intensity.

"You're a darned fool! You have no hooting idea what you're dealin' with," spat Randilin bitterly. Dunstan, who seemed momentarily to have forgotten that anything else existed in the desert apart from him and the Book, looked up and smiled. "Oh, my dear little friend, loud and feisty to the end, aren't you? However, you are also mistaken. If only you knew the man I am working for. I assure you, we are extremely well equipped."

"To the grave wit' being equipped! And to the grave wit' you, too! That Book will destroy you! And that's only the beginning!" yelled Randilin, his voice growing raspy.

Dunstan stood still, seemingly amused by the comments. "Well, time will tell, will it not? Chance keeps life exciting!" He nodded to the gun wielding man, who stepped toward Randilin. "Unfortunately for you, my dear friend, you will not be around to see your gloomy prophecy play out. I'm terribly afraid that I'm going to have to have you killed. Nothing personal, of course, but as they say here in America, business is business!" Cody watched in panic as the bald man raised his gun flush with Randilin's forehead, his finger tightening on the trigger—then chaos broke out.

Cody dove forward and collided with the man, knocking him off balance. A loud bang echoed in the night sky as his shot discharged just wide of Randilin's head. The second, bulky assailant jumped forward to grab the fallen gun, but Randilin wasted no time. He lowered his head and charged. A loud *Umph!* sounded as the wind was squeezed from the large man's lungs.

The darkly-tanned man was overpowering Cody on the ground. Jade dashed in and unleashed a solid kick to the man's ribs and he let out a loud groan. From above a humming sound droned and the wind escalated, sending sand flying into a whirlwind. Cody glanced upward to the sky to see a black helicopter. In the driver's seat was the blond-haired sentry from the hotel lobby. *A helicopter? These guys are serious!* From the ground he felt legs whisk past him, Dunstan was dashing to the chopper; in his hands was the Book.

BANG!

A thunderous crash erupted over the commotion. The wind softly ceased to blow. A thick silence settled in on the desert like a fog. Then, as soft as the twilight breeze, came a skin-tingling sound—a soft growl.

Cody felt the warmth of his body drain out; he began to shiver. He cautiously peered toward the abandoned vehicles on the road. Perched on top of the van, like a horrifying gargoyle, stood a menacing, colossal shape; it was cloaked in a dark purple robe. Dunstan and the dwarf both cried out in terror. Cody attempted to do the same, but his mouth had run completely dry—the Beast had found them.

The terrified crowd stood lifelessly, paralyzed by fear. Suddenly, in a blinding instant, the large fiend lowered its head—and sprang forward. With a sharp crunching sound, its giant mass came crashing down on the chest of the scar-faced henchman. The man screamed in agony. With a wild squeal the Beast sank its fangs into the man, silencing him instantly. Rearing its head up, blood smeared across its black lips, it's burning red eyes locked onto Cody.

Jade watched in horror as the gigantic Beast galloped on all four legs toward her friend. She opened her mouth to scream, "Run!" but no sound came out. Instead, she stood disoriented as the Beast closed in. To her astonishment, Cody dropped to the ground and curled his body into a tuck position. *Playing dead!? What are you doing, Cody! Run! RUN!*

The Beast lowered its shoulders and lunged. Jade couldn't handle it; she squeezed her eyes closed, a salty tear running down her face. She waited for Cody's agonizing shriek. Silence. She slowly opened her eyes; Cody was lying on the ground just as he had been before, untouched. She turned toward the helicopter, and in an instant, she understood why.

The Beast had jumped over Cody, and was now in pursuit of the stampede of men racing toward the helicopter. Dunstan was in the lead, closely pursued by Randilin. The two remaining goons trailed several feet behind. The sound of the Beast's claws ripping into the dirt brought Dunstan's head around. His face was ghostly white. The crowd had almost reached the helicopter, which was hovering above the ground, but the Beast was closing in. Still looking behind, Dunstan's foot unexpectedly caught a rock and he tumbled to the ground; the Book flew out of his hands and skirted across the dirt floor.

The bulky henchman scooped it up like a baton and continued the mad dash. He fired a round of wild, blind shots at the Beast, but they had no effect in slowing the rabid predator. The man crunched down and launched himself toward the helicopter—half a second too late. With remarkable grace, the colossal Beast lunged over the fallen Dunstan and punctured its large claws into the man's back. He let out a sharp scream as he came crashing to the ground.

From where Jade stood she couldn't make out what happened next. Below the helicopter erupted a fury of motion and yelling. Dust ascended like a spirit and clouded the scene. From within the dust shield she heard an unmistakably gruff voice calling out, "Start the van! Start the wretched van!" Randilin came billowing out of the haze, a bloody gash oozing across his left cheek, and legs chugging away with all his might. Nestled in his arms was the Book.

Cody whizzed past her and she instinctively turned to follow. Judging by the heavy sound of the feet trampling across the desert ground, Jade knew that the Beast was chasing Randilin. What she didn't know, or want to know, was how close that chase was.

As they reached the van, Jade heard the roar of the helicopter as it cruised over their heads, the sound of the propeller slowly softening as it raced across the skyline and out of sight. Jade jumped into the front seat as Cody filed into the passenger seat beside her. *Thank heavens! They left the keys in the ignition!*

Cranking the key, the engine rattled loudly before settling into a low hum. Jade glanced out the window; Randilin was huffing and puffing, his face beet red. The Beast was not far behind and rapidly gaining, but Randilin had a jump on it. Cody reached over his seat and slid open the side door. Jade braced herself, she had her learner's driving permit, but had yet to drive anywhere farther than a stone's throw of her house, and never without her mother in the passenger seat. She had no time to ponder the situation; a loud thud shook the van—Randilin was in.

She slammed the gas pedal to the floor. The tires spun franticly, searching in vain for traction. For a moment the van sat still as the tires spun like treadmills. Jade's eyes raced to the window where she saw the chilling red eyes of the Beast sailing toward the open side door, blood smeared around its gaping jaws. With a loud screech Jade's head was hurled back against the seat, and the van shot off, not a moment too soon.

"Drive! Drive like your whole ruddy life depended on it!" yelled the breathless Randilin from behind her. Jade didn't need to be reminded; she knew her whole life *did* depend on it. Looking into the mirror she saw the horrifying Beast in the middle of the road, charging after them with amazing speed. It was gaining—and fast. *I don't believe it! What IS this thing!* Sparks ignited as the creature's razor-like talons scraped fiercely across the pavement. It reared its large hoggish head and released a wild, piercing squeal that echoed in the night air. *Faster! Come on—faster!* The creature's red eyes were boiling with savage hunger as it galloped feverishly closer and closer and closer. The warmth from its heavy breath began fogging up the rear window. "Jade. For heaven's sake, step on it!" Randilin screamed. With a hard jolt the car kicked into a higher gear and rocketed forward. Jade exhaled a sigh of relief as she watched the large robed figure fade into the distance behind them.

They had escaped.

Its two glowing red eyes squinted as the vehicle disappeared into the horizon. The creature's long black tongue ran slowly over its lips, lapping up the smeared blood. The taste produced a moan of pleasure. It had been close, but the Book Keeper was proving more difficult than it anticipated. The creature smiled. After three thousand years of hibernation, the sport of a good chase was exhilarating. A growl came from its stomach.

Raising its head it sniffed the air, a pleasant smell carried on the breeze: the smell of fresh blood. Its sharp eyes found the fat figure of a man lying on his back, fighting for breath. The Book Keeper wouldn't get far, but for now . . . it was meal time.

19

The Diner Lady

The steady hum of the tires racing over the smooth dessert road lured Cody into a dreary trance; he entered somewhere into the neutral zone between sleep and wakefulness. Cody made out the light sound of snoring. Looking ahead, he saw Jade sprawled out gracelessly in the passenger seat. After their frantic getaway, they had driven several miles without slowing. Eventually satisfied that they were free, they had pulled over and Randilin had relieved Jade of her driving duties. Few words had been spoken during the drive; Randilin had explained nothing. Before they had even refastened their seat belts the van had screeched away, eventually settling into its steady pace.

Cody knew that Jade would be horrified to realize she snored. He smiled. He couldn't bring himself to wake her. She needed the sleep. *So do I.* Looking out the front window, he watched as the road raced beneath the vehicle. The two faint headlights offered the only light to the thick Nevada sky. Cody felt his eyes drooping and jerked his head to stay awake. His hand ran across the smooth surface of the object in his lap: the Book. He pulled it tightly against his chest.

He glanced up to Randilin, who gazed forward with a blank stare. Only the thick, clotted, bloody wound across his cheek distracted attention from the otherwise humorous sight. Due to his short stature, he looked to Cody like a child pretending to be grown up behind the wheel.

The encounter with Dunstan and his men had proved that the situation was more involved and dangerous than Cody had thought. Dunstan had mentioned his employment, but for whom? Cody shuttered. By the sound of it, the employer seemed like a man Cody hoped never to meet. As for the Beast, it left no mystery as to how it fit in. It was on its own side. Cody remembered the pale, horrified look on Dunstan's face when he saw the Beast. *How much more about this creature do we still not know?*

And then there was the question of Randilin. He remained a mystery to Cody. *Whose side is he on? Are there even sides anymore?* He had proven himself a valuable ally, having already saved them several times. Still, though, maybe Dunstan was right; maybe they *had* been too quick to label good guys and bad guys. Maybe Dunstan was trying to save them from Randilin? Cody didn't even know where Randilin was taking them. There was one thing he did know: Dunstan knew something about Randilin that Randilin was determined to keep secret. Cody recalled how Dunstan's reference to Randilin's past had impacted the dwarf. His face had become a tapestry of fear, shame, and anger. However, the emotion overarching all these feelings on the dwarf's face had been the unmistakable look of pain and regret.

Cody felt frightened. For the first time since discovering the Book, he also missed his home. He thought of school. No doubt Ms. Starky had already phoned his mom to inform her of his absence. *Mother.* Due to the rush, Cody had not informed his mother of his whereabouts. *Not that she would believe me anyways.* He could picture his mother arriving home and finding him missing. She would panic. He was all she had left in the world. Cody knew she would have gone directly to the police to arrange a search party. He then remembered that there most likely already *was* a police search party for him, as he was the lead suspect in the Wesley murder. *Life has become so complicated!* He fought back tears. He would trade anything to be back in 'Slacker Row' dozing in his desk . . . dozing in his desk . . . dozing. . . .

Cody opened his eyes. The sun was shining brightly through the windows. A bag of sour cream and onion chips plopped into his lap. Following the path of the toss, Cody's eyes arrived at Jade's smiling face; she seemed rejuvenated.

"We stopped to fill the van a few miles back, got you your favorite chips for the road, thought you'd be hungry." *Actually, barbeque is my favorite, but it's the thought that counts!* Chip crumbs flew everywhere as Cody inhaled them.

"So . . . where . . . are . . . we?" Cody asked between bites. After a moment of silence, Jade reached down and pulled up a map as it seemed that Randilin was in no mood to repeat their earlier conversation.

"Well, we're about in here somewhere," Jade pointed to a northbound highway road, "and we are heading here." She pointed up the map to a large blank desert zone. "Which, although nothing shows up on the map, Randilin says it is the location of . . ."

"Area 51," Cody finished. The sound of the name still seemed more fairytale than reality to Cody. He looked to their driver, who had yet to utter a noise. "You seem quiet today Randilin? I think Jade and I have been very accommodating up until now, but it's time for some answers."

When Randilin finally spoke, his voice no longer resembled the sarcastic whip Cody had become accustomed to; instead it was distant and shaky, almost nervous. "It's none of your business if I decide to be quiet. And, I heartily agree, it's unfair of me to leave you in the dark. . . ." His voice trailed off, following an unseen rabbit. Jade cleared her throat, reminding him of the conversation. Randilin blinked. "But not now. We will need to brainstorm a strategy for entering Area 51, as well as gather equipment, and well . . . there's someone we need to see."

By the silence that followed, it was crystal clear to both Cody and Jade that no further explanation was to be given. Without any other choice, they settled into their seats to rest, and to wait.

Shawn was bored out of his mind. Every second that clicked on the obnoxious clock was yet another reminder to him how mundane his life was. School had seemed like such a waste of time; however after a month working at Fingo's Gas, he was beginning to reconsider. The lone bright spot in the day had occurred several hours ago when a strange midget of a man had come barging in. He had rambled on incoherently in a thick smoker's voice, had grossly overpaid for his gas, and then waddled out the doors again. The female accompanying him, however, had not been hard on the eyes. Speaking of eyes, those green eyes of hers had been like nothing he'd ever seen before.

Ding. Shawn turned angrily toward the door to see the customer whom had ruined his daydreaming. He gulped. The figure in the doorway was seven feet tall and cloaked in a dark purple robe. A rank smell intoxicated the room. Shawn stood petrified, unable to utter a word. The large figure sniffed the air and turned to face him. From beneath the robe, two chilling red eyes burned into Shawn's with unbearable intensity as though branding onto his very soul. The sun flowing through the window reflected off the creature's large talons as they tapped against the floor. With lightning speed the creature pounced. There was a painful scream—and then all was silent.

The van slowed to a stop. After the bizarre events of the past few days, Cody had definitely expected more from their mystery detour. In front of the van sat a rickety building, resembling more of a trailer than an actual structure. Above the door, painted in messy yellow paint was: Sally's Diner—Best Hot Chocolate in the Desert.

Filing out of the van, Cody glanced over at Randilin; his face was pale and he looked sick to his stomach. As they neared the steps, the front door burst open. Standing in the doorway was a woman; and like the diner, she was far from what Cody had expected.

To his surprise, she stood at roughly the same height as Randilin. Billowing out, stringy and un-kept beneath her white lace bonnet, were two long, frizzy, dirty-blonde pig-tails. Her face was not overly beautiful, but it had a friend-ly warmth to it. Her lips were caked with several lays of clumpy, bright red lipstick and, even from a distance, the smell of her potent perfume congested their noses. Her blue eyes were welcoming, and her large dimples gave her a youthful appearance.

"Well, blow me over. If it isn't Mr. Randilin himself; what a pleasant surprise! And you brought friends, you adorable young dearies! Come in; come in! I'll have a fresh batch of hot-chocolate out in a jiffy!"

"Oh, that really won't be necessary," argued Randi-lin, but Sally paid no attention. Randilin leaned over, and whispered in a shaky voice, "Keep your heads about you lads. This woman is not to be messed with. I'm warning you, don't look her in the eye, she'll suck out your soul."

"I heard that Randy! Fortunately for you, you have no soul in that heartless carcass to suck out!" she called out the window, over the clinking sound of mugs. Once inside, they grabbed a table. They were the only customers in the homely diner. Apparently hot chocolate wasn't a popular commodity in the smoldering desert.

After a few moments, Sally came shuffling back from the counter with a teetering stack of hot chocolates in her hands and slid a mug to each of the visitors. "Now," she began, plopping herself in a chair next to Randilin who, apparently feeling the close distance was unsatisfactory, scooted his chair away several inches. "I believe Mr. Randilin has yet to offer the courtesy of introducing us." Randilin opened his mouth to speak, but Sally continued, "My name, as you may have guessed, is Sally Peatwee. And, who might you two youngin's be?"

Jade introduced the two of them. Meanwhile Randilin sat silently with a dejected look on his face, wavering between pouting and humiliation. His attitude did not seem to hinder Sally's good spirits in any way; she continued to chatter on.

"And, so what are two children such as yourselves doing out here in the Nevada desert? And with this black-sheep?" She winked over to Randilin. Cody looked to his two traveling companions, unsure as to how much to reveal to the lady. Randilin saved him the trouble, speaking for the first time, "I'm afraid it's not good news. They come carrying *the Code*." Randilin's answer had a visible impact on Sally's face. Her happy-go-lucky expression warped into a look of terror and confusion.

"Good heavens! Randy, this is no time for jests," she exclaimed, troubled. Randilin's silence confirmed that her fears were true. "How? When? What are we going to do? What about the Hunter? Are you here on your way to the Second Passage Way? How much do they know about A . . ." Randilin's hand shot up, placing a finger on her lips. She stopped talking.

"Sally, there is no need to speak of things," he glanced toward Cody and Jade, "which do not need to be spoken of. I know it's an impossibility for you, but try to hold your tongue." He took a deep breath, showing, for the first time, heavy signs of fatigue. "It is true. That is where we are heading. As for the Hunter . . ." Randilin paused before finishing, "he has already feasted."

Sally gasped, holding her hands over her mouth. "Then it has finally awoken? Please don't tell me, what of Wesley, I'm afraid to ask, is he . . . did he . . ." Randilin nodded slowly, "Unfortunately, Wesley is the first casualty of the coming war." All the while, Cody and Jade sat stunned, listening intently, but unable to make sense of the conversation. Suddenly, Sally stood up, surprising her three guests. The look of terror was gone, a look of determination shone on her face. "What's our first move?"

Cody gave a sly smile to Jade; they both realized the value of their newly-gained ally. Randilin, too, was unable to suppress a grin, "Oh, Sally, you old harpy, you make a wretched dinner companion, but I sure wouldn't want to be your enemy! We have little time to waste. We pack the gear and head for the passageway . . . tonight."

20

A Brewing Storm

Thunder shook the sky as the clouds exploded into a fury of rain. Pulling down his hat tighter to block the on-slaught, a man trekked across the street, his feet splashing in the accumulating puddles. *I don't have time for this!* Crossing the street, he entered into a brisk walk down the empty pathway. He checked his watch: Quarter 'til midnight. *I still have fifteen minutes.* He picked up the pace knowing full well that his night's business would not allow him to be a moment late.

Spinning down another dimly lit street, the man was relieved to see his destination before him. Glancing around quickly he ensured that he was, indeed, alone before crossing the street. A rickety, abandoned house towered before him; the doors and windows had been boarded up. Whatever ancient use they once served was long since lost. Crossing around to the side of the house, he knelt down, fumbling with the keys in his pocket. The heavy rain left red streaks across his face as it pounded relentlessly against it.

Finally, with key in hand, he unlocked a sturdy wooden door, which was mostly concealed by the un-kept foliage swallowing up the house. Stepping into the darkness, the man pulled the door down firmly above him.

Scurrying down the ladder, he flicked a match and lit several torches around the perimeter of the room. The warmth of the fire felt instantly soothing on his soaking wet skin. The thought of removing the heavy clothes sticking like glue to his damp skin gave him pleasure. *But after, only after.* He had no time to spare. Having lit the final torch, he walked to the corner of the room. Without looking down, he stepped over the crumpled lump on the floor. *Hello, Charlie.* Against the wall was a table, upon which sat a solitary phone. Taking a deep breath, the man picked up the receiver and pressed the speed-dial, there was only one. The phone rang once—then twice. When the phone rang a third time the man became uneasy. *I know you're there, just answer the phone!* The man got his wish. Following the third ring a voice came over the speaker, "Report."

The voice was a male's voice, but not overly deep. It had a chillingly steady tone to it, completely purged of emotion. The rain-drenched man's voice faltered slightly as he spoke, "My Master, the Book is still in the possession of the children. They appear to be guided by a native—Sir Randilin. Also, Sir, our men have encountered the Hunter, unknown casualties."

The man on the other end spoke in the same emotionless tone, "Casualties are of no concern. I sacrifice their lives willingly for the cause." The indifference of his words sent a chill down the caller's spine. "What of the children?" asked the icy voice.

The caller's mind raced over the memorized report in his mind, but the words still came out slow, hesitant, and clumsy, "Cody Clemenson and Mari Shimmers, Sir." There was a long pause. The caller held his breathe.

At last the man on the other end responded, "Curious . . . this is a fascinating development. Don't underestimate them. Any leads on their course of action?"

"Yes, Sir, we are tracking them now. We have reason to believe they will lead us directly to the entrance. It should not be long."

"Indeed. I believe it is time for CROSS to handle the situation personally. I will dispatch one of our agents. Success is crucial." The rain-drenched man shivered; he did not like the direction the conversation was leading, "What of the hired mercenaries? Shall I dismiss them?"

"No. We cannot afford to leave any traces. CROSS does not exist . . . ," the cold voice paused as though savoring the words the way one enjoys a juicy thanksgiving turkey, ". . . eliminate them."

"Yes, Master," the man responded dutifully.

"Well done, Dunstan. You have played your role well; the world will remember you for it. See to it, for your sake, that there are no mistakes. "

"Yes, Sir." At the sound of the dial tone, the man exhaled loudly. He had done well. He stripped off his drenched clothing and collapsed onto his bed. He needed his sleep. Tomorrow was going to be a busy day. Tomorrow—the war was going to begin.

21

The Break-In

A chorus of howls sailed on the midnight desert draft. With the retreat of the sun, a cool air settled in, driving away the tyranny of the day's scorching heat. The soft breeze slithered across the earth like the rhythmic breaking of ocean waves. The setting sun had ushered in the ritual nighttime circus of creatures, predator and prey alike, basking in the luxurious night chill. Joining the animals in their festivities was a boy, standing on a sandy dune as though the captain on the bow of his ship.

Cody gazed across the eternal sea of sand. Off in the distance he could faintly make out the dim flickering of light, a dying candle illuminating through the darkness. At the sight of the distant lights, Cody shuddered. On any other day the cool air and the solitude of the continuous desert would have been a welcome, soothing experience. However, on any other day he would not have been preparing to break into the most protected, dangerous location in America—Area 51.

A subtle cough crackled to his left, startling Cody, and announcing that his privacy had been forfeit. Randilin ascended the sand dune and joined Cody in his lookout. For several minutes, the two soaked in the view, watching as a lone star raced across the sky before quickly vanishing from sight.

"Well, son," Randilin began, "don't waste a single glance. You people foolishly take this sky for granted every single second you hustle to and fro underneath its splendor."

Cody knelt down, grasping a fistful of sand and allowing it to slowly trickle through his fingers. "You keep mentioning *you people* as though I am so different from you. I've been lugging this Book around with me for days now and still have no idea why. Dunstan was right you know, I *am* just an ignorant child." Reaching around to his back, Cody pulled the Book out of his backpack. He rubbed his fingers across the smooth leather of the cover and felt the familiar surge of energy rush up his arm. So many questions remained unanswered. He had now witnessed the Book's power twice; and on both occasions it almost seemed as though the Book was somehow *protecting* him. He shook his head. "Maybe Jade's right, maybe I'm just seeing what I *want* to see and letting my imagination get the best of me. Perhaps it really is nothing more than a stupid Book."

Randilin's face flushed. His mouth shot opened but paused hesitantly, and remained silent. Taking a deep breath he continued in a softened tone, "My boy, it's true that I'm not particularly fond of you. But you're going to have to just trust me. Things will make sense in the end. I can promise ya that."

"But why can't you just explain yourself now? Isn't it better that I understand what this Book is if I'm going to try and protect it?"

Randilin crouched down beside Cody. "Do you know how to swim?"

Cody was startled by the randomness of the question, but nodded his head in affirmation. Randilin continued, "Good, good. Okay, so imagine you go for a swim in the ocean. While swimming a big fish pops up beside you and starts talking to you. It asks you what those strange two appendages are that you have in place of your tailfin. What do you tell the fish?"

Cody rolled his eyes, "What does this have to do with anything? I'd tell the fish they were obviously my legs and . . ."

"But what if the fish then asked you what legs are? And why you would ever need them? Isn't it better to have a fin if you're going to swim?"

Cody was growing irritated. "I'd tell the stupid fish that I didn't use them to swim, I used them to walk across land. . . ."

"Land? The fish asks you what this strange word *walk* means, and then what you mean by *land*?"

"Ah! I don't know, I'd put the fish in a bowl and bring it back to the shore with me and show it . . ."

"Exactly!"

Cody raised his eyebrows skeptically. "So, we're going fishing now? I don't follow. This is a waste of time."

Randilin stuck his chubby index finger between Cody's eyes. *"YOU* are my fish, boy. Don't you get it? Do you see how pointless it is to explain something to somebody that has no point of reference? The person cannot understand because they have nothing to compare it to. The only way to make them understand is to *show* it to them. Well, right now Cody, you are in my fishbowl. And pretty soon we are going to make it back to the shore and everything will make sense to you. Understand?"

The lecture was put to an abrupt end by the sound of Sally's voice calling through the diner window, "Oh, Randy, you never did have a way with words. Anyways, we are ready to go. If we hurry, we can reach the passageway before the sun rises and we lose our advantage of nightfall. Come along boys. Chip, chip!"

Cody followed Randilin back toward the diner; the only building laying claim to the desolate landscape. They passed by their stolen black van. Cody stopped for a moment to examine it. After the heat of their frantic escape died out, they had taken time to meticulously search the vehicle for any clue that could identify the origin of Dunstan and his gang. What they had found had been horrifying.

Cody looked to the ground to where three familiar faces were staring hauntingly up at him—one of the faces was his own. He bent down to retrieve the fallen piece of paper. He shivered as he recollected Jade's piercing shriek the moment she had first discovered the document. She had entered into a state of hysteria. As Cody examined the paper again he began to feel the same terror gripping him; his portrait was flanked by an image of Jade and one of Wesley. The latter had a bold red 'X' through it and the word 'EXTERMINATED' written below. Below the photos were lists of biographical information about each—systematic detail from eye color and height to miniscule facts such as favorite candy bar and color. The document had been signed by only one word: CROSS.

They had debated the significance of the word to no avail. *Just one more piece of the puzzle that I don't understand,* thought Cody bitterly. What he did understand, beyond all doubt, was that CROSS, whomever or whatever it was, clearly knew who they were, and would not think twice about killing them to get what they wanted. *We need to get moving.*

He entered the diner, ducking beneath the newly-erected sign that read: Closed—Indefinitely. Jade and Sally were waiting for them, both cloaked in black jackets with the hoods pulled up over their heads, casting a shadow over their faces. Sally tossed a matching outfit to Cody, her frizzy pigtails billowing out of her hood in a tangled mess. Cody quickly put on the jacket. With a soft click the lights in the diner were extinguished.

"Okay, from here on out we speak only in whispers. Follow me." Sally walked over to a table at the far end of the diner. A large red "Out of Order" sign was taped to its mustard and coffee-stained surface.

Stretching out her arms, she grabbed hold of the table. With a grunt she twisted it hard, the blood vessels bulging in her plump forehead. It didn't budge. She whipped several beads of sweat off her brow and brought her arms to her hips. "Silly little thing is wedged on tight! Gosh, this thing hasn't been used in centuries." Randilin stepped forth meekly to offer his help, but an icy glance from Sally sent him scurrying for cover behind Cody and Jade. "Oh Randy, don't you be disguising yourself as a gentleman now. I'm perfectly capable of handling this myself." She pulled her sleeves up above her stocky elbows.

With another deep breath she grabbed hold of the table and heaved with all her might. There was the sound of cracking; and the table began to move. Cody watched in amazement as ground below the table began to rotate in a circle. Jade grabbed her head as the sound of scraping rung in her ears. Sally continued to corkscrew the table until they heard a loud popping noise. With one final grunt she pushed the table aside. Where the table had once stood was now a hole.

A thick murky air filled Cody's nostrils. "Wow . . . it's . . . an underground tunnel?" he proclaimed, bewildered. Randilin huffed, and tossed a flashlight at Cody's face, who caught it just in time.

"Well, you didn't bloody well expect us to skip merrily though the front Gate of Area 51 now did ya, you dimbo." Flicking on his own flashlight, Randilin motioned for them to follow him down, "and be careful, this ladder is rather . . . old. You fall down here and you save us the trouble of burying you. Now snap to it."

The ladder felt fragile under Cody's feet. Looking down there was only darkness. With a loud thud the entrance of the tunnel was re-covered, leaving the foursome engulfed in blackness. Cody began his descent. He started counting the rungs of the ladder but abandoned his efforts somewhere after passing 362. The light from their flashlights struggled to fight though the density of the air. Randilin had led the way, followed by Cody and Jade. Sally had taken up the rear. The ladder swayed underneath their steps, sending a rattle down the wooden structure like a shiver down a spine.

After what seemed like an eternity, Cody felt the much-welcomed solid ground underneath his foot. Jade and Sally landed beside him with two soft patters. Cody held his flashlight out and illuminated the path in front of him.

The corridor was not wide. Cody could stretch his arms to both sides and place his palms flush on the cold rock sides. The walls were not rough, but smooth as though sanded by ocean waves.

"Let's go." Although spoken in whisper, Randilin's voice was amplified as it echoed down the narrow passage. The convoy set out down the pathway in single file. Any initial excitement stemming from the pending break-in to Area 51 was dulled by the mundane march. Two hours came and went and Cody began to feel a cramp forming on his side. The thick air had made it a challenge to maintain steady breathing.

"Ouch!" The shout exploded down the corridor. Cody's left pointer finger throbbed. Randilin threw a glance toward him that clearly communicated several nasty cuss words all at once. Cody pointed his light toward the wall. There was a deep rut in the surface that had jammed his finger. He followed the path of the rut up the wall. Jade gasped behind him. It was not a rut at all: it was a carving.

Carved into the wall was a large "A." It matched perfectly the marking on the cover of the Book. Below the letter was an inscription. Cody recognized the letters as that which he had seen in the Book during his ill-fated reading. As with that time, he could not translate the meaning. To the right of the "A" were two dashes, similar to the Roman numeral II. Randilin's finger shot up to Cody's lips, as if in anticipation of his questioning. "Fishbowl," he whispered. Without another sound he pointed his flashlight to the end of the passage. There was a second ladder—they had reached the other side at last.

Cody's heart began to pound. If they had reached the end, then it meant that he must now be standing directly below Area 51. He felt Jade's cool breath pulsing on the back of his neck. Even in the dark he could tell she was frightened. Cody clenched his fists; the time for questioning was over. He was ready for some answers. He grasped the ladder firmly and began his ascent—each rung inching him closer and closer to Area 51.

22

Future War, Iron Décor

The monitor screen was still—as always. Wilson reclined in his chair, severe boredom seizing control of every fiber in his plump, disproportionate body. He lazily brought a coffee mug to his lips. The sparse liquid not soaked up by his bushy mustache tasted unappealing on his tongue. Cold. He checked his watch. Still two more hours until he was free from his night-watch duties and once could again enjoy a steaming hot java. They weren't paying him enough for this.

The idea of working in Area 51 had exhilarated him. The reality had failed to live up to his ideals. He sacrificed all connections to the world in order to stare at a security monitor day in and day out. Twelve years into the job he now understood his position to be a mere formality.

He checked the monitor again. His coffee cup went soaring into the air. He craned his neck toward the screen. *Could it be?* On the screen he watched a floor tile jiggle and pop to the side. Out of the hole four figures in black coats emerged, quickly scurrying from sight. Wilson stared at the monitor bewitched, his world becoming surreal. This was the moment he had been dreaming of for twelve years! Adrenaline burst through his veins. Puffing out his chest he reached his hand for the alarm switch.

He paused. In the reflection of the monitor screen he saw another cloaked figure. A crest symbol covered the front of the cloak. Stenciled underneath was a singular word: CROSS. He never got a chance to dissect the meaning. Two arms grasped the side of his head and he felt quick pressure.

Jade's senses were overloaded. Every inch of the building was screaming out for her attention. She had expected to emerge from the hole onto the far outskirts of a military base. Instead she had found herself in some sort of giant hanger. The room was absolutely massive. Jade estimated the ceiling to be around thirty stories high and the room equal to at least four football fields—and not an inch was wasted.

The room was bursting with objects like a forsaken attic. Metal crates, engraved stone obelisks, and glass-encased display cabinets filled the room like a city skyline. The chamber looked to Jade to be more of a museum than a top-secret military intelligence base. Various artifacts such as tall stone statues and pillars looked surprisingly similar to the ones she had seen in the British Museum the last time she had visited her father. There was one object in the giant space that held her gaze. The crown jewel of the room: a towering stone statue, fifty-feet high. What captivated her was not the immensity of the structure or the masterful sculpting; it was the shocking familiarity of it. The aged sculptor did not depict a human at all. Jade immediately recognized the great, ominous jaws; how could she ever forget them. She felt a rush of terror—the statue was of the Beast.

The sight of its grotesque beetle-like back brought vomit into her throat. Cody appeared to have come to the same realization; the color had drained from his face. *PSST!* Both their eyes followed the sound back to Randilin, who was crouched down low behind a tall glass-encased shelf of stone tablets. Scanning the room Jade found Sally with her back pressed against a large granite monument a dozen feet from the dwarf's position. She was waving them forward.

Elevating the balls of her feet off the ground, Jade scurried from her hiding spot toward Randilin's location. She had never been very graceful. Her mother had constantly scolded her for her resistance to "be a lady." Dresses and makeup had no appeal to her. She allowed herself a quick smile as she recalled the memorable day her mother enrolled her in dance class. It had been disastrous. She had danced with the elegance of a clubbed-foot rhinoceros. Her teacher had literally fallen on her knees *begging* her mother not to bring her back. That was the end of her mother's 'lady-izing' attempts. *Always a daddy's girl* she thought with pride.

By the painful expression on Randilin's face, Jade concluded that her attempted stealth was every bit the atrocity she expected from herself. Cody reached them with the silence of a morgue. *Show-off,* Jade groaned bitterly. Sally quickly held out the palm of her hand motioning them to freeze: the coast was no longer clear. Muffled voices engaged in tired conversation but Jade couldn't pinpoint their location. She leaned her back against the shelving. Inside of it were tablets that looked exceedingly ancient. While the language seemed incomprehensible, at the top of each tablet were recognizable scripted 'A's.

She leaned forward for a closer look—and lost her balance. Instinctively, she grasped the sides of the shelf for stability but immediately wished she hadn't. The shelf began to wobble back and forth. Jade looked helplessly to a stone tablet teetering hazardously on the top shelf, inching closer to the edge with each of the shelf's tremors. With one last sway, the stone tablet tipped and came freefalling toward the ground. Jade let out a muffled shriek and covered her ears.

In the next instant, Randilin was on top of her. Disdain dripped like rain from his face onto hers. Jade's eyes slowly worked their way down his outstretched arm. He had caught the tablet inches from the floor. For the next few minutes nobody exhaled. Jade fought to hold her breath. She could feel her face turning purple and her eyes beginning to haze.

At last, another whistle from Sally broke the silence and Jade found herself scurrying alongside Cody and Randilin to join up with her. They had reached the corner of the room. Peering out from behind the cover of the stone block, Jade saw a long hallway the size of a six-lane highway. The lights were off and the hallway was empty. She checked her watch. *5 a.m. Soon this place will probably be bustling with activity.*

Randilin's thick arms folded around Jade's shoulder and pulled her into his side. Cody was likewise entrapped by the surprising strength of the dwarf. "We only have one shot at this, kids. If you want to be stupid and waste your own lives then be my ruddy guests. However, for the sake of the Book, I want you to listen to me. I'm going to count to ten. When I say ten I want you to run your flabby hind-parts off. Understand? *NO* stopping under *any* condition."

Cody and Jade nodded their consent. Randilin began his count. "One . . . Two . . ."

Jade looked back down the hall, wondering where their run would lead them. "Six . . . Seven . . . Eight . . ." It was now or never. Jade lowered herself into a running stance, "Nine . . ." The muscles in her leg tensed. "Ten!" Jade took off.

Her arms swung like pendulums, propelling her forward. She kept her eyes focused straight ahead. Her peripheral vision caught the sight of doorways lining the side walls, but she dared not stop and look as they shot past. Instead she ran with all her strength. Despite her determinacy, she had fallen to the back of the pact. *Wait? Where's Cody!* She slowed down. He was nowhere to be seen. *Oh, you idiot!*

Horrified, she turned around. There was Cody, standing transfixed in front of one of the doors. She looked ahead; Randilin and Sally were still sprinting away. *Why can't you EVER listen, Cody!* Jade twisted and raced back down the hall toward Cody. The door in front of him appeared to have been accidentally left slightly ajar. The temptation had seemingly proven too great; Cody's arm was extending slowly toward it. *Nooo! Stop!* She lunged forward—but she was too late. Cody's hands made contact with the door. A loud alarm exploded through the intercom: Intruder Alert! Intruder Alert!

The blaring alarm jerked Cody out of a trance. He groggily reoriented himself as if waking up from a sleep walk. Then he remembered—and groaned. The sign had been too much for him: **EXTRA-TERRESTRIAL/UFO/ ROSWELL EVIDENCE.** He had urged himself to continue running, but curiosity had mutinied his common sense and he found himself approaching the door as though pulled magnetically. One quick, harmless little peek was all he had wanted.

He felt himself being thrown to the floor. Jade collapsed on top of him, her explosive green eyes burning a hole through his head. Despite the situation, he couldn't help thinking how beautiful she looked. Her un-kept black bangs swaying across his face and her thin pencil lips gave her a dainty quality that he had never realized in her before. He smiled—and immediately regretted doing so.

SLAP! His cheek stung under the force of her hand. "You idiot! What are you doing! Are you out of your . . ." Her voice was cut off by the sound of gunfire. Sparks flew off the wall beside them. Cody wrapped his arms around Jade and rolled her to the ground. Another gunshot echoed down the hall. This time there were no sparks.

"Ahhh!" Cody screamed out. He felt his left pant leg grow wet. It burned like fire. Jade was on her feet, waving her arms wildly above her head. "Stop shooting! For heaven sakes, we surrender! Please!" Her voice was desperate. Cody rolled his head toward their attackers. His every movement sent violent jolts of pain to his leg. Two security guards were approaching vigilantly, both with guns raised.

Where are you Randilin! Cody frantically searched for the dwarf as the two guards approached. Their fingers rested tightly on the trigger of their AK47s. Cody knew that Area 51 was no haven for forgiveness. The guards exchanged a few muffled words to each other. Cody understood what the outcome would be. He and Jade were about to be eliminated. *Randilin! Now would be a nice time for a rescue!* He was nowhere to be seen. The guards concluded their huddle and turned back to their captives. Their guns rose to their shoulders. Cody winced.

Thud. Thud. Cody grabbed his chest. He was untouched. He glanced up to Jade, who was standing with an equally confused look on her face. There was a faint, wet, gurgling sound. He looked back to the guards; two glimmering metallic objects were protruding out of the wall behind them—they looked like some kind of circular blades. The hallway was deathly silent except for the gurgling. The two guards swayed back and forth for a moment—then a dark scarlet gash appeared across their jugulars and they crumbled lifelessly to the floor.

Cody retched at the disgusting sight and fought to keep vomit down his throat, "Randilin! You sick, twisted, barbaric, disgus . . ." Cody shut his mouth. The man emerging around the corner into the hallway was not Randilin. He was a tall man cloaked in a black robe. In his hands were two circular, throwing blades. On the front of his robe was one word: CROSS.

23

Down the Rabbit Hole

Run. That was the only thought occupying Cody's mind as he stared at the hooded man fifty paces from his position on the floor. The searing pain in his leg reminded him that this option had been eradicated from his sparse repertoire. Jade's shadow was unmoving on the floor behind him. She too had gauged that the price of running was the loss of her head. *Where are you, Randilin?* Biting back the pain rearing from his leg, Cody called out,

"Who are you? What do you want with us? We're not scared of you!" He had intended the last part to come out brave and valiant. Instead it had flopped out of his mouth with the ferocity of a crippled mouse. He felt a nudge in his back and heard Jade's voice, "Just tell us what you need and we can work something out. What do you want?"

The hooded man stood completely unmoving. Only the steady breath exhaling from under the hood gave signs of life. At last the hooded man spoke with a soft, youthful voice that surprised Cody. "What I want to give you, both of you, is a life of a meaning. A life of grandeur and importance. But to do so, I'm going to need that Book."

"How do we know you aren't lying? And what if we don't *want* a life of meaning, grandeur, and importance? What then?" Cody responded cautiously, trying to buy time until he came up with an escape plan.

The man chuckled softly, "Oh, but you *do*. You always have. It's in your blood. . . ." The last words collided with Cody hard, knocking his wind out. The man noticed and spoke again, "Isn't that why your father abandoned you and your mother? Tired of his mundane life of being a nobody? Just another face in the crowd?"

Cody wanted to respond. He wanted to tell the man to stop talking, but the words in his head kept spinning away out of reach.

The man continued, "Isn't that why you've always felt that you don't stand out at school? You share your father's fate. But most of all, you want to prove to yourself that your father was wrong, and that you aren't worthless."

It was Jade who finally came to Cody's rescue. "Shut up! You think you know us, but you don't! You don't know anything about us! You think you can aim some blades at us and we'll just hand over the Book? Do you think we're that simple?" There was a blur of motion and a light thud. Jade felt a burn on her cheek. She immediately knew it was bleeding. She looked behind her; one of the man's blades was sticking into the wall. It had grazed her face. She didn't need any convincing that the man hadn't missed.

"My boss is not a man known to give second chances, so I'm going to ask you one more time, Cody, hand over that Book and I promise you a life that surpasses even your wildest imagination. The life . . . your father always wanted."

Cody pushed himself up onto his feet and steadied himself with Jade's help. His leg felt numb and staggered under the pressure of his body. He felt dizzy and his vision blurred. For the first time he looked down to his wound; blood soaked the floor. He unzipped his backpack and pulled out the Book. A tingling sensation ran up his arm. "Okay, here's the Book. Just leave us alone and it's yours." Cody held it out in his hand. The man took several long strides and reached out for it. Cody smiled—and tossed the Book into the air.

The hooded man froze in surprise. For a split second he raised his eyes to follow the path of the soaring Book. It was all Cody needed. He hurled his body toward the man. His head smashed into the man's chin, causing the assassin to stagger back. Jade jumped up and caught the falling Book, "Let's get out of here!"

Cody's head butt had stunned the man only momentarily. He shook his head and raised his remaining blade. However, the cavalry had arrived at last.

Appearing from nowhere, Randilin came flying through the air and landed a solid blow against the man's cheek. The man staggered again before collapsing under the power of Randilin's uppercut. Randilin screamed toward Cody and Jade, "To the end of the tunnel! Now!" They took off after him down the tunnel. Cody hobbled as fast as his gimped leg would take him, wincing with each step.

As they neared the end, he saw Sally's head sticking out from around the corner shouting for them to hurry. At last they reached her. She quickly led them down another corridor until they were standing in front of a door. Above the door was a simple sign: **WISHING WELL.**

As they entered through the door Cody was startled to find that it did not lead to another room. He felt the rays of the morning's rising sun spray down on his forehead. They were now standing in a large, open-roofed courtyard. In the middle of the courtyard was a water well. Of all the mysteries in Area 51, this one perplexed Cody the most. As if reading his mind, Sally leaned her head toward his, "We are standing at the center of Area 51. In fact, the base itself was *built* around this well. Employees here are not allowed to leave, so this is their source of fresh air."

The tone in her voice suggested that the story was much more complex than she revealed, but for the moment, Cody didn't care. He was too focused on the ancient structure. It was massive. A circle of stacked stones made up the base with the perimeter the size of a paddling swimming pool. The water was dark and still. It was impossible to guess how deep it stretched into the ground. Cody cupped a handful of liquid. It had an almost gooey, silk-like texture as it drained through his figures.

Jade was less interested in the ancient well. "Okay, so what now?" she questioned. "We need to get to this passageway before *somebody*" her gaze zeroed in on Cody, "does something stupid and gets us all killed. What are we waiting for, Randilin? We're wasting valuable time. Cody needs medical help!" Once again Jade had spoken the voice of reason. Cody knew she was right as he felt his eyes blur and his leg go completely numb. He looked to Randilin and Sally who stared reverently toward the well; Randilin smiled toward Jade. "Once again, buttercup, you have used your wonderfully rational brain to jump to wrong conclusions. We are exactly where we want to be," he rubbed his hand along the smooth stones of the well. "Ladies and gents . . . welcome to the passageway." All eyes moved back to the ancient well.

"The well? I don't understand, I . . ." Jade stammered. Sally wrapped her arm around her back. "Just wait and see."

Randilin jumped up onto the ledge of the well and began muttering a chant of unrecognizable words. When he finished, everything was still. Cody stared hard at the dark water unsure of what to expect—was that a bubble? Sure enough, a bubble had risen to the top of the water. Then, another and another. Cody stepped away from the well, propping himself up on Jade's shoulder. The bubbles were coming rapidly now, larger and larger. Soon the well looked like a boiling pot of water. Vapor began rising into the air—and the water began to swirl.

Slowly at first, the water began circling the perimeter of the well as though somebody had pulled the plug in the bathtub. The water tornado was picking up speed, forming a violent whirlpool. Randilin jumped off the ledge, "Well, kids. Who's gonna be the first one to dive in?"

"What!? Surely you must be kidding?" Jade uttered in horror.

Cody was no less enthused, "If anyone is going first, it's you, Randilin!" Cody had expected the comment to set off the fuse on another one of Randilin's cuss-littered rants. Instead, his eyes went momentarily heavy. The voice Cody heard next was not the firey, snappy one he was accustomed to, but a broken one full of heartache. "Unfortunately, this is the end of the road for me. This is where we part. I will be . . . unable to accompany you any farther. But you can trust Sally, she knows the way, I'm sorry."

Sally reached behind him and grabbed his hand, "Randy, perhaps it's time to move on. You can't live this life forever." Cody fought back his desire to question. Even Jade's held in check her impatient need for answers. They both realized the conversation taking place before them ran much deeper than they were welcome to know. Sally was now looking Randilin straight in the eyes and speaking softly, "Randy, what happened back then, that was a different lifetime ago. We all have regrets. . . ."

"Not like I do!" exploded Randilin angrily. "You have no idea what it's like to live with what I've done. Or spend every single second of restless sleep reliving my mistakes and wishing so hard that my blood vessels pop for just one chance to go back and undo what I've done. Don't pretend you understand." His cheeks were burning red. Cody understood that Sally was not the target of Randilin's self-inflicted anger.

Sally grabbed hold of Randilin's other hand, "I'm not pretending to. But you can't live forever in regret. You need to face your demons. And I'll be right beside you."

Randilin was perplexed. The weight of the decision was evident in his slouched shoulders. "I . . . I. . . ." Randilin's answer never came; Jade's voice interrupted his thoughts, "Look out!" With unhesitant obedience, Randilin dropped to the ground, pulling Sally down with him. Sparks flew as a circular blade skimmed off the stones of the well where Randilin's neck had been moments before.

"Down the passageway! Hurry!" Randilin ordered. Cody felt himself being guided to the well's edge; his arm was over Jade's shoulder. Behind her neck he could see the cloaked figure standing in the open doorway to the courtyard, another blade in his hand. Weary from the loss of so much blood, Cody used his last burst of strength to hurl himself over the edge. *SPLASH!*

Water rushed up and clogged his nose as his head was completely submerged. He fought to steady himself with his arms, but the force of the whirlpool was too strong and he felt himself being flung around in circles against the stone walls. He struggled to keep his eyes open, but the water bashed forcefully against his face, blinding him. For a moment he was suspended in time. He could not distinguish up from down, left from right. He felt his lungs straining for breath. He flailed his arms around in search of the surface but came up empty. The pressure of the whirlpool had dragged him deeply down the well. Then a thought dawned on him. *I am going to die.*

Strangely, the thought did not scare him. In fact, he was comforted by it. The last week of his life had destroyed everything he thought normal. Cody relaxed his muscles and released the final storage of air in his lungs. His limp body tossed and turned in the water. He thought how nice it would have been to see Jade one last time. Then everything went black.

PART TWO
THE CITY

24

Breached

Approaching your superiors is always a nerve-inducing occurrence. But doing so to proclaim bad news is even worse. This was exactly the position that Dace found himself in as he marched up the long steps to the assembly hall. As always, there was no wind blowing. Yet he still felt a chill as the dampness of the air clutched to his heavy clothes. Reaching the top of the stairs, four guards stood between him and the giant, twin, wooden doors. This was of no concern to Dace. He gave the guards a slight nod and they stepped aside, pulling the doors open as they parted. Dace gave another nod of thanks before entering.

The room was one he had entered only a handful of times in his life, and the grandness of it once again startled him. The immense room was supported by twenty large, stone pillars, arranged in rows of ten flanking the path across the chamber. The ceiling rose into a giant dome that stretched across the whole room. On the ceiling was a magnificent painting full of lush colors and intricate details. He had, of course, seen the painting many times in books during his childhood, but seldom in person. Now, standing under the gigantic masterpiece, his breath was drawn from his lungs. The painting depicted a bright light, fire and lighting busting forth from it. To the side of the light was a sphere: Earth. However, the sphere was not complete; only the lower hemisphere was visible. A second bright light radiated from within the hemisphere. Chunks of dirt and earth swirled above the half-earth in a whirlwind. Dace was lost in thought recalling his professor's comments on the painting.

A cough sounded from across the room and stole his gaze away from the painting. He flushed, realizing he had been standing in the middle of the room staring at the roof with the wonder of a child. He inwardly kicked himself with embarrassment. *This is not the way for a trained soldier to behave! Especially now!*

Regaining his cool, he continued his march across the room, dwarfed by the giant pillars that towered over him on both sides. Across the room was a platform, and on top of the platform was a large chair. It was not elegant nor was it fancifully decorated. Instead it looked like one that would be found in the corner of any humble carpentry shop. Dace slowed as he approached the chair. It was empty.

The movement of shadows drew his attention to the left. A lady gracefully appeared between two of the pillars. Dace gulped. She was breathtakingly beautiful. Her pale skin had the fairness of a child. She was veiled in a long, ice-blue dress which followed behind her in a train. The dress fluttered across the floor with smooth magnificence.

When she spoke, her words had the soft innocence of a dove, "Welcome to the Great Hall, captain Ringstar. My father is attending to other matters. I, however, will handle your concerns. What is the purpose of your coming?"

Dace's jaw tightened as he stood hypnotized by the lady's beauty. He fumbled as he attempted a clumsy bow. *Why did beautiful women always make him act the fool?* When he rose back up he saw that the lady made no reaction to his awkward bow—whether out of grace or annoyance was unclear,

"My Lady, the Second Passageway has been breached." Whatever emotion this proclamation stirred in the lady was a mystery. Her face remained perfectly cloaked in her calm demeanor. When she offered no words, Dace decided to continue, "Scouts have reported that five bodies appeared an hour ago. The gatekeeper is among them, accompanied by two children. One of the men was unidentified and the fifth one . . . well . . ." Dace suddenly felt very small in the large room. He thought he would melt under the steady gaze of the beautiful lady. Taking a breath, he forced out the final words of his report, "It looks as though Sir Randilin has returned. What course should we take, my lady?"

The lady's face remained stiffly neutral; leaving Dace to speculate what was going on behind her glazed eyes. When at last the lady spoke, it was with the same steady tone, "This is certainly unexpected . . . and ill timed. I will consult my father at once. Take a troop and retrieve the intruders. Do not take Randilin lightly; he is extremely dangerous. Bring him here . . . dead or alive. Dismissed."

25

Captured

S tars. They sparkled overhead in the dim sky. *Am I dreaming?* Cody sat up slowly. He did not know where he was; neither could he remember where he had come from. His foggy eyes soaked in the newfound dream world. The landscape was rocky and uneven. It was a desert dune comprised of flaky red rocks and dirt. High above his head he faintly made out a rough, rocky surface. *Am I in some sort of cave?* Light radiated from the sun that was nestled low on the horizon. Cody smiled. His dream world had a tranquil peace about it; the only sounds that could be heard were his own steady breathing and the rushing of a nearby river. Water?

Suddenly a wave of remembrance crashed over him. He remembered being tossed around in the whirlpool. Images of the experience came rushing back rapidly. *Did I die?* Surely he had, which meant that he was now standing in heaven. He had to admit, he wasn't one to have given a great deal of thought to death, but he had imagined that dying would be much different.

"Cody! Cody! Cody!" He heard his voice being called from some unknown location. *God?* No, wait! The voice was a familiar one. It was Jade's. *Did she die, too?* Cody craned his head around in search of his friend. "Jade! I'm over here! Jade!" He heard the loud thumping of footsteps approaching. He smiled; even in heaven Jade hadn't lost her less-than-graceful feet. The footsteps morphed into a person as Jade came running over the rock dune.

"Cody! I didn't know where you had gone. Where are we? I haven't seen Randilin or Sally anywhere. Oh, my gosh, look at your leg!" Cody glanced down at his legs. They were perfectly normal.

"Um, Jade, I think you bumped your head a bit too hard, there is absolutely nothing wrong with my . . ." he stopped. It was true. His legs were undamaged. There was not even the slightest trace of a bullet wound or blood. Then it occurred to Cody that both he and Jade were completely dry. "I guess we get free healing once we get to heaven?" he concluded with a shrug. Without warning Jade's fist came flying toward Cody and crashed into his cheek. "Ouch! What was that for!" His cheek throbbed.

"It was to snap you out of it. How does your face feel? Sore? We're not in heaven, you doofus. Heaven doesn't even exist. We're just on the other end of the passageway. That whirlpool led us down here. We need to regroup with Randilin and Sally and find out where exactly *here* is. Come on." She grabbed hold of Cody's hands and pulled him to his feet before whipping the dust off his back. Cody smiled. Jade frowned, "Oh, and don't think that I'm not still immeasurably furious at you for touching that door in

Area 51. That was the stupidest thing you've done in your entire life, and believe me, that's saying a lot." Cody was no longer smiling. They began walking along the river, occasionally calling out for Randilin or Sally.

Cody had, in fact, been banking on the hope that Jade, in the heat of the action, might have forgotten all about his earlier foolishness. Fate had thrust the Book into his possession and along with it a mountain of responsibility. Yet, it seemed to Cody that all he had accomplished since then was to leave a trail of dumb choices and put people's lives at risk. His thoughts went back to the words the mysterious agent had spoken in the Area 51 corridor. The part that hurt the most was that the man's words had been true. At first, Cody had secretly cherished the excitement of discovering the Book. It had given him a sense of purpose, of significance. It was his moment to prove that he wasn't a worthless, plain, ordinary boy, that he was special. But now he wanted nothing more than to throw the Book into the bottom of the ocean and return to his ordinary life; back when beasts weren't trying to consume him, assassins weren't trying to murder him, and things made sense. Most of all, he wanted to go back to a time when Jade didn't know how weak he really was.

"Hey, Cody." He was pulled away from his thoughts. Jade was looking directly at him, and despite her noticeable attempts to conceal it, a very slight smile had formed on her thin lips, "Thank you for taking that bullet for me. It was very brave." Any dismal thoughts taking up space in Cody's head evaporated quicker than they had come. He was on top of the world. And, just when he felt his usual swagger returning to his bloodstream, Jade shook her head, "Don't let it get to your head, you moron." But her voice lacked her previous harshness. She had to admit, it was almost impossible to stay mad at Cody.

Although they didn't talk any further, the tension between them had vanished. Jade halted, holding out her arm to halt Cody. "Do you hear that?" He did. The sound of feet moving at a rapid pace; or were they hooves? "Look!" A cloud of dust was rising from behind the rock dunes and heading their direction. "Run!"

They took off sprinting down the river. The sound of hooves was getting louder. "It's no use, they're too fast. We need to hide!" They looked around them for a hiding place, but they were surrounded by endless rocky terrain.

"Hide where?!" *Thud*. Between Cody's feet landed an arrow lodged into the dirt, its shaft still vibrating. He heard the sneering of horses behind him.

"Slowly turn around and put your hands behind your back, or the next one finds a home in your back." Cody raised his hands and cautiously turned to face the speaker. Before him were ten men on horses, several of them had bow and arrow leveled at him. The men were all broad shouldered and clothed in light chainmail armor. Hanging from their sides in scabbards were large swords. Cody recalled the bizarre image of Wesley running toward the stairs with a similar sword. *Who are these people?* Even stranger than the men were the horses; their faces were oddly stubby and narrow with their muzzles coming to a point in a wet black nose. The hair covering their sturdy bodies was longer and shaggier than Cody had ever seen.

There was a scraping sound as one of the horses pawed the rocky ground with its hoof—and Cody suddenly realized that it wasn't a hoof at all . . . it was a paw. Instead of hooves, all the horses' front legs had furry paws like that of a badger. *Things just keep getting stranger!*

The speaker smoothly dismounted his unusual horse-like steed and noiselessly landed on the ground. Off the horse, Cody could see that the man was not very tall. He had a youthful face that was aged only slightly by the presence of light stubble on his chin. His wavy hair hung neatly down to his shoulders. The features of his face gave him an almost mousy appearance. In that moment, it suddenly occurred to him that they *all* had subtle rodent-like qualities. Until seeing the mounted strangers, he had been unable to pin-point what made Randilin and Sally's appearance somewhat abnormal. *Where are we?*

The man approached Cody with a confident strut, his voice was confident and calm, "Hello, my friends. My name is Dace Ringstar, captain of the Outer-City guards. Identify yourselves."

Cody looked over to Jade, but her eyes were already fixed on him, indicating that this time it was up to him to choose the course of action. Would there be any benefit of lying? Finally, Cody spoke boldly, "My name is Cody Clemenson and the girl with me is Jade Shimmers." Dace smirked, "Yes, I know, we've learned that much already from your friends. I just wanted to test your honesty. Wolfrick, Hex . . ." He signaled to two of the guards behind him who dismounted their horses. They too were of shorter stature.

"What have you done with our friends? They're innocent!" yelled Jade. At this, Dace gave a puzzled look. "Innocent? Are you in jest or in earnest?" Jade's defiant stare confirmed the latter. "I think it's time you learned with whom you've been running, Sweetheart. Your friend Randilin happens to be the most wanted, dangerous criminal in the world."

Several of the guards pulled their horses aside to reveal a man shackled by both his arms and feet. The back of his shirt had been torn open and the fresh scabs of lash marks lined his back where his flesh had been torn off. The man was Randilin.

"You let him go! I don't care what he is; he's saved our lives and he's our . . . friend." Cody began to lunge forward but stopped as the guards tightened their grip on their bows. Dace held up his hand to stop his bowmen. "Unfortunately I have orders to follow. And your friend Randilin is now under arrest . . ." he paused. Cody felt his arms being grasped from behind, ". . . as are you."

26

Beneath the Dirt

Cody's wrists burned as the rope binding his arms rubbed against his skin. Fortunately, Sally had thrown a lively fuss and convinced Dace to allow him and Jade to ride in the pulled carriage with her instead of walking. However, her fit didn't persuade Dace to provide Randilin with the same courtesy. Delirious from pain and blood loss, he had been bound by his hands to the back of Dace's horse and forced to stagger behind. Sally had tried her best to free him; knocking two guards completely unconscious before she was eventually subdued. She had finally conceded to stay in her carriage, but the look of rage and disgust never left her face.

The caravan departed. Cody had no idea where they were headed, but then again, there seemed to be very few things that *were* known to him of late. Yet, there was one particular question that was perplexing him the most. Why had Wesley sent him here? He was getting used to accepting the unexpected, but after all the tension and dangers of the journey to arrive here, wherever *here* was, he hadn't expected to be treated like a criminal and subjected to torture. *What were you thinking, Wesley?*

Sally continued to rave about the injustice of the situation and Cody decided it was unwise to interrupt her tirade. Instead he looked across the carriage at Jade. Her head rested against the window as she looked out over the rocky terrain. She was unaware of Cody's stare. The one bright spot of their adventure was that it had drawn him even closer to Jade, a feat he previously thought impossible. The picture of her slight smile as she told him he was brave ranked as one of the greatest moments of his life; although he would never, under any earthly circumstances, hint of it to Jade, of course.

The carriage came to a halt. Cody opened his eyes; he had dozed off, but was unsure of how long. Jade had an equally groggy look on her face. Outside the carriage, they heard raised voices engaged in heated argument, although Cody couldn't make out the words. Finally the disagreement stopped and the carriage door opened. Dace stuck his head in. "We have decided to stop for the night. We are almost within sight of the city, however, Randilin has slowed our progress and I do not believe he can reach the city in his condition. Tents will be provided for you." Before Cody could question, Dace disappeared.

Cody stepped out of the carriage. The sun's light was still shining bright, leaving Cody to question Dace's concern for nightfall. He quickly searched for Randilin, but he was nowhere to be seen. A lone tent had already been constructed and a gruff looking guard wielding a spiked mace stood at attention in front of the entrance. Cody guessed that Randilin was contained inside and hoped he was okay. Jade joined his side; she, too, was thinking of Randilin's safety.

"Hey, Jade, come make yourself useful. We need to unpack the supplies for breakfast tomorrow," a guard called across the clearing. Cody remembered the man's name as Hex. Jade followed in obedience as the soldier led her through the camp and out of sight. The other guards assembled their tents and bustled around. Cody stood dumbly and watched, unsure whether to help or stay out of the way.

"Cody, over here. I wish to have a word with you." It was the youthful voice of Dace. Cody walked over to where the captain of the guards was standing. "Follow me." He led Cody a good distance away from the camp and up one of the rocky dunes. Reaching the top of the dune, Dace flopped down and sat upon the ground. He motioned for Cody to join him.

"First of all, I wish to offer an apology for the treatment of your friend, Randilin."

Cody sneered disdainfully. "An apology is sure easier now, after you've already whipped him to death and dragged him half way across this god-forsaken desert. You're nothing but a bully."

A wave of irritation passed over Dace's face, but he took a deep breath and the harsh lines on his brow once again smoothed. "I ask you not to be so hasty to jump to conclusions. While I am in command of this troop, I am far from being in command of all. Decisions regarding the fate of your friend are far beyond my sphere of influence. In fact, by the very act of stopping and giving him rest tonight, I am disregarding my orders, a decision I will be harshly reprimanded for."

Cody could read the sincerity on his face and instantly felt guilty for his haughty accusations. "I'm sorry, I didn't know. Thank you."

A cocky expression returned to Dace's face, "Don't mistake my decision as care for Randilin. If anyone deserves the fate he has received, it's him. However, there is a fine line between justice and barbarianism and my conscience won't let me cross it." Cody stared down at the red dirt beneath him. As much as he hated himself for it, he was beginning to have an involuntary liking for Dace.

Dace looked toward the sky, back to the horizon, and then back to Cody. "Good night." This peculiar statement rattled Cody. By way of answer, the entire sky went pitch black. "What's going on!" cried Cody. The sky had instantly transformed from sunny midday to late evening in the span of an instant.

Dace laughed, "Don't worry. It's perfectly normal down here. It will make more sense tomorrow. Trust me." Cody hoped so, because it certainly didn't make any sense at the moment.

"Wait." Cody pondered, "What do you mean it's normal *down here*?"

Dace looked honestly surprised by the question. "You mean you genuinely have no idea where we are? Neither Randilin or Sally told you where they were leading you?" Despite the images of Randilin's bloody back, Cody couldn't help but feel some resentment toward the dwarf for having kept him in the dark. Then again, he was starting to learn that Randilin was a man accustomed to secrets.

"No, they did not. They didn't tell me a single thing. I've been carrying this B . . ." he paused. He realized that so far there had been no mention of the Book. *Perhaps Dace doesn't know?* Cody decided that it was best not to bring it up. He stumbled on his words, "this b . . . b . . . burden of not knowing for awhile. So where on earth are we?" Dace caught the awkwardness but, to Cody's relief, did not question it.

"Actually, it is not a question where *on* earth we are, but rather, where *in* earth we are." Dace allowed a moment for his words to sink in.

"So you mean, we aren't . . . on earth? But that whirlpool in the well at Area 51, it couldn't have led anywhere. It could only have led . . ."

"Down," Dace finished.

"Surely you don't mean that, I mean, you can't be seriously saying that we're, that we're . . ."

Dace flashed a mischievous smile. "Oh, I am absolutely serious. I guess I should take a moment to offer you salutations. Welcome—to the center of the earth."

27

The Lost City

Cody stared at the shadows as they danced across the roof of his tent like a puppet show. His conversation with Dace had come to an abrupt end when Dace was called to attend to a dispute between several guards accusing each other of cheating in a gambling game. The reality of being in the center of the earth had not shocked Cody as drastically as it probably should have. Perhaps he had finally thrown in the towel and opened his mind to the many unknown, crazy realities that were now his *new* reality.

After Dace left, Cody wandered back to the camp in search of Jade. Being unable to locate her, he decided to retire to his assigned tent. The commotion outside slowly died down and one by one the lights had been extinguished. However, he could still make out the shadow of a man sitting at the entrance to his tent. The man had an axe. *I'm being guarded.*

Lying alone in his tent, out of touch from Jade, and enclosed in the center of the earth, Cody began to feel very claustrophobic and very alone. He closed his eyes. He had the feeling that tomorrow would require all his strength.

The sound of voices awakened Cody from his sleep. Stretching and rubbing his eyes, he pulled himself out of his sleeping bag and exited his tent. Men were scurrying around and packing up the final pieces of equipment, leaving no sign of last night's campsite.

"My boy, bout time you got up, you sluggard. Don't know what Dace has me guarding ya for, can't escape if ya ain't ever gettin' out of bed!" The comment had come from Wolfrick, the guard who Cody remembered had captured and bound Jade's wrists the night before. Of all the troops, he was the biggest. His hefty size came from bulkiness, not fat. His reddish hair hung greasily over his eyes and formed a messy pony-tail that reached his mid-back. A thick, bushy beard that was fashioned into two, tight braids covered his face.

"Then again, it must be pretty exhausting being a criminal fugitive, I reckon."

Wolfrick smacked his large hand onto Cody's shoulder. "But lazy cow as ya might be, you sure got good taste in women, I'll give ya that! Your pretty girlfriend's practically running the place already."

Cody flushed bright red. "She's not my girlfriend. We're just friends."

Wolfrick gave him an exaggerated wink. "If ya say so, captain. She's over on the north end helping out Hex and Sheets last time I saw. Asked me to send ya over when ya woke." The large man turned and walked back into the camp, muttering to himself, "Just friends, he says. My mother-in-law's false teeth, they're just friends."

Cody dashed in the direction that Wolfrick had pointed but immediately slowed himself. He didn't want to appear desperate or concerned. He looked to the sky. In the daylight he could see the rocky surface stretching out as far as his eyes could see. They were literally in an enormous cave. Colossal stalactites hung from the ceiling like gobs of thick tar ready to break. Cody shuddered. One break and they all would be smashed into bloody pancakes. Something glittering above his head caught Cody's attention; hundreds of shimmering sparks flashed before his eyes. It was as though he was looking at a starry night sky. One of the passing guards slowed down and followed Cody's eyes. "Ah . . . I see you've taken notice of our stars. Beautiful, ain't they?"

Cody shook his head. "But I don't understand, how can there be stars if we are in the center of the earth?"

The guard laughed, "More so, how can there be a sun? Nah, they ain't real stars. Can't get rich off a real star now, can ya?"

"How so do you mean? If they're not real, then what are they?" responded Cody.

"Gems. Pure, perfect, gigantically gorgeous gems. You bring just one of those stones up to Upper-Earth and you're a king." Cody made a mental note to himself: *Get sky gem = become king.*

He continued on his way. True to Wolfrick's words, he found Jade packing up some cooking materials with the slight guard known as Hex, and an older, redheaded man with a thick mustache that Cody assumed was Sheets.

When Jade saw Cody approaching she gave a large smile and motioned for him to come.

When Cody arrived, Hex and Sheets were clutching their bellies and laughing hysterically. Sheets stuck a finger out toward Cody. "Well, if it ain't the valiant hero of the story himself!" Hex let out another laugh before tossing his arm around Cody's shoulder. "Indeed it is, my good man, Sheets! Although he appears to be wearing more than his usual *mighty warrior armor*!" The two men burst into another fit of hysteric laughing. Even Jade chuckled in good humor. Cody stared uneasily between the three of them, apparently missing the joke.

Jade smiled. "Good morning, Cody. I've just been entertaining these gentlemen with the heroic tale of you dashing for your life through Wesley's apartment wearing nothing but tighty whities." At this the two guards entered into more wheezy laughter.

Cody's skin became clammy and he suddenly felt cold. "Well, what are you telling them that for? You think you can just go around talking behind my back? You're a real friend, aren't you, Jade!" Without waiting for a response, Cody stormed back toward his tent. The moment the words had exited his mouth he knew he was over-reacting, but he didn't care. Jade had embarrassed him in front of the masculine troops and turned him into the butt of jokes. In fact, his *butt* had become the butt of jokes. He was furious at her for mocking him that way. He knew he should go apologize, but he wasn't going to give her the satisfaction. Not after the way she humiliated him. And what was she doing acting so cozy and flirtatious with those men anyways? Nope, she would receive no such apology from him. He was the victim.

As the convoy resumed their trek Cody found himself walking alongside some of the guards on horses. He overheard that Randilin had contracted blood poisoning from his whip wounds and was in rough condition. As a result, he had been given the carriage for the trip. Sally eventually had worn down Dace and had been allowed to ride in the carriage with him. Several yards in front of him, Cody watched as Jade's black hair swayed back and forth with her steps. She was engaged in a conversation with one of the other mounted guards; it was a conversation that looked a little too friendly for Cody's liking. Cody had not spoken a word to her since their morning scuffle. Nor did he have any desire to.

As Cody walked behind the pack, Wolfrick apparently decided that no more supervision was needed, and had trotted off to ride beside some of his peers, leaving Cody alone. Cody spent the next hour making systematic lists of all the ways Jade had mistreated him over the years. Only when Dace trotted up beside him on his paw-footed horse was Cody's focus distracted. Dace coolly dismounted the horse with a single hop and began walking alongside Cody. "Rough morning, eh, brother?" Cody glared at the guard captain irritably, but the good-natured smile on his face slowly dispelled his frustration.

"I've had better." Dace followed Cody's eyes toward Jade. "Ah, things not so peachy with the lady friend, I take it. Chin up; once we arrive at the capital, you'll have enough to divert your mind."

"The capital? Of what? It seems like I have three million questions but no one ever answers them. So you guys have *cities* down here in the center of the earth?"

The captain ran his fingers through his long, sweat-damped hair. "Well, unfortunately, I must add to your growing list of disappointments, as I am still the captain guard and you are still my prisoner. However, I do think you have earned some explanation. Besides, things are a bit tense in the capital of late and it's best that you are prepared."

Dace clenched his jaw as he debated where to start. Cody waited anxiously, eager to finally receive some understanding. At last Dace began, "Okay, much of this will probably not make sense to you right now . . ."

"Don't even think of telling a story about fish," snapped Cody.

Dace raised his eyebrows in amusement before continuing, "Just bear with me and be patient. Also, there are several crucial details that I am unauthorized to divulge, further adding to my inability to explain things to you. However, I will do my best with what I have. As to where you are, as I informed you yesterday, you are in the center of the earth, or as we locals call it: Under-Earth. You arrived here from Upper-Earth through the Second Passageway . . ."

"So I've heard several times. If the water well within Area 51 was the Second Passageway, then where is the First Passageway?" Cody questioned. A mysterious smirk molded onto Dace's lips, "Where is it, indeed? And furthermore, where are the Third, Fourth, and Eleventh Passageways? Our two worlds are not as divided as you may think. However, the exact location of these passageways is restricted information; so much so, that I am unaware of them myself." An image of a groundhog's complex network of tunnels flashed in Cody's mind.

"Well, why would you keep an entrance in the middle of Area 51? It's impossible to get in or out of there!"

Dace grinned. "True. It is. I believe the answer is already in your question. The difficulty of entrance is precisely why it *is* there. Sometimes the best way to keep something hidden is to hide it right under the nose of those searching for it. We don't even bother with guarding it; you people are doing a fantastic job of that already. You also assume that the passageway was placed within the complex, and not vice-versa, with the base being built *around* the passageway . . ." Cody had to admit it was clever. Area 51 was the destination for supernatural objects once they were found, not a place where one looks to uncover them.

Cody believed Dace was telling the truth. His mind rattled around, brimming with all the other countless questions that haunted his mind. "What about these people calling themselves CROSS. Are these your people? Why are they trying to kill me?" The question produced a blank stare on Dace's face. "If there is a group called CROSS, then it is news to me. I know of no such group."

Cody was now shooting rapid fire: "And how could a water well possibly bring us all the way down here alive? What did Randilin do that was so bad as to be treated this way? And what kind of unholy creature is this . . . demon-like Beast that's been chasing me . . ." Dace's face became deadly serious. Cody noticed Dace's fingers had made their way around the hilt of his sword.

"What was that you just said?" Dace's voice was shaky and sullen. Cody bit his lip. He did not mean to disclose any information that might lead to the discovery of the book. He stammered, "Um . . . the beasty man in the CROSS robe I meant. He's a monstrous killer." Cody knew his lie had fallen completely flat. Dace sat perfectly still, his intense gaze unbroken. Cody was trapped. Thankfully, luck was once again on his side. The rest of the company had stopped at the top of a large rock dune and Wolfrick was calling out for him, "Hurry up, son, come feast your eyes on the breath-taking beauty of the capital!" Dace gave Cody a nod to go, but the look in his eyes revealed that their conversation was only temporarily on hold.

Cody ran up the dune to join the guards, thankful to at least be momentarily liberated. When he reached the top, he gasped. Resting at the peak of a giant sand mound was the capital. In fact, it did not look like a city at all, but rather a gigantic walled fortress. A thick, stone wall rose forty feet high and stretched out for miles. Situated periodically behind the walls were giant towers. At the front of the wall was a thick stone gate. Encircling the wall's perimeter was a water-filled moat the size of a small river.

From his position, Cody could not see much behind the walls, only the odd roof tip or tower peeking over the fortifications. However, two structures towered above the rest. One was a large, white-walled building constructed in a circular shape, forming into a large red dome on top. But this structure was not that which stole Cody's gaze. A giant oval-shaped formation dwarfed the rest of the structures. The unorthodox building resembled an egg resting on a golf-tee. It was made from some smooth, shiny metallic substance that Cody couldn't pin-point. Along the sleek surface of the structure were large engravings and designs. The base of the structure must have stood thirty-stories high. In all, the futuristic design looked noticeably out of place within the otherwise ancient, medieval looking city. A blinding light glowed from the oval causing Cody to squint his eyes.

"Never seen anything like it before, have you?" whispered Dace. It was not a question, but a fact.

Cody kept his eyes fixed on the marvelous metropolis. "What is this place?" Lights shone from within the city as it began to wake for the day. Dace held his hand out. "Believe it or not, I have no doubt that at some point in your life you've actually heard about this great city before. It's the most famous city in the world, surface or not. . . ." The comment startled Cody.

"No way. I have never heard of anything as amazing or beautiful as this before. What do you mean?"

"Oh, don't be so sure of yourself. It is commonly known in Upper-Earth, or at least speculated about. To you surface-dwellers it is simply known as the *Lost City*. However, for us underlings, we know it by another name. It is the illustrious capital city of Under-Earth . . . the majestic city of Atlantis."

28

The Rumblings of War

Atlantis. The fabled city. Lost since the beginning of time—now found. The sight was surreal to Cody. Humankind had scoured every inch of the globe in search of this legendary metropolis, and as Cody's caravan inched closer and closer to the colossal city he realized they would continue to search forever in vain. Atlantis was not a city of the earth, it was one with*in* it. Now Cody found himself thousands of miles underground approaching the greatest archeological discovery in history.

He desperately longed to share the excitement with Jade, but he wasn't going to give her the satisfaction of watching him crawl back apologetically like a meek child. The moment she decided to come apologize to *him* for mistreating him in front of the guards, he would be happy to resume the friendship. Until then, he was on his own.

The closer to the city the convoy reached, the more Cody began to appreciate the immensity of it. However, he also had the foreboding sentiment that the scarlet 'A' on the cover of the Book and Atlantis were somehow linked. Did the Book belong to them? Was it written by them or about them? Should he re-turn it? Or keep it hidden? These questions remained unde-cided, but Cody knew he was running out of time.

Cody looked up at the immense stone doors and then down at the moat which now separated them from the city. From a distance the moat had seemed flush with the ground, but now that Cody stood directly in front of it he could see that the water was actually at the bottom of a twenty-foot crevasse. Cody imagined that any attempts to siege the city would be ill advised and disastrous for the attackers. The city was an impenetrable fortress.

Dace trotted ahead and stopped at the foot of the moat. Suddenly the heavy doors began slowly creaking open. Dace reared his horse and brought it alongside Cody. "When we get inside," Dace commanded, "I want you to follow close. Don't stop moving for any reason. Under-stood?" Cody nodded in affirmation. He didn't need to be told twice; not after the fiasco in Area 51.

There was a loud thud as the city doors were opened fully. The sound that followed was a cranking noise of something sliding over a pulley or some such contraption. Cody watched in amazement as a large wooden plank began emerging through the doors. It was a retractable bridge that slammed into place. Dace whistled loudly and the caravan began filing over and into the city.

Walking through the gate Cody felt like he was passing through a time machine into some forgotten ancient era. All the accounts Cody had ever heard of the fabled city told of its far superior advancement. They spoke of how it had evolved into a higher form of species than any on earth. And yet, as Cody stepped through the gate, he saw a dusty, old-fashioned city. The houses were constructed of stone and latched with straw roofs and the streets were comprised of primeval cobblestone. Along the walls torches were mounted, wielding flame. *The most advanced city in history doesn't even have electricity?!* The thought stunned him.

The houses and buildings seemed run down and poorly kept. Cody felt a tug on his pant legs and turned to see an elderly man sitting against the wall. He shoved a tin can in Cody's hands. "Spare some coins for a poor man? Spare some coins?" Cody's mouth went dry.

Wolfrick knocked the can back to the man. "Leave the boy alone, Gelph. He ain't from these parts." The old beggar grinned, revealing several lost teeth. "Wolfrick, you know me. It matters not where the boy's from, just as long as they have coins there!" Wolfrick laughed and placed a copper coin in the man's can. "Now scram! And if I find out you've spent my coin on booze I'll have your head hanging on the wall of Yanci's pub!" The beggar scampered off.

Wolfrick leaned down to Cody. "Atlantis is divided into three tiers; this here is the Outer-City. It's Dace's domain to oversee. It's full of dust, beggars and thieves. But, I'll tell ya, here are some of the greatest people in all of Atlantis. Just people who need to catch a break."

As they passed through more of the Outer-City, Cody couldn't help but have increasing respect for Dace. He seemed to know all of the residents on a first-name basis, and despite his government position, treated each of them kindly and with dignity. It was clear that Dace did not receive the obvious admiration of the residents by chance. It was also clear that his mousey features were not an oddity in Under-Earth. All the citizens they passed were equally short in stature and rodent-looking.

Suddenly, a loud gong rang over the city. Instantly each of the guards dismounted their horses and knelt down on one knee. The citizens of the Outer-City joined in the action, all facing toward the massive oval structure towering above all the other buildings. Cody felt like a giant soaring above the mob of kneeling people so he hesitantly bent down onto his knee. All at once the people raised their voices to chant in unison, "Hail, the Orb of holy light, humbled we by its eternal might. Hail the Orb, let it shine forever bright." The chant repeated seven times before the crowd uttered, "Amen" in unison.

The guards stood and remounted their horses and the citizens resumed their business as though nothing had happened. Raising an eyebrow, Cody looked to the burly mustached guard, Sheets, for some kind of explanation. The guard grinned. "You will quickly come to understand that Atlantis has its own share of rules and customs. All in good time my boy. No worries; even the AREA won't put an ignorant Surface-Dweller behind bars until you've had the customs fully explained."

"The AREA?" questioned Cody.

Sheets grunted and leaned in close to Cody. "I keep forgetting you Surface-Dwellers are a little slower than us Underlings. The AREA is a powerful lot down here. It stands for the Atlantis Rule Enforcement Association. They ensure that the religious rituals are performed up to snuff; as well as stick their pointy noses into everyone else's business. A bunch of pompous pigs, if you ask me, which, of course, you didn't. Superficial rules and codes are more useless than a legless horse at the racetrack out here in the Outer-City where folks are scraping just to get by."

"Then why do people follow them still?" asked Cody.

Sheets gave a sarcastic laugh. "Because all are created equal, and then live according to class systems. You will soon see that not all folks in Atlantis are like us Outer-City misfits. Trust me; the General was doing Dace no kind favors by expelling him and our troop out here. Ol' Dace has never been a soul constrained to his commands or orders; he lives by his own strict code of principles. Admirable, but not a great recipe for promotion! However, in the Inner-City the AREA is supreme. Not to mention that the price for disobedience is a good flogging or a date with the gallows. A monopoly on the death business has a curious way of enticing people to obey." Cody looked to the dusty faces of the citizens with tattered clothes scurrying by in the shadows. *This is the mystifying, great city of Atlantis?*

The caravan stopped as it reached another gateway that was closed with a solid iron cage door. Dace nodded to the two guards peering down from the overhanging lookout towers. The gate slowly elevated. As Cody followed the troops away from the Outer-City, he saw a wooden sign on the wall: Mid-City.

The contrasts between the Outer-City and the Mid-City were significant. Whereas the Outer-City was dirty and rundown, the Mid-City was clean and well maintained. The streets were crammed with people going to and fro. Actually, Cody suddenly realized that most of the residents were heading in a unified direction—they were following directly behind them. The dissatisfied looks on their faces made Cody uneasy.

Sheets leaned toward Cody again. "Here in the Mid-City are the working folk. It is here where the gears of the city turn. They're a hard-working lot, but not the most pleasant of people as you'll find here in Atlantis. They're in constant tension with the AREA. Claim they have too much work to worry about such strict, fluffy religious practices. Industry is the divine being in this part of the city."

Every glance back over his shoulder revealed to Cody that the assembly of followers had increased. There were now almost thirty men and women behind them. He noticed that all of Dace's troops had casually brought their hands to rest against the hilts of their swords. Cody glanced behind him again. One of the followers was carrying a sign above his head. The words on the placard read: **THE TIME FOR WAR IS NOW!**

"If we don't strike first, *they* will!" yelled the man with the sign. His cohorts echoed his cry. A woman with frizzy hair tossed up her hands, shouting, "It's time for the king to stop hiding in his castle and face reality!" More cheering. A large man in the crowd called out, "Let the people vote! As for me, I vote war!" The man received a loud burst of applause for his statement, and slowly the loud chant, "We vote war" was picked up by the mob. "We vote war! We vote war! We vote war!"

Hex and several of the other guards starting yelling back at the mob. Cody heard the sound of swords being pulled from their scabbards. Wolfrick appeared by Cody's side wielding his giant axe, "Not everyone is seeing eye to eye in Atlantis these days; things are a bit . . . unstable." As the yelling behind him continued to escalate Cody inched closer to the bulky guard. "What do they mean, they vote war? War with whom?"

Wolfrick shook his head. "Don't mind them. As long as our good king remains on the throne, you need not waste your time worrying about war. Besides, we're almost at the Inner-City." They soon reached another gate similar to the one between the Outer and Mid-City divisions. However, Cody noticed that this gate was blockaded with several armed guards and that two fortified towers flanked each side. Cody could see the tips of arrows aiming down at his company from within the small, slit-windows of the turrets.

The gate opened and they filed through a door that was just wide enough for two men to pass simultaneously. Cody guessed this was yet another defensive mechanism. The moment Cody passed through the archway his jaw dropped. The towering futuristic, circular structure that appeared to be visible from any part of the city was even more magnificent up close. The structure was gigantic. The base was constructed in a massive hourglass shape. Even so, the foundation looked minuscule compared to the structure itself. The immense oval's smooth metallic surface glimmered in the light. Actually, Cody realized that it was *producing* the light. Bright beams of illumination were being broadcast across the city and beyond. *What's inside there?*

Cody was still lost in thought as the company reached the long stone staircase ascending to the grand dome-shaped building he had seen from the sand dune. He noticed that a crowd of people had gathered to witness the commotion. The residents were clean and dressed in long tunic-like garments made of fine fabric. Compared to the citizens in the Outer-City, they looked like royalty. Cody's eyes halted; at the edge of the crowd was a girl. She had flowing blonde hair and ruby red lips. She stood out in the crowd like an angel among a pack of ogres. Her eyes were staring directly at him. He felt his skin heat up and his palms become clammy. Blushing, he dropped his gaze to the ground to break the stare. When he glanced back up, the girl was gone.

29

Interrogated

Something big was about to happen. He didn't know what, but the very marrow of Dace's bones proclaimed it with upmost certainty; his solder's instinct was seldom wrong. He gazed out over the crowd of people who slowly engulfed his band of troops at the foot of the palace. They too seemed to sense it.

Dace took a step up onto the first stair of the palace before pivoting to face his troops, "Lacen, Hoffin, Didet, and Hex, I want you to escort Randilin down to the holding cell until further instruction. Sally is to be put on temporary probation until her association with Randilin is cleared. Kingsty and Tyrin, you will return to the Outer-City and rendezvous with the others. Wolfrick and Sheets, keep the crowd away. Let's move." The soldiers immediately set about their orders. Cody felt the shadow of Wolfrick fall over him, urging him up the stairs.

With the majority of the company dispatched, Cody suddenly felt uncomfortable walking beside Jade as they ascended the stairs. He stole a glance at her. She seemed completely at ease and unconcerned. His frustration toward her reached a new high. "Everything's just business as usual for you, isn't it, Jade." The words snidely exited Cody's mouth before he could stop them, but he was pleased that they had. Jade shook her head but kept her eyes focused ahead. This ticked Cody off even more. "What, too good to even talk to your best friend anymore? You seem to have no trouble batting those eyelashes of yours and chatting it up with the guards . . ."

"Oh, that's what you think, is it? You're such a child." Cody was about to lash back in retaliation when he collided into Dace's back. Jade chuckled under her breath. There was a thud as the opened front doors slammed into place.

Dace whispered over his shoulder, "Be ready to bow and give respect. You are about to enter the presence of the King." Without further instruction, Dace led them into a large room with a dome roof. A large painting on the ceiling transfixed Cody. He did not understand its meaning, but was captivated by the beautiful artistry. "Psst! Come on." Jade was waving her hand and Cody jogged to catch up. They came to the throne—and found that it was empty.

The sound of voices came echoing forth from some unseen hallway. As the speech approached nearer, Cody began to comprehend some of the words. It seemed to be a heated conversation between two people: "I'm telling you, I don't know how much longer we can hold them off. We'll have a full-grown riot before long. War is brewing. What could have provoked such a bold ultimatum after all these years . . ."

"It doesn't matter. We are not prepared to engage in a war of this magnitude. Not without a champion, one who is knowledgeable in the way . . ."

"I know, but time is scarce. Our scouts report that enemy troops are gathering east of Lilley. If they strike through the pass we will be completely unprepared, our father . . ." The voices halted. A man and a woman appeared from behind the throne. Dace bent into a bow which Cody attempted to mimic.

"My lord and lady, I have returned with the captives." The woman stepped forth from the shadows; she was stunningly beautiful in an elegant blue dress. Her eyes sparkled like glimmering stars in the night sky.

"So, I see," she said smoothly. Her accomplice joined her in the light. Like the lady, the man was strikingly handsome. His features were dark and exotic.

"What of Sir Randilin and the gatekeeper?" he asked in a flatly serious voice. As he spoke, he began slowly circling the visitors like a leopard eyeing its prey.

"He is being contained as we speak. His health is poor, but not critical. The gatekeeper is in holding." Cody noticed that Dace's usual swagger was hardly visible; instead he seemed nervous and fidgety.

The exotic looking man completed his inspection. He noticed Dace glancing over to the empty throne, and stepped into the captain's line of sight. "The King is not to be bothered. He has many pressing matters to attend to with the rumors of war catching like wildfire."

The woman glided in front of the man. "As such, we have been given authority in this matter. Where is the fifth intruder?" Cody shot a worried glance to Jade. *What fifth intruder? Had the assassin with circular blades followed them down the Well?*

Dace squirmed uncomfortably under the lady's gaze. "Unfortunately, he has temporarily evaded us. My men are in pursuit as we speak. He will be caught."

"I expect so. There is also the matter of your delay and apparent disregard of my commands." Dace opened his mouth to apologize but the lady silenced him with a raised hand. "We will deal with that later. As for now, we have other matters to attend to . . ."

She leaned toward Cody. He blushed; the perfection of her silky skin was intoxicating as it came close to his. She had an alluring scent to her like the water of a desert oasis. He was entranced. "I believe introductions are in order. I am Lady Cia, daughter to the King of Atlantis. This pessimistic fellow behind me is my brother, Prince Kantan."

The man didn't flinch, keeping his gaze on Cody. His voice was slow and calculating. "Now, by authority of the crown, I order you to identify yourselves and your business in Under-Earth. Speak." Cody felt the vast weight of the Book in his backpack and wondered why it had not yet been confiscated.

"Um . . . My name is Cody, from the small town of Havenwood. This is my friend Jade . . . your highness," Cody added hesitantly.

Kantan peered unwaveringly at Cody. "Havenwood you say? Interesting . . . my knowledge of Upper-Earth geography is admittedly limited but I too know a man who lived in a town called Havenwood, His name was Wesley

Simon." Cody focused all his energy to maintain his unaffected facial features. Their chances of escaping the situation were balancing on the tip of a knife.

"What a coincidence," Cody responded with forced coolness.

"Indeed," the man smirked, "as, I have no doubt, is it *mere coincidence* that your current traveling companion, Sir Randilin, is Under-Earth's most wanted criminal . . ." Cody continued to hold the man's heavy gaze. The Prince stepped so close to Cody, he could feel the mint in his breath.

It was Lady Cia who finally put an end to the misery, "Oh, Kantan, enough with your games. Let's cut to the point. It is clear to everybody in this room that the secret is resting within the boy's backpack." At that moment Cody realized that both his hands were reaching behind his back and clutching the backpack. The scam was up. "Captain Ringstar, empty the sack."

Cody felt Dace's hands pull the pack off his shoulders. The look in his eye was almost apologetic. He unzipped the bag slowly and reached his hand in. Cody held his breath; this was the moment of truth. Dace pulled out several empty Granola bar wrappers and sent them fluttering to the floor. When his hand appeared again it was holding the ruby pocket-watch; the small red hand on the clock was now spinning rapidly in circles, out of control. Dace reached in again; this time his hand pulled out a dusty, worn, leather-bound Book—a large scarlet 'A' radiated from its cover.

Silence hovered over the room with such thickness that Cody thought he would choke on it. The appearance of the

Book silenced every tongue in the room—until the dam finally broke:

"*The Code*! Here in Atlantis? In the hands of a boy! Explain yourself!" Blue veins pressed softly against Cia's suddenly sweaty forehead. Kantan's firm hands grasped Cody on the shoulders. "Boy, what is the meaning of this? Speak at once. This is not some childish game. What dark frowning of fate is this?"

To Cody's surprise, Dace spoke up, "Prince Kantan, forgive me for speaking out of line my lord, but I can vouch that this boy is no criminal. Perhaps it would be more beneficial to allow him a chance to explain his story?" Kantan's eyes burned with disdain that seemed ready to burst into flames.

Cia laid her hand on his arm to calm him. "The young captain is right. Perhaps fate has smiled rather than frowned. This could prove crucial in the unfolding circumstances. We must hear the boy's tale from the beginning—but not here. Let us retire to the privacy of the royal chambers."

Kantan held his grip on Cody's shoulders for a moment longer before exhaling and releasing him. "Wise, as always, my sister. We must consult the King immediately. Captain Ringstar, escort the children to the royal chambers to await our return. We will, however, keep the Book with us." Kantan retrieved the Book from Dace and the two siblings hastily disappeared through the columns the way they had come. The moment they had departed, Dace's arms shot out and grabbed Cody's mouth, muffling his scream. Cody saw that Jade was captive to Dace's other hand. With a harsh jerk, they were dragged into the shadows.

"Shhh!"

Dace was hunched down and pulled them into a huddle, "Cody, Jade, listen closely. I don't have time to explain. All I can say is, if I'm correct about that Book, you have instantly become the most powerful man in Atlantis. Listen to me, the royal family is noble, but they are also desperate. We are on the brink of war. Stay alert. Your power will make you a very valuable pawn, or an insurmountable threat. The line between the two is razor thin. Keep your head about you. And remember . . ." Dace stopped, they were no longer alone. Two palace guards had joined them in the shadows. Cody looked to Jade; her face reflected the thought burning into his own mind: *What have we gotten ourselves into?*

30

A Tale of Two Cities

The room was not large. The decor was simple but elegant. Cushioned sofas surrounded the perimeter, and rich cherry-toned drapes hung down from the center of the roof, transforming the room into an indoor tent. Cody's leg muscles twitched. Dace's words clogged his mind. He felt Jade's arm brush against his own. They were alone in the room. The relief he felt from her presence was overwhelming. Although neither of them had spoken or offered an apology, Cody knew from the closeness of her body on the sofa that their clash was ancient history. They needed each other; now, more than ever.

The door abruptly opened and caused Cody to involuntarily grab Jade's hand. Four bodies entered the room and positioned themselves onto the adjacent furniture. Lady Cia and Prince Kantan were joined by two others. The first was a plump looking young man with a rounded, freckled face. His clumpy hair looked as though a dirty, wet mop had been placed upon his head. The other was a youthful looking girl. Her appearance was defined by simplicity.

Her straight blonde hair draped over her shoulders in two tight French braids. Her face was pleasant, complimented by two oversized blue eyes, but her expression was glazed as though unaware of her surroundings.

It was Kantan who began the conversation, "The King offers his sincere apologies. He is unfortunately still engaged in war council meetings with his generals and unable to join us. However, he invites you both to his chambers tomorrow morning for breakfast." Kantan motioned to the stalky boy and plain girl. "Our younger brother, Prince Foz, and younger sister, Lady Eva." The young girl smiled timidly and the plump prince offered a clumsy wave.

Cia spoke, "We apologize for the way you have been treated. However, we ask you to tell us your story, the whole story, so that we can understand each other." She laid the scarlet-lettered Book down onto the center table. All eyes narrowed in on Cody. He remembered Dace's warning, and began slowly telling of their adventures. When he got stumped, Jade would offer details and fill in the gaps.

Cody told of their discovery of the Book. Mention of Wesley's death brought a gasp from Eva. He detailed their return to Wesley's and narrow escape from the Beast. Even stone-faced Kantan's skin went pale at the mention of the creature. Cody explained their decision to flee and their meeting with Randilin. However, Cody failed to mention anything about Dunstan or CROSS. For some reason he didn't feel right about divulging those details. Perhaps it was because he still didn't know which side CROSS was on. Regardless of the reason, he was happy that Jade had followed his lead and had apparently made the same decision. Finally, Cody concluded by describing their break into Area 51, their journey down the Wishing Well, and eventual capture by Dace and his troops.

When he finished he held his breath. He felt the sweat between Jade's fingers press against his as she gripped his hand. Kantan leaned forward. "Cody, can you please pick up the Book?" Cody nodded, and cautiously reached out his hand. He felt a tingling sensation on his fingers. His hand closed around the Book. The moment it did, a jolt of energy shot through his fingers, up his arm, and into his head. He dropped the Book and grabbed his head. Cia flashed glance toward Kantan. "Fascinating."

She moved her focus toward Cody. "You just felt a strange sensation, didn't you? Have you felt this sensation before?" Cody recalled the bizarre experience in Jade's bedroom. He also remembered the two unexplainable times that the Book had mysteriously worked through him.

"Yes. Every time I touch it, it feels as though this Book, whatever it is, sends some sort of electric shock into my brain. Don't you feel it?"

Kantan shook his head. "I feel nothing. Only the texture of leather under my fingers." Cody was irritated; he was tired of feeling like he was crazy.

"So why me?" he asked with a raised voice.

Cia smiled. "Because you are very special Cody. It affects you differently than us because the Book did not *choose* us."

"It didn't what?" cried Cody and Jade in unison.

The roundish brother Foz spoke for the first time, his voice was surprisingly solid and affirming, "Brother and sisters. Perhaps it would be wise to explain our history to the boy. If he is indeed who we suspect him to be, then he deserves to know the power he possesses. Don't you agree, little Eva." The youngest sister blushed and merely nodded her head in affirmation.

Cia leaned forward in her chair. When she spoke her voice was an airy whisper, "Foz is right. You deserve to know. Our history is a long one, full of tragedy and betrayal, so listen carefully. Many things may not make sense at first, but you need to know the facts." She drew in a deep breath, and then began,

Our story begins at the dawn of time, where a pack of twelve skilled hunters battled through a violent sandstorm. Ishmael, the chief, knew that they would certainly perish in the tempest, so he ordered his men to set up camp. For seven long days the storm raged relentlessly against their thin tents. The weary hunters were on the verge of death from starvation and dehydration when at last the monstrous storm subsided and they staggered weakly from their tents. To their disbelief, directly outside their tent was a water well. None could recall the existence of the well before the storm. Ishmael took this to be divine preservation. As chief, he was to take the first drink. Yet, the moment his hand pierced the liquid, a great whirlwind appeared and Ishmael was dragged into the water, disappearing under its tempestuous surface.

It was then that the younger brother of Ishmael, driven by a deep love of his brother, led the remaining hunters down the well in pursuit of their beloved chief. Certain death awaited them. Yet, somehow they eluded death's snare. When they awoke, they found themselves in a giant cave. Miraculously suspended above them on the surface of the cave's roof was a gentle pool of water. Not a single drop trickled down to the ground from the mystical portal. The well had dragged them to the middle of the earth.

Ishmael and his brother saw that a bright light radiated from the horizon. It seemed a sun of sorts, burning in the core of the world, the earth's center. Drawn by curiosity, Ishmael led the hunters on a seven-day journey toward the glowing Orb. When they arrived, Ishmael fell on his face in fear and in reverence of the shining essence. His brother, however, being the more logic-minded brother, sought answers. It was he who discovered, hidden in a nearby cave, seven stone tablets. Their writings contained a language unknown to him, but the brilliant combined intellect of the brothers managed to slowly unveil the mystery of the tablets. To their great surprise, through the words on the tablets, they discovered that they were able to access immense power from the Orb. Using its power, they could create mountains and valleys. They could cause a river to form in minutes and even gained power over light and darkness. They had obtained the power to become gods.

The power terrified Ishmael. He concluded that this Orb was the very thing that the creator of the universe had used in designing the world. He saw the Orb as no less than leftover paint remaining in the master artist's pallet—and that it should be strictly left alone. His brother, on the other hand, saw the power as an opportunity to better the world; the Orb was a gift to mankind. The two brothers argued for several days over this disparity. At last Ishmael compromised, declaring that his brother had free will to pursue his own path, and that the remaining hunters were free to pick whom to follow. Six sided with Ishmael, while three joined with his brother, departing to the far, uncharted lands of Under-Earth. The remaining hunter, torn between the two leaders, opted to remain neutral and walked away from the others, never to be seen again.

That very night, Ishmael founded the city of Atlantis. A majestic kingdom, built around the Orb itself. Slowly, Atlantis was populated with offspring. The king himself bore forth four children. He also came to the startling discovery that the Orb did more than just give power—it prevented death. For the next several hundred years the population grew and the city flourished, until one fateful day when Ishmael's brother returned to Atlantis.

Like his older brother, he, too, had founded and populated a city. Unlike Ishmael, however, whose city of Atlantis was formed to honor and protect the power of the Orb, the brother's city had exploited the power for its own gain. The streets of his city were paved with solid gold, and trees of diamonds grew in its gardens. The city became known as the 'City of Gold', ruled over by the self-proclaimed Golden King. The city is also known by its more common name—El Dorado.

Yet even with all this, the Golden King was not satisfied for his unquenchable greed had corrupted his mind. He protested that it was unfair that Ishmael had claimed the land around the Orb, while he had been banished to the distant corners of Under-Earth. He demanded that Ishmael surrender Atlantis. Ishmael promptly refused, and again urged his younger brother not to abuse the power. The Golden King was enraged. He returned to El Dorado and raised an army to overthrow his selfish brother.

Before the walls of Atlantis, the power of the Orb was used as a horrifying instrument of bloodshed. The war lasted only three days. Many lives were lost in the bloodbath and Atlantis was left in scorched rubble. In the end, it was Ishmael who emerged victorious over his brother. Yet, the powerful love for his brother drove Ishmael to ignore the urges of his counselors and spare his brother's life. Instead he had his brother sign a covenant.

In the aftermath of the dreadful war, Ishmael realized the danger of the Orb. As such, the covenant proposed to limit the Orb's access to only a select, trusted few. In order to restrict and keep the knowledge secret, the ancient words of power were copied down into two different Books and the seven stone tablets were destroyed. The first Book contained only the ancient words; it is known as *The Code*. The second Book contained only the translations and instructions on how to read *The Code*. It is called *The Key*. To appease the Golden King's demands, the Books also served a second purpose—to funnel power. By using the Orb's power, the brothers infused the Books with the ability to channel the Orb to the individual keeper of the Book. In a way, he who held one of the two Books also held the Orb. They then contrived a fail safe to prevent anyone other than that single owner from ever using the Book's power; a terrible evil that was never to be spoken of, and only released in dire circumstances.

The Books were divided between the two kingdoms, allowing each city to possess only one half of the whole. The Golden King and his ravenous lust for power designated himself as the Book Keeper of *The Key*. However, Ishmael, who had been devastated beyond healing by the loss of his wife, as well as over two thirds of the city's population, never wanted to be tempted to use the Orb's power for violence ever again. He therefore refused to become the keeper of *The Code*. Instead, he entrusted the Book to his more trusted member of The Twelve, a noble and reliable man.

Both men knew that the soul of the Golden King had been corrupted beyond repair, and that even as the supernaturally binding covenant was being made, he was secretly scheming to steal *The Code*. He dreamed of gaining the full knowledge of the Orb for his own purposes. Desperate to prevent the Golden King from uniting the two Books and obtaining endless power, Ishmael ordered his trusted ally to flee above ground with *The Code* and keep it forever hidden. The power of the Book ensured the longevity of the man's life. The name of that man was Wesley. For a thousand years the Book remained hidden and in his care, that is, until now, when it has been brought back to the one place that Ishmael never wanted it to be: Atlantis.

Cody shook his head disbelievingly as Cia finished her tale. He did not want to believe it, but he knew in his heart that it was true. He recalled the bizarre picture he had found framed in Wesley's bedroom and suddenly the pieces all began to fit. His eyes focused on the Book lying in the middle of the restricted room. *The Code.* For most of the last week Cody had hauled the Book around in his backpack, completely oblivious that he possessed the gateway to accessing the power of the universe; the power to become a god. Cody looked up at the four royal siblings staring intensely at him. Jade laughed.

"So, this water well just *magically* appeared out of thin air? And just so happened to lead to the center of the earth?" she challenged suspiciously, raising her eyebrow slightly. "And this power . . . this orb. Where is it now? If it's even real, then it's obviously some sort of high-energy concentration of friction caused by heavy gravity in the earth's core. Energy pockets in the earth are not uncommon. This is fifth grade-level science. Besides, what else could it be?"

The siblings stared back at her knowingly. "What else, indeed?"

Jade cast a skeptic look to Cody and back to Kantan. "Are you seriously suggesting that you think this orb is some sort of . . . *tool* used to create the earth? Left here by the creator of the universe? There is absolutely no logical proof, not to mention there is no creator. Who would ever believe such a ridiculous explanation?"

"I would," answered Cody softly. Jade's face flushed. Kantan held up his hand. Getting up, he retrieved several books from the corner of the room and returned to his seat. "Before you accuse us Underlings of being so senseless, perhaps you'd like to hear something that hits . . . a little closer to home."

He held up the first book and opened it. "This here, is the Koran, the holy book of the Muslims. Allow me to read it for you," he cleared his throat. "'Then turned He to the heavens when it was smoke, and *said* unto it the earth: come both of you, willingly or loth. They said: we come, obedient.'"

He set the book down and lifted another. "This scroll is *The Hymn to Atum*, one of the Egyptian gods. It reads: 'At the moment of creation, Atum *spoke*.' Later it reads: 'When the almighty speaks, all else comes to life.'"

The prince picked up a third book from the pile. "This here is the Holy Bible, the sacred book of Christianity. Perhaps one you're more familiar with." Jade groaned and rolled her eyes. Kantan continued, "It reads: 'by the *word* of the Lord were the heavens made, all the host of them by the breath of his mouth. For he *spake*, and it was done.'" He flipped through several pages, "or simply put: in the beginning was the *word*." The Prince motioned toward the table of books. "I could go on, but I hope you are beginning to understand."

Jade shook her head. "I'm not following you. What is your point?" she demanded.

Cia smoothed out the folds in her dress before answering, "Words. Religions tend to disagree with one another, but no matter what you believe about the formation of this world, one of the underlying themes in almost all belief systems, above ground, or below it, is the power to create by words. What Ishmael and the Golden King found on those seven stone tablets were those words; words which unlocked the chest containing the pious power to create!"

"At least in your belief," added Jade unenthusiastically.

Cody's eyes gleamed. "The large oval structure in the center of the city, the one made from smooth metal, is that . . . the Orb?" he asked eagerly.

"Yes," answered Kantan. "Well, literally, it is the shelling *protecting* the Orb. The Sanctuary of the Orb. Are either of you two familiar with the concept of *ex nihilo*?" Cody scrunched his forehead tight giving it the look of ocean waves. He wasn't even sure he could *spell* the word, let alone understand it. Luckily, his best friend happened to be a world-class science nerd.

"*Ex nihilo*?" replied Jade unimpressed, "It literally means *out of nothing*. A ridiculous belief that many religious nuts apply to the creation of the universe. I can't even count the number of scientific theories that discredit such an outlandish idea."

Instead of frowning, Kantan grinned. "Let's suppose you're right. Suppose creation *ex nihilo* is entirely impossible. What if the universe *wasn't* created out of nothing. What if the creator had a box, so to speak, to unpack it and organize it as he pleased. What if he had . . ."

"An Orb," finishing Cody, his eyes bulging from their sockets.

"Precisely. An Orb that we can still access by using the words of creation, the High Language, as we call it. What if, as Jade mentioned, the Orb *isn't* caused by gravity . . . but rather it's *causing* gravity. No, Jade, we don't have the proof you desire. We can't *prove* what I say is true . . . but what if it is? Are you beginning to grasp just how crucial this Book is? The Orb is sacred. Only the Brotherhood of Light and the King himself are allowed access into the Sanctuary of the Orb."

"Brotherhood of Light?" Cody questioned, raising his right eyebrow slightly.

"Worshippers of the Orb. Men dedicated to respecting its power, and only using it for good and life. They have preserved the High Language," explained Foz in his steady voice.

"And," Kantan added, "they will oversee your training. You will report to the Monastery of the Brotherhood tomorrow evening where the high priest, Reverend Lamgorious Stalkton, will begin your instruction. Our servant, Poe Dapperhio will be assigned to you and will meet any of your needs. *The Code* will be sent . . ."

"Hold on," Jade cut in firmly, "What training? Instruction for what exactly?"

"Training on how to harness the power of the Book, of course. On how to use the High Language. To learn how to become a Creator," answered Cia patiently. Jade stuck her finger in the princesses' face, "Or to become a puppet in your war campaign. Don't assume we're stupid just because of our youth. I can see what's going on here. You are going to exploit Cody for your own gain. To become a vessel for a king that hasn't even shown his face since we arrived."

"Jade, stop." Cody pleaded, "I want to learn. I want to be trained."

Jade stood up from her chair, her voice shaky with disbelief and frustration. "Cody, what are you doing? We don't even know these people. You can't seriously believe all this garbage about orbs, gods, and creation power, can you?" She turned to the royal family, "I mean, how is it that you could possibly know all this? Give me one good reason to believe you."

For the first time that night the answer came from the soft, meek voice of Eva, "We know this . . . because Ishmael is our father." The revelation hit Cody like a bolt of lightning. He squinted his eyes shut tight before opening them again. He felt dazed by the overload of information.

"Then, the Golden King is your uncle?" Jade asked in a surprised tone. Cia nodded slowly.

"Is he . . . still out there?" Jade said in an unusually timid voice.

Kantan's focus fell to the floor. "Oh, yes, he is still very much out there. Not only is he out there, but his forces have been amassing on the Atlantis border. The forces of El Dorado are strong. The Golden King has grown impatient in his search for *The Code*. Something appears to have finally woken him from his dormant slumber. When he learns that *The Code* has returned to Atlantis, he will bring his armies crashing against the walls of our city like a flood. He will stop at nothing to gain the united strength of the two Books and the unending power of the Orb. A second

Great War will take place, and this time, we don't know if Atlantis will be strong enough to win."

Cody jumped up, grabbed the Book off the table, and shoved it out toward Kantan. "Then take it! I don't want it. Give it to the King. Take it! Please!" Kantan swatted Cody's hands away, "As much as I want to take it, I can't. Our father will be devastated to learn of its return. Don't you understand, Cody? The deal our father made with our uncle a thousand years ago was that only one person would be the keeper of the Book. After Wesley's murder, somehow, by ways unknown to us, all of Wesley's powers and responsibilities transferred to you. Cody, like it or not, *you* are the Book Keeper."

31

The Area

The Book Keeper. It had a nice ring to it. Cody's initial horror at the revelation of his unique connection with the Book had transformed into gleeful pride. The power was *his*. Even the mighty royal family seemed nervous around him now. He was special. He and Jade had been escorted to two rooms in the palace that were to be their lodgings in Atlantis. The rooms were spacious with fluffy, oversized beds. Cody belly-flopped onto his mattress and was engulfed in a sea of pillows. The warm comforter felt refreshing after the last couple nights of slumber on cold dirt ground and train seats. He reached to the side table and lifted the ruby pocket watch from it. The short hand continued to rotate franticly. He watched as the gold and purple hands inched slightly before resuming their petrified state. *Where did they lead?* If the taller red hand led toward *his* Book, *The Code*, was it a logical guess to presume that the golden hand would lead him toward the second Book, *The Key*? Perhaps. But then, where would the purple hand lead? He set the pocket watch back on the nightstand; his mind was too preoccupied for any more problem solving.

At the request of Cia, *The Code* had been taken to the Monastery to be watched over by the Brotherhood of Light until Cody could begin his training the following evening. Cody happily obliged; he knew they wouldn't be able to use it anyways. It was his.

There was a soft knock on his door. When Cody opened it Jade was standing in the doorway. She was wearing a long white tunic and a thin, matching white headband. The paleness of the outfit illuminated her darker features giving her an almost exotic appearance. Cody suddenly realized he was staring at her. Jade smiled. "It's the clothes they left us in our rooms. Guess they think we stand out too much with all our *surface dweller clothes*." She laughed; it was the first time Cody remembered hearing her laugh in days. He was glad. "Anyways, Poe, the servant Prince Kantan assigned to us, has offered to show us around the city. He's waiting downstairs. I'm anxious to get out and see if the rest of Atlantis is as wacko as its royal family!"

"Yeah, it will be good to get out and walk around a bit. Give me a second." On the side table by his bed was a similar stack of new clothes that had been left for him. He quickly removed his shirt. The moment he did so he felt the beams of Jade's eyes slicing into his uncovered body. He felt embarrassed and vulnerable. He hastily changed into the rest of the clothes. They were surprisingly plain; just a baggy, brown tunic with a cloth belt. He felt slightly disappointed. He had hoped for something a little more majestic; a little more befitting of a Book Keeper. Perhaps even a gold B and K embroidered onto it. He made a mental note to ask Cia about it next time he saw her.

By the time Cody reached the lobby Jade was already waiting. With her was one of the oddest-looking people Cody had ever seen in his life. Even Sean Schneil would have looked shockingly handsome next to this strange specimen. His body was shaped in the distinct formation of an overripe pear. His chubby head perfectly mirrored the shape of his body, only in miniature, as though the pair were part of a Russian Matryoshka doll set. A lonely regiment of scattered hair hung like string from his otherwise balding head. The sparse hair was tucked behind his oversized ears, which stuck out like kites. His face, like all the other inhabitants of Atlantis, was mousey. The man turned to Cody as he approached and gave a nervous smile. "G-g-greetings, most noble Master Cody," he stuttered, "Poe Dapperhio at your humble service . . ."

"Oh, Poe," said Jade, "I've already told you, there is no need to be calling us master or noble or anything of the like. A simple Cody or Jade will do." Cody sighed with disappointment. Most noble Master Cody—he had liked the sound of that.

"You are most kind, Master Jade. If it pleases you, I will show you around Atlantis, our lovely, perfect city." With an overly deep bow, the peculiar man waddled to the door. Cody and Jade followed close behind.

The city took on new life in Cody's eyes now that he understood some of its history. As he gazed over the people and buildings he tried to imagine what it must have been like when the twelve hunters had first come to the spot, back when it was just them and the Orb. Cody cranked his head around to see the crown-jewel structure behind him.

"B-b-behind you," stuttered Poe, "is the heart of Atlantis. The Sanctuary of the Orb."

Directly on cue, a loud gong sent sound waves streaming across the city. Instinctively every visible citizen knelt down to their knees and began chanting, "Hail the Orb of holy light, humbled we by its eternal might. Hail the Orb, let it shine forever bright." As the crowd began chanting the phrase for the seventh time, Cody risked a glance up. Several men with dark red sashes across their chest and matching red headbands had remained standing. They were walking through the kneeling citizens as though inspecting them. The chant ended with a loud, "Amen."

As Cody stood he tugged on Poe's sleeve. "Who are those men? The ones with the red sashes." Poe's face lit up and he gave a slight bow in direction of the men.

"Those are the Enforcers. They work for the AREA, which of course stands for . . ."

"The Atlantis Rule Enforcement Association," finished Cody.

Poe's face gleamed with delight. "Y-y-yes! Well done! Splendid folk!"

Cody eyed Jade curiously. "So you are in favor of the AREA? We've been given the impression that the Association is not well loved by the citizens . . ." Cody's voice trailed off.

Poe's face looked as though he had just witnessed his favorite pet fall victim to the plague. His eyes watered under his eyelids. "Not well loved? Rubbish! The AREA *is* Atlantis! Without them our city would fall to chaos! Nobody would know how to worship the Orb! Let us not speak of such horrors. . . ." Poe's disproportioned body shook like a wet dog before waddling forward. As their tour of the Inner-City continued, Cody grew increasingly irritated by Poe's stutter. He had the annoying tendency of stuttering only on the first word of his sentences, as though his tongue was incapable of smoothly pushing off from the starting line.

They were shown all the workings of the Inner-City. Poe explained that because the majority of the actual industry took place in the Mid-City, the Inner-City acted as the metaphorical brain of Atlantis. All the most important citizens lived in spacious houses and all the headquarter buildings were in close proximity to the Royal Palace.

Poe stopped abruptly to show them the Atlantis Food Processing Center. "Y-y-you can probably guess that here in Under-Earth we are not accustomed to the same vast food options that you Surface-Dwellers are." Poe continued, "Although several nutritional elements have been imported from Upper-Earth, our main source of food consists of insects and deep-earth animals. But, for those with money, there is also the practice of *de-fossilization*."

"What's that?" asked Jade curiously.

Poe took in a deep breath; he seemed exceedingly pleased with himself to be the know-it-all-expert on the city. "W-w-well, *de-fossilization* is a practice which recycles what Upper-Earth is finished with. The ground of the Earth is not static; rather it is fluid, constantly in motion. Every time one age of life ends, another one is quick to take its place, reestablishing itself on top of the previous. As a result, the earth is like what you Surface-Dwellers call a tomato . . . or is that an onion? I always forget. Upper-Earth history was never my strongest subject; never really saw the point. Anyways, like your tomatoes, the earth is made of many layers. *De-fossilization* is the delicate art of going into these layers as they reach us and removing the fossilized objects, such as animals, nuts, fruits and so on. At our Food Processing Centers, such as this one, these fossils are rehydrated and the nutrients are regained. As they say, one Surface-Dweller's three thousand year-old trash is an Underling's dinner!" Cody shivered. The thought of three-thousand year old, rehydrated woolly mammoth meat had suddenly caused him to lose his appetite.

Next Poe led them to another large building. "T-t-the Atlantis Stone-Clothing Textile Factory," announced Poe cheerfully. "Y-y-you both can thank this very center for the clothing you currently don!"

Cody rubbed his hands along the soft fabric of his tunic. "What do you mean, *stone-clothing*?"

Poe once again entered into professor mode. "O-o-one thing you may have noticed is that here in Under-Earth we do not have access to the wide variety of fabrics you do in Upper-Earth. But one thing we do have an abundance of is rock. It was the great Gorgo Tallsin who invented the first rock-tunic. In essence, the process has been going on since the beginning of time in the depths of the oceans, but Tallsin devised a way to speed up the process. By a continual breakdown of the rocks into granites smaller than sand, and by a simultaneous polishing of the granites by water compression of enormous proportions, he was able to produce a material that felt soft to human skin. By welding the tiny granites together, a pain-staking procedure, as you can imagine, our designers are able to produce any article of clothing. Not only is it soft and stylish, but it is also exceedingly more durable and tough than the flimsy, tacky clothing worn by you Surface-Dwellers."

As their tour continued they saw other fascinating places. Out of reverence, Poe refused to lead them too close to the Sanctuary of the Orb; but he did point out the Monastery of the Brotherhood nestled at the top of the base below the Sanctuary where Cody was to begin his training

They were toured through the Pure-Air Plant: a center that, through intense light energy and a complex matrix of shoots and pipes, mimicked photosynthesis and recycled the air, maintaining breathable levels even in the center of the earth.

They were also shown the Strategizing Center for Roof-Mining, which organized the mining camps that hung from the ceiling of the cave and harvested the mammoth sky gems. Next, Poe showed the tunnel-phone: an elaborate communication system in which tunnels dug miles beneath the ground stretched from one location to another. Due to the perfect design of the tunnels, they would amplify the sound and carry it great distances to another location. "A-a-although call options are obviously limited, the sound quality is unhindered," explained Poe. "It is an effective way to communicate between distant cities . . . that is, if you have the patience to wait for a response."

The trio came to the last stop on the tour which Poe had obviously saved until the end for dramatic effect: the AREA headquarters. The building looked like a magnificent temple. A row of pillars lined the perimeter of the structure and the roof elevated high, meeting in a sharp point. A big open window framed the large hanging cymbal within. Above the large double front door was a small, wooden plaque that read: Rules Are The Foundation of Worship.

A large signpost stood next to the building. Written in small print, the sign read: **ESSENTIAL RULES OF ORB WORSHIP.** Cody read aloud:

1. Recite the Orb's Hymn seven times every 2.5 hours while facing the Sanctuary
2. <u>Never</u> under <u>any</u> circumstance enter the Sanctuary of the Orb. To do so is punishable by death
3. Walk barefoot on the fifth day of the week in reverence to the Orb
4. <u>Never</u> wear a headband when walking within the shadow of the Sanctuary. To do so is to disrespect the Orb
5. <u>Never</u> challenge the authority of an AREA Enforcer

Cody scanned down to the bottom of the list that numbered 232 rules. Poe skipped merrily up beside Cody. "S-s-splendid aren't they? I can recite each one by heart. All Atlantis citizens can; we are taught to as children." The mention of children jerked something in Cody's mind. It suddenly occurred to him that he had yet to see a single child in the entire city. He opened his mouth to inquire about it but a shriek from Poe cut him off, "It's him!"

Cody followed the servant's eyes to a man approaching the building. Like the Enforcers he had witnessed earlier, the man had a dark red sash across his chest. However, instead of a red headband, he wore a large red hat. Cody had to fight to suppress a chuckle at the ridiculousness of the head attire. Poe leaned over and whispered gleefully, "T-t-that man there is Sli Silkian, head of the AREA. Outside of the royal family, he is the most powerful man in Atlantis."

The man had a face like a panther and walked with a cool confidence. As he reached the building he gave one quick glance to where Cody and Jade were standing. His beady raven eyes connected with Cody's. In that brief instant Cody felt as though a wave of disdain was passed into him. He shuddered. The man quickly disappeared through the door and was gone.

Poe was rambling on excitedly about how Silkian had revolutionized Orb worship, but Cody tuned him out. His contact with the stranger had been brief, but for some reason Cody couldn't escape the sickening feeling in his stomach that in that one short stare, he had just made a very powerful enemy.

32

A Secret Rendezvous

Her lush, blonde hair flowed across her face as her eyes gazed longingly at Cody. He smiled back, winking and flicking his bangs to the side. The blonde beauty blushed and motioned with her finger for him to approach. Cody smiled confidently as he strutted toward the girl. He slipped his arm firmly around her back and pulled her body into his. She closed her eyes. Slowly Cody lowered his face toward her, his lips almost touching hers . . . just as a hard knock banged against his door.

Cody screamed. The beautiful blonde girl suddenly transformed into his pillow. He wiped the drool off of it; with a sigh of disappointment he realized he had only been dreaming. He closed his eyes again. The girl from his dreams was real, he had seen her the first time he had entered the Inner-City. *Who was she?* He was determined to find out. But another loud rap on the door brought him back to reality. Cody groaned and rolled off his bed. His legs were still aching from Poe's exhaustive tour of the city. Cody didn't know how long he had been napping, only that it hadn't been long enough. Groggily staggering to the door he pulled it open. It was Jade.

"Cody, do you do anything other than sleep? Hurry up, you're coming with me for a walk through the city." Cody felt another throb from his aching legs. He opened his mouth to protest but his brain felt like scrambled eggs. Jade smiled. "Great, let's go." *This girl will be the death of me* thought Cody bitterly as he followed Jade out the room.

As they exited the palace they crossed paths with Princess Eva. She gave a quick smile before looking back down to her toes as they passed her. Cody and Jade exited down the palace stairs. "That Eva is not a girl of many words, is she?" Jade observed.

"Who can blame her? I'm sure she's not the only one to feel a little intimidated around the new Book Keeper," said Cody, puffing up his chest. Jade rolled her eyes but didn't say anything; some things weren't worth wasting words on.

Cody couldn't help but notice the parallels of their situation. After all the craziness, it energized Cody to be back alone once again with Jade exploring unknown alleyways and streets. Although now instead of the slow-moving, small town of Havenwood, they were exploring the fabled lost city of Atlantis.

A loud gong rang over the city. Cody fell to his knee robotically and recited the Orb's Hymn seven times. He could make out the shadows of the Enforcers and knew he was being inspected. Finishing the chant, Cody jumped back up and ran after Jade who had already resumed their hike.

"Where exactly are we going, Jade?" Cody asked, breathing heavy as he jogged to keep up with her. By way of answer, they reached the gate dividing the Inner-City from the Mid-City. Being only late afternoon, the gate was open. Once inside the Mid-City Jade resumed her brisk pace.

Cody was wheezing. "Hey, what's the hurry? I mean, it's not like . . ." Jade's hand flung up to his mouth, and Cody was dragged to the ground behind a stack of crates. She held a finger to her lips, and slowly pointed over the boxes. As silently as he could manage, Cody peered over the top. Across the street and down an alleyway a group of men were assembling. Cody squinted; the men looked familiar somehow. Then it hit him. They were the men who had protested for war during their initial journey into the city. The big man who had held the sign came into view and it was obvious by the way the men interacted that he was the ring leader.

Cody felt a hard tug on his tunic; Jade motioned toward the other end of the street. A man with a hood was walking briskly in their direction with his head downcast; Cody couldn't make out the face. The man reached the alley and turned down it. At the sight of the hooded man, all the protestors froze. The large ring leader gave a slight bow, rose and walked toward the man. A smiled formed on his face and he threw his arms around the hooded man, embracing him in a hug. They exchanged several words and the protestors began filing through a door into one of the buildings. The ring leader held the door open for the hooded man, who gave one quick glance down the alley before disappearing through the entrance.

That one glance had been enough. For a split second the man's face had been exposed. There was no mistaking that face. The man in the hood was Prince Kantan.

33

Reunion

Neither Cody nor Jade stopped running until they reached the gate to the Outer-City. When they arrived they collapsed against the wall breathing heavily. "What reason could the heir to the throne possibly have for attending secret meetings with the city's biggest war mongers?" Cody asked, trying to wrap his brain around the scene they had just seen.

"Perhaps he was just trying to make peace with them?" Jade offered weakly.

"Well, then he's doing a darn good job. He seems awfully cozy with their ring leader." Jade knew it was true. The situation had a suspicious aura to it.

Jade pushed herself off the wall, "Well, perhaps it's nothing. We can ask Dace what he thinks. He's who I've been leading us toward; I have a few questions for him." The Outer-City was like a ghost town. They were completely alone on the barren streets. "I don't doubt this is the nocturnal part of the city. Let's get in and out before it gets crowded." They began walking in search of Dace.

Turning around one corner they collided with a man coming the other way. It was Gelph, the beggar. He flashed his crooked teeth, "Well, well, well! Didn't scare you off last time I take it. Your pockets any more full with beautiful golden coins this time, eh?"

Cody laughed. "Only American currency and that won't get you much down here. We are looking for Dace, have you seen him?"

The beggar thought for a moment. "As a matter of fact I have. Passed by bout an hour ago. Said he was on the way to Yanci's pub. Just go down this street and take your second left; you can't miss it. If you get lost, just follow your ear in the direction of the most ruckus." They thanked the beggar and followed his directions down the street. As they got closer they heard the sound of music, laughter, and yelling.

"Must be getting close," Cody said with a grin. They took the second left and at the end of the street, situated all on its own, was Yanci's pub. Despite it only being late afternoon, the tavern already was full. As they walked timidly to the front door they heard raised voices and the sound of crashing.

"Perhaps we should catch Dace at a better time," suggested Jade as she took two nervous steps backwards. It was good that she did. Moments later the pub door crashed open and a body came hurtling out, crashing face first in the spot where Jade had been only seconds before. With a groan, the man pulled himself off the ground.

"Wolfrick?" The surprised, bulky guard looked down at Cody. A large bruise encircled his left eye and blood streamed from his nose.

"Hey'o! If it ain't Under-Earth's latest unwanted intruder! How's life as a fugitive, son?" The smell of ale reeked on his breath. An angry yell came from within the bar, "Get back in here Wolfrick, you lousy, no-good, two-timing, cheat! These are loaded dice! I want my money back!" Wolfrick opened his mouth to respond, but instead of words a loud belch came out. He staggered to his feet. "Well, it was good seeing you again Jody and Cade!" He stumbled back up the steps and through the door. The sound of crashing and yelling promptly resumed once again.

Cody let out a huge sigh of relief when Dace came strolling through the front door and approached them. He was smiling.

"Yanci's isn't exactly kid friendly. I saw you two from the window. What brings you to these parts?" Cody quickly recapped the mysterious episode they had just witnessed with Prince Kantan. Dace listened carefully. When Cody finished, Dace shook his head. "I won't pretend like that doesn't sound fishy. But let me assure you, Kantan may be cold as morning ice, but one thing is for sure. He is not a traitor. He is cut from the same cloth as his father, the good King Ishmael."

"Well, if you ask me, that's some pretty cheap cloth," Cody proclaimed. "We've been here all day and your noble King has yet to show his face. I'm the *Book Keeper* for heaven's sake, think he might want to meet me of all people."

Dace gave him a serious glance. "That is not a fact that you would be wise to spout off in public, boy. It is not something that should become common knowledge; at least not yet. Fortunately for you, I am already aware of your position and its implications. Secondly, don't undervalue the King. He is a remarkably great man. If he has decided not to show his face, then he has good reason for it. As for Kantan, I trust him, and so should you."

"Ahhh!" Jade screamed, "What happened to your back?! There's blood soaking through your shirt!" Dace gave a cocky smirk and turned around, lifting up his shirt to reveal five deep whip wounds. The scars were black and clumpy as mashed potatoes where the blood had clotted.

"Yeah, General Levenworth wasn't too pleased with my extra rest day on the way here. Was actually only supposed to be three lashes. Word of advice, if you ever find yourself on the whipping pole, don't insult the torturer's grandma." He gave a wink and Cody and Jade laughed. "Was there anything else you two trouble makers needed?" Jade leaned in and whispered something in his ear. Dace frowned, but whispered something back.

"What was that all about?" asked Cody as he followed Jade away from the pub having said farewell to Dace.

"Just wait. I'll show you." Cody opened his mouth to protest but Jade stopped him. "And don't you dare pull the *'but I'm the Book Keeper'* card on me." Cody closed his mouth; point taken.

Crossing through the Mid-City they paused by the alleyway where they had seen Kantan with the rioters. There was no light coming from the building. With Jade leading the way, they returned to the Inner-City. They came upon the palace, but instead of entering the front doors, Jade led Cody around to the back. "Where are we going?" asked a surprised Cody.

"Shush, just keep up," spouted Jade as they circled the palace. Slipping through a back door they found themselves in the royal kitchen. They made their way through the crowded room swiftly and without being noticed by the focused cooks. Exiting the kitchen, they reached a staircase and began to descend. Down six stories they ran into a barricade blocking their access to the next level. A sign there stated: **RESTRICTED. MILITARY PERSONNEL ONLY.** Jade hopped over it without hesitation and continued down the stairs. Cody sighed. They seemed to be making a habit of breaking into restricted sections. He jumped over the barrier and followed after her.

They reached the basement. It was a small room with only one solid steel door that was bolted three times and braced with a horizontal iron bar. Two armed guards stood blocking the door. "Hey, what do you think you're doing down here? This is a restricted area. Leave at once!" ordered one of the soldiers as he sprang forward, his hand on the hilt of his sword.

Jade took a step back. "Dace sent us, and we just want a quick visit. Please." The guard grunted, "Dace has no authority here. Get out."

Suddenly there was a knock from the other side of the door. The second guard grunted, unfastened the bolts and removed the latch. The door swung open and Prince Foz stepped out. Seeing Cody and Jade he stumbled over his feet, bumping into the guard.

"Oh my! What are you two doing down here?" he asked, regaining his balance and adjusting his mop-like hair.

"We just want a quick visit, Foz. Please." Jade pleaded. Foz looked hesitantly at the door, and then back at Jade. "Make it quick."

The guard, clearly displeased, held open the door. As Cody passed he couldn't contain himself, out the side of his mouth he whispered, "How's *that* for authority." Once inside the room the door closed with a crash behind them and Cody heard the locks being fastened. "Jade, what are we doing. Where are we?"

"We are doing what we *should* be doing if your head wasn't so ballooned about being the all-mighty and powerful Book Keeper."

Jade's words stung. "Jealousy doesn't work for you, Jade. Just because the Book chose me and not you doesn't mean you have to take out your envy on me."

"Envy!?" cried Jade, "Is that what you think this is about? You heard Kantan, the Book didn't *choose* you at all. By stupid luck your useless hand touched the Book first after you got Wesley killed. So cut the chosen-one talk."

As Cody prepared to retaliate another voice spoke instead, "Must be the bloody dim-witted, village idiot of the whole blasted book-world to have even thought of choosing either of you mindless-goats. Now stop your incessant yakking before I rip my own stinking ears off to silence you."

Cody smiled and looked to the direction of the voice. "Well, glad to see imprisonment hasn't dulled your charming personality." On the other end of the room, behind two sets of bars, and latched to the wall with chains by both hands and feet was Randilin.

34

The Perpetual No-Show

Randilin's face looked thin and colorless with thick black bags hanging under his heavy eyes. His forehead was swollen, puffing down over his left eye. He had changed a lot since Cody had last seen him. He was almost unrecognizable. There was a squeak in the corner of the cell where two small rodent-looking creatures fought over a bone. Randilin's head hung limply on his neck, "So, you kiddies miss me or something?"

Jade's hand was over her mouth, a salty tear rolled over her upper lip. "This is awful. Barbaric even! What are these people doing to you?"

Randilin let out a deep, coarse cough, "Nothing more than I deserve. Could have been worse. The ever-cheerful Prince Kantan argued to have me executed immediately. It was Prince Foz who arranged a fair trial and this five-star luxury suite." He tried to laugh but entered another deep coughing fit.

"Well, surely the jury will spare you. I mean, if it wasn't for you we'd both be dead. If it wasn't for you the Book would have been stolen. Surely that is enough to erase . . . whatever it is you've done," said Cody exasperatedly. Silence hung in the air. It was a question that had been burning in his mind since Dunstan first broached the topic.

A spark of pain flashed over Randilin's face. "Well, I sure ruddy hope so, right?"

Cody decided not to push the issue any farther. "So, when is the trial? How can we help?" he asked.

Randilin shrugged, "Two days from now. Foz seems hopeful that my recent actions can sway the jury. Sally has already volunteered to testify in my defense. I know I can be a bit rough toward you two lads, but I was hoping, you know, despite my lack of tact that you might, well, might . . ."

"We would be absolutely honored to testify for you. You have saved our life; now it's our turn to repay the favor," answered Jade firmly.

Randilin grinned. "Perhaps you two aren't as dense as I thought . . . perhaps."

Cody suddenly realized how glad he was to see Randilin again. During their time above ground Cody had felt no emotional loyalty to Randilin whatsoever. He merely had been a last resort; somebody with more answers than he had. Yet now, thousands of miles in the center of the earth, surrounded by strangers in a strange city, Cody saw that Randilin was perhaps their only true ally.

Cody and Jade filled him in on all the events that had taken place since his capture. They told of Dace's sacrifice, the brewing war between Atlantis and El Dorado, Kantan's suspicious meeting with the activists, the King's continual absence and even of Cody becoming the Book Keeper.

Randilin listened attentively, only interrupting a few times to clarify points.

When they finished, Randilin spoke slowly, "These are interesting times. There has not been a full-fledged war between Atlantis and El Dorado in centuries. I have no doubt that the royal family will attempt to exploit your power as Book Keeper to tip the scales in Atlantis' favor. I warn you, Cody, think for yourself. Everybody is a friend to somebody with power. People will try to use you. Don't let them." He paused for a moment, his eyes rolling into the back of his head as though reminiscing about some invisible time. After a brief moment, he continued, "Princess Cia is as cunning as she is beautiful, and Princess Eva appears harmless and innocent, but she's never been the same since the accident. Be especially wary of Kantan; he is sly and powerful. I don't know what he was doing with those malcontents, but I suspect it isn't good."

"What do you mean Eva's never been the same? What accident?" asked Jade. Randilin began to respond but was stopped by the sound of loud knocking. "Time's up," bellowed a voice from the other side of the door.

Jade gave one last look to Randilin. "We won't forget about you. The trial's going to be okay. I promise." Her last words never reached Randilin as the door was slammed and all three latches were tightly locked.

"Wake up, you sleepy head."

Cody rubbed his eyes. There appeared to be three of Jade's faces fluttering above his head.

"What time is it? Why are you in my room? I'm going back to bed." Cody rolled over and pulled the covers up to this chin. His body went cold as the blankets were yanked off his bed.

"Get *up*! Don't you remember anything? We're meeting with the King this morning, and I'm not about to keep him waiting." Cody had indeed forgotten about the meeting. *What is one supposed to wear to have breakfast with a king?* He thought as he rolled out of bed, collapsing on the floor,

"Can't we just reschedule?"

A pillow came flying over the bed and smacked against his cheek. "Five minutes. That's how long you have to meet me in the common room. Poe is meeting us there to escort us. And don't you *dare* go back to sleep," she ordered over her shoulder as she exited the room.

Cody reached for the pillow that Jade had thrown at him. He tucked it snuggly under his head. He had four more minutes to sleep.

Jade was frowning when Cody came dashing around the corner into the common room. His tunic was on backwards and his hair was sticking straight up as though he had chewed on an active power line. Jade shook her head in disgust. Wetting her fingers with her mouth, she attempted, with a dismal lack of success, to tame Cody's wild hair. They waited fifteen minutes for Poe, but the servant didn't show.

"Do you think we should just go on without him?" asked Cody, his stomach growling with visions of a kingly breakfast. Reluctantly, Jade agreed. Luckily, after their trouble with the guards at Randilin's cell, Prince Foz had given both Cody and Jade a royal seal which granted them access to any part of the palace, no questions asked. They hastily made their way down several long corridors and up two tall staircases. When they reached the royal chambers they found Princess Eva wandering down the hall, humming to herself.

"Lady Eva, we are supposed to meet your father this morning for breakfast but our servant Poe never showed up to bring us. Could you escort us in?" Jade asked, eyeing up the red double doors. Eva looked concerned, her eyes fixated to the floor. Her delicate lips parted, yet no sound came through them.

Suddenly the red doors opened, and Kantan stepped out. He looked flustered and in his hand he was cupping a small glass object. A flash of surprised showed on his face to see Cody and Jade and he quickly slipped the glass object into his pocket.

"I am sorry, but unforeseen events have arisen. The King has asked for complete privacy until further notice while he meditates and deals with these urgent issues. El Dorado is on the move. If you would please leave the royal chambers." The tone of Kantan's voice suggested that it was not a negotiable request.

As Cody turned to leave, he caught something in his peripheral vision. Kantan exchanged a knowing look with Eva, whose face registered deep concern. Her nimble body slipped past them and into the King's chambers. The door was only open for a second, but from the crack came forth a potent smell that disappeared as quickly as it came.

35

Murder in the Air

Word of Randilin's capture was no longer secret. Rumors of the trial suffocated the afternoon air as Cody and Jade strolled through the Inner-City. A gangly man with dirty clothes and an odd rock-clothing hat stood on the ledge of a fountain calling over the streets, "Get it here! Your *Under-Earth Rumblings!* Home to your up-to-date city gossip! Get it here, breaking-news about El Dorado's possible next move! Rumored to have been leaked from the Golden King's own mouth! Also, Under-Earth's most wanted fugitive returns! Randilin, back in Atlantis! Get all the latest information about his trial!"

Jade approached the man. "Excuse me, sir, could I purchase a copy?"

The gawky man jumped off the fountain ledge and landed next to her, "You could have *two* if you got the money. How could I refuse business with such a charming young lady? The name's Tople, Fincher Tople. But you can just call me Finch," he said, giving an exaggerated bow. Grabbing Jade's hand, he planted a wet kiss on it. Cody pulled Jade away and stepped between her and the man.

"Just give us the paper." He shoved several of the coins that Foz had given them into the man's hand. The man reluctantly handed over a paper, never looking away from Jade.

"What a hack-job," exclaimed Cody once they were out of earshot from the paper salesman. Sure enough, the front-page headline read: **"TOMORROW'S TRIAL! UNDER-EARTH'S MOST WANTED TO FACE JUSTICE."** A sketch of Randilin with a foul face accompanied the headline.

"It's unfair for them to use a picture of him looking so nasty. It will sway the jury!" cried Jade as she flipped through the paper to the article. Cody laughed. "Good luck trying to find one where he *doesn't* look downright spiteful." Jade's stern face broke and she joined in laughing. "True, true."

She pointed to the opened paper, "This article doesn't say anything about what Randilin's standing trial for, only that he is an awful, vicious man who devours babies for his late-night snack. I'm worried for him." They came to an open city square where a mob of people were scurrying around. Lined around the perimeter of the square were a dozen booths, each sheltered by a tarp. A variety of goods were being sold, from foods to beautiful looking rocks.

"It's an outdoor market! Let's go have a look!" Before Cody could even answer Jade had pranced off and disappeared into the crowd. *Just great,* thought Cody, *even at the center of the earth Jade managed to find shopping to do.* He strolled over to the closest booth where an old lady was slow-roasting something on a stick. He skidded into an abrupt stop. Directly across from him, moving gracefully in his direction, was the blonde girl from his dream.

Cody immediately dropped to the ground, concealing himself behind the vendor stall. He cautiously lifted his head above the booth and peered back into the clearing. The girl had stopped, and was now engaged in a friendly conversation with one of the vendors. Cody carefully examined her for the first time. She was every bit as beautiful as she had been in his dream—maybe even more so. Her light olive-toned skin was alluringly fair and her thick blonde hair hung straight down to her mid-back. Unlike the pale-toned robes of the other residents, her attire was a wild blaze of color, complemented by various tribal-looking rock and bead necklaces that hung around her slender neck. Cody watched as the girl's ruby lips moved elegantly, causing the light to shimmer off the coating of gloss. He leaned his head forward and strained for a better look. At that precise moment, the girl pivoted her head and her deep blue eyes stopped directly on him. His heart jumped . . .

A hand grasped Cody's shoulder. "Ah!" he yelped in surprise.

The arm belonged to the dowdy vendor lady. "Here, son, instead of all this hide-and-seek, why don't you fill your stomach with some grub!" she said cheerfully, pushing a blackened skewer of meat toward his face. Cody looked franticly back to the clearing—but the blonde mystery girl was nowhere to be seen.

Cody sighed and turned back to the vendor. The meat skewer smelled crispy and his stomach gave an involuntary growl reminding him of his missed breakfast. And, thankfully, it didn't look like *de-fossilized* grub. He dropped two gold pieces into the lady's leathered hands and grabbed the long slender piece of meat. It was tender in his hands. Putting it to his mouth he took a large bite. An unpleasant liquid squirted onto his tongue. The meat was chewy in his teeth and the taste was bitter.

"Lady, what meat is this exactly?" he asked, cringing from the flavor.

The old lady laughed, "Where are you from, son? It's only the most popular snack in Under-Earth—blackened earthworm!" Cody felt his face go green—and then he threw up.

Something brushed against his side, knocking him off balance. Looking up and wiping his mouth, he caught a glimpse of a hooded figure dashing into the crowd and disappearing into the mob. There was something familiar about the man. Then he saw it, the glimmer of a circular blade dangling from the man's side. Cody turned his head away from the crowd and was startled to find that in his own hands he was holding a crumbled slip of paper. How he had gotten the paper he could not remember. When he looked back to the crowd, the hooded man was gone. Glancing cautiously over his shoulders, he unfolded the paper and read:

Trust no one.
Things are not as they appear.
Murder is in the air.

Cody stared intensely at the paper, rereading it several more times. He flipped the paper over and choked. The note had been signed by a single word: CROSS.

Cody's arms were towering full of woven rock-clothing, undistinguishable snack foods, and a flute-like instrument sculpted entirely out of dark violet gemstone. Jade had succeeded in living up to her reputation. "The people were all so nice, I could have spent all day there! Maybe Atlantis isn't so bad after all!" Jade chatted excitedly as they walked back toward the palace. Her excitement had melted Cody's resolve to show her the note. He didn't want to worry her. *I'll show her at a better time.*

The streets emptied as dusk set in. Or at least Cody thought it was dusk, as the weather never changed in Under-Earth. As usual, the air was damp and cool. As they neared the palace, Cody stared at the large egg structure: The Sanctuary of the Orb. The excitement of being the chosen Book Keeper was evaporating as the time for his official training neared. *What if the Book chose incorrectly? What if I'm not good enough and let the city down?* These thoughts weighed heavily on his mind as they reached the palace.

"Well, Cody, I guess this is where we part ways. I'm meeting Sally in her room tonight to talk strategy about the trial tomorrow. Good luck with your training. Try not to get yourself blown up or something." *Thanks for the confidence booster, Jade,* Cody thought grimly.

Poe had explained the shortest way to the Sanctuary was through the palace. Cody quickly navigated his way through the ancient castle's long, winding corridors. Coming to the end of a narrow hallway, he found a door—it was ajar. Reaching to open it, Cody halted. There were hurried whispers from the other side.

"You have my guarantee for the murder. I don't make mistakes," came the first voice smoothly. It was a familiar voice, but Cody couldn't connect it with a face.

"You're an ice cold man," replied a second, gruffer voice. "That look in your eyes—I've seen it in men before; and every time the night ends with blood-stained hands. Are you sure this is the path you want to take?" Cody held his breath.

"I'm positive," replied the first man emotionlessly. Cody took a step slowly back. The sound of his shoes on the stone floor echoed down the hallway. The whispers stopped. Cody was trapped. He looked behind, but the hall was too long to escape. The door before him swung open, and through the archway stepped Prince Kantan. Cody's eyes were immediately drawn to the serrated dagger resting in the prince's steady hand.

Kantan's cool, calculating eyes were burning a hole into Cody's forehead. A second man stepped out from behind him; he was a large man with a grayish beard, thick sideburns and a stone face. He was wearing full body chainmail and a heavy broadsword hung by his side. He too was staring intently at Cody.

"I was just trying to find the High Priest Lamgorious Stalkton at the Monastery. Sorry. . . . Could you tell me which way to go?" Cody blurted out nervously.

Kantan's expression remained frozen. "Just through this door. I'm sure he is anticipating your arrival." He motioned to the man behind him. "Allow me to introduce

General Gongore Levenworth, captain of the Inner-City guard and head of city defense." Cody gave a slight nod to the man, but the man merely stared blankly back.

"Um, well a pleasure to meet you. I will just be going now. Bye." Cody put his head down and walked to the door only to find it blocked by the large general who seemed in no hurry to move. Cody awkwardly pushed his body against the wall and squeezed past the man. Face beet-red, Cody hurried down the hall.

"Oh, and Cody," Cody stopped, turning back to face Kantan, who was still peering suspiciously at him. "I can trust that you will keep your ears to yourself, can I not?" Cody felt a knot twisting in his stomach. "Yes, Sir, of course."

As he scurried away, he felt the eyes of the two men pierce his back like a knife. Finally, turning the corner of the lengthy corridor, he flung his body to the wall and slid down into a squat; his breath was hoarse and erratic. His hand unconsciously slipped into his pocket, fingering the warning note from the marketplace. His head was spinning, but he was certain of one thing. The brief encounter had made one fact unmistakably clear. *Before the sun sets tonight . . . somebody is going to die.*

36

The Low Priest

The lights of the city shrunk to the size of a thousand fireflies as Cody ascended the base of the Sanctuary. A wooden pulley system constructed of worn timber and frayed rope worked as a primitive elevator guiding the small square platform along the outside wall of the building. Cody held his breath as the lift swayed gently left and right; Cody did not have an intimate relationship with heights and now he remembered why.

With a jerk the lift stopped, sending Cody stumbling against the railing; he had reached the top. The metallic sphere of the Sanctuary overhead cast a dark shadow over him. He quickly jumped off onto a large balcony, anxious to get indoors and put some distance between him and the antique elevator. At the other end of the balcony were two rustic wooden doors. Between his position and the doors, standing tall in the middle of the balcony, was a large steel sculpture of a man. The steel man was dressed in a robe and kneeling, head downcast and arms raised high. In his hands was a sphere resembling a globe. Cody had arrived at the Monastery of the Brotherhood: Refuge to the Brotherhood of Light—holy protectors of the Orb.

The sound of the doors opening drew his attention away from the statue. A young man wearing a long black robe emerged from the open doors. His hood was down revealing him to be a boy around Cody's age with short black hair and a mischievous face. Reaching Cody, the boy gave a slight bow, "So, you are Cody, the one Prince Kantan informed us of?" he asked in a monotone voice balancing between indifference and irritation. Cody nodded. The young man sighed. "Well, you are late. What a splendid beginning for the new savior of Atlantis to start his training. Master Stalkton is inside. Waiting." Without allowing time for Cody's reply, the boy turned and disappeared through the doors from which he came. Cody's stomach tightened: *Strike one.*

Cody quickly followed after the boy's fading footsteps. The room where he now stood was breathtaking. A dome ceiling stretched ten stories high. The assembly hall itself was circular with ten balconies spiraling around the elegantly adorned walls, one for each story. The mosaic floor was decorated with thousands of tiny, colorful stones that fashioned a beautiful swirling design. Inside, several robed men held books, although none appeared to be reading. Instead, every eye focused on Cody. The expressions on their faces were not ones of welcome.

Following the boy, Cody passed through another door which led him into a second circular chamber, although much smaller than the previous. The room was completely empty. Nothing hung from the walls, and even the floor consisted of simple gray stone. There were no windows in the dark room. Only a single lit torch provided its meager lighting. The lone object in the empty room was a cushion lying in the floor's center, and on that cushion, was a man.

The man had his back to Cody, his thick snow-white hair rested against his neck. He was muttering softly to himself as though engaged in an urgent conversation. "Sit," the man murmured, keeping his back to Cody. Cody looked to the young boy, who rolled his eyes, and motioned with his head for Cody to obey. The stone floor was cold against Cody's legs as he folded them on the ground. He hesitated, waiting for the white-haired man to address him again, but the man had returned to his incoherent muttering.

Cody cleared his throat, "Um, Sir," he began, "I have been sent by Prince Kantan and Lady Cia to be trained in the power of the Orb. I am looking for the High Priest Lamgorious Stalkton," Cody finished softy.

No immediate answer came from the man. Slowly his muttering ceased. "Then you foolishly have come looking for the wrong thing," replied the man finally, his voice smooth like the gentle rush of a river.

"Excuse me?" asked Cody confused.

The elder man remained still as he answered, "You come in search of a Lamgorious Stalkton, a meek, humble servant to the Orb. Not worthy of any seeking, except I guess for those questing for meek, humble servants." The man paused and inhaled a wheezy breath before continuing, "You also come at the command of others to be trained, a puppet in the war effort of the nobility."

Cody threw up his arms in frustration. "Well, then, why *should* I have come? And who are you anyways?" he asked bitterly.

The soft sound of chuckling came from the man's hidden face. As the man slowly turned to face him, Cody stumbled back, startled by what he saw—the man sitting before him was an albino. His pale skin mirrored his pure white hair. His face was smooth and unwrinkled, and pressed tightly against his pointy bones.

"I am he whom you seek; the Low Priest, Lamgorious Stalkton. And the only reason one should enter this Monastery is to unlock the wonders of the universe." The albino paused, sighing, "Although you are a special case. Very special, indeed." A grunt came from the boy standing in the doorway.

"Oh, that is enough Xerx; leave us. Return to your studies." With another snort, the boy stomped out of the room, closing the door with a bang. An uncomfortable moment ensued.

Cody squirmed on the rough ground. "Sir, did I do something wrong?" he asked hesitantly.

Stalkton unexpectedly smiled. "Son, you have done a great *many* things wrong! As have we all. But don't you worry about Xerx. He'll warm up to you." Stalkton was interrupted by the sound of an angry shout followed by a loud crashing noise outside the door. The priest grinned. "Or at least stop brainstorming ways to murder you in your sleep! You see, young Xerxus has been my pupil for many years now. He is, how shall I put this . . . less than enthused about me taking on another pupil. To be quite frank, he loathes your very existence. I would suggest that for now, you lock your bedroom door before you sleep."

Cody gulped. "Great. Just great. I've been here only sixty seconds and I've already made an enemy. I'm not off to a great start, am I?"

"Oh, no, not at all. Absolutely dreadful, actually." The man took a sip from the wooden cup in his hands, and shook like a wet dog as the liquid ran down his throat. "But, if it's any consolation," the man continued, "things aren't as bad as they will be soon. At least for now only one boy hates you and not legions of people petitioning for your brutal death," the man concluded matter-of-factly.

"What! Why would anyone want to kill me? What have I done wrong? I don't want people to hate me!" Cody asked desperately.

The pale-skinned man chuckled. "Oh, *want* really has nothing to do with it. You see, as the Book Keeper, you have become powerful, and power and hatred go together as inevitably as lava-shakes and crisp earthworm *de-fossilized* cucumber sandwiches."

Cody had no clue whether this was a positive or negative example, but was anxious to change the subject.

"Sir, just a moment ago you referred to yourself as the *Low* Priest; did you not mean *High* priest?" Cody asked.

The pale man brought his boney finger up to his left nostril as he answered, "No. Well, yes. You see, I am high only to the extent of my lowness." Having depleted the mine, the old man sought new fortune in his right nostril. "You will soon learn in your training that to be low is to be high, and to be high is simply another reminder of why we must be low. I actually knew a lad once whose birth name *was* Low. But then he died . . ." The man's voice trailed off.

Cody shuffled himself forward. "So, I am to be your pupil?" he asked excitedly, feeling it best to push the conversation along.

Stalkton nodded. "Yes and no. But perhaps more yes than no."

Cody looked puzzled at the white-skinned High—*or was it Low?*—Priest who stared absently at the wall behind Cody's head. Cody glanced down at the wooden cup in the man's hands and arrived at several logical conclusions as to what must be in it.

"So, you are going to train me?" Cody pressed, slowly feeling his patience fading.

The old man sighed. "Youth. So passionate and yet so reckless. Did you expect to come in here and learn how to become a creator of worlds in one day?" The old man said in a soft tone pointing his finger at Cody. "You have much to learn, but I suppose that is why you have come . . . or are you that Jack fellow who delivers my mail? I've never been much of a wizard with faces . . ."

"Um, no, Sir, my name isn't Jack. It's Cody."

The pasty-skinned man leaned forward, his face an inch from Cody's. "No, no, you must be Jack. It's that lumpish double chin of yours . . ."

"Sir," Cody interrupted impatiently, "I am not Jack, I am Cody. I am the Book Keeper. I am here to receive your training." The old man gave one last examination before sitting back down, finally at peace that the boy before him was indeed *not* Jack.

"I will not train you. . . . Unless you desire my wisdom on the perfect earthworm and cucumber sandwich, which you undoubtedly do. . . . But with regard to the Orb, I will not train you. . . . I shall merely guide you to discover the power for yourself. Speaking of which, I believe this belongs to you." Stalkton reached behind his back and produced a familiar Book, the scarlet 'A' illuminating in the darkened room.

A familiar jolt of energy ran up Cody's arm as he took the Book into his arms. He looked down at the simple leather cover with a deeper appreciation than he had had during his flight to Atlantis. He now felt that he and the Book were connected, as though the Book was alive.

"What do you know about this Book and the Great Orb?" questioned Stalkton, taking another sip from his cup.

Cody paused, in truth he did not know a lot about either.

"Well, I know that it is called *The Code;* that it has a sister called *The Key* which resides in El Dorado. I know that it was created by King Ishmael and his brother, the Golden King. I know that it funnels the power of the Orb."

"It doesn't just funnel the power," cut in Stalkton, leaning his head forward, "it funnels the power to *you.*" He pushed against Cody's chest with his long, boney index finger, "Only *you* can access its power."

Cody stroked his hand across the Book's leather cover. "So only I can use the power of the Orb?" he asked.

Stalkton shook his head with impatient disgust. "No, no, no. Your mind really *is* slow. Anyone can use the Orb's power assuming, of course, they are within a reasonable distance from it. Think of the Book as an extra boost. It funnels the power directly to you, effortlessly giving you more power than even the most skilled man could ever obtain without the Book. You see, using the power is a straining activity. Even the good creator of the earth rested on the seventh day, did he not? The Book functions as your energy reserve. Do you follow?"

Cody nodded adamantly. "So, how do I use it?" he asked eagerly.

Stalkton frowned. "Slow down, son. We will get to that in time. However, your first lesson is that everything functions according to rules. We live in a world constructed to function by rules. The Orb is no different. The first rule is that the Orb is responsive to the High Language, and to it alone. In order to create, you must know the creation language."

"Which is contained within the two Books created by Ishmael and the Golden King," concluded Cody attentively.

Stalkton shook his head, "You are partially correct. The words contained within the Books are indeed the High Language, or more specifically, the *forbidden* High Language."

Cody raised his eyebrow as the old man continued, "You see, the words in your Book contain the instructions on how to create worlds. Endless galaxies full of suns, stars, and moons. Of course, these words are useless without the second Book, *The Key*, to decipher them. But if ever these two Books should be brought together it would give its Keeper endless power—even the power to create and control human life."

Cody noticed a serious expression come over the man's frail face. "Well, if you don't mind me asking, it seems that without *The Key*, this Book is useless. I mean, how can I create without knowing what the words are?" he asked, feeling a sense of disappointment. "That is where I come in," Stalkton replied mysteriously. Cody was no longer blinking; he was a complete slave to the old man's words. "You see. Not all of the language was strictly forbidden. While Ishmael and his prodigal brother agreed to restrict the knowledge of creating worlds, they overlooked the small areas of life. For example, the High Language for human life was prohibited and slowly forgotten from human thought, but the words for things, such as water and light were not. Yes, for most people these words were lost to their memory and faded out of their lexicon, but not for all. The Brotherhood of Light is dedicated to preserving this knowledge. For example, *seamour!*"

At first nothing happened. Cody froze. A drop of water spilled out of Stalkton's cup. Another splash rolled over the edge. Suddenly water was pouring out like a fountain. It continued to gush out, soaking the floor. *"Gai da Gasme."* At the sound of Stalkton's voice, the water ceased. Cody stared in amazement at the tiny streams of water that ran like rivers across the floor. His gaze rose to the small wooden cup in Stalkton's hands, the same cup that produced several gallons of water.

"How did . . . how is that even . . . how could . . ." Cody stuttered as the floor streams collided with his foot like a dam. He lifted his shoe to allow the water to flow past.

Stalkton took a sip from his now-full cup. "It is possible because of the Orb. You see, the word *seamour* is the High Language for water. By using the word, and focusing on the inside of my cup, I brought the energy from the Orb together into the form of water. You see, all of life is made up from energy. Even your distastefully scrawny body is merely a dense compression of energy that forms together to appear as a body to our naked human eyes. Fire, or *fraymour* in the High Language, is also just high concentration of energy producing friction. That power, that energy— that is the Orb. By using the High Language we can control that energy."

"And, how did you make it stop?" asked Cody, biting his lip and trying to make sense of what he was hearing.

"Gai da Gasme," responded Stalkton. "Its literal meaning is impossible in our human tongue. However, it is roughly the equivalent to 'done it be', or 'good it is'. Whatever the translation, it serves as a plug, stopping the flow of energy. It ends the process of creation. Had I not uttered it, the water would have simply remained flowing out of my glass forever, or at least until the extensive use of the Orb drained and killed me, which for most common folk, would be only five minutes of continual creating. This, of course, is the second rule of creating: that you can only use as much power as your mental strength allows, a rule that has less significance for you as the Book Keeper. Now, do you see the water on the floor?"

Cody nodded; he also saw a towering dune of dried boogers on the floor, but he tried focusing on the water. The old man continued, "Note how it did not disappear even after I cut off my creating. The final, and most important rule of creation, is that it cannot be undone. Let me tell you a tale: There was once a young creator who was lounging in his luxury palace that he had just created. It was perfect and he was extremely content. Suddenly a large spider crawled across the floor. The man detested spiders. He uttered a few quick words and created a frog to eat the spider. After some time, the croaking of the frog became unbearable, so the man created a large bird to devour the frog. However, after some time, the bird's flapping wings made a large mess in his beautiful palace so out of irritation he created a giant boulder to fall from the sky and crush the bird. The boulder, which landed in his bedroom, was too heavy to be moved. Frustrated, he hastily created a great hurricane to come and blow the rock away, which it did. Unfortunately, in the process, the hurricane completely leveled his beautiful palace and buried him beneath the rubble. Why do I tell you this story?" asked Stalkton seriously.

Cody shook his head. "I don't know. To tell me that it's best to just step on the spiders in my room?" Cody answered with a laugh. Stalkton did not join in the laughter. Seeing the deadly serious look on his face, Cody's laughter died.

"I tell you this because when abused, the power of the Orb will bring destruction. It's easy to solve any problem by casually using the High Language. But," he warned, "what you do cannot be undone. The power should never be used thoughtlessly, and *never* for personal gain or pleasure. I've seen with my own eyes the horrible consequences when one starts down that dangerous path." His voice trailed off in grim thought. It didn't matter. Cody could read his mind like a paperback novel—*the Golden King.*

37

A Strange Scent

"S*eamour! Gai da Gasme. Fraymour! Gai da Gasme. Seamour!*
Gai da Gasme." Cody watched as water rose in his wooden cup and burst into flames before being extinguished by a geyser bursting three-feet high. At Cody's final words, the water subsided and Cody poured the full cup out his bedroom window into the garden two stories below. His mind felt tingly and his face felt flush. He placed his palm directly on the scarlet 'A' of the Book and felt a reviving rush of strength flow into him. He had to admit that being a creator of worlds certainly had it perks.

He looked down at the garden below. It felt nice to see greenery again. He guessed that gardening in the center of the earth had its complications. When he and Jade had first been shown to their rooms, Cia had explained that the garden was the only garden in Under-Earth. Looking at the rocky terrain beyond the city gates to the distant mountains painted on the horizon, he had no reason to doubt her claim.

He heard the creaking of a door as it opened and closed from beyond the wall. "Cody? You there?" came the soft voice of Jade out her window.

"Yeah, I'm here. Any luck on tomorrow's trial? Were you able to uncover anything that might help us win Randilin's release?" Cody asked, propping himself up onto the ledge of his window.

"Nada. I went to the library to find some history on him. Absolutely nothing. Not a single, solitary reference to Randilin in any of the historical records. Don't you find it just a little odd that the number one criminal in the whole land is not recorded anywhere? It's like he doesn't exist." Cody frowned; it *was* odd,

"What about Sally? Surely she has some answers," suggested Cody curiously.

"Strike two. I'm *positive* she knows something. She became nervous and fidgety the instant I brought it up. Unfortunately, what she *does* know, she's not sharing. Any time I even hinted about the subject she would quickly change the topic toward the techniques for perfect hot chocolate or the delicate art of flawless toast. Whatever Randilin did, Sally's keeping tight-lipped. But enough about that; how was your training? I see you didn't get yourself blown up; that's a nice surprise. What about reverend Lamgorious Stalkton?"

Cody couldn't suppress a laugh. "Low Priest Stalkton is, to put it delicately, a crazy hermit. He hasn't left the Monastery in about fourteen centuries."

"Oh, Cody, don't exaggerate again. You're making him out to be another Ms. Starky. I'm sure Monastery matters keep him occupied. He probably doesn't have a lot of free time to go out gallivanting," replied Jade in a motherly tone.

Cody let out another uncontrolled laugh. "No, Jade, I mean the man has *literally* not been out in centuries. His skin is blindingly white. Reminded me of the time you joined my mom and me at the beach house after having spent the entire winter with your father in cloudy London. We needed sunglasses just to look your direction!" He laughed. Although he could not see Jade, he knew her cheeks were burning bright red. "But, yeah, despite being completely bonkers, Priest Stalkton is a good guy. Even though six thousand years of minimal social interaction have left him with an utter lack of tact. I feel like I'm talking to Wesley all over again!" Cody waited for Jade to laugh, but no reply came. "You okay? What are you thinking about?"

"Home," answered Jade in a quiet, sober voice. "Don't you miss it? Don't you wonder about what's going on up there while we're down here?" Cody cringed. His cheery mood was overthrown by a sense of guilt. With all the excitement and adventure he had completely forgotten about his life back on the surface. His world had become a blur, and he couldn't remember how many days had passed since he and Jade had fled on the train to Las Vegas, but he had no doubt that, by now, his mother would have received word of his absence. It also struck him that his disappearance would cement the accusation that he murdered Wesley; Sheriff Messiner probably had patrols all over Utah looking for him.

"I miss home, too, Jade," he responded quietly, wondering if he had seen Havenwood for the last time, or if life could ever return to the way it was before all that had happened. "Maybe we should get some sleep. We need our energy for tomorrow evening's trial," responded Jade, who retired into her own room. Cody was quick to agree. Walking over to his bed he flopped limply on top and smothered his face with his pillow as the tears began to pour.

Tick . . . tick . . . tick . . . tick . . . tick. The moment Cody woke a strange scent evaded his nose. He looked around his room. It was empty. The ticking sound was coming from beyond his walls. *A clock? No.* Cody knew Atlantis didn't use electricity. *Jade?* He pulled himself out of bed and went to the window. He could hear the peaceful snoring of Jade in steady rhythm. With Atlantis' bizarre morning-night changes he couldn't tell what time it was, but only a few lights still flicked in the city.

Scratch. Scratch. Scratch. The sound was like a knife carving away at a block of wood. Cody's heart froze. It was not coming from out his window—it was coming from the other side of his door. Cody inched forward, grabbing *The Code* in his arms. The strange smell seeped under the crack and into his room. Cody pressed his ear against the wood surface. He heard a grunt as the scratching continued. Somebody was standing just outside. Cody was suddenly thankful that he had taken Stalkton's advice and locked his door. *Was it Xerx trying to get through? Had Stalkton been in earnest when he had warned him?*

Cody took a deep breath. He had never been a very big kid, but Xerx was only an inch taller. By going on the offensive and opening the door, it would give him the element of surprise on his intruder. He counted in his head: *Five . . . Four . . . Three . . . Two . . . One!* With a war cry he swung open the door—and immediately knew he had made a horrible mistake. The strange smell had finally registered, but a moment too late. An imposing figure stood before his open door; two familiar, glowing red eyes peered directly at him.

38

A Treasonous Accusation

The Beast. The looming dome of its cloaked exoskeleton rose and fell steadily with its heavy breath and its two snake-like eyes illuminated with a reddish glow from under its hood. Its six talons clicked softly against the stone floor from its scale-covered, bird-like feet. Cody's lungs emptied as he felt the heat of the creature's dense breath.

"*Fraymour!*" yelled Cody instinctively. Suddenly the archway of the door burst into wild flame. The Beast let out a piercing squeal. Cody dashed to the window, "*Gai da Gasme!*" He looked down the ledge of his window at the distant ground below. He glanced back to the door; with another cringing squeal the Beast came gliding through the flames into the room. Cody felt beads of sweat burning down his forehead, the heat of the flames pressing against this face. The Beast lowered itself, and pounced.

Swinging out his hand, Cody swiped the wooden cup from beside his bed and aimed it toward the Beast, "*Seamour!*" A burst of water sprang forth from the cup like a water hose, colliding with the Beast and sending it crashing against the wall. *"Gai da Gasme,"* Cody muttered as he climbed onto the window ledge, *The Code* under his arm.

Looking across the palace wall he saw the ledge of Jade's window balcony ten feet away. There was a clutter of noise from behind and Cody knew that the Beast was once again on its feet. It was now or never. Taking a deep breath, he propelled himself out the window.

He felt a gust of wind as the Beast's jaws clamped the empty air where he had stood. His stomach felt suspended without gravity as he soared through the air. Reaching out his hands, he tossed the Book through the window before his fingers clutched onto Jade's ledge, sending his body slamming against the wall. He felt a burn in his hands. He was hanging helplessly by the tips of his fingers, swaying in the wind. He looked back to his own window; the Beast's silhouette was like a giant gargoyle perched on the ledge.

"Help! Help!" Cody began yelling desperately. The Beast crouched down again, ready to jump. "Help! Help!" Cody closed his eyes. He felt a firm grip on his arms and the sensation of flying before crashing on the ground.

"Cody?"

He opened his eyes. A circle of people surrounded him. "What in heaven's name is going on?" asked Prince Foz with a look of concern on his face.

"Indeed. Explain yourself," questioned Kantan suspiciously.

Cody looked to the remaining person. "Jade, we need to get out of here, we're not safe!" He attempted to push himself off the ground, but Kantan's firm grip held him prisoner.

"Explain yourself," Kantan demanded impatiently. There was a stampede of footsteps and Cia, Eva, and two guards appeared over him.

Cia was clothed in a long, white night gown; her usually straight hair was curled and knotted. "Brothers, what is the meaning of this?" she questioned, kneeling down beside them.

"It's the Beast! It's here! In my room! It attacked me. We're not safe!" Cody yelled exasperated, squirming to break free from Kantan's grasp.

Foz yelped, but Kantan's grip tightened as he leaned in close. "Silence boy. You had a nightmare. Nothing more. Come here."

Kantan pulled Cody up by his collar and led him into the hallway, the others crowding behind. "Look here; does this look like a battleground?" challenged Kantan. Cody stared at the door. There were no burn marks. Looking to the ground he realized that it was completely dry.

"It was here, I know it was. I fought it! I'm not lying!" Cody cried with a raised voice.

Cia placed her hand on his shoulder, "No one is accusing you of being a liar, Cody. You had a bad dream. After what you've been through we don't blame you. But you are in the safest place in all of Under-Earth. There is absolutely no way the Beast could have gotten into the palace."

Cody sneered. "Unless somebody let it in," he muttered.

Cia's eyes widened. "What are you talking about, Cody? Who would ever do such a thing?"

Cody felt a jolt of pain as Kantan pinched his shoulder, but Cody was tired of being intimidated. He swatted the prince's hand away and turned before the crowd.

"Who would do such a thing you ask? I know who did it." The crowd held their breath intensely.

Jade anxiously stepped forward, "Cody this isn't the time for this. We don't have any proof for our suspicions. It was probably just a nightmare . . ."

But Cody wasn't listening. He pointed his finger to Kantan. "Here he is!" The crowd cried out, Eva turned her head away. Jade brought her hand to her eyes and shook her head.

"Cody!" exclaimed Cia, "this is treachery to the throne. You had better have solid evidence to make such an outlandish claim."

Kantan stepped forward. "Indeed, you had better think extremely carefully about what your next words are going to be," said Kantan, the words slithering smoothly from his mouth.

Cody could feel all eyes on him. "He's...planning to murder somebody. I heard him speak of it. And he's been secretly meeting with the war activists. I've seen it myself. He's a traitor, and now he wants to kill me and take the Book!" Silence hung in the air.

Kantan circled around Cody like a vulture eyeing up its dinner. "And what is your proof?" Cody felt a clump forming in his throat. He looked to Jade for help, but the minute their eyes met she turned her head away.

"I . . . I . . . just know," Cody finished lamely. Kantan gave a victorious smirk. Foz ran his hand through his matted hair.

"Cody, Cody, Cody. I don't know what has possessed you to tell such lies tonight, but Book Keeper or not, treachery is treachery. By my royal rights and medical expertise, I suggest that punishment of death be suspended, citing a disillusionary state of dream due to special circumstances. But boy," his voice was dropped to an almost inaudible whisper, "we won't be able to overlook this type of action again." Prince Foz turned to crowd that had amassed. "I think it is best for all of us to forget this incident and return to our sleep."

The crowd began to depart, casting Cody sideward glances as they passed. Cody had never felt so small. He felt his cheeks smoldering. He had been humiliated. Worst of all, Jade had left him out to dry. She had seen Kantan's secret meeting just like he had, hadn't she? *Always too scared to break a rule or resist authority,* Cody thought bitterly. Jade gave Cody an irritated look. "Why can't you *ever* just *listen* . . ." Without another word, she slipped into her room, closing her door behind her. Cody cast a deathly glare toward her door—and that's when he saw it.

At the bottom of the wooden door, caught in the hinges, was a small, dark purple thread. *It was no dream. The Beast WAS here.* It suddenly made sense. *Someone is trying to cover up the evidence.* Panic struck Cody. He turned to examine the now-silent hallway. The entire crowd had departed. All except one. Kantan's conniving face glared back at him. For a moment their eyes locked. Kantan grinned, and disappeared around the corner like vapor in the wind.

39

The Nature of a Beast

Randilin's face looked even more pale as he hung weakly by his chains. His unkempt beard and greasy hair had transformed him into a wild Neanderthal. Despite his horrid appearance, his swollen lips curved into a slight smirk. "You called out the prince to his own flea-picking face? Cody, I hate to admit it, but blast it all, I'm proud of you!"

"This is not a joking matter!" cried Jade sternly. "One doesn't just accuse a prince, to his own face no less, of being a traitor and murderer, and then walk away unscarred. Kantan will retaliate. This is not what we need right now. Not with a war looming and your trial this evening."

Randilin's smile subsided. "Suppose you're right . . . but it was still bloody brilliant of you, Cody."

Jade hung her head in defeat.

Cody propped himself up against the wall in front of Randilin's cell. "So, what is this Beast anyway? How could it possibly have made it past the guards to my room?" he asked, shuttering at the memory.

Randilin's eyes rolled to the back of his head and he inhaled a heavy breath. "To be honest, kids, I don't know. Not sure there's anyone other than perhaps King Ishmael who does. All I know is that we first got sight of it around the time of the Great War. It was like a shadow. No one ever got a good glimpse of it, or at least no one who stayed alive long enough to tell of it. It started with the priests. One by one they disappeared; some in their houses, some in the streets at night, some in the very Monastery itself. Never a trace of evidence left behind other than the mutilated victim himself. Rumors began to spread. It seemed that something was systematically hunting down the Brotherhood of Light. People began referring to it in hushed whispers as—The Hunter. All of the old order of Brotherhood Priests fell victim to its merciless hunger. All but one. A boy, the newest member of the order. His name was . . ."

"Lamgorious Stalkton," finished Cody. "How did he survive when none other could?" he asked eagerly.

"That's the thing. Nobody knows. All I know is that Stalkton lived. And after the Great War no one saw the Beast ever again. Centuries passed and The Hunter became a myth, a ghost story even. That is, until now. Did you know that before he was murdered by the Hunter, Wesley sent me a message attached to the leg of a hawk?"

"No, I didn't; you've never mentioned it," Cody answered in surprise.

Randilin continued, "Oh yes, that old man was crafty as they come. He knew he was in danger. I received the message that the Book's location was compromised. By the time I arrived at the house, it was too late. Wesley's body was in all four corners of the room. By the brutality of the killing, I feared the worst. But even in the face of death, Wesley was using his head. He left me a note . . ."

"Hung by a dagger to the wall," recalled Cody, remembering his initial shock at watching the elderly Book Keeper pulling out a menacing knife. In hindsight, he realized there was so much he didn't understand about the man. He wished he had known him more.

"That's right, hung by a dagger. The note was brief; it simply said *Cody Clemenson now holds the code of fate. The torch has been passed.* Obviously, by *code of fate* he was tipping me off that you now possessed *The Code.* I knew I had to find you before The Hunter did. I began asking around the city about you. I knew you would eventually flee town, so I waited at the train station and followed you on board. I was going to join you in your compartment but that British fool, Dunstan, beat me to it. Instead I tried to round you off in Las Vegas, and now here we are. All cheerfully awaiting my death sentence."

"Don't worry, Randilin. I'm sure the trial will go okay. As you've just told us, you've done more than your part in keeping the Book safe," said Jade with more confidence than she felt.

Randilin smiled. "Thanks, kid. Don't worry about me. Men like me are destined to depart the world with a noose around our necks. But kids like you two give me faith that hope in this world is not an extinct reality."

Cody's knuckles were still white as he passed through the large wooden doors of the Monastery. *Atlantis possessed the power to create the universe, so why was it that he still had to put his life at risk every time he rode that flimsy elevator to the Monastery* thought Cody bitterly. "Heads up!" came a shout from above and Cody quickly dropped to the floor. A large rock whizzed over his head and skidded across the ground. Cody tucked his head into his body and rolled over. Xerx was on the first balcony. "Oops! Guess my aim was a bit off. I wouldn't want to be sending boulders at the high and mighty Book Keeper now would I? He might send them flying back . . . oh, wait, he doesn't know how to. I guess merely being a keeper of the Book doesn't do squat for your knowledge of what's inside. Pity." Xerx gave a mocking smirk. Cody bit his lip; he didn't have time for petty mind games.

Entering into the training room Cody found it exactly as it had been before. Stalkton's back once again faced Cody as the elder man muttered away. Cody sat down cross-legged on the floor. "Master, I'm here to continue expanding my knowledge of the Orb under your guidance."

The pale man turned around slowly. "Now, that's more like it. Oh, my heavens! What a hideous zit you have on your nose, frightening almost. It's like a mountain was dropped onto the prairies," exclaimed Stalkton, leaning forward curiously to examine Cody's nose.

Cody pulled his head away. "Sir, we don't have much time. I am participating in Randilin's trial this evening."

"Randilin . . . the funny midget of a man? So, he has returned at last," said Stalkton thoughtfully.

Cody inched himself closer to his teacher. "What do you know about him, Sir? About Randilin?"

Stalkton took notice of his pupil's anticipation. He paused and collected his thoughts for a moment before answering "Randilin is a prime example of humanity's curse; an example that even the greatest men have a darkness in them, buried deep inside. But enough of this, you are here to learn. I want you to practice the word *byrae* . . . oh, and you might want to hold onto something."

Cody shrugged disappointedly at the change of topic, but obeyed. *"Byrae,"* he stammered half-heartedly. A howling whistle came from the dome ceiling. Suddenly a powerful gust of wind billowed down from the roof like a waterfall and collided with Cody, sending him flying against the wall, and pinning him two feet in the air. He tried to raise his head, but the force of the wind held it tight.

"End the creation. Remember the words!" called Stalkton from the other end of the room in a mixture of worry and amusement.

Cody struggled to open his mouth against the wind. *"Gai di gasme!"* The wind died immediately, sending Cody crashing to the floor with a thud. He pushed himself back to his feet. "You're a cruel man, Stalkton, you do know that."

Stalkton gave a breathy laugh. "To be quite frank, I had forgotten the joys of new pupils. So much fun," he said giddily.

Cody rubbed his sore hip. "Master Stalkton, so far, these words you've been teaching me. I can't help but notice that they all involve creating or controlling the elements. Isn't there more? I mean, can't the Orb's power be used to create tangible, material objects?" he asked, still clutching his bruised side.

The old man's hazy eyes widened. "Oh, yes. The Orb is limitless. The vast depths of your creative mind would only flirt with the surface of its capability. You see, our creativity is merely a mirror of that which already exists. You can create water, fire, and wind. But are you really *creating* them? Or are you merely *mimicking* the reality that you already know? If you create a rose, are you *inventing* a rose? Of course not, you are merely creating a reflection of the beautiful rose you previously beheld in the garden. Regardless of how far your ability reaches, you must remember that you will always be incapable of being anything more than an *imitator*, never an *inventor*. Do you follow? "

Cody nodded his head slowly, rubbing his tongue along his upper lip. "I think so. But I don't understand what relevance this has to do with my training. Who cares if I am just mimicking?" Cody replied indifferently.

The old man's hand shot out and stung across Cody's cheek. "It is of *complete* relevance. It is the very essence of being a creator. Let me tell you another tale boy. There was once a brilliant young creator who had become so skilled and powerful that one day he claimed to be the god of the universe. The divine creator heard of this and challenged him to a contest in order to determine who would hold the title of god. The divine creator suggested that the highest pinnacle of his creation had been making man out of dirt. So the young creator, confident in his ability, bent over and grabbed a handful of dirt to create a human life. The divine creator laughed and simply said, 'Get your own dirt.' Brilliant as the young creator was, he was still trapped within the framework of the world he lived. Don't forget this parable, son. By using the Orb's energy we gain power, but we are still limited. Unfortunately, there have been some who have let the Orb's power infest them like a cancer; distorting and twisting their minds until one day they wake up and believe that they are no longer merely man—but a god. Can you think of anybody?" Stalkton prodded.

Cody looked down. "The Golden King."

Stalkton nodded. "Oh, yes, the Golden King he calls himself. It makes me sick to my stomach to hear of such blasphemy to the Orb . . . then again, it could also have been the two dozen rock-cakes I consumed this morning. They tend to give me the worst gas . . ."

"Sir," Cody asked, suddenly remembering the question that had been floating around his mind since his meeting with Randilin, "I was wondering if you could tell me about something . . . about . . . the Hunter."

Cody suddenly wished he could retract his words. The pupils in Stalkton's eyes grew as he stumbled backwards, coughing. His head started jerking as though he was having a seizure.

"The Hunter is a demon," he finally coughed out, his voice shaking like a flag in a hurricane. "An unholy Beast; the literal embodiment of evil. But it has been banished. So we have no need to speak of it. Ever!" he spit out, an unfamiliar edge in his voice.

"Banished, you say? How was it banished, if you'll forgive me for asking? I mean, theoretically, could it ever come back?" Cody pressed cautiously.

An almost demented appearance seized Stalkton's stern face. "Back? Why would you even bring up such an outrageous idea?" he snarled harshly. "It was banished by the Good King Ishmael himself during the truce with the defeated Golden King after the Great War. It was a compromise. The Hunter cannot be killed; it can only be contained. The Golden King agreed to trap the Hunter at the bottom of the Great Sea of Lava where it would rest for all eternity. His one condition was that, as a fail safe, if ever a man should read from *The Code* or *The Key* whom was not its rightful keeper, the Hunter would be awoken from its slumber," Stalkton finished softly. Cody gulped,

"And, if someone were to read from *The Code* other than its rightful keeper, what would the Hunter do to that person?" Cody asked timidly.

Stalkton shuttered. "It would hunt them without ceasing. The Hunter needs no sleep; it only needs flesh. It is a flawless predator. When it catches a scent, inexorable doom awaits its wretched prey . . ." the priest's voice faded to a whisper, his thoughts carrying him back to ancient memories. After a moment he shook his head. "But enough of this; it is only hypothetical talk. You didn't attempt to read from the Book before it was yours, right? Surely you weren't foolish enough to have read from it while Wesley was still alive . . . were you?" Stalkton asked, the terror bursting from his eyes.

Cody felt his palms sweating. "No, Sir, absolutely not. You have nothing to worry about," he lied.

Stalkton's shoulders slumped and he let out a long sigh. "Thank the maker. You had me worried. If you had read the Book before it was yours, then we'd all be doomed. But as it is not the case, we are never to bring up this topic again. Is that clear?"

"Yes, Sir" Cody responded tensely. A sharp cramp formed in his stomach. *What have I done?*

"Now, was there anything else you wanted to learn, our time is nearly up?" asked the priest as he lowered himself back to the floor.

Cody shook his head as he walked to the door, but stopped, and turned back to Stalkton, "As a matter of fact, there was one more word I was hoping you could teach me."

Stalkon's white eyebrow rose, "Yes, and which word was that?"

Cody closed the door behind him, once again leaving his elder teacher alone in the room of darkness. Cody walked into the middle of the hall and scanned the balconies. He found the object of his desires on the third level. "Hey, Xerx," he called up.

The irritated young face of Xerx stuck over the ledge. "I'm busy, what do you want?" he called down angrily.

Cody grinned. "Just to warn you to keep your head up. *Gadour!*" A fist-sized rock whizzed toward the ceiling, pounding Xerx square on the forehead.

40

Soul Snatcher

"Guilty or Innocent? Find out all the latest on this evening's dramatic trial!" the voice of Fincher Tople called over the sea of people filling the streets, "Get your *Under-Earth Rumblings!* Containing exclusive, classified information from the jury themselves!"

Cody rolled his eyes. *That guy's really starting to get on my nerves.* As he walked the steps into the palace, Cody could see a large line of people waiting to enter the courthouse. Life in Atlantis was being put on hold in favor of the trial. Several men stood outside the courthouse holding signs: **Don't Let History Repeat Itself, Send Randilin to the Gallows!**

Cody closed the palace door behind him, blocking out the noise of the crowd. He paused at the stairs to his chamber. He was still ticked off at Jade for not standing up for him and his accusation of Kantan. He knew their lives were at too much risk to stay mad for long, but for the moment, he couldn't bring himself to make peace. Walking back down the stairs he set off aimlessly into the palace. Anywhere quiet would do.

"Cody! My dear, sweet, little thing!" came a friendly voice. Cody felt two pudgy arms wrapping around him and heaving him off the ground. "I've been wondering when I'd see you again!" Cody turned to face the voice. Sally Peatwee looked just as she had before, rosy cheeks and her two frizzy French braids hanging down to her waist. However, the redness and bags under her eyes proved that she'd been doing a lot more crying than sleeping of late.

"Oh, hey, Sally. It's great to see you again! I wasn't sure if you had stuck around here or gone back to your café."

Sally's eyes squinted, foreshadowing another crying fit. "They've allowed me to remain here until after the trial. I just couldn't leave Randy. Not now." Tears started streaming down her face. "It's just not fair! Randy isn't evil inside. We've all made poor choices! Randy's dark incident was . . . I mean, I was *there*! I saw the horror with my own eyes! He wasn't himself that night! He didn't know what would happen! I mean, he *couldn't* have . . ." Sally's voice was suffocated by fierce hysteric crying.

Cody gave her another hug. "It's going to be okay. We have a strong testimony for his defense. I'm sure we can convince the jury. But we should both probably rest for a bit and go over our stories. Do you know anywhere quiet I can go around here?"

Sally grabbed her left braid and dried her tears with it. "Hard to find anywhere quiet on this ghastly day. But the garden should be empty; the entrance is just at the end of the hall," she replied jittery. Cody thanked her and set off down the hall, hoping that what he had told her would indeed be the truth. Reaching the end of the hall, he came to a set of royal purple doors. On each door was a golden figure, a winged creature with a human head. The creatures were wielding flaming swords.

The potent aroma of pine and timber welcomed Cody as he passed through the doors. His eyes widened. The sight before him was not so much a garden as it was a rainforest paradise. Thick green foliage and bright multi-toned leaves and flowers filled the dense courtyard. Up the sides of the walls, leafy vines had slithered up, completely covering the bricks in rich greenery.

"Ah, I see you have discovered the beauty of Atlantis at last." The plump-faced Prince Foz emerged from the trees, carrying a bucket of water. "Come. Follow me."

Cody caught up to the short prince. "What are you doing out here, Foz?" Cody asked. His strides fell into sync with the Prince's as they walked deeper into the forest. Foz stopped at a patch of beautiful, red flowers and poured some of the water from his bucket on them. "I'm here for much of the same reason I suspect you are; to relax and gather my thoughts. I'm going to be testifying for Randilin this evening, did you know? It's a choice that will not sit well with my family, but I can't let other people stop me from doing what I think is right. Besides, these plants aren't going to water themselves, eh?" he laughed, throwing some more water onto the greenery.

"Are you the gardener? I thought you were the doctor here in Atlantis?" Cody asked curiously as they came to a stop in the middle of the garden.

Foz laughed. "The answer is yes. I'm both. Although my official duties are as city doctor, let's face it, living in a city of immortals that are incapable of even catching a common cold does not result in a very full schedule." Foz extended his arms to the forest. "*This* is my real passion. Beauty. *This* is what the power of the Orb is all about. Perfection, the way it was always intended to be."

Cody looked around at the plants surrounding him. He knelt down and picked a bright green flower with large, smooth petals. "It's called a jade flower," Foz explained excitedly. "One of my personal favorites."

Cody smiled, and tucked the flower gently into the sash of his garment. It would make a perfect peace offering to Jade.

Another plant caught his eye. The plant had thick, sky-blue leaves with yellow and orange blotches on it. All the leaves together reminded him of a stained-glass window. Cody reached out to touch it. Foz's hand came slapping down on his with a smack. "Don't touch that one; it's not safe!"

Cody grabbed his throbbing hand and gazed curiously toward the panting Prince. "What do you mean, it's not safe? What kind of plant is this? It's the most beautiful thing I've ever seen." As the light danced off the plant's leaves, Cody felt the uncontrollable urge to touch it. *It is so beautiful . . . just one touch . . .*

Foz clutched onto Cody's arm and guided him back toward the entrance of the garden. "That plant is called the Derugmansia. But its more common name is the *Soul Snatcher.* I can't tell you how many times I've tried to remove it from the garden, but despite all my attempts, it always grows back. Within those beautiful leaves is an immeasurably high concentration of poison, equivalent to roughly twenty bites from the adult black mamba snake on Upper-Earth. One of those leaves makes contact with your lips and twenty seconds later you're being ushered into the afterlife. Now here we are." They had returned to the palace entrance. "We both need to change before heading over to the courthouse. Guess I'll have to return afterwards to finish watering all the plants."

Cody looked back at the garden and smiled, "You know what, Prince Foz, I think you have a busy enough day as it is. Why don't I save you some trouble?" Cody held out his arms and cleared his throat, *"Seamour!"* A thick rain poured down upon the plants. Foz gave a sly grin.

"Show-off."

41

The Trial

The courtroom was filled to capacity. The back of the room was like a can of sardines as more and more people attempted to squeeze into every inch of unoccupied space. Despite the mashed-together crowd, the room was silent. The air was growing toxic from lack of carbon dioxide; the masses held their collective breath. The anticipation leading up to the trial had been fanatical. Now that it had finally arrived, people seemed unsure how to handle it.

Cody looked across the sea of people from his reserved seat. At the end of his row was Sally; the bags under her eyes were freshly red. To Cody's direct left was Prince Foz, and beside him was Jade, a green flower tucked daintily behind her ear. All the *who's-who* of the city were in attendance. Cody saw General Gongore Levenworth and Dace standing with a bald man with tanned skin who Cody assumed must be the captain of the Mid-City guard. Poe Dapperhio sat at the front of the courtroom proudly holding a feather quill; he would be the trial scribe. Cody hoped he wrote more eloquently than he spoke.

Even Xerx was in attendance, leaning against the back wall with his arms crossed; a large purple bruise bulging from the center of his forehead. On the adjacent side of the room was a parallel boxed seating compartment. In it sat Lady Cia, looking radiant as ever, and her sister, Princess Eva. *Where was Prince Kantan?* Cody realized that the Prince wasn't the only one missing. In the middle of the box was an empty throne. Cody felt his anger toward the King rising. War or no war, Randilin's life had value and deserved the respect of the King's presence.

"Excuse me, Sir, excuse me. Ma'am, if you'll excuse me. Official business. Reporter coming through!" Fincher Tople climbed over chairs as well as any unfortunate people who happened to occupy them as he worked his way toward the front. The crowd glared at him as his gangly limbs scurried overtop.

"All rise." The doors at the front of the room opened. The first man who came through was a man with the conniving face of a panther: Sli Silkian—head of the AREA. His fine, black hair was slicked smoothly back and his eyes were cool and calculating. There was something about the man's appearance that once again gave Cody the creeps.

Behind Silkian, and escorted by two guards, was Randilin. Looking worse than ever, he hung limply against the guards as they ushered him to his seat, binding his hands securely to the chair. Following him through the door was a plump, little man with only a few strands of hair still clutching the top of his head. The man waddled over and took a seat beside Randilin. His name was Geoffrey. Cody had been briefly introduced to him the night before; he was a member of The Brotherhood of Light. He was also the lawyer for the accused.

The final man walked through the door and Cody felt his face heat up. Prince Kantan approached the bench looking as smug as ever. Cody clenched his fists, *so that's where he was!* Kantan would be the prosecutor in the case. Cody reached behind and felt his backpack, the indentation of the Book pressing against it. All it would take was one simple word. Cody imagined the pleasure he would get from watching Kantan burst into flames.

The panther-faced man took his position behind the pulpit. "I am Judge Silkian, overseeing the trial of Sir Randilin Stormberger, for the offense of high treason to the Crown," the judge paused, his black eyes squinting under his bushy eyebrows, "and his role in countless, premeditated murders." Jade cried out, covering her mouth with her hand. All eyes in the room shot her an angry look. *A murderer?* Cody stared at Randilin sitting in the front row; his head resting on the table as though sleeping, oblivious to the trial all together. Cody couldn't believe it. Randilin was a rough man, but a murderer? *It just couldn't be . . . could it?*

"Will the prosecutor please call the first witness?" Silkian asked with his smooth purr of a voice.

Kantan stood up and walked to the front. "Ladies and gentlemen. Today is truly a monumental occasion. The accused is a man who really needs no introduction. I could offer you shocking numerical data of the atrocities that this man has committed, but what is a number anyways? When we reduce precious life to a mere number, we become no greater than the man accused today. Instead let us examine the issue . . . a little closer to home. Will Ms. Sky-tin please come forward?" Cody began to panic. Kantan's smooth voice was captivating, his serene words weaving a hypnotic spell over the audience.

An elderly lady took the stand. Cody noticed that it was the same lady that had sold him the blackened earthworm in the marketplace. Kantan glided over to the stand. "Ms. Skytin, do you know the accused?"

The lady's eyes narrowed. "Oh, yes, I know him. I've thought about him every day for a thousand years. He visits me . . . in my nightmares," she answered in a timid, shaky voice.

Kantan held his hand out to the audience. "I know it must be hard, but can you tell the audience how your life has been different because of the accused?"

The women shuddered. "It hasn't just been changed, it's been ruined! Because of this wicked man I have to live with this gimpy knob instead of my right arm!" she pivoted her body to display her missing appendage before continuing, anger infecting her voice. "My husband was killed in the war, so I've been forced, even with my handicap, to work overtime selling worms in the market just to support my family. My daughters, they can't even remember having enough food on the table. Oh, but they remember him." The lady pointed her trembling finger at Randilin. "They remember him all right." The woman burst into tears and Kantan helped her off the stand and back to her seat.

When Kantan returned he approached the jury. "As you can see, the actions of the accused continue to devastate the lives of innocent people today; even blameless children."

Suddenly Kantan's eyes narrowed toward Randilin, his voice quivering with hushed rage. "Oh yes . . . I think it's safe to say we've *all* been affected by the *dark incident* that took place that day . . . some will never recover." An expression of anguish flashed over the Prince's face before quickly vanishing. His devious grin returned. "I have arranged for three other individuals to share their tragic stories. Shall we continue?"

With each new witness Cody felt all hope seep from his body. Kantan was no fool. Half the audience was in tears, the other half looked ready to pounce over the railing and strangle Randilin themselves. When the last witness left the stand Kantan sniffed as though caught up in emotion. "Hasn't this trauma gone on long enough? Isn't it time to turn the page and prevent the next generation from sharing our hurt. Evil men don't change; they only contain the vice for a short while. Randilin should be executed before that evil breaks out again. I rest my case."

The crowd burst into applause as Kantan took his seat. One member of the crowd stood up and yelled out, "Why wait? Send him to the gallows right now!" Two guards escorted the screaming man out of the building. Cody saw that Randilin's head was still resting on the table. *What are you doing Randilin? Don't give up now!*

Judge Silkian slammed his mallet onto the podium. "Order! Order! The trial has not been completed. Reverend Geoffrey, you now may take the stage and call your first witness." As Geoffrey stood his large belly lifted the table. Stumbling backwards he knocked his chair to the ground. Several muffled laughs went out from the crowd.

Cody hung his head; compared to the smoothness of Kan-tan, Geoffrey looked like a hippopotamus at the queen's tea party.

"Ladies and gentleman," he began in trifling, clumsy voice, "we have just heard about the tragic effects of evil. Let us also not pretend that we haven't all also heard the rumors of a threat growing out of El Dorado. Acts carried out by a merciless king, unwilling to forgive and let be. I ask you now, how much different are we than he?" Geoffrey let his question hang in the air like a vapor. The rambunctious crowd had been silenced. Cody had underestimated Geoffrey due to his appearance. A sense of hope slowly returned.

"I will now call on several witnesses to testify on the transformed nature of the accused. For my first witness I call on Sally Peatwee, gatekeeper of the Second Passageway, and first-hand witness of the accused's . . . *dark incident*. Sally, please approach the stand."

Between muffled sobs Sally recapped how, upon Randilin's banishment, he had aided her in the protection of the passageway and provided her with valuable information about the current events of Upper-Earth. She shared how on several occasions he had aided Wesley in the security of the Book, often at the peril of his own life. Jade was next to take the stand. As always, she delivered her speech assertively. She recalled several of the events of their journey to Atlantis and how Randilin protected them and provided invaluable guidance. Prince Foz followed after Jade. His testimony was jumbled and often incohesive, but he passionately recapped how Randilin had displayed perfect compliance with the guards during his imprisonment. The young Prince reminded the crowd of the days before Randilin's crimes, and how he had played such a valuable role in the very founding of Atlantis. Throughout his entire testimony his brother's eyes never blinked, glaring wrathfully toward him. As Foz returned to his chair Geoffrey called his final witness—Cody.

Cody nervously approached the stand. He could feel every eye in the room following him down the aisle. He took a deep breath; he had thought out a strategy for his testimony. Now that the moment had come, he just hoped it was the right one.

Taking the stand, Cody looked out over the crowded room. It appeared to Cody that Geoffrey had the upper hand over Kantan. Cody crossed his fingers. *Don't blow it.*

Geoffrey paced back and forth. "So, Cody, we've heard some of your story from Jade's testimony. But please, tell us in your own words how Randilin has proven his repented heart."

Cody took a deep breath. He told of Randilin's rescue from the hotel in Vegas, and how he had saved them from Dunstan and his gang at risk of his own life. Cody stopped, and looked up to see Jade staring at him. He hoped she would approve of what he was about to do next. Cody began slowly, "I have a confession to make . . ." He paused, taking a deep breath. *Well, here goes nothing.* He pushed himself up to his feet. "*The Code* has returned to Atlantis. . . . *I* am the Book Keeper!"

A loud gasp burst from the crowd, followed by rapid muttering and commotion. Cody continued, not daring to look back at Jade, "Simon Wesley died to protect this Book, and in his last breath of life, he gave his trust to Randilin to carry on his work. Wesley believed in Randilin, and so do I. I am the Book Keeper, and I say forgive and forget, and let us honor the dying wish of a founding father of this great city." Cody flopped back in his chair, awaiting the detonation of the bomb he had just recklessly lobbed into the room. But the unexpected happened.

A man in the back of the room stood to his feet and began clapping. Another man joined him, and then a woman. Soon the whole room was standing in applause. "Forgive and forget! Forgive and forget!" the crowd began chanting.

Cody risked a look back toward Jade. Her face was neutral, but beside her was Prince Foz who had an enormous grin on his face; he gave Cody two thumbs up. "Order in the court!" yelled Silkian as Cody returned to his seat.

Foz grabbed his arm, "That was absolutely brilliant Cody!" he whispered into his ear.

Jade leaned into the huddle. "And rash! Isn't it dangerous to reveal our secret in this manner? Dace warned us not to mention it," she probed sternly.

Foz waved his hand. "Forget Dace. What Cody just did was leverage his position and power to sway the audience. His announcement has created a shock. Without much time to consider its implications, no one in Atlantis, including the jury, is going to want to stand up against the new Book Keeper right now. Don't you understand? Cody has become more influential than the King himself! Cody, I think you may have just saved Randilin's life."

Judge Silkian stood and raised his long fingers to silence the crowd, "Court is adjourned. The jury will discuss the evidence from *both* parties and make its decision. The ruling will be issued tomorrow. Court dismissed."

Chatter and gossip flooded the room as the crowd filed out. Cody scanned over the chamber for one man in particular—Prince Kantan. Their eyes locked, Cody gave him a smug grin, "Got you!" he mouthed victorious. Kantan raised his eyebrows and tilted his head like a curious dog. He motioned toward the jury box. Cody's heart sunk. He suddenly recognized the jury—they were the dissenters whom Kantan had secretly met with in the alleyway. Kantan gave a mocking grin.

"Got you."

42

Giana

Mornings to Cody were appalling on the best of days. When the fate of his friend's life was to be decided, a fate which rested largely on the repercussions of his own rash actions, it was utterly dreadful. Cody tossed and turned in his bed. By the calm wafting through his window, he knew it was still early morning. He was due for a training session at the Monastery at noon, but he was lost in other thoughts. The previous day's trial ran through his head over and over on repeat. He could recite the entire session verbatim. His shocking announcement had caused a rippling stir in Atlantis. Within an hour the entire city was abuzz with the news. Fincher Tople eventually had to be subdued by three guards as he chased down Cody for a desired interview.

Cody rolled over and pulled the covers above his shoulders. He had become an instant celebrity; people were taking notice of him. It was everything he had always dreamed about, but as his eyelids drooped he wasn't sure he had the energy to deal with his new status. He closed his eyes; Atlantis had waited centuries for a Book Keeper to return to the city, they could wait a few more hours.

Cody took a deep breath. Only the front doors of the palace stood as the division between privacy and whatever craziness the day held for him. It was still early and Cody was hoping that most citizens, at least in the Inner-City, still were lying harmlessly in their beds. Cody crossed his fingers and pushed open the door. The moment he did so, he realized that his hope had been in vain. Several hundred people had assembled as a mob at the bottom of the stairs.

Recognizing Cody, they started cheering and yelling, "Let us see *The Code!*" "Prove yourself to us, create something!" "Our roof has a hole, if you just had one quick second to stop by and create a new one . . ." "Hail the savior of Atlantis! Let's use our Book to crush El Dorado once and for all!" "Create! Create! Create!" Cody stood dazed as the mob rushed the stairs. The two front guards crossed their pikes and stepped into the path as a barrier to separate Cody from the crazed crowd. Cody felt overwhelmed. Then he saw her.

The rest of the crazed multitude dissipated into a blurry mist as he stared dumbly at the beautiful specimen before him. It was the girl he had seen the first day he arrived in Atlantis and again in the marketplace. He had been dreaming of her striking blonde hair, mesmerizing blue eyes and glossy red lips. She was perched casually against a wall, segregated from the rest of the crowd, and eyeing him curiously. Cody's heart started to pound. The girl had a slender body that was covered in a tight snowy tunic and fastened with a silver belt. She was stunning.

Mustering up all the smoothness he could manage, Cody puffed out his chest and strutted down the remaining stairs, heading straight toward her. She watched him with amusement, but made no sign of moving away. Sweat rolled over Cody's neck. When he finally stopped, he was only inches from where she stood. Her warm breath rolled gently over his face. From close range he could see the sparkling flash of glitter on her two painted cheeks. Cody's mouth felt sticky, as though all the moisture had been vacuumed out. Besides Jade, none of the other girls at school had ever given him as much as a second glance. *Those days are over.* As he had seen the jocks at school do many times, Cody ran his fingers through his hair coolly and opened his mouth, "Hi, the name's Cody . . ." On the last syllable his voice erupted into a horrifying, mousy, squeak; like grating pointy fingernails being dragged roughly down a chalkboard.

His face flushed; he could feel his heart thrashing in his forehead. He wished he was dead. The blonde girl's thin lips parted into a half-smile. "That was precious," she said casually in a teasing voice. Cody felt dizzy. There were many ways he would categorize himself in that moment, but *precious* was not one of them. *Moronic,* perhaps, but not *precious.*

"It's the . . . power from the Book. . . . Sometimes it's flowing through me so intensely that it affects my voice," he stuttered weakly trying to salvage his decimated dignity.

The girl reached out her hand and wrapped it around his. Her skin was silky and warm as it pressed against his.

"My name's Tiana. Although the way you've been spying on me I'm sure you already knew that . . ." The words floated from her scarlet lips like a song and sank into Cody's pores. He tried to come up with a witty reply but, coming up empty, merely gave a dumb grin. The girl pushed herself off the wall so that her body was almost pressing against his. "Word has it that you're our new Book Keeper now. That's impressive . . . I think," she added playfully. Without lowering his gawky grin, Cody turned back to the stairs, sighing deeply and relaxing his muscles.

"*Gadour!*" With a flash of light a pebble appeared on the steps; it was slowly growing in size. Cody closed his eyes in concentration and waved his hands in the air. This action wasn't necessary, of course, but performance was everything. The crowd inhaled as the pebble grew into a rock—a rock formed in the unmistakable shape of a heart. The heart reached the size of a human heart. Cody opened his eyes. "*Gai di Gasme!*" The rock instantly stopped expanding. Cody glanced back at Tiana who returned an irrepressible grin. He winked. "*Fraymour!*" The rock heart burst into flames.

The crowd cheered boisterously at the sight. "*Gai di Gasme.*" Cody sensed Tiana's soft hand cup the back of his neck, pulling him toward her. He then felt warm, moist pressure against his cheek. The crowd erupted even louder.

"I'm surprised. You are quite the romantic, aren't you?" said Tiana in her tranquil voice.

"Yes, truly amazing," came a straight voice. At the top of the stairs stood Jade with a blank expression on her face. "Unfortunately, Barbie here is going to have to wait until later to see a few more childish magic tricks. Because, if I'm not mistaken, Romeo was supposed to be at the Monastery almost an hour ago for training."

Tiana eyed Jade humorously. "Well, it looks as though someone didn't have enough time to primp this morning. Although, as they say, even a master sculptor's final statue can only be as lovely as the original stone he is given to work with. Anyways, I'm sure I will see you around, Cody," she planted another lingering kiss on his cheek, keeping her eyes focused on Jade the entire time. Pulling her lips away, Tiana disappeared into the crowd.

"Jade, I was just . . ." Cody called up the stairs, uncomfortably trying to stomp out the flame from the flickering stone heart, but with an echoing bang, the door slammed behind Jade and she was gone.

43

Germinated

The nerve! A pillow catapulted across the room, collided with the wall, and fell to its final resting spot on the floor beside other discarded items such as an opened book, a dirty shirt, and several coins. Jade's burning red face surveyed her room in search for any other object that might be chucked. Realizing she was out of bullets, she instead released a venomous shriek. Yanking her left shoe off her foot, she sent it to join the pillow. Her right shoe was quick to follow.

She shivered. The thought of those puffy red lips made her feel queasy. Those. Stupid. Ugly. Red. Lips. She wanted to peel them off the Barbie's pale, plastic face and smack them across the fiend's cheek. The thought of the girl's face sent another shiver down Jade's back. She felt dirty. She needed to shower.

The warm water soothed as it rolled over her gawky shoulders and fell down onto her toes. How Atlantis had managed to have working showers was beyond her comprehension. She focused her mind on this mystery; she desperately needed a solvable problem. Something that she could accomplish. Something that would make her feel competent. Anything to get her mind off that prissy girl. That girl. Jade grabbed a wad of soap and smeared it over her body, rubbing it hard against her skin until it began to burn. The blonde girl had polluted the air and made it toxic. Jade felt contaminated.

She was happy for Cody, of course. Honestly. When she had first met him, he was an awful sight. He was plump as a globe; a kid who continued to put on weight in preparation for a growth spurt that had gone on strike. He was quiet and mostly kept to himself; a solitude that all his classmates had been happy not to disturb.

She never really could pinpoint what exactly had drawn her to her unexpected future best friend. All she knew was that something about him was different. Underneath his quiet demeanor was a boiling passion and a free spirit chained by insecurity. Over the next six years she witnessed that spirit break free. He gained confidence; so much so that even the other classmates seemed willing to accept him back into the world of the living. He was rough around the edges, but Jade always knew he had more character than any of the dimwitted, bimbo jocks all the girls batted their fake-eyelashes at. Now one of those girls had finally noticed what Jade had seen all along; she should feel happy for him—but she was miserable.

You're acting like a jealous child! She ran her fingers through her long dark hair as it fell heavy against her back.

It wasn't fair. Cody was hers. She had been by his side when no one else had. Most importantly, she had seen his worth before he became the wretched Book Keeper! *That stupid, ugly Book!*

Now, it wasn't that Jade desired him in any romantic way. Never. He was like her little brother. She cared about him sure, but love? She remembered how cute he had been on the train to Las Vegas after she had spent the night on his shoulder. He had played cool with the skill of a first-grade drama student. His eyes were beaming and no matter how hard he tried, his mouth kept sneaking into the shape of a smile. That night he had been hers. His shoulder was hers to lie upon and she was his to protect. But those days had come to an abrupt halt. Barbie's disgusting, vomit-inducing kiss on his cheek had been the termination of that contract. Over. Gone. Done.

Now that that phase of their relationship was gone, she realized how much she had enjoyed it. The way Cody looked at her for the last several days felt good. It made her feel like a lady. For once, she felt attractive, and she liked the feeling. But she was going to be a big girl. So what if Cody and his new ditz were friends? She wasn't so weak that one lousy kiss on the cheek would ruin her. She was strong. Jade slid to the ground and pulled her knees into her chest. Only the shower water washing over her masked the tears that poured down her face.

44

Sentenced

Cody stepped into the Monastery unevenly, his head still dizzy from the elevator ride up. He rubbed the back of his hand where Tiana had touched—perhaps the elevator wasn't the only thing that made him dizzy. Cody could still hear his heart beating. It was growing louder . . . and louder. *Wait. That's not my heart . . .*

Suddenly a huge wave of water came crashing over the third story balcony. Cody threw his hands above his head, "*Byrae!*" A gust of wind came billowing through the front door and collided with the crashing water, sending it splashing against the wall. "*Gai di gasme,*" Cody surveyed the now completely soaked room.

From the third balcony Xerx glared down at him. "Not bad, Book Keeper. That was some testimony at the trial. You just couldn't wait to announce your secret to the world. Well, have fun rolling around in your newfound fame and bliss, because very soon everything is going to change. When that time comes we'll see what you're *really* made of. As for me, I'm not holding onto too much hope."

Xerx let a large gob of saliva drip from his mouth and drop toward Cody's face.

"*Byrae!*" Cody yelled again, just in time; a gust of wind sent the clump of spit flying out of harm's way. "*Gai di gasme*".

"Ooff!" came a startled voice. Cody followed the trail of the spit across the room—right into the surprised face of Lamgorious Stalkton who stood in the open doorway. Cody looked back to the balcony; Xerx was nowhere to be seen. *Great, just great.*

"Cody, word has reached me from a little bird that you have been using the Orb's power for less-than-righteous purposes. I trust that similar rumors will never find my ears again," lectured Stalkton firmly. Cody had no doubt that the little bird had been none other than the rare Xerxbird, seemingly indigenous to Cody's private life. He nodded apologetically.

"Then let us move onto more important matters. First, I am sorry to inform you that I have been suffering from severe constipation." Cody took a small step back from his master. "Secondly, your training progress report. So far you have impressed with your ability to master the High Language and its application effortlessly. I'm not yet sure if this is due to your natural talent or simply the leather Book in your backpack. Either way, I am ready to take your training to the next level. Although, perhaps, it would be beneficial first to teach you a creation word which you can use to wash those two lipstick marks off your cheek." Cody quickly rubbed his face with the sleeve of his shirt. He felt his heart beat faster again at the memory of his morning.

"The word I am now going to entrust to you is a significant one. Indeed, in some religious traditions it was the first word in the High Language ever uttered—light. The word in the language of creation is *illumchanta*. Now there is one very important thing you must know about this word . . ."

"*Illumchanta!*" cut in Cody eagerly. A flash of light burst above their heads, floating under the dome ceiling like a star. "*Gai di gasme,*" he finished. The new light reflected off Stalkton's pale skin like a mirror.

"You impatient fool. How a clumsy, reckless boy such as you manages to get lipstick marks on your cheek while I haven't enjoyed the company of a lady friend in two thousand years is beyond me! What I was about to finish explaining is that there is no entity of anti-light. This creation cannot be reversed!" Stalkton said angrily, taking a step back into the shadows.

"What do you mean? Can't you just teach me the word for darkness?" Cody asked bashfully, looking up at the glowing ball floating above their heads.

Stalkton shook his head. "What *is* darkness? Is it the opposite of light, or merely the absence of it? We cannot *make* darkness, although it is always present. Indeed, it is impossible for us to even *stand* in the light without projecting the dark shadow of our silhouette onto the floor. It is only when we *understand* the ever present darkness that we can appreciate the light. However, fortunately for us, your creation skills are noticeably amateur and this light should fade away within several minutes."

"How long would it have lasted had I been more skilled?" Cody asked nervously. Stalkton brought his eyebrows together. "I'm not sure. How long has the sun given light?" he asked, opening the door while his stomach gave a deep growl. "I suddenly feel as though I have gained the upper hand in my fierce battle with constipation and must cut this session short. The last word I wish to leave with you as you go is *bauciv*, the creation word for wood. Practice these words. Know them well. They are the building blocks into a deeper understanding. Tomorrow we will advance to the next stage. Wish me luck!"

Cody couldn't help but walk with a slight strut in his step. Not only was his training going well, but as he walked down the streets of Atlantis back to the Palace, he noticed that all activity froze and voices were silent. He loved being a celebrity; someone interesting who had a purpose. Even as the gong rang over the city and citizens recited the chant of the Orb's Hymn, Cody noticed that many had kept their eyes on him. An image of his father unexpectedly flashed into his mind. *Would he be proud of me now? Would he still have left?* A guilty desire took control of Cody's heart. He wished his father could see him right now, the pride and joy of Atlantis. He knew that if his father were there, he would walk right past him and never look back.

"Cody!" the voice pulled him from his daydreams. He puffed out his chest, and turned to the speaker, hopeful that it was Tiana. It was not. Jade came running down the street directly at him, her eyes red and puffy. He couldn't remember ever seeing her cry. In fact, he often had suspected that she had been born with sterile tear ducts. *Wow, who knew?*

The tear-stained cheeks gave Cody due warning that it was not an appropriate time for joking. "Cody, it's an outrage! I can't believe it; we've got to do something. It isn't right!" Jade stammered. Cody had rarely seen his emotionally-reserved best friend in such hysterics. *Is this about Tiana's kiss? Is there more lipstick on my cheek?*

He grabbed her shoulders. "Take a deep breath, Jade; back up for a second. What is an outrage? What has happened?"

Jade's green eyes bulged. "Then you haven't heard yet? It's all over Atlantis!" she cried, grabbing her temples and breathing in stuttered breaths.

"What haven't I heard? Spit it out, Jade" said Cody shaking his friend by the shoulders.

Jade pushed his arms away. "You selfish boy! How can you not have heard? It's the trial. They've come to their verdict on the trial. Kantan won. That sick, twisted man has won. Cody, don't you get it . . . Randilin's been sentenced to death!"

45

The Inauguration of Death

Death. A word known by all but understood by few. Indeed, there was not a living person on earth, or *in* earth who truly understood it. To Cody, the word was hollow, void of meaning. On some days he thought that perhaps his father, wherever he had gone, was now dead. If true, the irony gave Cody grim satisfaction; his father had abandoned his mother and him in search of life, and instead found death.

But now the abstract idea of death had materialized into a tangible reality. His friend, in some distorted sense of the word, was to be put to death. Randilin. Cody had never learned so much about a man while knowing so little. The man had gone from villain, to guide, to captive, to friend, to convicted mass murderer in the time-span of just over a week.

"What are we going to do? We can't let this happen. Kantan rigged the trial from the beginning. Surely somebody must believe us!" pleaded Jade desperately. She was right; Cody only wished he had realized Kantan's strategy sooner. But whom could they trust? Prince Foz? The brotherly relationship with Kantan made him less than ideal. Dace? Perhaps, but did he hold enough power in Inner-City politics to help them? Sally? Too emotionally compromised. They were alone.

Suddenly Cody's eyebrows drifted up. "There *is* perhaps one person who has the power to overturn Kantan's villainy," he whispered mischievously.

"And, who would that be? Dace?" questioned Jade.

Cody grinned, determination taking full control of his thoughts. "Even better . . . don't you think it's time a certain King came out from his hibernation?" he uttered slowly.

Jade staggered backwards. "Oh, Cody, you can't be serious? Do you expect to just barge into his chambers unannounced?"

Cody's smile widened.

"Oh, my. You're actually serious about this?"

Cody nodded. "The King may disdain conflict, but his city seemingly doesn't. It's time he faced up to things and started acting like a real king. Follow me." Without waiting for a reply, Cody took off running down the streets. Jade caught up to him and their strides fell into sync. For a few moments only the pattering of their soft footsteps filled the void of awkward silence.

After a few speechless blocks Jade cleared her throat, "It seems as though we hardly see each other anymore with all your training," she said meekly. "What's new with you?" Before Cody could answer they reached the palace steps. Cody almost tripped. Looking down he saw his stone heart, blackened by the flames. "Oh, yes. How could I forget?" added Jade coldly. Cody quickly shuffled the still glowing stone aside with his foot and flashed Jade an apologetic look. Jade rolled her eyes, "Forget I asked."

They reached the palace entrance and passed through the large wood doors. Without stopping, they ran up the winding flight of stairs to the royal living quarters. Reaching the top, they saw the King's chamber door at the end of the hall, flanked by two guards. "Well, well. This is an unexpected surprise." Cia circled in front of them. She was wearing a glittery blue dress made of soft blue pearls that mimicked rolling waves as it swayed back and forth. "What brings you two up here in such a hurry?" she asked, eyeing them curiously; her voice flustered and short of breath.

"We . . . we're supposed to meet Prince Foz in his chambers. Which ones are his?" Cody lied.

Cia examined him as though trying to determine between truth and bluff.

"His chambers are two from the end. But, unfortunately, Foz is out of Atlantis right now on diplomatic duties. I shall tell him you stopped by."

Cody grabbed Jade's sleeve as he took slow steps down the hall. "Cody, I said Foz is not here. I order you to leave the royal chambers at once."

Cody pointed toward Cia, "Speak of the devil, there's Foz right there!" Cia spun around to find an empty hall behind her. She grinded her teeth; by the time she spun back around Cody and Jade were already halfway down the hall, running for the door.

"Guards, seize them!" demanded Cia.

Jade gave Cody a desperate look as two guards carrying large axes sprinted toward them. Cody looked to the floor in front of them. *"Bauciv!"* Suddenly a pile of sticks appeared, catching the lead guard unprepared. Stepping on the sticks, his feet slipped out behind him and he flew into the air. There was a loud thud as he landed on his face. The second guard leaped over the sticks and raised his pike.

"Byrae!" shouted Cody.

The sentry cried out as a jolt of wind caught him from behind and sent him soaring down the hall and crashing against the far wall. Cody turned back to see Cia and the first guard back on his feet, running toward them.

"Fraymour!" Cody shouted next as a wave of heat burst the sticks into flame, forming a blazing barrier.

"Gai di gasme," Cody whispered, feeling slightly dizzy and lightheaded.

"Stop now, Cody! If you take one more step, it will be treason" yelled Cia angrily through the fire. Cody approached the King's chambers which were now unguarded. *There's no going back.* With a deep breath, he pulled the doors open. A sickening smell attacked him as soon as he did. The horrendous stench brought vomit to Cody's throat.

He pulled up the front of his shirt and covered his nose. The room was not at all what he had expected. It was a simple, modestly sized, stone walled room with only a few lit torches providing light. Cody saw shadows moving in the corner, "King Ishmael? Is that you? I am the Book Keeper of *The Code.* I request an audience with you," he called into the shadows.

"Cody? What are you doing here?" came a familiar voice from the shadows. Stepping into the light was Prince Foz, "What is the meaning of this? How did you manage to get in here? You must leave immediately!"

"Let them stay. Perhaps it's time they knew the truth," came another voice. Prince Kantan stepped into the light. "You want your audience, Cody? Our father is just over there," he said pointing into the shadows.

Cody took a timid step forward. Something didn't feel right. The ghastly smell was making his stomach turn, but he knew there was no turning back. The silhouette of a bed came into view. A figure was kneeling beside it. Eva. Her eyes were swollen. Mustering up all the resolve he could find, Cody took a final step toward the bed. Lying in the bed was King Ishmael. He was dead.

46

The Lie

Ring Ishmael was dead. There was absolutely no doubt. The wrinkled skin on his face was course and blotchy like molded cheese. His lifeless eyes had sunk into the back of his head and his mouth was gaping open as though his final breath of life had been devoted to a fearful scream of agony. Both his teeth and his lips had turned a flaky black color and white larva had laid claim to his rotting body. Yes, King Ishmael was very much dead.

"You lied to us. Why?" asked Cody looking away from the wraithlike body.

"There was no other choice. It was the only way we could keep Atlantis safe," answered Cia softly as she entered the room, shutting the doors firmly behind her.

"How did he die?" asked Jade somberly, sticking her head out the open window and welcoming the fresh air into her lungs.

Kantan joined her by the window. "He died a rare death. One so rare that never before has anybody in Under-Earth ever experienced it."

"And which way was that?" asked Cody gravely.

Kantan paused for a moment, looking back to his siblings for confirmation, before turning to face Cody. "Our father has died . . . from old age."

The revelation was shocking to Cody. "But, I thought that was impossible? I mean, you guys live forever. The Orb, it makes it so. I saw the picture in Wesley's house; he should have died centuries ago, but he didn't. So everything you've told us has been a lie? Some elaborate conspiracy?" Cody demanded, feeling anger consume his body.

It was Foz who answered next. "Oh, no, no, no. We have never meant to deceive you. We *do* live forever. Sure, men and women died by the scores during the Great War and there is the odd case of unfortunate events resulting in sporadic death from time to time, but none of our kind has *ever* died of natural old age before. At least—not until our father," he finished painfully.

Jade looked back to the horrifying scene of the decaying King. "Why have you kept this secret? If your father is half as good as we've heard, then he deserves better than this. He deserves a royal funeral instead of having his undignified body decompose slowly."

"We agree. He was every bit the man you've heard. But it's not as simple as that," said Cia, "You see, by dying of old age, the power of the Orb is proven to have lost its strength somehow . . ."

"Or proven to have never had any divine power to begin with," cut in Jade. "Perhaps the Orb really *is* nothing more than an energy build-up. Isn't it perfectly logical to accept that you have all lived so long simply because you live under the earth, several thousand miles worth of dirt and rock separating you from any human diseases? Maybe your life has merely been prolonged and Ishmael, being the oldest, is the first to reach the end of the rope?"

"Blasphemy!" yelled Cia. "How *dare* you shame the Orb's power by trying to force it into your childish box of rationality! You disgrace our father by . . ."

Kantan held up his hand to calm his sister, "Quiet sister. The girl speaks reason . . ."

Cia's jaw dropped in disbelief.

"But . . ." continued Kantan, "If I may, allow me to point out that Wesley managed to live quite comfortably up on the earth's surface. How does your logic deal with that fact? Or that your friend Cody here has been able to form objects out of nothing and control the elements with only a few words and a tattered Book?"

"I . . . don't know. But there is obviously an explanation. I'm sure, if you would just give me some more time to work it out I could . . ." Jade mumbled.

"STOP! The one thing we don't have in all of this is *time!*" yelled Cody over the crowd. "Regardless of whether or not the Orb is a divine essence or merely a scientific energy; we still have a rotting corpse lying on this bed that needs to be buried. What are we going to do about it?"

Cia brought her face down an inch from Cody's, "We will do absolutely nothing. As we have said, people don't die here; we don't exactly have many burial options. Our only cemetery is in tribute to the Great War, and I'm not about to defile my father's life by burying him like a common solider. Nor will I allow the faith of our city to be broken by the announcement of his death."

"You kids must understand," continued Kantan, "Atlantis is on the brink of war. If our people were to think that the power of the Orb was fading or even non-existent, as fabricated a thought as it might be, then we would not stand a chance against El Dorado. There no longer would be the need to keep the Orb's power sacred. People would flood toward El Dorado like cattle, free to use the power as they desire. Don't you understand, the truth of our father's death would be disastrous! We will continue to operate as we have. The lie must not be broken."

Kantan held out his long hand. Cody hesitated. He felt the pressure of all the eyes on him. The soft hand of Cia pressed onto his shoulder, "Please, Cody . . ." Cody looked back to Kantan who remained unblinking. Finally, with a sigh, Cody reached out and shook the Prince's hand. "The lie will not be revealed."

Kantan gave an arrogant smirk. "I am glad we can all agree. Now, I think it's about time we gave our father some privacy."

Cia opened the door for Jade to exit before filing out behind her. Kantan stood unmoving, staring at Cody. Cody reluctantly turned and moved toward the door. As he exited he took one last glance at the dead King's agonizing slumber. For the first time something caught his eye. In the King's gaping mouth Cody thought he saw something illuminating in the light. Something he had seen before. He squinted to make out what it was but Kantan's body pushed against him, forcing him out of the room. The door closed with a slam, leaving the good King Ishmael to lie alone in his stone-walled tomb once again.

"I can't believe the guards wouldn't let us see Randilin. His execution is in *two* days! We need to tell him about Ishmael. There's got to be a way to overturn the ruling," spouted Jade as they returned to the palace. "You know what? I'm starting to think that maybe we're on the wrong side. Maybe El Dorado is the good guys. I mean, look at how corrupt and manipulating these people are."

Cody stopped at the door to his chamber. "I don't know, Jade. They aren't all bad. Let's not give up hope on Randilin. Tomorrow we will come up with a plan. But we're going to need our sleep." A deep yawn from Jade added the exclamation point to his statement.

She took a slight step forward, her arms reaching hesitantly toward Cody. But then, as quickly as the motion had begun, it was abandoned, and Jade scurried awkwardly into her chamber. Cody suddenly found himself standing alone in the corridor. He shrugged. *Women.*

Cody pulled off his sweaty shirt, which was damp from the busy day, and flopped down onto his bed. Tomorrow was going to be critically important and he was anxious to get to sleep and recover his strength. The moment he laid his head on his pillow, there was a knock on his door. *Who could that be? Maybe Jade was coming to apologize for embar-*

rassing me in front of Tiana? Or maybe it was Tiana herself? Cody's palms started sweating. He rolled out of bed and walked over to door, pulling it open. Standing bashfully in the hallway was Princess Eva.

"Oh, my goodness," she exclaimed quietly and looked downward to the floor.

Cody uncomfortably felt every square inch of his exposed bare chest. "Um, do you want to come in? I mean, one second, I'll go change." Cody quickly retreated into the room and threw on a fresh tunic. When he returned to the door, Eva was still standing timidly with downcast eyes.

"Why don't you come in?" Cody asked. She gave a humble bow and shuffled into the room. Cody took a seat on the corner of his bed and patted the mattress beside him. "Come have a seat."

Eva's eyes widened and Cody immediately realized his mistake. "Or, you can stand if you'd prefer," he muttered. Eva didn't move. By the look in her eyes, Cody could see something troubled the simple girl. She looked up, and for the first time he was able to look closely at her face. Without Cia's radiating presence beside her, Cody realized that Eva possessed a unique beauty of her own. Not flashy or eloquent like her sister, but still very warm.

"I loved my father," she said in her gentle voice, "He was not a perfect man. But he always took a stand for what he believed was right . . . and he was a good father." Cody was blindsided by the unexpected turn of events. Jade had always teased him that he was the sensitive one in the friendship, but he had never been good at comforting people, especially with issues relating to fathers.

"I'm sorry for your loss, Eva. I am sad that I was never able to meet your father," he offered, squirming on the bed.

Eva smiled, "I'm okay. Most daughters in your world only get fifty, maybe sixty years with their father. Is that not so? Who am I to complain about spending three thousand years with mine? Don't worry; I have not come here seeking comfort. I have come . . . to warn you."

Cody jerked his head. "To warn me? Warn me about what?" Cody asked surprised.

Eva dropped her voice to a whisper, "To warn you that my family is not in their proper state. They have contrived this lie to conceal my father's death, but I fear they do so for selfish reasons. Fear has corrupted their thoughts. They no longer mourn for our father; they seek to use his death to gain power. Did you know that Kantan and Cia are twins? They are also equal heirs to the throne. I fear that they will suck you into the lie. They will use your power to further their games," she finished firmly. Cody couldn't suppress a smile; he was genuinely surprised. Eva shook her head, "I am not crazy. I may be the youngest of my siblings and have no heart for their politics, but I have walked for longer than your Upper-Earth history spans. I have to go, if my siblings were to discover that I've been here . . ."

Eva froze. There was a scratching sound outside the door. Cody jumped off the bed, and shielded Eva with his arm. "Shhhhh, get behind me!" The door-knob began to jiggle. Cody stepped over to his nightstand and placed his palm on the scarlet 'A' of the Book. "I'll block the door with stone. *Gadour!*" he yelled. Nothing happened. The door-knob shook more violently. Cody yelled again, "*Gadour!*

Gadour! Bauciv! Seamour!" Still nothing happened. "Something's wrong! The Book isn't working! It's like something is preventing me from using the Orb's power. I don't understand. . . . Quick, to the window, Eva!" But he was too late. The door flung open.

Cody squinted, "Dace? What on earth are you doing here? You scared the bejibbees out of me!" Cody yelled in irritation, exhaling a deep breath.

Dace gave a quick grin before returning to an unusually stern expression. "Just keeping you on your toes. But I'm afraid we don't have time for any more fun and games. Foz sent me to retrieve you; General Levenworth has called a secret war council. As the Book Keeper your presence is required."

Eva stepped out from the shadows of the room. "A council? At this time of night? What's happening?" she questioned timidly.

Dace's lips folded into a grin as he saw the Princess, looking from her to Cody, and then back to Eva. "We suspect an El Dorado invasion. That's all I know. We will be briefed at the council. Cody, they are waiting." Dace gave Eva a low bow, and Cody awkwardly followed the example. The two exited the chambers, walking briskly to the war room.

Once out of earshot, Dace elbowed Cody hard in the ribs. "Ouch! What was that for?" Cody exclaimed, rubbing his side.

Dace winked at him, "First the cute green-eyed girl, now a royal princess? You *are* a sly devil! Although I should warn you, I'd be careful with that one. Ever since . . . *the accident,* during the Great War she's been . . . different. Although I'm guessing you probably don't need me to tell you that . . ." Cody nodded silently. "Yeah . . . different . . ." he uttered distractedly, the image of Eva's innocent eyes immobile in his mind.

The tingling sensation in her skin prickled like the aftermath of a resilient fire. She held up her arms and examined the invisible feeling. *It's happened again.* The faint voices of Dace and Cody could still be heard as they drifted away down the corridor. After several moments the voices faded into silence. It didn't matter—she had already heard enough. Eva squeezed her eyelids closed, releasing a lone tear. She was different; a fact reiterated for her with painful frequency. Always spoken to as though a child, always spoken about as though invisible. She sighed. *One day they will understand.* Slowly the tingling in her skin faded away, leaving a slight glow in its wake.

47

A Growing Threat

Invasion is imminent! The only question is: when?" The rich, booming voice of General Gongore Levenworth rang authoritatively over the small room. To his left sat the bald man with ivory skin whom Cody had first seen during Randilin's trial, and beside him sat Dace. To the General's right were Kantan, Cia, and Foz. Silkian sat in the corner of the room silently, looking as slimy as ever. Two other men sat across the table from the General. They were both rugged in appearance and donning full soldier armor. Cody sat at the other corner of the table, sinking into his chair and feeling completely out of place.

"The Golden King surely plans an invasion. It is no coincidence that he has mobilized his troops after centuries of peace. Clearly, this comes only because our foolish Book Keeper announced so dramatically to the world *The Code's* location." Cody melted even farther into his chair.

"Objection!" called out Dace, "The odds that Cody's proclamation could have reached the Golden King already are unlikely. Even with tunnel-phone the chances are slim. Besides, there has been troop activity for months now."

Levenworth strolled around the table, stopping in front of Dace. "Indeed, there has . . . but not like this." Levenworth motioned to the two soldiers sitting across from Cody. "These two scouts have just arrived from the borderlands with fresh news. Private Tat Shunbickle, report."

The taller of the two soldiers stood. "Several months ago we began noticing increased activity around the border. One night we went to sleep staring out over the great desert divide, clear as the horizon. We woke to the sight of tents in the distance. Forty, maybe fifty. A day later, there were well over one hundred just sitting out there. Day by day the tents multiplied like a spreading cancer. Before long, thousands of them were dotting the desert like house flies. Captain Talgu ordered us to take a closer look. Under cover of nightfall, we crossed the border and got in close to the camp. There is no doubt that this was a camp built for war."

"And what makes you say so? There are plenty of nonwar related reasons for such a camp, are there not?" questioned the Captain of the Mid-City guards.

The Soldier nodded, "True, Captain Eagleton, however, several observations convinced us otherwise. For example, the men in the tents were undoubtedly warriors. Their skin . . . it was . . . armored . . . so-to-speak."

"Their *skin* was armored?" asked Kantan, crunching his stern face as though mishearing the report. "Don't you mean their skin was *covered* in armor?"

The Private shivered. "No, Sir. We didn't get a good look, but it appeared as though plate mail of gold was literally fused into their body. I've never seen anything like it before in all my years. It was as though the skin and the armor were one," the soldier's voice tailored off retrospectively.

"Thank you, solider, for your report," said Levenworth.

The once silent soldier began to squirm, muttering softly to himself, "Demons from below. Demons. Eyes that do not see . . ." The entire table turned to the soldier who was verging into hysteria. The first soldier put his hand on his partner's shoulder to silence him.

The Private turned to the General, "Sir, I'm afraid there's more. The golden men are not the only beings in the camp. There is . . . something else." The second soldier's eyes bulged and his face began to twitch violently; the Private continued, "On the second evening my comrade and I managed to infiltrate the camp. Our mission was to gauge the number of warriors. However, when we reached the center of the camp we discovered something." The soldier stopped, attempting to calm his partner.

"Well, what was it?" demanded Kantan impatiently.

The soldier's face was full of fear. "I don't know. We only got a quick glance. But that one look was enough. There were men in the center of the camp, or at least they looked like men."

Lady Cia stood from her chair. "What do you mean they *looked* like men? What else could they be if not men?" she questioned.

"I don't claim to know what they were, honorable lady, only what my eyes saw. They had the bodies of men, yet there was something missing. They were . . . empty. I don't know how to explain it, but they looked like hollow bodies.

Soul-less wraiths. They were just standing there, not sleeping or blinking. Just staring at us with empty eyes. Excuse my honesty, but it was the most terrifying sight I had ever seen. My comrade here is still suffering from shock."

"How many?" demanded Levenworth sternly. "How many of these, hollow men were there. Five? Ten? How many?"

The soldier shook his pale face, "Hundreds."

A chill flowed through Cody's body. He watched as that same chill circulated the room.

Foz broke the cycle. "I believe there is only one possible course of action. Atlantis' troops should be sent immediately to the city of Lilley to bolster the strength of our border. An attack is coming," he said firmly.

Kantan brought his fist down onto the table with a crash. "We send out troops to Lilley and we *guarantee* an attack. The moment the Golden King senses that we are preparing for an assault he will move quickly. He will not sacrifice the advantage of first strike. Gathering our troops at the border is nothing but an invitation. No offense, little brother, but not all war strategy can be learned from your silly books. I ask you to leave the decisions to those experienced in war. If we have a question of gardening you will be the first one we ask . . ." mocked Kantan cruelly.

Foz sat back into his chair dejectedly.

Levenworth paced back and forth. "I agree with Kantan. It is too risky to take any action that might provoke an attack, especially while we are vulnerable and unfit for combat. Captains, your stance?"

Captain Eagleton nodded without hesitation. "Our forces are not yet ready to fight should El Dorado take our reinforcement effort as a threat. We should not take the risk."

Dace nodded as well. "I agree that the wisest action is to remain as is. However, if I may insert a personal concern, I fear that Prince Foz is correct as well. The city of Lilley is not fortified or equipped with enough men or resources to repel an invasion of this scale. If El Dorado strikes, Lilley will be massacred. Would it not make sense to . . ."

"Opinion heard, Captain Dace. That will be enough," ordered Levenworth, silencing the captain. "We will stay the course for the time being and let the situation unfold. Council dismissed."

"Wait, what about our Book Keeper? Shouldn't his voice be heard?" objected Foz, motioning to Cody.

Kantan sneered. "The Book Keeper is not one of us. Mere unexplained luck and inherited power does not constitute the right of a political voice. This is a matter of Atlantis and is of concern to Underlings, not Surface-Dwellers. We've already seen how their knowledge of war has turned out."

"Yes, because you wouldn't know anything about inherited power now would you, Prince Kantan?" Cody blurted out before he could catch his words. The three royal siblings gave him intense looks of caution. He had struck a chord too close to the truth. He was still bound by the lie.

Kantan stared disdainfully at him. "Council dismissed."

48

A Record-Setting Sunset

Cody wiped the sleep from his eyes as he jogged after Jade. She was less than interested in his recap of the previous night's war council meeting as more pressing concerns plagued her thoughts. "That's unimportant right now. All that matters is that we have a friend who has an appointment with the gallows in two days. Stay focused, Cody!" she blurted as she led the way toward the prison. After his conviction, Randilin had been transferred to maximum security.

A gong sounded over the city. Cody knelt down but Jade dragged him forward by his sleeve. "We don't have time for silly ritualistic nonsense." Cody scanned around for Enforcers. Thankfully there were none to be seen.

They reached the prison. It was a square structure constructed entirely of stone. Other than the barred and bolted front steel doors, there was no window or access inside. Six armed guards stood stiffly upright outside the entrance. Cody nodded as he approached, giving the sentry a good look at his face; the face of the Book Keeper. Without any return motion, the guard unbolted the gate. With the help of two other guards, they slowly pulled the heavy door open. Cody followed Jade inside.

There was a slam as the door closed, concealing the room in total blackness. "Hello? Who's there?" came a feeble voice. It was Randilin. *"Illumchanta,"* whispered Cody. An orb of light rocketed from his fingers and crashed into the ceiling forming a star. Bright rays sprinkled down into the room like fireworks.

"'Bout time you goats stopped by," snarled Randilin. If he had looked in rough shape before, he now seemed only moments from death. Dark purple bruises covered the entire left side of his face, and dried blood coated his bottom lip. His arms were bound by chains, which had completely rubbed off the skin on his wrists.

"What have they done to you?" cried Jade, softly grabbing his arm to examine his scars.

He pulled his arm away violently. "Let me be. Our mutual friend, Prince Kantan, and his muse, General Levenworth, have paid me a few visits. They seem to think my execution will prevent them the future joys of torturing me, so they are getting in their fill now. What news have you from the land of the living?"

Cody told of the reported activity in the borderlands. Like Jade, Randilin showed little concern, "Well, unless El Dorado attacks tomorrow, I won't be around to see it," he concluded grimly.

Jade felt anger welling up within her. "Surely there's something we can do to prevent your hanging. Think guys, there's got to be something."

Randilin's head rolled back and rested on the iron bars of his cell. "I'm afraid not. The only one who can reverse a ruling is the King himself. And I wouldn't count on Ishmael to interfere, he didn't even show up to the trial."

Cody looked to Jade and swallowed. "They don't own me. If they want to lie then power to them, but I've had enough," Cody said with release.

"What are you talking about? Lie about what?" Randilin asked, bringing his bloated face to rest between two iron bars.

"Randilin . . . the King is dead." Cody explained about their break-in to the King's chambers and their horrible discovery. Randilin listened silently.

When Cody finished, Randilin hung his head low. "Long live King Ishmael. He was a good king, and a better man. Unfortunately his death is untimely. The only man with the power to prevent my death is a man dead himself. The sun sets on Randilin, and the world says good riddance."

There was a crash as the steel door was slammed closed, once again leaving Randilin to his solitary purgatory. Jade brought her black hair over her shoulder and stroked it like a cat. "Perhaps we can convince the royal family to pardon him on their father's behalf?" she suggested as they sauntered gloomily back toward the palace.

Cody shook his head. "I wouldn't count on it. One of them would have to be appointed as the new ruler, which is impossible while they continue to lie. And besides, they hate Randilin, especially Kantan. Cia seems indifferent, Foz has no real influence in the family and Eva is . . . well, Eva. She's treated by her siblings like a child. If we are going to save Randilin, it won't be through them," Cody concluded.

"Well, well, well, if it isn't the famed Book Keeper himself! What an excellent surprise." Stepping out from the market was Tiana. "And, hello to you too Jade," she finished in a tone of boredom. Jade stared unflinchingly ahead as though she didn't hear the greeting. Cody felt the lump in his throat return,

"Tiana!" he blurted out with childish delight. His face flushed as he cleared his throat. "I mean, hi, Tiana . . ." his eyes dropped down to his feet. "Well. Anyways. I was just on the way to my training. I'm busy. I mean busy right now. Well. Not like *right* now, obviously, because that wouldn't make any sense . . . wow . . . um . . ." Cody continued to splutter on, helpless to stop the catastrophic train wreck unfolding before him, and completely inept to think of anything even remotely interesting to say. He felt his face grow redder with each agonizing syllable.

Tiana held her skinny finger to Cody's lips. "Shhh. Just meet me back here after your training. . . . I've got something special planned. If that's okay with Jade, of course?" she asked in her singsong voice. Jade grunted, pivoted, and walked away without responding. Tiana grinned and gave Cody a wink. "Well, I guess I'll see you tonight."

"I hope you are free of any distractions! Because today's lesson is one of the most imperative of all!" lectured Stalkton, "Indeed, the life-altering significance this lesson had

on me in my youth was immense—not equaled until that delightful night I accidently misplaced my clothes and discovered the blissful comfort of sleeping in the nude . . ."

Cody nodded attentively, although he hadn't soaked in any of the words. Instead he was swimming in a hurricane. *What did Tiana have planned?* The feeling of her soft finger on his lips still tingled . . .

"Up until now, you have been limited to one creation product per one creation word," continued Stalkton. "This, however, is not a limitation of the words, but only of your mind. When you used the creation word, *bauciv*, for example, what happens?"

Cody shrugged. "I create a stick. It's pretty straight forward."

Stalkton folded his hands together. "Is it? And, why is it that you make a stick?"

Cody shook his head. "I don't know, because it's the word for stick . . ."

"Wrong!" exclaimed Stalkton. "The word *bauciv* is only the word for stick because in your *mind* it is the word for stick. Do you follow?" the priest questioned, flailing his arms around as he lectured. "*Bauciv* is actually the word for a specific particles of cosmos energy which, when highly concentrated, forms the material essence that our human understanding classifies as wood. When you use the word, your subconscious pre-understanding of wood equaling a stick results in the creation of a stick. Let me ask you, when the divine creator used the Orb to create the world how many sticks were around?"

"I guess there were none," Cody answered.

Stalkton nodded. "Exactly! You see, by his infinite creative imagination the word was used to form trees and forests. He was not limited to a preconceived image. The words are not cookie cutters; they are paintbrushes. You must unlearn your mind to achieve the full heights of your creative potential. Try using the word, but allow your mind to float away from a rigid understanding. Unchain your mind . . ."

Cody cleared his throat. "*Bauciv! Gai di gasme.*" In the blink of an eye there was a patter as a strange object appeared on the floor.

Stalkton chuckled. "Perhaps I should have been more specific. Class dismissed. I think it's safe to say your mind is elsewhere." With another laugh, the teacher picked up the object and tossed it to Cody. Cody grabbed it and instantly blushed. The object in his hand was a smooth, polished, wooden carving the size of his palm. The wood was in the shape of two, puffy lips.

Glistening red lips were the first thing Cody noticed as he rounded the corner. They rose into a grin. "I was beginning to think you weren't coming. That you were too nervous . . . ," Tiana said playfully. Cody smiled back as coolly as he could. "What's that in your hand? Some kind of carving?" Tiana probed curiously.

Cody looked down to the wooden lips. "Oh, nothing," he uttered in a panicked voice while shoving the carving into his backpack. "You said you had something planned for tonight?" he asked, changing the subject.

Tiana ran her fingers down Cody's cheek. "I do . . . but I can't tell you about it. You'll just have to follow me." She took off running down the street. Cody smiled. Tiana was unpredictable—and he loved it. He rushed after her, her thick blonde hair swaying as she ran.

She led him down alleys and through crowds of people. When she eventually stopped, Cody was out of breath. They were standing underneath a very familiar structure. "Here? The Sanctuary of the Orb? We're back at the Monastery!" Cody exclaimed in surprise, "Surely we aren't allowed in here. I thought access to The Orb was forbidden on penalty of death?"

Tiana laughed. "You worry too much. It is against the law to go *into* the Sanctuary . . . but nobody said anything about getting *close*." She winked, and disappeared around the side of the building. The moment Cody caught up, his heart sank. She was standing on the pulley elevator. *Might as well be eating spaghetti tonight,* he thought hopelessly.

Luckily for him, Tiana was too captivated by the view to notice his terrified face and white knuckles on the way up. They jumped onto the balcony as they reached the top. "You had me join you just to bring me back to where I already was? What are we doing up here anyways?" Cody asked, confused.

Tiana grabbed his hand. "Shhhh. There's a lot about me you don't know. But relax, I'm not doing the crazy, albino priest's dirty work by retrieving you for a second lesson, just follow me." She took off running again, jumping up on the thin stone ledge and prancing across the edge of the balcony.

"Get down, it's not safe!" called Cody instinctively.

Tiana looked over her shoulder. "You are such a *wimp*. Loosen up! Here we are." Tiana jumped gracefully from the ledge. They had reached the end of the balcony that had been concealed by shadows. Cody stepped into the shade and stopped.

The stone wall was not a wall at all, but instead a rustic door. Tiana heaved it open to reveal another elevator, similar to the first. "I discovered this years ago. I'm not sure what it was used for. Perhaps it's merely a maintenance access. Or maybe it was a secret route to The Orb for the priests of old! Either way, it's ours now. Come on!" She jumped on and it swayed beneath her weight.

Cody took a slow step forward. "Are you sure we're allowed? I mean, what if we get caught?" Cody asked timidly.

"What if you get caught, indeed?" came a voice from behind. Xerx stepped into the light, "Being the *all-powerful* Book Keeper does not give you exemption from the rules. Take one more step and I'll report you to Master Stalkton," he warned mockingly.

"Oh, step off Xerxus, you cowardly muskrat. We both know you will do no such thing," laughed Tiana.

Xerx's eyes bulged. "Ti? What are you doing here? I didn't see you . . . what are you doing with Cody? I didn't know, I mean, I hadn't seen. I . . ."

Tiana put her arm around Cody's waist and pulled him onto the platform. "When you finish gathering your thoughts, Xerx, let us know," she called back mockingly. She unhooked a rope and Cody found himself soaring above the balcony. Xerx's bewildered face slowly shrunk into a spec on the ground far below.

Cody was speechless as he looked out over the city thousands of feet below him. Lights flickered and people the size of dots moved about the streets. The elevator brought them to the very top of the building. They were now standing on the roof of the Sanctuary.

Cody's fear of heights was defused by the surprising sight before him. "Tiana. Do you . . . *live* up here?" A bed of feathers and blankets was laid out like a bird's nest beside the remains of a small fire. Several woven baskets sat on the other side of the bed filled with clothes and various other trinkets. Hanging over the bed like a tent canopy were banners of soft, transparent silk sheets. Cody felt the warmth of Tiana's body as it pressed beside him. "It's not much, but it's home . . ." she said with a quiet laugh.

"It's lovely. But I don't understand. Why live all the way up here? Why not in the city like everyone else?" asked Cody in bewilderment. Tiana shrugged. "Where in town can you get this kind of quiet privacy? Or this view? Besides, I have everything I need up here."

"But don't you get lonely? Don't you have any family you could stay with . . ." Cody stopped; an unfamiliar look had transformed Tiana's face.

"I said I have everything I need up here, okay?" she responded coldly. Cody opened his mouth to apologize but Tiana's face broke back into grin. "Don't worry about it. Anyways, we don't have much more time until it happens. I want to show you something . . ."

"Before *what* happens?" questioned Cody, but she had already scampered away. When he caught up to her she was standing on a small balcony. Cody stepped out beside her and for the first time he got a full view of the massive size of the city as it stretched out all around him. Beyond the city gates Cody could see for miles across the flat landscape. Tiana's arm pointed over his shoulder. "You see that, those are the Labyrinth Mountains; they separate our land from El Dorado's. The Borderlands." The mountains were almost invisible off in the distance, but even from such a distance, they looked immense. They were not so much mountains as imperial pillars that stretched up and connected with the earth above, as though holding up the cave's roof. Cody rarely looked toward the sky, as it gave him the uncomfortable feeling of being trapped in a cave, although Dace had assured him that the ceiling of the cave was actually hundreds of miles high.

There was a soft humming and clicking noise behind him. "What's going on?" Cody asked.

Tiana giggled and pointed to the floor. "You don't think I brought you all the way up here just to show you my meek dwelling did you? Have you not wondered about Atlantis' sunsets?" Cody nodded, remembering the bizarre, instantaneous changes between night and day. Tiana answered her own question, "Well, obviously as Underlings we don't have access to the sun light you Surface Dwellers do. Any light we have in Atlantis is provided by the Orb itself. Think of The Sanctuary like a giant eye. When the eye is open, the light from the Orb shines out to the very ends of Under-Earth; when closed, it is night. What you are witnessing now—is an Atlantis sunset."

The light from the structure burst forth over the city in a blinding flash—and then the landscape went pitch dark, as though somebody had flipped off a light switch. One by one the lamps in the city were lit like a lightshow of fireflies. "It's beautiful!" exclaimed Cody as the lights danced across the city. "None of this feels real! To be up here and seeing all this . . . with you." For a moment his words hung in the air as the lights of the city continued to flicker like a giant wave rolling across land. Cody began to feel uncomfortable. "Well I guess I should probably get back now that it's dark, I'm sure Jade will be wondering . . ."

Cody stopped. He felt the warmth of Tiana's hands as they wrapped around his waist. The hands guided him slowly around. The air around him was pitch dark; all he could see were shadows and silhouettes. "Um, Ti, are you there?" he asked, peering into the blackness. He felt the warmth of breath upon his face, and then the tender wetness of lips pressing against his. "I think Jade can wait a few more minutes, don't you?"

Cody gulped; his insides were a tangled mess. He didn't respond—he couldn't, his parched throat wouldn't let him. Instead, he stumbled dizzily away, his lips still tingling.

The next thing Cody knew, he was riding the pulley elevator back to the surface. He rubbed his sweaty temples, the veins pulsating in rhythm with his pounding heart. *What just happened?* Everything was a blur. But there was one thing Cody *did* know. Either he was dreaming or he had just experienced the best moment of his life.

49

The Prince's Chambers

Cody's shoes squeaked against the stone floor as he tip-toed toward his bedroom. He paused before Jade's door; light still flicked from underneath. She was awake. Cody reached for his door-knob and opened it with a creak; he went to step inside but paused. He stepped back out and closed the door again. Moments later the light from beneath Jade's door went out. *She was waiting for me to return.* Quietly opening his door again he slipped back inside.

Although, the way his heart was pounding, he did not expect to get much sleep.

"How was last night; exhilarating I suppose?" asked Jade as she casually munched down on a soft piece of rock cake.

Cody buttered his own piece. "It was enjoyable, yes. And yours?" he asked without looking up.

Jade swallowed her bite. "Same. I said goodbye to Sally. She is returning above ground to her post at the café. Foz offered to let her stay until tomorrow, after the execution, but she refused. She said she wanted to be as far away from here as possible. Who could blame her? After that, I returned to my room and slept soundly. I didn't even hear you return last night."

Cody risked a look at her, but didn't push the issue. "What are you doing today? More training? Don't suppose that blonde-haired Barbie will be able to keep herself away for a whole day. Not now that you're the powerful Book Keeper," she muttered with a trace of sarcasm.

Cody stood. "Her name is Tiana, by the way. And she's not like you think. She's a free spirit. She's wild, unpredictable even. We have a lot in common. But yes, I have another training session; although I have something I need to do first."

"And what is that?" asked Jade defensively.

Cody shrugged. "Not sure exactly, might be nothing. But I have a hunch and I want to check it out." Grabbing another loaf of the surprisingly tasty rock cake, he left the room. He was glad to be alone. After experiencing a night of Tiana's *take-life-as-it-comes* attitude, he found Jade's strictly-scheduled personality draining.

He returned to his room. Shutting the door he quickly fastened the lock and went to his open window. He looked down upon the garden; there was no sign of Prince Foz or anyone else. Cody examined the outside wall. If he had done his calculations correctly, his target should be two stories up and four down from his room. *Cody, I sure hope you know what you're doing.* He held out his arms like a cross, and taking a deep breath, he jumped off the balcony.

"*Bauciv! Gai di gasme!*" Suddenly, he felt the texture of tree bark in his hands. The wood was in the shape of wings. "*Byrae!*" A blast of wind came billowing from below. As it collided with his wooden wings he felt himself soaring through the air. His stomach was suspended in his chest. He held out his arms to steady himself, and then began flapping the wooden wings around his arms. Slowly he began to rise. Grinning, he gave one powerful flap and his body soared through the air toward his target.

Tucking in his arms, he went flying through an open window. With a loud crash he face-planted into the floor and skidded to a clumsy stop against a cushioned chair. "*Gai di gasme,*" he muttered with a groan. *My landings are going to need a bit of work!*

Cody stood up to examine the room for the first time. It was spacious, with a bulky bed in the middle, satin curtains draping the sides. Against one wall was a polished oak desk. A grand stone fire-place claimed the other wall. Above the fire-place was a vast painting: a portrait of Prince Kantan. *How fitting.*

He didn't know how much time he had; he needed to work fast. *There has to be proof of Kantan's guilt somewhere in here!* He went to the desk cluttered with papers and various trinkets. Prince Kantan did not strike Cody as the sloppy type, which meant there was only one reason why his desk would be messy: *He's still working.*

Cody franticly began pushing aside papers until one caught his eye. Stopping, he picked it up and began to read.

It was a letter. The ink was still setting—it had just been written. As Cody read, his hands began to sweat. It was exactly what he had hoped to find. It was perfect. Folding it carefully, he stuck it into his pocket.

Suddenly a noise sounded from the hallway. Cody's body became rigid and unmoving. He held his breath, but heard nothing more from the corridor. At last, assured that the coast was clear, he exhaled. *If I get caught I'm dead! I better hurry.*

He quickly opened the top drawer of the desk. Reaching in, he pulled out a serrated dagger. The razor sharpness of the blade pricked his finger, instantly drawing a bead of blood. *Ouch!* As he returned the knife a glimmer caught his eye. His fingers wrapped around a small, smooth object. He pulled out a glass vial containing a colorful object of blue and orange. *I think I've seen this before, but what is it?* He didn't have time to ponder. He slipped the vial into his pocket alongside the letter. Turning to leave, he stopped. His eyes fell to the bottom drawer of the desk. It was the only drawer to have a thick deadbolt fastened to it. As Cody looked closer he realized that the bolt had not been locked and the drawer had been left slightly open. *He must have just been in there. Why only lock THAT drawer?* Cody wondered.

Drawn by his curiosity, he swiftly returned to the desk and drew open the drawer; the lone object inside was a framed picture. Lifting it out Cody realized that it was a painting of two people. On the right was Kantan, although he looked much younger and there was surprisingly no trace of his stern demeanor. Instead he was flashing a boyish grin. Cody hardly recognized him with such a foreign, jubilant appearance. On the Prince's left was a woman. She was beautiful. Her face was plump and merry with long, frizzy blonde hair. Her expression was warm and inviting. She too had a playful smile on her face. Her hand was intertwined with Kantan's. The bottom of the painting had a simple caption: Kantan and Arianna. *Who is she?*

He froze. His ears perked up: the soft pattering sound of footsteps approached. Somebody was coming. The sound was getting nearer. Cody flung the picture back and pushed the drawer closed. The door-knob began to jiggle. *Oh, no!* In horror, Cody saw that the blood from his finger had left blaring smears all over the desk. *Nothing I can do about it now!* Grabbing his wooden wings he dashed across the room. There was a soft creak as the door opened. Without hesitation, Cody dove headfirst out the window.

The air pounded against his face as he freefell like a boulder. He opened his mouth but no words came out. *Oh, no.* He opened it again—nothing. *What's the creation word for wind!* His mind had gone blank. The earth rushed rapidly toward him. Cody flapped his arms desperately as he plummeted to the ground. He squeezed his eyes shut. **Thud**.

50
Yanci's Pub

———

Pain. Excruciating Pain. Cody felt every square inch of his battered body throbbing in unbearable pain. "OO-OUUUCCCHHH!" He screamed again—and again; each time attempting to somehow one-up the previous scream in level of anger and anguish.

"Good heavens, what in the name of all that's holy happened to you!?" came a raised voice. Cody felt his body being turned over. *Oooouch!*

Foz stared down at him with a look of utter bewilderment. "My gosh, Cody, it looks as though you've had a mountain fall on top of you."

Or dove out of a third-story window into a face-plant. He cringed; even thinking somehow made his body ache. "I'm fine. Just doing some . . . practicing. I better get going though, nice to see you again, Foz." With a grunt Cody pushed himself to his feet and headed toward the street.

"Gelph, have you seen Dace?" Cody asked impatiently as he came across the beggar.

Gelph fell against the wall in a fit of laughter. "Tell me again, son, how'd your face get so purple and puffy like that? I mean, you look worse than me and *I'm* the homeless one!" he laughed again as he turned and headed on his way without answering Cody's question.

Cody heard another noise—the sound of shattering glass followed by jeering and laughter. Cody took off jogging. Why had he even bothered asking where Dace was? There was only one place he would be—Yanci's pub.

Cody turned the corner and entered into the heart of a brawl. The front window had been shattered and Cody didn't have to look hard to see why: the limp body was draped over the ledge. Cody ducked as a bottle of ale soared over his head. He scurried across the street, hoping to escape the fight entirely.

A thick hand slapped him on the back. "Well, looky here, if it ain't our new Book Keeper." The large bodies of Hex and Sheets blocked Cody's path. "Take a look at this here, Hex, the boy's gone and gotten his face turned into a plum! I think Wolfrick is rubbing off on the boy!"

Cody's nose flared at the comment. "Well, what are you guys doing here anyway?" Cody asked, hoping to change the subject.

Sheets laughed. "Oh, we're just here in case things get out of control" he responded matter-of-factly. Cody's eyes widened as an unconscious body flopped down at his feet.

"In case things *get* out of control?" Another ale bottle soared toward Cody's head; Hex reached out and caught it before it struck. Popping the cap, he took a hearty swig. "Yeah, it's a bit of a slow night for us tonight. Nothing like last night; ol' Timon still hasn't regained consciousness. But don't worry, look over there, Wolfrick's sure *on top* of things!" he laughed. Cody saw the flailing body of Wolfrick hoisted into the air by the mob who carried him down the alley.

"What are they going to do to him?" Cody asked worriedly.

Sheets and Hex shrugged at the same time. "Oh, nothing he doesn't have coming. I'm sure he'll show up again in a day or two. Anyways, if you're here to speak to Dace he's inside." Cody watched the crowd of drunks carry Wolfrick's limp body farther away, his slurred cursing echoing into the night. Cody shook his head; these Outer-City folk were of a different breed.

He stepped into Yancy's and found it surprisingly calm after the violent showcase outside. He scanned the crowded room for sight of Dace and found him sitting at a table in the corner. Cody approached the table but paused, realizing that Dace was not alone. There was an attractive female under each of his arms and he appeared to be entertaining them with a lively tale. Cody started to walk back toward the door.

"Cody? Hey, it's Cody! Where you sneaking off to? Come here!" called Dace. Cody walked hesitantly back to the table. "Well, ladies, I'm afraid this tale of bravery will have to wait for another time. The boy and I have some business." The two ladies sighed, planted two solid kisses on Dace's forehead, and left the table. Cody took a seat across from Dace, who leaned forward. "Ouch. What happened to you? You look like a walking plum!"

"Story for another time. How are things with you?" Cody asked quickly.

Dace brought his two hands behind his head and leaned his chair against the wall. "If you mean with me *personally* . . ." he pointed across the room where the two girls were still staring at him and batting their eyelashes. Dace leaned in close to Cody and whispered, "But if you mean for Atlantis, then the answer is not good. Word has reached us by tunnel-phone from the border city of Flore Gub that more tents have appeared on the horizon."

Cody stared blankly. Dace again leaned forward, "Let me give you a quick geography lesson. The Labyrinth Mountains stretch across the borderlands of our two provinces, Atlantis and El Dorado. There are only two passes through the mazelike mountains into our land. The first is impassable over the Great Sea of Lava. The second is blocked by our fortress at Flore Gub. However, the peaceful outpost village Lilley lies beyond the fortress, on the border. It is a small, but indefensible settlement. These camps are not mere coincidence—El Dorado is preparing a full-scale invasion."

"What are we going to do? Should we send out troops to the borderlands to protect Lilley?" Cody asked.

Dace swallowed a sip of ale. "That's the thing; it's not as easy as that. General Levenworth refuses. Even if he *was* willing, Prince Kantan has forbidden it. He says he will not risk the safety of Atlantis by vacating the already meager troops from the city. With all the unrest, he feels our soldiers are better served in the capital."

"So, he's willing to sacrifice two of his other cities? Kantan is a mad man. What if he isn't sending troops because he *wants* there to be a massacre? I think he's in league with El Dorado," Cody declared rashly.

Dace held his finger to his mouth, "Shhh! Even in the Outer-City it is unwise to make such a treasonous accusation. I'll admit, I think he is acting unwisely. I agreed with him at first, but since the reports from Flore Gub I think only a fool is blind to see that the Golden King has his black heart set on invasion. He can't resist, not with *The Code* back in Atlantis. But to say that Kantan is *deliberately* acting this way to aid the Golden King, that is a far stretch."

"What about General Levenworth? Surely he has the power to do something? Won't *he* listen to reason?"

Dace shook his head. "Old Gongore is without question the most brilliant warfare tactician who has ever lived. He could challenge an entire legion of elite enemy troops with nothing more than a handful of rookie recruits welding wooden play-swords and still strategize his way to an outright rout of the enemy. He is also extremely old school. He obeys the royal family's orders, no questions asked. I'm afraid all we can do is sit and wait. It's like closing your eyes and jumping off a cliff. You know you'll eventually hit the ground but you don't know when. The anticipation is almost worse than the actual landing."

Cody winced; his throbbing face begged to differ. "Well, I've actually come to see you for a different reason. Will you be attending the hanging tomorrow?"

Dace nodded. "Yes, as the officer responsible for Randilin's capture, I am obligated to oversee the execution. And before you ask anything further, there is absolutely nothing in either my desire or my power that I can do to prevent it from happening."

"I don't expect you to. I only ask that tomorrow you are . . . prepared. I need to know I can count on you."

Dace tilted his head quizzically. "You had better not be planning on doing something stupid, Cody. Randilin forfeited his life by his actions; don't become his last victim. Don't waste your important life in some idealistic rescue crusade."

Cody stood up from his seat. "Just be prepared, Dace. That's all I ask."

Cody followed the echoing sound of pounding nails to the market square. There was no trace of the lively people or the colorful sales tents. In their place sat a wooden stage. The gallows. Several hooded men crept over the structure like insects, making final adjustments. Cody watched as the men hoisted a wooden mannequin onto the stage. They placed the noose around its neck. One of the hooded men held up three fingers. *Three . . . Two . . . One.* There was a clatter as they released the trapdoor. The noose tightened around the wooden figure's neck. There was a loud crack as the body crumbled down the trapdoor, leaving the head in the vise-grip of the noose. Cody cringed.

The gallows were ready.

51

A Perfect Day for a Hanging

⸻

The morning had arrived. Rabid butterflies were swarming the inside of Cody's stomach. His legs twitched restlessly. His arm sprawled over the edge of his bed, brushing against a smooth object. He closed his hand around it—there was still hope.

Rolling out of bed, he threw on his rock-cloth tunic, wrapped the brown sash around his waist, and left his room. Light shown from under Jade's door; Cody knocked. When the door swung open, Cody noticed that Jade's eyes were bloodshot and her hair frizzy. She looked as though she had spent much of the night awake. She gave a slight nod. No words were needed; they both understood the grim significance of the morning. The next time their heads laid down on their fluffy pillows, their friend Randilin would be dead.

The silence spread like a contagious disease. Throughout the palace people went quietly about their business. Cody looked down at his shoes as he followed Jade. Exiting the palace they stopped on the front step. People were mutely pouring out of the alleyways like a nest of ants, solemnly staggering toward the gallows. Cody was shocked by the transformation in the crowd. The same people who had cheered for Randilin's pardon in the courthouse mere days earlier were now resolved to the reality of the noose. As far as Cody could tell, there hadn't been a public execution in many, many years, if ever. He ran his fingers along the smooth texture of glass in his pocket, *and that's the way I intend to keep it.*

By the time Cody and Jade reached the gallows, there was already a sizable crowd. Cody felt the warmth of Jade's hand press against his. "We've failed. Cody, we've failed. We promised him we'd help him. We gave our word that we would save him. Yet, in an hour, he will be killed all the same. I can't watch this; I'm going back. Not just to the Palace, but home; above ground. I'm sick of all this. This crazy cult and their mythical Orb. I'm done with it all." Jade turned to leave but Cody grabbed her wrists.

"Wait, Jade, you can't leave. These people need me. What about the Book? What about me being the Book Keeper? What about . . . Ti? " he asked hurriedly.

She pushed his arm away. "What about your mother? School? A normal life? Cody, these people don't need you at all, *you* need these people to need *you*. I know you're caught up in all their talk of destiny, but Cody, it's just a tattered Book. Isn't it curious that no one is actually allowed to *see* the Orb? Instead we're all supposed to blindly believe that within that Sanctuary is some awesome power. Do you know what I think? I think that there *is* no all-powerful Orb. As I see it, we have two choices: believe all the lies from these desperate people or go home to our normal life. I choose the latter, what about you?"

Cody dropped his shoulders. "You're wrong, Jade. Perhaps I can't prove it right now, and perhaps I never will be able to. But someday you will realize that there's more to this life than we can understand. I don't ask you to believe right now, but please stay at least until after the hanging. I need you right now. You're going to have to trust me." Cody held out his hand and smiled. Jade reached out her hand. She locked pinkies with him. "Pinkie shake, never break, or all my books are yours to take," they said in unity. The crowd pressed in behind them. It was almost zero hour, and still there was no sign of Randilin.

"Cody? Thank heavens it's you!" Tiana's head popped between Cody's and Jade's. Stepping forward she squeezed her body between the two. "I've been looking for you. I knew you'd be here early. This is dreadful." Her face looked tired, lacking the usual explosiveness of life that Cody had become accustomed to. Cody could feel her body pressed up against his. *Not now, Cody! Focus!*

He looked up across the crowd. He knew Randilin's only possible chance of ending the day alive rested in him alone. He could not afford to be distracted by anything—no matter how tempting. To Cody's surprise he saw Stalkton in attendance. A red-faced Xerx stood behind him holding an umbrella in each hand; they were meant to block the Orb's heat from reaching Stalkton's glowing white skin.

Cody scanned the crowd further. He clenched his fist. Fincher Tople was drifting through the multitude with a cheerful disposition peppering people questions. He stopped before Cody. "Splendid day! Good to see you, Cody, Keeper of the Book. I just have a few questions for tomorrow's issue of the *Under-Earth Rumblings* that I've been asking, if you three wouldn't mind. Firstly, in your guess, how long do you think Randilin will hang by the noose before his spine snaps? For strictly editorial purposes, of course! The common consensus has been three to four seconds. Care to weigh in?"

Like a loaded spring, Cody's hand launched out and clobbered the journalist square in the chin. He fell backwards and was engulfed by the crowd. A loud hush passed over the mob, followed by a chorus of whispered murmurs. Cody looked up to see the cause of stir. Randilin approached the stage.

With bound, swollen hands and his head hung low, several guards led the dwarf toward the platform. A hooded man followed behind him. Reaching the top, the man grabbed the noose and began pulling on it to inspect its strength. After the tremendous build-up to the execution, the sudden arrival of the actual event was surreal. A round of cheers broke the quiet comatose feeling as Kantan jumped up onto the stage. He motioned to the guards flanking Randilin to bring the prisoner forward toward the rope.

"Ladies and gentlemen. We are gathered here today to witness the carrying out of justice." Kantan unwrapped a folded scroll in his hands. "The felonies committed by the convicted are long in nature, numerous in occurrence, and brutal in severity. Of these crimes committed against the crown, and against humanity, the most notable are as such:

direct treason against the King, disclosure of secret information to our enemies during time of war, and a central role in numerous deaths of innocent civilians. As such, by the power and authority investing in the court, Sir Randilin Stormberger has been sentenced to hang by his neck until dead."

The guards pushed Randilin forward. He didn't resist or struggle. The hooded man placed the noose around Randilin's neck, pulling it tight. Cody felt both his hands squeezed. Standing on both sides of him, Jade and Tiana's fingers intertwined with his. He could sense their rapid pulses through his fingers. Time seemed suspended. Then with a simple clatter, the trapdoor fell, the noose tightened, and Randilin was hanged.

PART THREE
AND SO IT BEGINS

52

The Truth

Fraymour!" Sparks exploded before the shocked crowd and Randilin's limp body fell to the stage; the frayed end of the rope blackened from the fire. Bound by surprise, not a person moved a muscle as Cody leaped onto the stage. *"Bauciv!"* he yelled. Vines made completely of wood burst through the floor. The wooden tentacles shot out toward the guards and wrapped themselves around their ankles, paralyzing them. *"Gai di Gasme!"*

Cody jumped up onto the ledge of the stage. "People of Atlantis, you have all been deceived!" he shouted over the silent crowd.

Kantan stepped forward. "What is the meaning of this atrocity? You have aided a convicted criminal and assaulted the guards. This was not a wise decision, boy . . ." he threatened.

Cody's eyes scanned the crowd. Jade's head was in her hands; Tiana was beaming with pride. Finally his eyes found Cia, Foz, and Eva standing to the side. Foz was adamantly shaking his head, but Cody had come too far now to turn back.

"People of Atlantis, rumors have spread that your righteous King has been in hiding. Others say he is sick, and still others say he has abandoned his people. I wish to put these rumors to rest. Your good King has not abandoned his city—at least not by choice . . ." Cody risked another glance toward the royal family who were staring at him with pleading eyes. "It's time you knew the truth. Your King . . . is dead."

Cody braced himself for the outcry of rage and confusion—it never came. People continued to stare dumbly back at him, as though they had not heard his words. "You're lying. As long as we live in the presence of the Orb, we cannot die!" called out an elderly lady. The crowd echoed her cry.

General Levenworth emerged. "Indeed, the boy is obviously delusional, brought on by the trauma of watching his friend be executed. It appears as though we are going to require a second noose. Guards . . ." He motioned toward two soldiers who pulled swords from their scabbards and approached.

Cody scanned the crowd again quickly. *Where are you?* The two guards stepped onto the platform. Cody's eyes stopped, locking with Dace's. The young captain's face sunk as realization set in; but for Cody he was past the point of no return. *Please be a man of your word!*

"People, hear me out! You are all buying into the assumption that your king died a natural death . . ." urged Cody.

"How else could he have died? You're just a liar!" yelled another man from the crowd.

Cody cleared his throat, "Your King—has been murdered." At his proclamation he finally received the reaction he had expected. Chaos erupted. Women began screaming and men began muttering incoherently.

Prince Kantan raised his hands to silence the outburst. "The King, murdered? And in your fabricated tale, who could have had the desire and the ability to have accomplished such an assassination?" There was something unusual about the Prince's face that Cody couldn't decipher. Almost as if the Prince was warning him to stop. *Not this time.*

"The King has been murdered . . ." Cody paused, "by his own son—Prince Kantan!" he exclaimed pointing his finger toward the Prince.

The crowd gasped, but Kantan merely laughed. "Oh, is that so? Prove it. Or do you *just know* again?" he snarled.

Cody reached into his pocket and pulled out a glass vial. "Contained in this vial is a small specimen of the highly poisonous plant Derugmansia, or *Soul Snatcher* as it is called. This is the same deadly substance that can be found ground against the surfaces of the King's molars. This vial was taken from Prince Kantan's office only yesterday, where several more samples can still be found."

Kantan's eyes bulged. "You don't know what you're doing boy. This proves nothing . . ."

Cody gave a smug smile, "Perhaps not . . . but *this* does." Cody reached into his pocket and pulled out a folded piece of paper. "This is a letter recently written in Kantan's own handwriting, and contains a signature verifying it as indeed the product of Prince Kantan. Allow me to read it for you:

You must trust me, the deed has been completed
as we had previously discussed. My father has been
murdered. I must have your word that this deed is
kept secret. Right now, no one has discovered the
truth behind his murder. You must keep it this way. I
feel deep remorse, for a father to be killed by his own
flesh and blood is heartless. Meet me tomorrow. It is
time to move to the next phase of our plan.

Sincerely, Prince Kantan.

Cody lowered the letter and sneered at the Prince, "How's that for your proof?"

He turned to the crowd. "The correspondent of this letter is none other than General Gongore Levenworth. These are the men responsible for the murder of your innocent king! They would have us distracted by punishing the ancient crimes of Randilin while their sinister actions go unnoticed! I ask you, where is the justice?" Like a talented maestro, Cody stepped back to listen to the beauty of the symphony he had conducted. The crowd exploded in rage. "We want justice!" "Blood for blood!" "Send the Prince to the gallows!" Several of the mob begin rushing toward the stage.

Kantan screamed out, "You don't know what you're doing!" His face convulsed into a demented wraith. With a shriek he lunged forward, grabbing Cody around the neck. "You fool!"

Cody's vision blurred. Suddenly he felt the pressure around his neck loosen.

Dace was standing with a knife held to the Prince's back. "I pronounce both Prince Kantan and General Levenworth under arrest for the suspected murder of King Ishmael," he proclaimed. His eyes found Cody. The perplexed look on Dace's face expressed more than a thousand words could ever do: *You had better know what you are doing.*

Levenworth grunted, "As usual, Captain Ringstar, your poor judgment disappoints me. This is way out of line. Don't think I will forget this abomination. Mark my words. Your military career is finished . . ."

Cody stepped forward. "Gag their mouths! Let us hear no more of their deceitful lies!" Kantan fought to break free from the guard's grasp, yelling, "Nothing is as it seems! I can explain! It's not . . ." The rest of his words were muffled by the cloth stuffed into his mouth.

A legion of soldiers, with Dace at the head, escorted the Prince and the general away to the prison. Cody watched as Wolfrick and Hex removed Randilin from the noose and lifted him away. He tried to make eye contact with Randilin, but the dwarf's head hung limply toward the ground. Lady Cia and Prince Foz stepped up onto the platform. Cody seized the opportunity to retreat from the spotlight. He rolled off the stage and fell onto the ground, surrounded by the still frenzied mob.

Immediately Jade's face hung suspended over his. "Are you insane! What you just did was borderline psychotic. How *dare* you keep me in the dark! You could have been *killed* for a stunt like that!" she yelled, clutching his collar.

The smiling face of Tiana appeared next to hers. "That was amazing! You just stood up against royalty and won!

I never knew you were such a rogue!" Each grabbing an arm, the two girls pulled Cody to his feet.

On the stage Prince Foz raised his hands and spoke, "People, what the boy says is true. The King, my father, is indeed dead." Cries of panic rose from the crowd again, but Foz silenced them. "This is indeed a dark time in our city and for me personally. I have just learned that my own blood brother is responsible for this dark atrocity. But all is not lost. We will rise up again from the ashes. My father always loved his people and cared about them until the end. I think it's time he received the honor and respect he earned through his many selfless years as reigning King. Two days from today, I propose that he is given a royal funeral, that we may give to him in death the way he gave to us in life. All hail the good King Ishmael!"

"All hail the good King Ishmael!" the crowd echoed, bursting into applause and cheering.

Lady Cia stepped onto the ledge, the light from the Orb shimmering off her white dress like the morning sun off fresh snow. "People of Atlantis. It is truly a dark day. Have my word; my brother's treachery will not go unpunished! Although it is an honor that I hoped never to have to accept, I present myself to you as heir to my father's vacant throne—Queen of Atlantis."

"Hail, Queen Cia! Hail, Queen Cia!" the crowd chanted. Cody couldn't help but smile, he felt relieved. For the time being at least, Randilin was safe and Kantan was behind bars. Things finally seemed to be falling into place. He felt a squeeze on his hand. He looked up to see Tiana smiling at him. She kissed the air softly with her ruby red lips. Cody felt a jolt of adrenaline pulse through him. He leaned forward . . .

. . . and felt another squeeze on his shoulder. *Jade, you really know how to ruin a moment!* He spun around, "What?" he spat in irritation. But it was not Jade who demanded his attention, it was Dace,

"Cody. I need you to meet in the war room immediately. We have just received another report from the borderlands. The news is not good."

53

Preparations

"The rumors are true: *The Impaler* has been sighted out-side of Flore Gub." The captain of the Mid-City guards, Eli Eagleton, paced before the crowded war-room, uncer-tainty and exhaustion evident in his every step. "El Do-rado's high general has not been sighted in the field since the Great War. His sudden appearance is troubling. I fear the worst."

Dace stood from his seat. "I agree. We can no longer turn a blind eye to the borderland. The Golden King has his mind set on *The Code*; it is no longer a matter of *if*—but of *when*. It won't be long until word reaches El Dorado of the good King's death and our weakened state."

Cia's melodic voice cut through the conversation. "I agree. However, we cannot spare troops from the city to aid the borderlands. With my father's royal funeral in two days, thousands of citizens will flock to Atlantis; our troops will be needed here to maintain order."

The panther-faced Silkian scratched his long, boney fingers across the table as though petting a cat. When he spoke, his beady eyes remained focused on the table. "Cancel the funeral. The King has already died; our citizens on the borderlands have not. When did the honor of one become more significant than the lives of many?"

At this, Prince Foz slammed his fist on the table. "This decision goes deeper than honor—the morale of the city has all but been demolished. In a single day they have learned that their beloved, immortal King has been assassinated by his own son. Moreover, that the treasonous Prince appears to have been in partnership with a well-respected general. Add this to an impending invasion—these people *need* the funeral. Preparations have already begun."

Cody timidly watched the scene play out. Just when things had been looking up again, they had, just as quickly, come crashing down. Cody was no politician, but even he could feel the tension building in the room. The two most influential positions in the entire empire had just been vacated. At a time when unity was needed, Cody hoped ambition could be set aside.

"Why don't we do both?" he said before he could stop himself.

Every eye in the room turned to him. "What do you propose, Book Keeper?" asked Eagleton attentively.

Silkian's black, marble eyes finally rose from the table. "Yes, indeed. Continue."

Cody's mind searched for an appropriate answer as the room waited for his response. "Well, perhaps either Dace or Eagleton could take the majority of the troops to aid Flore Gub and Lilley, while the other stays here to oversee the funeral processions."

Cia stroked her long hair as she sat unblinking. "The Book Keeper has spoken wisely."

The bald-headed Eagleton stood upright and saluted Cia. "I pledge my services to the Queen. If you deem me worthy, I offer my services to lead my troops, as well as Levenworth's legions, to the borderlands to aid their defense. Captain Dace will remain here with his Outer-City troop to oversee the funeral events."

Cia turned toward Dace with a raised eyebrow. "No disrespect intended, and I by no means wish to call into question the competency of your troops, but there will be thousands arriving here from the four corners of Under-Earth. It would be understandable if the sheer mass of people proved too large to . . ."

"I trust my men with my life. They will be more than able to fulfill this task," Dace cut in assertively. "In my military opinion, we cannot leave any more troops in the city than absolutely necessary. What is your final verdict, Lady . . . pardon me, *Queen* Cia?"

Although Cia's face showed no signs of stress or worry, Cody couldn't help but pity the beautiful Queen. She had begun her reign by being cast straight into the furnace.

"It shall be as you suggest. Captain Eagleton, in the absence of General Levenworth, I entrust you with full command over the defensive effort. You are to depart tonight. Ready the legions. Captain Dace, you will gather your troops and begin security preparations for the funeral. Dismissed."

Although no words were spoken, Cody felt the weight of Jade's presence as they stood together on the wall, overlooking the city. Not that long had passed since their unassuming, routine trip to *Wesley's Rare and Amazing Book Store*, but it seemed to Cody that everything had changed. For the first time in their long friendship, Cody felt awkward around Jade. He searched the depths of his brain for a conversation starter but found nothing. Jade seemed unaffected as she gazed at the city. Or was she feeling as uncomfortable as he was?

Jade had always had a competitive side to her. Was it jealousy over his new position and power as the Book Keeper that caused the tension in their friendship? Cody risked a glance at his friend who continued to look out at the city, obliviously. Cody wasn't sure how it had happened, but a vast crevasse had formed between them. He hated it. He missed having his best friend. Jade was one of the few people who truly understood him, weaknesses and all. When he was with Tiana he felt exhilarated, but he found himself unable to talk about anything important. It suddenly struck Cody just how much he needed Jade. He had been trying to hold down the mounting pressure. With the war to break any day, Atlantis was going to look to him as the Book Keeper to lead the way. Could he do it? Was he ready? Or was it all just another glorified amplification of Starky's classroom where he needed Jade to bail him out, over and over? Only time would tell—but, unfortunately, that the time was approaching swiftly as a summer breeze.

The transformation of the city in a single night was shocking. The front courtyard of the palace billowed with extravagant flowers of every color. Green vines crawled up the side of the building and radiating balls of light hung suspended in the air like little stars. Focused on the floating lights, Cody's foot caught a leafy vine. He tumbled forward and collided with something. That something was Xerx.

"I guess the great Book Keeper has far more important matters to attend to rather than acting as a lowly gardener. Or perhaps you're too busy running after more flighty blondes? Glad to know you're staying so focused on your responsibilities as Book Keeper." Xerx spit on the ground in front of Cody. "Now get out of my sight before I have these vines carry you up the wall with them."

Cody saw that several of the other Brotherhood Monks were moving around the courtyard creating greenery and decorations out of nothing.

As Cody exited the garden he muttered under his breath, *"Gadour. Gai di gasme."* Seconds later there was a scream followed by a curse, "Ouch! My toe!" yelled Xerx. Cody snickered as he walked away.

When the AREA gong rang, everyone routinely fell to their knees and began reciting the Orb's Hymn. Perhaps Cody just felt paranoid, but it seemed to him that the people were reciting the hymn with a noticeable lack of enthusiasm. *Were people losing faith in the Orb?*

Saying "Amen," Cody stood and continued on his way. It didn't take long for him to notice that already people were filing in from the outskirts of Under-Earth. The streets were packed. All in hooded black robes, the mourners had begun their grieving even though the funeral wasn't until the next day.

Up on the walls, Cody saw several soldiers watching over the crowd. Cody recognized Sheets and Hex as well as a few others from Yanci's pub. Cody was sure Dace was around somewhere watching over as well. Lowering his head, Cody weaved through the crowd toward the Monastery.

"Master Stalkton, I'm not ready!" Cody paced back and forth before his teacher, Lamgorious Stalkton, who was seated calmly on the ground. "These people are trusting in me to protect them in war. I don't even know if I can protect myself!" Cody rested his forehead against the stone wall, the coolness of the stone felt good against his sweat-soaked skin. "The training we have done. It is wonderful to be able to control elements and such, but what am I going to do against a trained army? I don't want to do this anymore."

Stalkton chuckled. "Oh, son, don't feel so singled out . . . I'm sure there are a great *many* people who don't want you to do this anymore. It's not illogical, you've been nothing but trouble since the moment you touched the Book. A bit of a disaster," the old teacher said conversationally.

"Thanks for the pick-me-up," Cody muttered.

Stalkton suddenly pulled his bony foot onto his lap and began picking his toenails.

Cody cringed.

"Unfortunately, unless you plan on dying, the responsibility for the Book is yours. We don't always choose our circumstances, but we always choose our actions. Therefore, let us move past what you don't *want* to do and focus on what you *need* to do."

Cody felt something flick onto his face and stick to his lip. He frantically brushed it off, exceedingly thankful to be in a dark room and unable to confirm his suspicion that he had been struck by a leaping toenail shard.

"So, what *am* I going to do? Learn more words?" Cody asked, still rubbing his now raw lip with his sleeve.

"Oh, words, words, words. Learning the words is not the issue. You want more words; the creation word for earth, or more specifically for dust, is *dastanda*. Another useful word is *sellunga*, which is the creation word for metal. The kind of metal depends on what specific elements you conjure up in your mind. Go ahead and memorize these words, but keep in mind that the paint is only as good as the painter using it."

"And, what do you mean by that? I thought the whole point of our training was to learn the High Language?" Cody asked confused.

Stalkton smiled. "That is because you are not particularly bright. Pity Wesley didn't pass the Book down to your green-eyed lady friend instead. No matter; to answer your question, my job is not to teach you to *know* the words; it's to teach you how to *use* the words. You are not special because you know some of the High Language. This Monastery has several knowledgeable in the language. Indeed, Xerx's depth of the language makes your sparse lexicon look like baby-talk."

"I know already. So why am I special then?" Cody asked, his irritation level ready to flood.

"Because the Book gives you the ability to use the words in a way that the rest of us can hardly dream. After hundreds of years, Xerx can create a boulder—after several weeks *you* could create a mountain! The problem is that you are still thinking too small. You still don't believe in yourself. *That* is how you will protect Atlantis; not by an excessive knowledge *of* the words, but by opening your mind and being able to *use* the words. When you reach that point, Cody, you will be virtually invincible."

54

The Swan and the Duck

―――――――

The coast was clear. She would have to be swift if she was going to make it in and out without being seen. With a quick glance behind, she tucked her chin to her chest and scurried across the clearing. Reaching the other side, she pressed herself against the wall. *So far, so good.* From across the way she could see her destination, the building seemed empty—she knew she was close. She took a deep breath and pushed herself off the wall—directly into Fincher Tople.

"*Oooff!*" cried the gangly man as the papers in his hands flew like confetti into the air. "Watch where you're . . . Madam Jade? Well, well, this is a pleasant surprise. A very pleasant surprise, indeed. And, alone I see?" he said smoothly, his hungry eyes devouring her.

"Just stay out of my way, Finch. I'm busy," snapped Jade, pushing Tople away.

The toad-faced man grinned. "Feisty, aren't you? Here, take one, as a token of my admiration." He handed Jade one of the papers, pressing his hands around hers as he did so.

Jade shook him off and briskly set off toward her destination; her advantage of stealth had been compromised, but there was still time. She brought the paper up to cover her face. The front page had a picture of Prince Kantan and the headline: **"BETRAYAL! THE SHOCKING TRUTH BEHIND OUR BELOVED PRINCE'S SINISTER ACTIONS! WHAT MORE ABOUT OUR ROYAL FAMILY DO WE NOT KNOW?"** Jade flipped through the rest and saw that the King's funeral occupied much of the pages as did El Dorado's imminent attack. She flipped another page and flushed; the headline read: **"UNDER-EARTH'S MOST ELIGIBLE BACHELOR—TAKEN?"**

"Several evenings ago Atlantis was treated to the touching birth of romance. Newly proclaimed Book Keeper, Cody Clemenson, was spotted wooing the lovely Tiana Hubrisa. Why can't these two lovebirds keep their lips apart? Read more juicy details on the next page . . ."

Jade crumbled the paper into a ball and flung it away. *It's just silly gossip anyways, right?* Jade reached the end of the clearing and stopped. She stood staring into the open door of the building in front of her. *This is stupid. I should turn back.* She glanced around again to make sure no one was looking. It was now or never. She stepped into the building. The minute she did so she felt exceedingly out of place. *What are you doing? Who are you fooling?* Just as she was turning to leave, a smiling young lady came around the corner.

"Welcome to Aunty Flora's Beauty Shop, can I help you find anything?"

Jade could feel her face burn red. She kept her eyes to the floor. "Um . . . I'm just looking for . . . some stuff for my face . . . and maybe something to make my lips look red," she muttered shyly.

"Is there any product in particular? Any tones or textures you prefer?" asked the lady.

Jade felt her heart beating against her temples, "I'm . . . well . . . I'm kind of new to this sort of thing."

The young lady smiled and put her arm around Jade's shoulders. "No problem, darling. Just follow me; I'll get you what you need. You'll be absolutely radiant by the time I'm through with you. I promise."

Jade pressed her face closer to the mirror, she was sure there was some sort of trickery in the works. There had to be. How else could she explain the dazzling princess staring back from the mirror.

The lady at the beauty shop had spoken the truth—Jade was absolutely radiant. Her cheeks had been powdered; her wretched freckles had been covered. Her eyelashes were dark as they shaded her green eyes. Her puffy lips looked brilliant in dark red. Her hair had been put into an up-do, which was, as far as she could remember, the first time in her entire life she had ever worn it any way other than straight down. Jade smiled, Cinderella had nothing on her; she felt gorgeous. *What will Cody think?* Thinking of Cody made her nervous. She didn't know if she was ready for people to see her like this—especially not Cody. Would he just laugh? Was she trying to be something she wasn't?

No. Jade smiled, allowing her face to shine. *I'm not letting that ditz steal my best friend without a fight. This is war. I've been an ugly duck for far too long . . . I'm ready to be a swan.*

The cool shade of the garden foliage comforted Cody as he went over his idea in his head for the thirteenth time. He had been asked by Foz to perform a special act of creation at the funeral to honor the King. Cody realized he only had one shot at it and that there would be no better time to win the much-needed confidence of the disoriented citizens. He picked up a wet cloth and pressed it against the side of his face. The soreness had decreased, but there was still a solid bump reminding him of the colossal failure that was his landing. He took a deep sniff, sucking the comforting scents of the garden through his nose. Randilin's words outside Sally's diner had finally sunk in; Cody, too, missed the feeling of fresh nighttime air and seeing real stars. He even missed the awful smell of horses that permeated Havenwood in the spring. How many rainy days had he complained and been miserable? Thousands of miles underground, he would welcome a bit of rain, or *any* weather for that matter. It was odd how some of the most wonderful things in life had been right in front of his nose.

"Hey, Cody," came Jade's soft voice from behind him. Cody turned his head around to greet his friend—and froze. Jade was standing at the entrance to the garden. At least he thought it was Jade. She was wearing a long flowing white dress that sparkled like stars. Cody felt an odd sensation come over him. He stood up slowly and took a step toward her. He was speechless. Jade's eyelashes fluttered up and down as her eyes gazed deeply into his. For a moment they both stood still, silently staring at each other. Jade's glossy lips rose into a smile. When Cody finally spoke his voice was flustered, "Jade, you look . . . I never thought . . . I mean . . ."

Jade giggled. "You mean what, Cody?" she asked teasingly, "go on . . ."

Cody shook his head, rubbing his eyes, "I mean . . . what's wrong with you?"

Jade shoulders fell and her face turned light red. "What do you mean? Nothing's wrong with me," she stammered, her chest rising and falling rapidly as her face darkened. "You don't like it?"

"You just look so . . . strange," said Cody as he reached his hand to her face and rubbed his fingers across her cheek. "What's all this on your face? It looks like you fell into a jar of cake icing."

Jade opened her mouth to speak but no words came out; her lips quivered as she fought to control her breath.

"And your hair," continued Cody, "Why isn't it down like it always is? I like it down. It looks like a beehive all scrunched up like that. Here, you can use my cloth; let's get you cleaned up."

Jade grabbed the cloth and threw it in Cody's face before turning and running out of the garden. Cody looked with confusion to the cloth and back to the door where Jade had exited. *What's gotten into her?* He shrugged. *Girls can act so strangely.*

Jade pulled the clips from her hair and threw them out the window. She looked in the mirror; her tear-stained face was smeared with make-up. Who was she kidding? She was no princess. She was just Jade. Ugly ol' Jade. The one no boys ever noticed; not even her best friend. She grabbed the leftover make-up bottles and dropped them into the garbage. Did she really think she could compete with a girl like Tiana? Her mother was right; she really was nothing more than an ugly duckling.

Jade crawled into her bed. She wanted to go to sleep and never wake up. She didn't want to face Cody, not after tonight. He was right after all; she *did* just look weird.

She pulled her blankets over her head; she didn't want Cody to hear her sobbing.

55

Randilin Stormberger's Secrets

The crowd expanded like rising bread. The number of grievers arriving from other parts of Under-Earth increased tenfold. Cody wondered how they would manage to house such a growing crowd. As the elevator brought Cody back to ground level, he spotted Tiana. "About time, hero, I've been waiting," she teased, gracefully gliding toward him and wrapping her hand around his. Cody's pulse picked up speed. He felt slightly awkward. After their sunset experience, Tiana acted like nothing had changed between them. *Was it not a big deal to her? Did she have other boyfriends? Was I just a really bad kisser?* All these thoughts filled Cody's head.

The truth was that Tiana had given Cody his first kiss; although he would always brag to the boys at school about other kisses he supposedly had shared with make-believe girls. Cody had been a late bloomer. He had never really differentiated between boys and girls growing up, which was perhaps why he and Jade had struck up such a quick and easy friendship. With Tiana, everything was different.

She was free-spirited. She was dangerous even. Every time she spoke to him he felt exhilarated, never sure what to expect. In his mind, a kiss represented a relationship; although Tiana seemed in no rush to declare commitment.

"Tiana . . . am I your boyfriend?" he asked awkwardly, hardly aware that he had verbalized his thoughts.

Tiana laughed and squeezed his hand. "Oh, you silly boy; you're a darling." With another laugh, she continued walking.

A darling? A yes or no would have been appreciated!

"So, where are you off to today? As the Book Keeper I assume you have been put to important work?" she asked as though the previous conversation had never occurred.

"Actually, with the funeral tomorrow I've been pretty much left alone. I was going to go talk to Randilin; haven't seen him since they hauled him away from the gallows. It's probably not a good idea for you to come, but I can meet up with you after and . . ."

"Oh, don't be ridiculous. I'm coming with you." It was not a suggestion. The two walked hand-in-hand to Randilin's original cell where he had been returned following the arrest of Kantan and Levenworth. Stepping into the cell Cody sensed that he was not alone.

"Oh, hey, Cody . . . Tiana" said Jade with free-falling enthusiasm.

Cody quickly let go of Tiana's hand. "Hi, Jade . . . didn't know you'd be here . . . just wanted to check on Randilin," Cody stuttered dumbly.

Jade rolled her eyes. "How thoughtful," she spat back venomously.

"Hey now, what's gotten into you lately? Too much sitting around unneeded by everybody? Bet it sucks to not be the one in charge anymore doesn't it?" Cody shot back. He watched helplessly as his words stung into Jade. The injured look on her weary face made Cody instantly regret speaking so haughtily. *What's happening to me? She's my best friend!* He didn't get a chance to apologize.

"Hey! I didn't die on the gallows last night, remember? Quit talking like I'm not here, you cowpies!" called out Randilin from his cell. He stuck his face against the bars; his neck was scabbed from where the noose had stripped away the skin.

"Sorry, how are you doing?" asked Cody slightly embarrassed.

Randilin grabbed the iron bars of the cell. "Oh, just peachy. Nothing gets me more emotionally juiced than being hanged! Although, I guess I owe you a thank you." He finished with a softened voice. Looking to Cody, Randilin caught sight of Tiana for the first time. He stumbled back a step. His head tilted to the side as his eyes strained toward her. For a moment the wrinkles on his rough face seemed to soften. He looked back to Cody as though in a trance, but Cody quickly shook his head.

"Don't mention it. It's all good now. The funeral is tomorrow, Kantan and Levenworth are in prison, and Cia has become queen. I'm sure we can persuade her to release you of the charges."

Randilin held up his finger. "Hold on, did you say that General Levenworth was imprisoned as well?" he asked tentatively.

"Yeah. Turns out he was working with Kantan the whole time. The two were scheming to keep Atlantis' troops away from the borderlands. You were there, surely you heard all this?"

Randilin rubbed his swollen neck. "I passed out. The next thing I knew I was back in this cell. I thought it was the afterlife until Jade started filling me in. But I hadn't heard the general was involved. Hmmmm . . ."

"Why is that troubling? We have the letter that Kantan wrote him, it's physical proof," insisted Cody.

Randilin retreated back into the shadows of his cell. "It's just that I never would have believed Kantan or Levenworth capable of such a horrible deed. They're flea-picking, royal elitists, but murderers?" pondered Randilin. "I agree the proof is substantive. I just don't know what they hoped to accomplish."

"Well, from what I've heard, the Prince seemed to be the most ready to accept the reality of another Great War. Perhaps he felt the only way to get Atlantis to defend itself was to eliminate a passive King?" suggested Tiana, speaking for the first time.

"If he wanted to defend the City, then why did he refuse to send the troops to the borderlands?" challenged Cody. "I think he knew a war was coming and he wanted to make sure he was on the winning side."

"Maybe . . . but that doesn't explain Levenworth's role. I'm telling you; I've known Gongore a long, long time.

Since before the discovery of Under-Earth. He was as loyal to the King as anybody in Atlantis. He was like a son to him," said Randilin.

"Well, after Kantan's actions, I don't know that that's such a compliment," added Jade pessimistically.

"I have a bad feeling about this. There must be more to the story," asked Randilin. "I'm obviously not going anywhere for a while," he said raising his arms and clinking together the chains bound to his wrists, "so you three need to keep your eyes open. And be careful."

"What do you think about what Randilin said? About there being something else?" asked Jade as they left the prison. They found themselves engulfed in a crowd of hooded mourners slowly walking the streets. Cody looked up at the man beside him; a tall man wearing all black. A glimmer reflected into Cody's eyes, blinding him. He rubbed his eyes but the man was gone. There was something unusual about the man, but Cody couldn't place it. Another wave of mourners surrounded him. Cody headed away from the crowd and toward Jade and Tiana who were waiting for him against the wall.

Jade raised her hands. "Well? What do you think?" she asked impatiently.

Cody shook his head. "I don't know. I have to admit; I don't feel good about the situation either. But I don't know what else there could be?" he responded as they turned down another road toward the palace.

Tiana took a few quick steps ahead and turned, blocking their path. "Has it occurred to either of you that perhaps it's your friend who's playing a role in all this himself, and just trying to lead you down the wrong road?"

"Randilin? Impossible. He's our friend. He's the one who brought us here safely," countered Jade firmly.

Tiana pulled Cody and Jade against the wall. "He also conveniently brought the Book back underground for the first time in a thousand years. He just happens to reappear from his banishment at the same time as the King's murder? And brings the Book within the Golden King's grasp on the dawn of war? Do you guys even know why this *close* ally of yours was banished in the first place?" Cody bit his lip. Jade stared at the ground not making a sound.

Tiana sighed. "I didn't think so. Would it help open your mind to my possibility if I told you that Randilin was banished because he switched sides during the Great War? That he leaked Levenworth's strategies to the Golden King. It was because of him that the Golden King managed to out-maneuver Levenworth and enter Atlantis."

"I don't believe you," stammered Jade.

Tiana rubbed her lips together. "The Golden King marched right through an open gate; a gate opened by Randilin himself. You see, your friend has a long history of switching sides. And that was only the beginning. That same night he committed his *dark deed*, an act so terrible they refuse to even tell us the details in school. Only that it resulted in the death of many. What makes you so sure he isn't willing to sacrifice innocent lives again for his cause?"

Cody leaned against the wall and slid down to the ground. Was it possible? Could Randilin really have been tricking them the whole time? It seemed there was still a lot they didn't know about Randilin Stormberger.

56

A Fateful Mourning

Cody inhaled guilt as he took a deep breath of city air. Is there a more humbling and unworthy action than breathing in a waft of clear morning air on the very same day you should be mourning the undeserved death of a good man? Cody had never met King Ishmael, but somehow he felt like he knew him well; as though they were somehow similar frayed threads to the same rope. Every time Cody touched the Book and felt its power surge through his fingers, he understood more than anybody the fear that led Ishmael to forsake his privilege and entrust it to Wesley. Although thousands of miles of dirt had separated Cody from the King, he still understood the King's greatness. Perhaps that is the very thing that made the King so noble.

Cody pulled on the black mourner's robe that Poe had dropped off the night before. There was a knock on his door, startling Cody. He opened it and immediately raised his hands into a defensive position.

"Relax man," said Xerx, dressed in a matching black robe. "I've been sent here by Master Stalkton. Lady Cia has requested that *The Code* be kept in the Monastery during today's events for safe keeping. I am here to retrieve the Book."

Cody instinctively stepped to his bed and pulled the Book out from under his pillow. "I'm sure you'd just love to get your hands on this," said Cody, holding it up, "but you can tell Stalkton that I will be dropping it off myself."

"Sure, whatever." Xerx turned to leave but paused. "Tiana. . . . She's not the girl you think she is," he added unexpectedly before disappearing from sight. Cody craned his neck. *What did he mean? What could he know about Tiana?* Cody grinned. *Oh, well, what was Xerx's opinion worth anyways?*

Cody had slept in later then he had wanted to. By the time he was out of bed, Jade's room was empty; she was already out preparing for the service. Cody headed toward the Monastery. Mourners were packed into the courtyard while thousands filled the streets. There was a solemn feeling in the air; today would be a big day.

"I don't know why I have to part with it. I don't like leaving it out of my sight," complained Cody, his fingers clutched tightly around the Book.

"I agree. But Cia feels that it is best left in the Monastery and, as she is now the Queen, we don't have much of a choice. When Prince Foz stopped by to relay her orders he seemed to share our concern for the Book's defense. But I assured him, as I assure you now, that The Brotherhood is more than adequate to ensure its safety," replied Lamgorious Stalkton. "It will be kept hidden on the upper floor. Only you, me, and the royal family will know of its location."

Cody stood still for several seconds before reluctantly handing the Book over to the elderly master. "Fine. But the moment the ceremony is over, I'm coming back here to get it." Cody turned to leave, but stopped, remembering something. "Master Stalkton," he said, turning back to his teacher, "You knew Randilin well. Do you think it's possible that he has something to do with the murder? Do you think he could have been working with Kantan and Levenworth?"

"Randilin is a flawed man," replied Stalkton simply, "as are we all. In each of us is the desire to commit evil. We all hear her seducing call lure us to action. Only for some, the call is too strong. Randilin is just as able as you or I to have done such a deed." *Glad I asked.*

"One second," Stalkton held out a book which looked identical to *The Code*, its large scarlet 'A' shining bright. "A decoy. It will be important for the people to see their new Book Keeper with the Book. Oh, and Cody . . ."

"Yes, Master?" asked Cody attentively.

"Make sure not to lock your knees when you're on stage. I've made a terrible habit of fainting at ceremonies . . ."

Cody vowed never again to fret over an oral presentation. He stood on the stage beside the royal family and other Under-Earth dignitaries staring out over thousands of black robes. As he had learned to do in all those school presentations, he stared straight at Jade who was standing in the front row. Stationed on a wooden podium at the front of the stage was the book—the decoy.

The sound of trumpets signaled that the ceremony was to begin. The crowd parted, as the coffin sliced through like a knife. Six soldiers, decked out in elaborate uniforms hoisted the coffin into the air. As the mass parted, not a single head rose to view the body of their King. For the first time it dawned on Cody that he was participating in perhaps the first funeral any of the thousands of mourners had ever experienced. For many of them, they simply didn't know how to respond or act.

The casket reached the front. It was lowered slowly into the ground. Cia stepped forward, her fair skin amplified against her long black dress. "People of Under-Earth. This is a day that none of us ever wished to see. We are shocked, but we are not defeated. We do not mourn a death: we celebrate a life. I stand before you as your Queen by title; but as a grieving equal. You do not see a crown atop my head because today the royalty, the honor, the respect, belongs to my father, your King, all hail King Ishmael!"

"All hail King Ishmael!" echoed the crowd in unison. Cia opened her mouth to speak but fought against her emotion; Cody saw with each passing second it was a battle she was losing. Her brother seemed to notice as well.

"My father always did what he believed was right in his heart. His body passes, but his legacy lives on," proclaimed Prince Foz boldly, "Now, what better way to honor that legacy than to have his body laid to rest by the one who has taken his torch. The Book Keeper, Cody Clemenson."

Cody suddenly felt very small. Foz motioned him forward. Cody stepped toward the front of the platform, his feet seemed like boulders. Dragging them across the stage, his foot caught the edge and he stumbled, nearly collapsing. The crowd didn't laugh or gasp. It was even worse—they were silent.

Cody looked down at the casket lying in the dirt. How odd that such a great man would leave the world in such a simple, wooden box. He deserved more; and Cody was going to give it to him.

He took a deep breath and shouted, *"Dastanda! Gadour! Gai di gasme."* The ground around the casket burst into a fury of motion. Cody raised his hands, and swayed them through the air. Dirt from the ground began spinning into a whirlwind, rising higher and higher. It stopped—and came crashing down like hail, concealing the casket in a blanket of earth. On the dirt was a stone 'A', marking the place. *"Bauciv!"* leafy vines burst forth from the earth, weaving across the grave and throughout the stone 'A'. Tiny buds pushed their way out of the vine, blooming into bright red flowers. *Time for the climax. "Illumichanta!"* he yelled, and from his hands he tossed a ball of glowing light. The light flew through the air and stopped above the grave, exploding like fireworks.

The crowd cheered. Cody bent over, gasping for breath and lightheaded. Creating without the Book's power to fuel him was exhausting. Cody looked eagerly to see the response to his handiwork. Jade was smiling. He glanced to the sea of mourners, and frowned. Many of their heads were still downcast.

One of the robed men in the front of the crowd looked up. A beam of light shot out from under his hood. Cody squinted his eyes, the light was not coming from in the hood—it was *reflecting* the light of the star. *Reflecting off what?* Cody focused his eyes—and his heart stopped. Suddenly everything hit him at once. The face under the hood smiled deviously—as the light glimmered off the gold platelets imbedded into the man's facial skin. Cody threw up his hands and screamed, dropping to the ground; and not a moment too soon, as an arrow whizzed over his head.

Atlantis was under attack.

57

Ambush!

Chaos claimed the courtyard. The sound of arrows whizzing and screaming filled the air. As the crowd de-hooded, rays of light blinded Cody's eyes. *What was going on?* The men seemed to be glowing. Crawling on all fours, Cody reached the edge of the platform and rolled off. The sound of steel scraping together pierced his ears. He heard an agonizing scream and a thud. A body toppled over the stage and collapsed in front of Cody. The man's face was familiar—he had been standing next to Jade in the crowd. A stream of blood was trickling from his mouth. He was dead. *Jade.*

"Jade!" Cody forsook his cover and stood. Across the entire courtyard a battle raged. Citizens fled while Atlantis' soldiers battled the glowing men. Already the ground had been stained red and littered with bodies—not all of which were soldiers. Cody looked to where Jade had been standing; in her place was now a pile of unrecognizable bodies. "Jade!"

"Cody! The royal family. We must get them to safety!" Cody followed the voice to the wall where Dace was galloping down the stairs with sword in hand. An arrow whizzed toward him; he dodged it effortlessly. Two attackers charged up the stairs to block him.

"Dace, look out!" Cody yelled. With lightning quickness, Dace sidestepped a thrust from the first attacker's sword. Without wasting a moment, he threw his shoulder hard into the other attacker, knocking him off balance. Grabbing the falling man by the sword arm, Dace pulled it up to block another blow from the first attacker. Before the man could recoup for another assault Dace's sword penetrated his neck. As the lifeless man collapsed, Dace pulled the other man forward by his arm. Twisting his wrists, he stabbed the man in the chest with his own sword. The sword vibrated, lodged into the man's stomach. With a hard kick, Dace sent the man flailing over the side of the stairs where he flopped onto the ground below.

"What's happening?" yelled Cody, pressing himself back against the side of the platform and crouching out of sight as Dace made his way toward him. Looking over his shoulder as he ran, Dace called out orders to where three guards were running along the wall. In the group was Wolfrick, Cody's old watchman, a bloody gash across his face. Dace ducked down beside Cody and instinctively wiped his bloody sword across his pant leg,

"We've been ambushed! Golden Warriors from El Dorado, disguised as mourners. We've been set-up! All our troops are at the borderlands; we're outnumbered! I need you to ensure that the Queen is safe. We can't afford any more royal bloodshed! Can I trust you with this task?" Cody nodded; his heart was beating faster. "Good. If we can surround them, then we may still have a chance. Go, find Cia!"

Dace stood and raced toward the crowd. Cody watched as two golden men pulled out swords from beneath their robes. Dace expertly parried the first swing; pivoting his body, he swung his sword back around and hammered it into the side of the other attacker. The man stumbled backwards, his hood sliding off his head. Without losing a step, he stabbed at Dace, unaffected by the blow. The solider was bald, with slabs of gold implanted into his skin like scales. The light from the Orb glittered against the smooth surface. The golden warrior brought his sword down upon Dace.

Jumping out of the chaos, Sheets raised up his axe and blocked the attacker's thrust just in time. Turned back-to-back, Dace and Sheets' weapons danced through the air, repelling the ferocious attack as the enemy closed in around them.

From behind him, Cody heard a piercing scream. His heart stopped. *Jade.* Cody dashed toward the sound. Arrows flew past his head and blades whipped through the air all around him. He ducked as a sword whizzed over his head. A golden warrior jumped in front of his path. Cody winced as the warrior's blade rose above his head. With a thud, blood splattered onto Cody's face. An arrow was lodged into the attacker's face. "These fiends can't shield their eyes with gold, can they!" called Hex from across the clearing, refitting his bow with another arrow and letting it fly toward another attacker. The arrow collided with the man's temple. The shaft snapped against the golden platelets and fell to the ground harmlessly.

"Ahhhh!" The sound of Jade's voice sent Cody back into motion. He jumped over several lifeless bodies and sidestepped an axe as it sliced through the air. "Cody! Help!" Jade was standing with her back to the wall, cornered by three golden warriors. Cody scanned the ground and snatched a sword from a dead man. The warriors spun to face their new attacker. At the sight of Cody wielding a sword, they laughed. Cody swung the sword uselessly through the air, the weight of it straining his arms. The soldiers approached, their unraised weapons by their side. Cody glanced around his surroundings franticly. He was no swordsman. Hand-to-hand combat with the warriors was suicide; but he knew he had one advantage . . .

Cody fell to the ground, scooped up two more fallen blades, and tossed them into the air. For a split moment they floated weightlessly. *"Byrae!"* A violent gust of wind caught the blades in mid-air and sent them soaring. Shock seized the warriors for only a second before they collapsed to the ground, a blade impaled into each of them. Cody wasn't sure how much more creating he could accomplish without the real Book. *The Book!*

"Jade, I need you to find the royal family. They need to get to safety! And so do you, you need to get to the palace!"

"What about you? Where are you going?" cried Jade, her voice quivering.

"To get the Book! It's still in the Monastery. We can't let it fall into the hands of El Dorado!" Cody turned to run but stopped. Four golden soldiers holding jagged-edged weapons formed a semi-circle around them. Cody and Jade were trapped.

"Quick, use the High Language again!" cried Jade as the four attackers inched closer. Cody and Jade were pushed against the wall.

Cody shook his head, "I can't do it again! I don't have the Book. I've never used the Orb's power without it; I don't know my limitations. It could kill me."

"Then what do we do?"

Cody had no answer. He reached down and pulled a blade away from the body of a fallen enemy. He knew he was no match, but he wasn't going to let anyone hurt Jade while he was still alive to protect her.

"Come get me, you golden wretches!" he taunted, swaying his blade back and forth in his hands. The attackers were more than happy to oblige. They raised their weapons and charged. *"Dastanda!"* With a quick shout one of the golden attackers disappeared—sinking into the pool of sand that instantaneously appeared below him. The other three attackers halted, glancing to each other uncertainly.

"Stop, Cody! You said you couldn't use the power, it's too risky!" shouted Jade, grabbing hold of Cody's arm.

Cody looked to her with confusion. "I didn't. That wasn't me."

"If it wasn't you, than who was it?"

As if on cue, Tiana appeared out of nowhere, somersaulting in front of Cody and Jade.

"Ti? What are you . . ." started Cody dumbfounded, but Tiana's shoulder rolled to the side.

"Seamour-fraymour!" she shouted. The ground in front of one of the soldiers bubbled, and a geyser of liquid burst out, drenching him. The man screamed, grabbing his face. The substance was lava. The golden scales on his body were glowing red; he collapsed to the ground still shouting. The remaining two guards looked to each other before charging at their new attacker.

"Tiana, look out!" Cody closed his mouth, and watched in awe as Tiana charged straight at them. As she reached them, she suddenly fell to her back, sliding across the ground, and passing between the two soldiers. Reaching out her arms on the way past, she took out their legs, sending them tumbling to their backs. Before they could recover, Tiana was back on her feet. She flicked up a lone sword and expertly caught it with her hand. Another quick blur of motion and the two attackers had been dispatched.

"Wh-w—what, what was that!" exclaimed Cody. "How are you so competent in battle! Actually, never mind that, you're a Creator? I don't understand. Why didn't you tell me!?"

Tiana smirked, and planted a quick kiss on Cody's cheek.

"Later," cut in Jade, "we need to protect the royal family, remember?"

Cody nodded. "Right, Tiana, take Jade and get Cia, Foz, and Eva into the palace. They *must* be kept safe. I need to get to the Monastery." As he looked at the two girls standing before him, a well of emotions turned in his chest. He wasn't sure what these emotions were; he only hoped that he wasn't seeing either of the girls for the last time. "You two stay safe."

He turned and left without looking back, wanting to leave before his emotions took control. He had only gone a few steps when he heard his name, "Cody!" Cody turned to where Jade was still standing beside Tiana. Her eyes were large and her body shook.

"Jade?" he called back, wishing he could forget the Book and return to her. Her green eyes locked with his. Instead of their usual fiery state they had a soft, tenderness to them.

When she opened her mouth, her lips quaked, "Cody . . . I . . . I . . . I lo . . ." The sound of clashing steel echoed in Cody's ears. A limp body fell against him. Cody shoved the body off and turned back to Jade and Tiana. They were gone.

What had she said? Cody could not find them anywhere in the crowd. He bit his lip, *please be safe.* Pivoting around, he ran back into the chaos. The fighting had spread throughout the Inner-City, leaving a pile of dead bodies in its wake. A sickening feeling came over Cody; he couldn't help notice that only a few of the golden warriors lay dead, surrounded by several dozen of Dace's men. The battle crept up onto the walls, and down through some of the side streets.

Dace ran past Cody, followed by several men. There was a deep gash across this forehead and blood was pulsing from a wound in his thigh. "Seal the gate! Must contain the enemy to the Inner-City! Regroup at the wall!" yelled Dace as he hurried by.

As Cody approached the Monastery, he looked up to the towering Sanctuary of the Orb. He hoped Stalkton was correct and that the Book was indeed safe within the walls of the Monastery. However, despite his desperate optimism he couldn't shake the sickening feeling in his gut that something had gone horribly, horribly wrong.

58

The Silent Sanctuary

The view from the Monastery elevator was alarming. The battle still raged below. Many bodies lay scattered on the ground, but from his distance, Cody couldn't distinguish how many were Atlantis' men and how many were El Dorado's. Strangely, the attackers had not pressed toward the Palace or the Sanctuary of the Orb; they appeared content to battle in the courtyard. What was the purpose of such an attack? Cody didn't have time to speculate, but hoped that Jade and Tiana had managed to reach safety in the palace.

Jumping onto the balcony, Cody paused; the front doors of the Monastery were wide open. Something wasn't right. Cody crouched down low and scurried to the entrance. All the lights were extinguished and an eerie silence rested in the room. Cody shuffled into the darkness, keeping his back against the wall. His feet bumped into something on the ground. Blinded by the shadows, Cody rubbed his eyes, urging them to adjust. Reaching down, he touched something wet. He brought his hand up to his face and gagged at the smell of fresh blood. Finally able to focus, Cody saw a face filled with terror. Cody recognized the man as Geoffrey, the elder monk who had defended Randilin during the trial. He was dead.

The hushed patter of footsteps raced across the floor, invisible in the darkness. Cody held his breath; somebody had infiltrated the Monastery. Cody crawled on all fours silently toward the stairs, he needed to find cover, and quick. Suddenly the sound of scurrying feet sounded again. There was a loud crash followed by an agonizing scream, and then—silence.

Cody's palms were slick with sweat as he hastily scampered up the stairs. Reaching the top, he dashed to his left and dropped down low against a desk. *Stalkton, where the blazes are you?* Why wasn't anybody fighting back? The monks were either hiding—or worse. Another painful scream cried out for only a second before the silence returned. Cody's mouth was dry and sticky. He had to do something quick, but what? He came upon a strange, sickening smell. All at once things made sense. The drumming of his heart quickened. History was repeating itself. The Brotherhood Monks weren't being attacked—they were being hunted.

Somewhere in the dark Monastery, the Beast was slaughtering the monks one by one. Cody heard a soft purring noise. The Hunter was close. The soft footsteps were growing louder. The creature was sniffing the air. Cody had to move quickly! Jumping up, something collided with him throwing him back against the wall. "Ahhhh!" Cody screamed in terror, swinging his fist around and colliding with the attacker. There was a grunt.

"Wait . . . is that . . . you, Xerx?" whispered Cody.

"You idiot, you just gave away our position! Run! For heaven's sakes, run!" A frantic Xerx grabbed Cody's collar and yanked him from the ground. A piercing, hog-like squeal came from above. The Hunter had zeroed in on its next victims.

"In here!" yelled Xerx. "We don't have much time. Master Stalkton is hurt and I think the rest are dead. We need to hide!" Xerx pulled Cody through a door leading to the library. The Beast's taloned feet scratched against the floor as it launched itself down the stairs. Cody frantically searched the room for a place to hide. He could hear the Beast approaching. Running down the long aisles of books, he came to a shelf of thicker, oversized books. "Xerx! Xerx? Where are you?!" he called. There was no reply.

Cody feverishly pulled the oversized books off the row. Rolling himself onto the shelf, he hauled the books back to conceal his body. As he brought the last book onto the shelf the awful stench entered into the room. The game of cat and mouse had begun.

The Beast moved like a ghostly wraith. From Cody's position he only had a slim view of the large room between the spines of two books concealing his face. He couldn't see any sign of Xerx or the Beast. He tried to hold his breath, but his heart was pounding like a gong. He fought desperately to stay calm.

He heard the flaring of the nostrils. The Beast was standing just on the other side of the shelf. The sensation of panic began to pump through his bloodstream. Cody involuntarily twitched, bumping one of the books with his elbow. The book staggered for a moment, before falling back into place. Cody let out a sigh of relief before biting his lip. It hadn't been quick enough. He heard the Beast lunge into motion from behind him.

Run! Run! Run! Yelled Cody's body, but he lay unmoving. He had lost a sense of the Beast's position; it could be anywhere now. *Xerx, please be safe.* Cody heard another sniff. The Beast was slinking down his aisle. Without any sound at all, the purple hood of the Beast's robe came into Cody's view; it was right below him.

In that moment Cody realized he was dead. His body was trembling uncontrollably. The Beast had stopped moving. Its mammoth head lifted to the celling. *Sniff Sniff.* Even in the darkness, its scarlet eyes burned. Cody braced himself for the sting of its fangs—but they never came. Instead he heard a loud clanking sound echo from across the room. The Beast's head shot toward the sound and its humped back passed by Cody's view hole. *Run!* He just needed to resist a little bit longer. . . . The Beast had disappeared from view, but Cody was not sure how far it had gone. *Just a little longer . . .*

He couldn't handle it any more. Before he could stop himself his body flailed. The books concealing him came crashing like thunder to the ground. Cody dropped off the shelf. Two red eyes pierced his from the other end of the aisle. The Beast squealed as it galloped toward him. "Help!" Cody yelled desperately. He stood to flee but tripped over the scattered books and came tumbling back to the floor. "Help!!" The Beast howled in ravenous ecstasy.

"*Byrae!*" yelled Xerx from the darkness. A gust of wind sent the bookshelf crashing down upon the Beast. "Let's get out of here!" cried Xerx as he jumped over the fallen bookshelf and bolted past Cody. Racing toward the door, Cody heard the angry wails of the Beast from behind. "*Byrae! Byrae! Byrae!*" Screamed Xerx. Three churning whirlwinds materialized behind them. Their violent gusts sent hundreds of books soaring across the room. There was a loud crash as the bookshelves begin to tumble over into each other. Cody lifted his hands to block the flying books as he leaped over the debris. The bookshelves came crashing down like dominos on both sides of them. "Jump!" Cody and Xerx dove through the open door as the shelves crashed to the ground behind them.

Cody spun around. "*Sellunga!*" An iron sheet formed over the doorway, sealing it.

"Good thinking," said Xerx, "but that won't hold it long. We need to get to Master Stalkton. Hurry!" They ran up the stairs. There was a loud crash as the iron shield rattled, leaving the deep indentation of a taloned hand. They didn't have much time.

Quickly ascending two floors, Xerx led Cody to a darkened chamber. The elder master was lying weakly on the floor; blood covered most of his white skin. "Master!" Cody bent down and lifted Stalkton's head. His eyelids were heavy as he dozed in and out of consciousness. Cody turned to Xerx. "We need to get him to Prince Foz soon or he's going to bleed to death!"

"What about Foz? What is going on here!" came a voice from the door. Cody turned around startled. Foz came running through the doorway.

"What are you doing here? We need to get out of here! We're not safe!" yelled Cody as the Prince knelt down beside him and examined Stalkton's bloody wounds.

"I came because of the Book, but I heard screaming," said the Prince in a flustered voice. There was a loud bang from below followed by a crash.

"The Beast has broken through the door. We need to get out of here!" yelled Xerx.

The Prince jumped to his feet. "It's too late, the Hunter is too fast." The Prince was right. Before they could move, the doorway was filled with the large silhouette of the Beast, its red eyes focused into slits, and its jaw hanging open, revealing each of its jagged teeth. The Prince stepped toward the entrance.

"No, Foz! Don't sacrifice yourself! We will fight to the death!" called Cody, bracing himself for attack.

The Prince looked over his shoulder. "Don't be foolish Cody; your life is far too valuable to waste in a suicidal fight. It doesn't have to be that way," said the Prince surprisingly calm.

Foz stepped toward the Beast, *"Flaymour."* A wall of fire burst in the archway forming a smoldering barrier. "We're trapped in here! What do we do now?!" yelled Cody in panic. Prince Foz turned back around, a demented grin on his face. "It's actually quite simple. . . . All you have to do is hand the Book over to me."

59

The Betrayal

W hat are you doing?" Cody whispered, a chill mani-
festing through his veins. "What are you playing
at?" Cody's eyes flashed between the Prince and the flaming archway, the towering silhouette of the Beast distinguishable through the inferno. "This is impossible."

The Prince smiled, although there was no joy in his action. "I'm afraid it's not. Now, hand over the Book, I can
only restrain the Hunter from a meal for so long." The
Prince raised his hands. "*Seamour.*" Water began to rain
down out of nowhere from the top of the door's arch, show-
ering down upon the wild flames like a sprinkler. "*Gai di
Gasme.*" The Prince, his face pale, turned back to the boys.
"I would estimate you have roughly five minutes before
the fire is extinguished. I can guarantee the Hunter will
not show you the same patience."

On cue, the Beast flared its nostrils and scraped its talons hard across the stone floor. Cody cringed and put his
hands over his ears. "Why Foz? Why turn on us? First your
traitorous brother, and now you? How twisted are you
guys!" Cody screamed defiantly.

Foz raised his eyebrows. "Oh, you don't still believe that the dogmatically loyal Kantan actually had anything to do with this, do you?"

Cody felt his resolve crumble under the comment. "But . . . the poison? And, the note to Levenworth? Kantan killed your father. He's in alliance with El Dorado!" Cody challenged weakly.

The Prince laughed. "No, boy. *I* killed my father. Who would know the wonderful usefulness of Derugmansia more than I? My father, foolishly trusting until the end, thought he was taking medication to relieve the stress. I wasn't lying; he's certainly not stressed anymore."

Cody shook his head in disbelief. "But the note. Kantan talked about the murder. I even overheard him mention it to Levenworth in person."

"That's because for all of Kantan's worthless traits, he is still admirably untrusting. He did not resign himself to the explanation of natural death as quickly as my brainless sisters. He suspected foul play right from the beginning. His suspicions lead him straight to me. Then, just when he was backing me into a corner, who should pop into Atlantis but you. Perfectly oblivious to everything. Your immediate hatred for my brother made it all too easy to turn you against him. All I had to do was earn your trust; you handled the rest, quite beautifully, I must say."

Cody's head was throbbing. "You set him up. You set us all up. But, why? Why murder your father?" asked Xerx desperately. The flames in the archway crackled; they were now sparse enough to see the Hunter in full view as it paced back and forth in anticipation.

The Prince took a step forward, backing the two boys toward the wall. "To do what your friend Randilin did many years earlier—what I thought was right. My father was weak. Look around you! Atlantis, the most advanced city in the world? It's falling apart! Beggars roam the streets. Thieves and gossips are multiplying. The citizens, much like the physical city itself, are caving in on themselves. We used to be great! There was a time when Atlantis was synonymous with glory, with power, with respect! What now? We are nothing more than a dusty old city, a shattered fragment of our former self. The power of the universe has been reduced to petty rules and chants. All the while, the greatest power ever discovered rests in a steel cage above us. My father had the power to make things right—and did nothing. Atlantis is ready for a change and I will be the one to give it to them."

"You're wrong," spat Cody. "Your father was a great man. He knew the power of the Orb better than anybody— and feared it. He didn't use its power because he realized that mankind was never meant to. All it does is corrupt!"

"Corrupt?" responded Foz venomously, "Is that what you think? You think my uncle, the greatest King to ever rule, was corrupted? Do you think it is corrupt to offer his subjects wealth and pleasure? Is it corrupt to provide his people with a utopia where everyone has, and therefore everyone is equal? No, what is corrupt is to have infinite power and not share it with anybody—not even your own flesh and blood. Times are changing. You don't want to find yourself on the wrong side. Now hand over the Book."

Cody looked to Xerx whose back was pressed against the stone wall, his face plagued with fright. On the floor Lamgorious Stalkon let out a soft moan of pain, the blood pumping slowly out his wounds. If Cody didn't move fast, Master Stalkton would be dead.

"What good will the Book do you anyways? Only I can read from it." For a moment Foz was caught off guard, his face reflecting a hint of uncertainty

"You're lying."

Cody took a bold step forward. "You know I'm not. If you read from the Book, that demon will be drawn with an uncontrollable frenzy to devour you. You need me alive."

The Prince snickered. "Maybe so . . . which is precisely why you will be coming with me to El Dorado. Do you think the infinite wisdom of the Golden King would act without a fail safe? I may need you alive . . . but I don't need your friends alive. Give me the Book and come with me now or I will leave the Hunter to feast on Stalkton and Xerx. Three . . . Two . . ."

"Stop! I'll give it to you. Just don't hurt anybody!" cried Cody. "But first you must call off the Beast."

"Give me the Book or you'll watch your friends eaten, one-by-one," responded Foz flatly. Cody took a timid step forward. He knew he had to think fast, but he felt as though his thoughts were trudging through a sea of molasses. He took his backpack off his shoulder and slowly unzipped it. The fire in the door still flickered weakly. The Hunter's jaws snapped as it sprang toward the flames before backing up. It would not be contained much longer.

"Don't be a fool, Cody!" yelled Xerx who lunged forward a moment too late; Cody had pulled *The Code* out of the backpack. He paused, staring strangely at the object in his hands.

Suddenly, Stalkton coughed, catching everyone by surprise. Through torturous, raspy breath he spoke, "No . . . use . . . lying . . . Book . . . decoy . . . real . . . Book . . . underneath . . . mat . . . corner of . . . room." His head fell back to the floor lifeless.

Foz laughed. "Clever Cody . . . but foolish. It was I after all who convinced my ignorant sister Cia to store the real Book here in the first place. Bring it to me or Xerx dies." Cody stepped over to the other side of the room, and came back carrying the scarlet lettered book.

The look on Xerx's face as Cody passed was filled with disgust. "You are selling us out. You disgrace Wesley's name," he said venomously, spitting on Cody's feet.

Cody looked into his eyes. "It's for the good of us all. I'm sorry." With his head hung low, Cody held out his hands, and Foz eagerly grasped his coveted prize. He greedily stroked the spine of the book.

"At last! The secrets of creation will once again be united!" There was a thump as the Hunter came billowing through the archway, landing beside Cody. Its long black tongue stroking across its dry lips. Foz grinned, "You falsely assumed that I had such authority as to control the impious will of the Hunter. It answers only to the Golden King. I'm sorry Xerx, but this is farewell . . ." The Hunter took a stride forward.

"Don't move!"

Cody spun around to see Dace standing behind him with a legion of soldiers, weapons raised. "Turn around slowly, and put the Book on the ground," ordered Dace, sweat glistening from his forehead.

Foz laughed. "Do you really believe you can compete with the power of El Dorado? Why resist when defeat is inevitable?" he challenged.

Dace stepped toward him. "We fight because the light has not yet been consumed by the dark. We fight to preserve the good and resist the evil misuse of the Orb's power. We fight, so that traitorous slugs like you do not go unpunished. Now stand down, you have no escape."

The Prince turned to Cody. "Don't think this is a victory. You've only delayed the inevitable. You *will* come to El Dorado. And when you do, the Golden King will be much displeased with your resistance. Until we meet again."

Without warning, the Hunter reared up onto its back legs and howled. The purple robe covering its body split apart with a loud tear. Two large bat-like wings spread into the room. A dozen insect trapper arms squirmed from its stomach. It thrust forward, grabbing Foz with its front arm. Cody dropped to the floor as the winged creature rushed over his head. There was a loud crash as the Beast smashed through the wall of the room. Cody looked up through the hole as the Beast flapped away through the night sky and out of sight.

60

A Prisoner of War

"Doctor! We need a doctor! Does anyone other than Foz know medicine? Quick!" Cody pulled himself out of the commotion to the corner of the room and propped himself up against the wall. He saw motion in his peripheral vision too slow to react. Xerx's hand came crashing against the side of his head. Another blow caught Cody on the chin, whiplashing his head against the wall. A third blow was halted as Dace's strong hand caught Xerx's fist.

"Stop! What is going on? What happened up here?" Dace demanded.

Xerx pointed to Cody. "He gave Foz the Book! He has doomed us all!"

Dace's face registered concern. "Is this true, Cody? El Dorado has possession of *The Code*?" Cody wiped the blood from his nose and motioned to his backpack. Dace handed it to him and Cody pulled out the decoy. He placed his hand on it, and suddenly his body began to twitch. The blood from his nose flowed slowly back up his nose, and his bruises began to fade away.

"What the . . . ?" stammered Dace.

Cody offered a weak grin. "Prince Foz only has a decoy . . . *this* is the true Book."

Xerx shook his head disbelievingly. "It can't be. I heard you and Stalkton fight. They wanted you to have a decoy at the ceremony to keep the Book safe. The real Book was hidden here. In this room. I watched Master Stalkton hide it!"

Cody nodded. "I thought so, too. That's why I tried to deceive Foz by giving him what I thought was the decoy from my backpack. It wasn't until I pulled it out that I felt the surge of power rush through my fingers. I didn't know how, but at that moment I realized that I had the real Book in my hands. Stalkton knew, too. It was all sleight-of-hand. He must have switched them back when I wasn't looking. He revealed the location of the other copy to Foz, leading him to think I'd been bluffing. Something tells me the Hunter wasn't fooled by the move, but thankfully you guys arrived just in time."

Dace's face lost its tension and became tired. "Fortune has smiled upon us. But we have much to do. We have several field-medics in my troop that can tend to Stalkton. But for now, you need to come with me, we need to talk."

Cody was surprised; the request was not spoken with confident authority, but rather as a tired plea. Cody was afraid to ask how the battle had fared outside the Monastery.

By the time Cody and Dace reached the central square, most of the dead bodies had been removed. However, the dried blood of brave men still painted the dirt with a wet scarlet coating. The air smelled of steel and flesh. The people of Atlantis were standing around the battleground in confused silence, as though they were waiting to wake up any second from some hellish nightmare.

As Cody walked alongside Dace, he recognized the greasy long hair of Sheets, who was kneeling down in the dirt. Cody placed his hands on the soldier's large shoulder. When Sheets turned around, his eyes were red and wet snot was running down into his beard. Cody didn't need to ask why. Below Sheets, lying on the ground with eyes closed was Hex—an arrow lodged into his neck. Sheets' lip was trembling. "He's . . . gone."

Hex was not alone. The pile of dead bodies rose seven feet tall. "This is horrible. El Dorado is going to pay for what they did here today," cursed Cody, fighting to hold his emotions in check. He stopped, a sickening feeling squeezing his stomach. "Dace, where is Jade?"

Dace's eyes were sympathetic; he looked to the ground. "That is what I wanted to talk to you about. It seems this ambush was not about an attack on Atlantis at all . . . "

"What do you mean? Answer me!" screamed Cody, feeling all eyes focused on him, "ANSWER ME!"

Dace put his hands on Cody's shoulders. "There was nothing I could do. I'm so sorry Cody. . . . They've taken her."

The words sliced through Cody like a dagger and seemed foreign, as though spoken in another, unrecognizable language. "What do you mean, they've *taken* her!? Who!?" Cody yelled, but his body suddenly felt too weak to maintain his fury.

"As the attack continued, I realized that oddly none of the enemy was moving toward the palace. In fact, they didn't seem to have any plan of attack at all. I knew that something was wrong. They began a full-fledged retreat just as they gained the upper hand. I thought maybe we'd beaten them. Then I saw her. They had Jade. I don't know why, but it was almost as if she had been their primary target all along. I tried to save her, but I was too late. They were gone before I could get to her. They have taken her to El Dorado. I'm so sorry."

Cody felt his legs wobble beneath him. Foz's words came rushing back to him, *"Don't think that this is a victory. You've only delayed the inevitable. You will come to El Dorado."*

The Prince was right. The Golden King *did* have a fail safe. Cody felt stupid. How had he not realized? Why had he *left* her!

"I'm going after her. If I have to take on all of El Dorado myself, I'm going to rescue Jade. I'm going to make sure Foz pays dearly for this," Cody uttered coldly.

"Yes, Cody, you have my word, we will *not* abandon Jade to the Golden King. But you must be rational. There is only one reason for them to kidnap Jade—you. They are trying to lure you to El Dorado."

"Well, they have succeeded."

"Cody, the Golden King must still not know what it meant when Wesley transferred ownership of the Book's power to you. He can't afford to kill you, without the Book

Keeper, *The Code* is useless to him. If you go to El Dorado, he will use you. It's what he *wants*. You will be dooming us all."

"So be it," said Cody with an empty voice. "Do you expect me to abandon Jade!? I will not leave her . . . I need her." Cody felt tears flowing from his eyes, but he no longer had the strength to hold them back. "It's all my fault! I shouldn't have left her. I should have stayed with her and protected her. I was so worried about this stupid Book because it made me feel important. Now she's gone. She's everything to me. She's always been there for me, but when she needs me the most, I run off on some selfish mission to build my own ego. It should have been *me* captured, not her. Never her . . ." Cody couldn't talk anymore, he was sobbing harder than he ever had in his life. His legs gave out from under him and he began to collapse.

He felt two arms wrap around him. Holding him up. Tiana pulled him close and Cody buried his face into her shoulder. He didn't know how long he cried, but Tiana never moved or spoke. She just held him tightly until his last tear was shed.

At last Cody raised his head. Tiana kissed him on the forehead. "It's okay. We are going to save Jade. I promise you," she whispered softly, "I promise you."

Cody nodded, clenching his fist. "And I can promise *you* something. . . . Prince Foz is going to suffer. You have my word."

The Second Great War between Atlantis and El Dorado had just begun.

61

An Unexpected Ally

The bedroom seemed strangely empty. Cody felt more alone than ever before. He glanced to the wall that separated his chambers from Jade's. He could sense the stark emptiness in the room beyond. He was truly on his own. For the first time since fourth grade, he was staggering into the future without Jade by his side. The thought was absolutely terrifying.

Tiana and Dace had finally convinced him that he needed sleep. He had been determined to start his pursuit of Jade immediately, but knew he was in no condition to fight. Where was Jade now? Was she okay? She probably was sleeping on the dirt somewhere, bound up and gagged. If one of the soldiers so much as laid a finger on her, Cody vowed he would regret it.

The final death count had been done. Fifty-four Atlantis soldiers had died—only twenty-three of El Dorado's golden golems had fallen. The deaths would be the first of many. Word had reached Atlantis just before nightfall that the borderland outposts were under heavy siege. The war between the two ancient cities was now well under way.

Lamgorious Stalkton was in critical condition with only a fifty-fifty chance to survive according to the medics. Cody felt like his four limbs were being pulled in opposing directions. Queen Cia expected to use him as a figurehead for the war, to rally the people together and provide hope. Stalkton desired him to continue his training, reminding Cody that he didn't stand a chance against the Golden King. Dace seemed unworried, and wanted Cody in the battlefield to give his men much-needed aid. But Cody couldn't do any of those without abandoning Jade, and that was the one thing that he would not, under any circumstances, consider doing.

He closed his eyes. He now understood why Ishmael refused to accept the role as Book Keeper. Everyone needs somebody with power. Well-intentioned or not, Cody was now under attack from the desires and needs of others. Instead of establishing an identity, the Book's power stretched him to the point of snapping. Cody heard a noise. *Jade? No, you need sleep Cody, your mind's playing tricks on you.* He rolled over onto his side and squeezed his eyes tighter shut, trying to block out his thoughts. He heard the sound of breathing. *Stop it! She's gone, let it go!* Cody squinted open his left eye; the shadow of a silhouette reflected off the wall.

Cody sat up, grabbed his head, and screamed, "I'm sorry, Jade!" He looked toward the window and stopped. Two figures were outlined by light.

The taller one held out a hand. "Do not panic. We are not here to harm you."

Cody started to jump up but paused; there was something familiar about the voice.

"Dunstan?"

One of the hooded figures stepped forward and removed his hood. "It is nice to see you again master Cody," said the familiar British voice. "It's been too long."

Cody put his back to the wall, feeling under his pillow for the Book.

Dunstan smiled. "We are not here to hurt you . . . we are here to help you," he responded calmly.

Cody's fingers touched the spine of the Book. "Give me one good reason why I should trust you?"

The second figure stepped forward; Cody saw the light flash off the circular blade hanging from his side.

"Because you are in desperate need of help; and help is one thing which we can offer you. And frankly, who else can you trust?" The thrust of the statement stung sharply. Indeed, whom could he trust? His only true friend had been stolen from him.

"How could you possibly help me? You've tried to kill me. You've tried to steal the Book. You're a thief and a murderer."

Dunstan raised his bushy eyebrow. "What I am or am not does not in any way affect your situation or your need to rely on my assistance. I guess I owe you a bit of an apology for our previous encounters. You must understand by now that the object so indiscreetly hidden underneath your pillow is of utmost importance. Things happened very quickly, and we were unsure of where your allegiance lay. Quite simply, we couldn't afford the Book to fall into the wrong hands. Your death was to be a necessary sacrifice to ensure that it was so."

Cody laughed sarcastically. "So, you're just a noble protector of the Book, then? Only concerned with its safety, completely un-desiring of its powers for yourself? I'm not biting."

"What you decide to bite or not to bite is entirely up to you," said Dunstan calmly. "But the truth is, you need us. And, to be honest, we need you."

Cody was taken aback. "Need me? How?" Cody asked. The lines on Dunstan's face tightened, reflecting an internal debate over how much information to reveal. When he spoke, it was slow and cautiously.

"For the same reason the Golden King won't kill you. We don't understand you. Until a month ago, there had only ever been two Book Keepers—Wesley and the Golden King. Whatever happened between you, Wesley, and *The Code* is something that has not occurred in human history: a change of Book Keepers. No one knows how it happened. But more importantly, no one knows what it means. To kill you would be to risk eliminating the only person who can access the information in the Book. That is a risk nobody is willing to take, especially the Golden King. Until somebody discovers how the transfer of power works, you must remain alive. Obviously, the Golden King has already discovered a loophole . . ."

"Jade," said Cody bitterly.

Dunstan nodded. "Indeed. If he cannot use the Book without you—he will force you to use it for him. He took the one thing he knew would draw you to El Dorado. The one thing he knew you would do *anything* to get back . . ."

"You can't stop me. I don't care what the Golden King is planning, I *am* going to rescue Jade."

"I never said anything about stopping you. I am here only to warn you. And, to give you this . . ." Dunstan held out his hand; in it was a stone tablet. Cody took it from him. The tablet was small, the size of an envelope. Carved into the tablet was writing. Cody wiped his hand across the stone sending a cloud of dust fluttering into the air. He slowly read the inscription:

THE POWER OF FULL DIVINITY,

RESTS ENCODED WITHIN EARTHLY TRINITY.

WHERE SACRIFICE OF THE PURE ANGEL WHO FELL,

IS THE WAY TO RETRIEVE THE PEARL WITHIN THE SHELL.

WITH HUMBLE HEART AND GOLDEN KEY,

THE UNIVERSE'S MOST POWERFUL FORCE IS REVEALED TO THEE

Cody quickly read the tablet again and then again. Finally he set it down on his bed. "Why give this to me? What does this mean?" he said turning back to Dunstan. Both he and the other hooded figure were gone. Cody went to the window, but there was no trace of either. The two men had vanished.

Cody returned to his bed. He gazed down at the tablet. Somewhere, entrenched between the roughly carved words, was an essential clue. But that clue remained a mystery. And this time he wouldn't have Jade to figure it out for him. He already missed her so much. What was it that she had called out to him the last time he saw her? A thought came to his head, but he erased it as quickly as it formed. It couldn't be. Jade saw him as a friend, nothing more. Didn't she?

He pushed the tablet underneath his pillow, nestled against the spine of *The Code*. He retrieved the ruby pocket watch off the side table and stared at the unmoving golden hand. He had many questions to answer—but they would have to wait until the morning. He pulled his blankets around his chilled body, and for the first time that evening his lips curled into a weak smile; how insignificant humans were. A catastrophic war was raging on, his best friend had been captured by a tyrannical ruler, and he had endless mysteries to solve. But still, his body was enslaved by its basic need for sleep. *How small we really are.* Pushing all thoughts from his mind, he rolled over in his bed, let his eyelids slide close, and fell fast asleep.

62

Golden

Voices. Sounding all around, as though they were being spoken a million miles away. Flying. That was the sensation she had, like her body had been grasped by the wind and pulled into the air to engage in a wild dance. Lost. She couldn't remember where she was, where she had come from, or where she was going. She was simply soaring through time in the land separating the living from the deceased. Heavy. Her eyelids felt heavy. She fought to push them open, as hazy shapes spun into focus. Strangers. Their faces were beautiful. Were they angels? Suddenly she stopped. She felt herself fall to the ground. She was no longer flying. The ground was soft. There was grass; and flowers, too! Wonderful flowers of all shapes and colors. Their petals looked like polished gem stones. She thought of how much she would love to smell them. She loved flowers. She looked up, hoping to find more pretty flowers. Beautiful. That's what she saw. It was the most lovely thing she had ever seen. It shone like the sun. She had to squint her eyes, but she couldn't look away. Down the lush green valley was a city. A wonderful city. A city like she had never seen before. A City of Gold. . . .

**To Be Continued in Book Two
of the Lost City Chronicles**

Visit Russell Media for our latest offerings:

www.russell-media.com

Find out more about Daniel Blackaby and
the next two books of the trilogy at:

www.danielblackaby.com

Be the first to read the Prologue
and Chapter One of book No. 2:

City of Gold

GO TO:

russell-media.com/cityofgold/chapterone